Destination Romance Series

While on a cruise to Jamaica, six couples discover *The Love Boat* is a lot more than a television series from the 1980s, and this time the destination is hot, steamy romance.

By

AlTonya Washington
Barbara Keaton
Deatri King-Bey
A.C. Arthur
Dyanne Davis
Niobia Byant

In 1995, Emma Rodgers, Ashira Tosihwe and Francis Ray gave birth to the ROMANCE SLAM JAM to demonstrate what Nikki Giovanni describes as "The Power, Passion and Pain of Black Love."

This anthology is dedicated to the Romance Slam Jam Family. Happy 15th Anniversary!
Thank you all for reading, writing and living Black romance.

This book is dedicated to all who have gone out of their way to give to such a wonderful organization the support and help they need to keep the community flurishing.

We wish to thank you for purchasing this book, as all of the proceeds go to South Side Help Center. So on behalf of the authors who have graciously given their all as well as the editor, cover artist and publisher, Red Rose™ Publishing, on behalf of those women and their families who need the extra help and support, if you would like to make a donation on your own please visit their site at http://www.southsidehelp.org/

If you would like to contact them or send a check or anything else please get in touch with them at the following address:

South Side Help Center
10420 S. Halsted
Chicago, IL 60628
Phone: (773) 445-5445

The mission of South Side Help Center (SSHC) is to provide families with positive and healthy alternatives for building better communities. In 1987, SSHC began its HIV/AIDS program as an outreach effort to African-Americans who were affected by AIDS in large numbers. Today, SSHC provides HIV/AIDS prevention intervention programs in various community venues and target populations on Chicago's south side. SSHC is especially proud of the unique and innovative educational and support programs for African American women. Below is a description of some of the programs we offer for women. Not only do they provide for women but also the youth of today. Please visit their website and see all the things that they have done and are doing for the community and people as a whole. http://www.southsidehelp.org/

Women Prevention Services
● **Shelter Women's AIDS Program (SWAP):** HIV Education via SISTA curriculum, Prevention Case Management (PCM), support group, onsite counseling & testing (CT), and referrals services to high-risk African American Women living facilities and homeless shelters.
● **Female IDU Street outreach Initiative** -Provides CT, individual and group risk reduction education and referrals services to African- American female IDUs.
● **Young Women's Project (BRIGHT)** –provides HIV Group education and PCM to young women ages 19 -29 who are at risk for HIV. Date started:1995
● **Women's Collaborative**- Provides HIV education and Testing in Beauty Salons across Chicago
● **Corrections Initiative**- Providing case management services to HIV positive women recently released from Cook County Jail.

In addition, South Side Help Center was the initiating and leading agency for the highly successful Illinois Women Preventing AIDS Campaign (IWPA).

Table of Content

This is a work of fiction. Names, characters, places, and incidents are products of the author's imagination or are used fictitiously and are not to be construed as real. Any resemblance to actual events, locales, organizations, or persons, living or dead, is entirely coincidental.

Destination Romance Series

Red Rose™ Publishing
Publishing with a touch of Class! ™
The symbol of the Red Rose and Red Rose is a trademark of Red Rose™ Publishing

Red Rose™ Publishing
Copyright© 2009 Destination Romance Series
ISBN: 1-60435-994-3
ISBN: 978-1-60435-994-7
Cover Artist: Shirley Burnett
Editor: Crystal Hubbard
 Line Editor: WRFG

Red Rose™ Publishing
www.redrosepublishing.com
Forestport, NY 13338

Thank you for purchasing a book from Red Rose™ Publishing where publishing comes with a touch of Class!

As A Whisper

By

AlTonya

Washington

Chapter One

Gulf of Mexico-

The maiden voyage of *The Destiny* had gone off without a hitch, so far. Every one of the spacious interior and ocean front cabins, plush staterooms and elaborate suites were filled. Every scheduled entertainer had shown ready to work. There had been no last minute cancellations. The chefs and their superbly trained staffs were quite pleased with the vast supplies on hand. All mechanical functions were given the green light. It went without saying that the executive staff of Datari Fleets and Engineering was very happy.

Correction: The majority of the executive staff of Datari Fleets and Engineering was happy. The man who ran it all was anything but. Gunther Datari's dark stare was focused and more narrowed than usual. Leaning against a gleaming silver rail of the ship he'd crafted, he studied the unending vista of blue and tried to train his thoughts toward his latest success.

His family's shipping fleet spanned into vast numbers. Gunther had assumed control a little over a year ago. Before that, his life encompassed an endless stream of tutelage at the hands of his father, Javaris Datari, and uncle, Oliver Datari. Following their deaths, Gunther had taken his subsequent control of the company very seriously. He'd launched several vessels, but *The Destiny* was all his— the first he'd designed.

Everything should have been perfect. It was anything but perfect. *It couldn't be her, it just couldn't be.* He wondered how many times had he repeated that phrase. He grimaced then, bowing his head while driving his thumb into the dent gracing his chin. They'd been at sea for almost a week, and this morning at breakfast, it had happened again.

She couldn't be there, but dammit...he slammed fist to palm that time. The resemblance was uncanny. Of course, the second he glimpsed her, she was gone. Like mist. Aside from turning the ship upside down to find her, he'd considered using every means at his disposal to seek her out.

So why was he hesitating? It would have been easy enough to scan the passenger manifest for the name. He swore silently, raking five fingers through his hair. Hell, he knew it was her. It had to be.

Whatever else he might misinterpret in life, there was no way he could misinterpret seeing her.

Izaya Charles was not a woman a man could easily forget. Fine-boned and fragile looking, her rich caramel skin was a perfect accompaniment to the striking gold-brown of her eyes. A head full of glossy onyx twists framed a small oval face.

A hand soothing across Gunther's back drew his attention away from the woman he'd spent eight years with. "Hey," he greeted the short, stout woman at his side.

Misty Terrell was grimacing in spite of the soothing rubs she gave her boss's back. "You know your being here is really just a formality. We really just wanted you here in hopes that you'd let go a little and have some fun."

Gunther's stare never wavered. "I have fun," he argued. The whisper soft quality of his voice, however, was flat as stone.

Misty hissed a curse and balled a fist on impulse before she calmed. "How can you possibly be in such a foul mood with a view like this stretched out before you?" She waved a jeweled hand towards the Gulf.

"I've seen her, Mis."

Misty's confusion was evident. The agitation in her brown eyes cleared as she watched Gunther's mount.

"Izaya." He clarified.

Misty pursed her lips as realization came to her face. "Honey, you closed the door on that, remember?"

Gunther buried his face in his hands.

"You let her walk away and did nothing to stop it." Misty tugged his hands away from his face. "Now, in the dead middle of the ocean, is not the time to be torturing yourself with thoughts of this, is it?"

Gunther turned to scowl down at his assistant of fifteen years. "I've seen Izaya. I know in my gut that she's somewhere on this ship. And correction," he pushed off the rail to tower over Misty, then, "I didn't *let* her walk away. I *told* her to." The agitation on his dark face glossed over to regret. "I ordered her out of my life and made her feel lower than crap when I did it."

"So then why are you preoccupied with seeing her?" Misty pretended to focus on a wayward string dangling from a button on her olive blouse. She heard Gunther mutter something inaudible and moved a tad closer. "And what the hell would she be doing on a cruise ship when she works just as much as you do?"

Gunther slanted a last lingering look toward the water, and then shook his head. "I don't know, Misty, but I'm about to find out."

Izaya Charles was working. What the hell was she doing on a sea cruise when she had a sea of unfinished tasks stretching out before her? It was Tammy and her bevy of henchwomen who bullied her into it, she remembered thinking of her Editor-in-Chief, Tammy Frinks, and her staff.

Nevertheless, the Romance Slam Jam event had always held a special place in her heart. She and the event went way back, ever since her days as an aspiring author. God, how long ago had that been? Twelve, thirteen years? She'd achieved modest success as an erotica writer, but it was a trip to Slam Jam 2003 in Atlanta where she'd realized her true calling. Meeting editor Suzette Aimes had provided her with both a friend and mentor. From then on, she'd been set on not only becoming an editor, but also the head of her own publishing house.

Now, seven years later, she'd achieved all of her goals to date. She'd become an author, editor and publisher of Charles House, the premier house for erotica publications. Now, the event where she'd found her purpose, was honoring her with a nomination for Publisher of the Year.

This year, Charles House was beginning talks for the start of a satellite network that would bring its steamy titles to film. To have the house receive a nomination in a category in which it had not been previously honored filled Izaya with a sense of triumph. Yes, she'd accomplished a lot. Still, she wasn't at all surprised by the irony that she hadn't accomplished the one thing she'd wanted most of all. With a quick shake that sent the glossy twists bouncing upon her head, she ordered that "thing" from her mind.

That was easier said than done since she'd had the most eerie sensation that he was near. Dropping the pen she held, Izaya began to pace the living area of her suite. Why couldn't she get him off her mind? How could she have any feelings for him after the way he ended things between them? It was useless to deny that she'd been going a little crazy each day since.

It had all happened over a year ago, yet in the last couple of days, she'd almost felt his presence in the same room. Not surprising, since Gunther Datari had commanded the bulk of her time when she wasn't working.

"Stop it!" Izaya tugged at the ruffled sleeves that fell past her wrists. She resumed her spot before the glass coffee table and tried to focus on the specs she'd brought along from her advertising department. She'd spent enough time pining over a man who cast her aside as if they'd had eight seconds as opposed to eight years between them. They had been close ever since the day they struck up conversation in a local Boston bookstore. What started as an easy friendship gradually transitioned into something deeper. Izaya didn't know how long it had taken for her to realize he was the man she wanted to marry. She knew she loved him and it was clear he'd felt the same.

Sadly, marriage would never be an option. Gunther had never made a secret of the fact that he wasn't inclined to that sort of commitment. In the eight years they had spent together, she had only met his family on a few occasions. It was enough to latch onto the distinct aura of disapproval from Gunther's father and uncle. Oh, she guessed they liked her well enough, but it was obvious they approved more of her and Gunther being nothing more than lovers. Still, Izaya hadn't realized how staunchly Gunther subscribed to his family's ideas until she had raised the issue of marriage. At that point, she had been shown the door without haste.

Again, she shook her head and grasped the specs more tightly, as if the action would help her focus. She blinked away unexpected tears clinging to her lashes and concentrated.

"She's gonna kill us when she finds out."

Charles House Senior Editor Jessica Hume sent an exasperated glare towards her assistant. "Dammit, Felecia, why didn't you check on this?"

Felecia Meyers rolled her eyes. "I'm sorry, but I didn't really think about asking who built the ship when I was booking the cruise."

Tammy Frinks answered with a sympathetic look, and then tossed back a swallow of her martini.

"Well, is it really such a big deal that her ex owns the company that built the ship?" asked Renata Hammond, one of the proofreaders seated at the table.

"No," Jessica waved a hand, "but it's a very big deal when it's the maiden voyage and he's someplace walking around."

"It was a pretty ugly scene between them when it ended." Tammy offered a condensed version of the relationship'sdemise. "Izaya was devastated. She really loved him." Tammy's voice took on a hushed quality as she recalled how lost Izaya had seemed right after the breakup.

Silence descended, the women regretting such a thing befalling someone they held so dear.

Renata gave a refreshing sigh. "This could still work out alright. Maybe they'll both be so busy, and hopefully the ship will be big enough to keep them traipsing around in their own worlds and out of each other's way.

The group raised their glasses in a toast.

Chapter Two

Captain Devon Reynard's contagious laughter seemed to vibrate clear across the luxury dining hall of *The Destiny*. At least, that's the way it sounded to the twenty dinner companions sitting on either side of the captain at the lengthy, impeccably set table. The delicious meal of chowder, cracked crab, lobster tails and peeled shrimp accentuated the joy of the evening. Bowls of vibrantly colored steamed vegetables and flaky biscuits rounded out the hearty meal.

Captain Reynard wasn't the only one having such a fine time. Spirits were high at the table due in part to the fragrant, flavorful white wine that filled everyone's glasses. Another factor attributing to the gaiety had much to do with the only erotica publisher dining at the table. It was no surprise that the rest of the group took great pleasure in picking her brain.

Izaya never expected to have quite so much fun when she accepted the unexpected invitation to dinner with the captain. She had already resigned herself to an evening alone in her stateroom with her own bottle of wine and a huge cheeseburger to nurse away her agitations.

Within minutes of introducing herself to her rowdy dinner companions, she was entertaining them with stories of how she broke into the business. Izaya's racy insights into the world of erotic fiction kept the group understandably intrigued. Not surprising, the delicious wines, champagnes and other alcoholic beverages loosened tongues and lowered inhibitions. As a result, the inquiries into the erotica writing profession almost made Izaya's cheeks burn.

"I put a few things down, but I've always been more of a reader than writer." Denise Parsons, a plastic surgeon out of Miami, Florida, shared her aspiring author dreams. "I have a few that I've written and thought about trying to publish. Nothing lengthy."

"You should go for it. There's always room for a fresh voice." Izaya encouraged and smiled when the rest of the group murmured uplifting words to Denise as well. "You've just got to be persistent and develop a thick skin—it takes that to deal with some of the agents, editors and critics out there."

"Izaya, tell us about your covers. Are those men for real?"

Izaya joined in the laughter roaring around the table. "They're very real," she told Marguerite Sparks, a college professor from Columbia, South Carolina. "If only there were more of them to go around." She shrugged. "But I'm happy to say that we've managed to arrange for several of the Charles House cover models to join us on the cruise. Hopefully, you'll have the chance to see them in person. Trust me, they're much more incredible *off* the cover."

"I agree!" Marguerite said once another round of laughter had quelled. "Although I have to say there've been times when I haven't been altogether pleased by what I've seen on the covers." She nodded when a few women at the table voiced agreement. "No matter how gorgeous they are, it just seems to fall short of what the author describes in the pages."

Izaya sipped her wine and nodded. "I remember having this same issue when I worked in the business as an author. As a publisher, I'm proud to say that my House was one of the first to provide authors with jpegs of the models the artistic teams were considering. We give authors the chance to confirm or deny in hopes of coming as close to the writer's vision as possible." She set down her glass. "It's a service we provide for *all* our authors. Not just the big names. Still," she sighed and grazed her nails across the scooping bodice of her jumpsuit, "No matter whose face is on the cover, we all have to accept the fact that it always looks better in your head."

Denise Parsons uttered a low whistle, her gaze skimming the dining room. "I may have to disagree with you on that one Izaya."

Following the woman's gaze, Izaya's golden-brown stare locked on Gunther Datari making his way toward the captain's table. She would've made the attempt to stifle her gasp, had she thought it might have been overheard.

She hadn't seen him in over a year, yet it was still easy to see that his manner was as cool and understated as ever. He wore the demeanor in practically everything he did. The results, on the other hand, were always explosive and about as far away from understated as one could venture.

Gunther Datari was as subtle as a whisper yet just as potent. He had yet to look her way and Izaya was glad, for it gave her the chance to reacquaint herself with his provocative features.

Tall, with a body that proved he enjoyed working out hard and often, Gunther's dark eyes and skin were simply accentuated by glossy midnight curls covering his head in thick ringlets. Izaya studied the dent in his strong chin, which drew more attention to the heavenly curve of his mouth.

She was remembering his voice. Like his manner, it was just as soft and subtle. The octave intermingled humor and an *understated* danger. When it rumbled through his chest and into hers, or past his lips and into her ear, the tone had the power to send her trembling toward climax.

Izaya's gaze and attention locked on the sexy dent, the strong chin, the heavenly mouth…his voice was inaudible amidst all the others rumbling around the table.

As if he knew she had been watching him all along—and he probably did—his dark eyes slid to her striking brownish gold ones.

"So tell us about all those love scenes, Izaya," Samuel Baxter asked.

With some—with *great*—effort, Izaya turned her attention toward the pilot from St. Louis. "What would you like to know?" Somehow, she managed to slip back into the easy manner she'd enjoyed before Gunther's arrival.

"Do they come from real life experiences?" Sam clarified his question once the wicked chuckles around the table had softened a bit. "All the detail you writers incorporate in your stories, especially in the love scenes." He shook his head and grinned devilishly. "Sorry, but some of them are just a little too thorough to come completely from imagination."

In spite of her former lover's presence at the table, Izaya's sense of humor hummed over the questions. "Well, Sam, honestly now, where's the fun in relying totally on imagination?"

The group burst into laughter and increased conversation on the subject. During all the discussion, Izaya sobered a bit to judge Gunther's reaction. He was still giving her his attention, yet no hint of a smile emerged on his face. Only when he dipped his head slightly in her direction did she realize she'd been holding her breath, anticipating his response. She wondered if he expected her answer to Sam Baxter's question to be a tad juicier, considering how much *real life experience* Gunther had given her.

The distinctive clink of silverware tapping crystal drew everyone's attention to Captain Reynard.

"We've been having such a good time here, I've fallen slack in my duties and neglected to introduce our host, Mr. Gunther Datari. And yes, our ship, *The Destiny*, is his company's creation."

Conversation swelled once more, Gunther and his line of work the topic of discussion. Izaya allowed herself more time to observe him as he answered the questions tossed his way. Greedily, her gaze absorbed the gorgeous features of his face. She'd forgotten how devastating he was, especially when involved in conversation. Apparently, every woman at the table shared her opinion, their eyes following Gunther's every movement. They watched his mouth while he spoke, as if they could feel the words tripping from the sensual curve of his lips.

"So, Gunther, tell us how your family became involved in the shipping industry. It's not every day you hear of such a family legacy."

Gunther graced Denise Parsons with a smile and nodded as though he completely agreed. "We have my great-great-great-grandfather to thank for that. Dou Datari came to this country a slave. After the Civil War, his master had lost everything except his ship. The man decided to pack it all in and invited any slave that wished to come along to do so. My great-great-great grandfather was one of them. When his master died, he was first mate, the ship became his and it became the first in the Datari family fleet."

"Fascinating," several diners at the table breathed the word in unison.

"That must be a real time consumer, Datari," Samuel Baxter said.

Again, Gunther nodded his agreement. "I've been in training for this job since I was old enough to read. The real work started when I was old enough to understand a map and globe."

"Such a demanding lifestyle, it's a wonder you have time for anything more...enjoyable." Denise Parsons inquired slyly, once laughter over Gunther's previous statement had died down a bit.

"It's true, the business keeps me very busy. But I've been known to make time when it appealed to me."

Izaya cleared her throat when his dark stare slid down the table toward her.

"Judging from the beauty of this place, I'm willing to bet that making that sort of time isn't a thing that occurs very often," Marguerite Sparks noted.

Gunther's eyes were still trained on Izaya. "It's a bet you'd win, but whenever I've made the time, I've made it count."His response roused even more interest and the inquiries grew increasingly detailed. Izaya participated only slightly in the conversation. She waited until the group was involved in their questions and then took advantage of that moment to excuse herself from the table.

God, why did he have to be here? Izaya's mind had raced with the question since she'd sprinted from the main dining room and back to her cabin. Now, enjoying a fraction of peace, she rubbed her bare arms and tried to ease the chill that had plagued her since seeing him. The fact that she'd suspected he was near in no way prepared her for his presence.

After the way things ended between them, he'd never believe her being there had nothing to do with him—with them. *Great goin', Izzy.*

She'd spent the last year going out of her way *not* to run into him in Boston. It was just her luck that she'd come all the way out to the middle of the ocean and done exactly that.

She jumped at a single knock on the door . *Moment of truth*, she acknowledged, knowing it was him. She didn't wait for a second knock.

Although she knew who waited on the other side of the door, seeing Gunther filling the doorway set her back a few steps. Her movement provided enough space for him to enter the suite, and he did so without a word. Izaya clenched her fists when the door closed behind him, and she prayed he'd break the silence. Her heart was in her throat, stifling talk on her end. She worked to display some sort of sternness in her expression. But when he walked toward her, all she showed was pure wanting. The look in his eyes was unreadable. When he moved past her, she silently cursed her weakness for wanting to swoon in reaction to his cologne. He wore sex appeal like a garment.

"Why are you here, Izzy?" Gunther bit his lip at the use of her nickname, which he only used when they were alone.

Izaya lost her ability to stand and took solace on one of the deep, sky blue arm chairs. "The, um," she cleared her throat when he turned to look at her. "The house is up for an award. My publishing house."

Gunther smirked, but the gesture held no trace of sarcasm, only softness. "I remember."

The smile beginning to tug at her mouth curbed when his gaze slid away to survey the suite. "Do I know this award?" He was observing the artwork adorning the walls.

Izaya had zoned out on the conversation, more interested in studying him. Silently, she appraised the cut of his trousers, loving the way they hung on his lean hips and long legs. Her gaze moved upward to savor the breadth of his back and shoulders beneath his black shirt. She blinked lazily more than a few times before realizing he was speaking to her.

"Slam Jam," she answered when he repeated his question about the award. Clearing her throat, she clasped her hands and focused. "The Romance Slam Jam Conference. Do you remember it?" she whispered while looked down at her lap, her lips pressed together.

"Ah right..." Gunther leaned against a wall and eased his hands into his pockets. "Ball gowns on Saturday night. I remember."

Izaya was remembering, too. Memories took her back to 2001 and the event in Orlando, Florida. On impulse, she'd asked Gunther to go with her and had been stunned when he'd accepted the invitation. He had business there that week, so the timing was perfect. They had only been seeing each other a few months, and Izaya remembered how she'd hoped the trip would bring them closer. She'd gotten all she'd hoped for and more the night he escorted her to the awards ball.

An unexpected moan edged its way up her throat, and she moved from the sofa to the bar cart where she poured a glass of water.

Gunther took advantage of the moment to indulge his own observations. His easy expression took on an intensity as he watched her across the room. He scanned her frame, loving the cut of the sleeveless jumpsuit and the way it cupped her full bosom and bottom. He'd almost gone mad missing her in the past year. To cope, he'd tried working himself to exhaustion, hence his staff *suggesting* his going on the cruise. He clenched fists inside his pockets when his palms tensed with the need to span her waist. He bowed his head and winced when his chest constricted with the same need that had caused his palms to ache. Memories of how she felt next to him threatened to singe his nerves.

"And you had no idea *Destiny* was mine?" he asked when she turned from the bar and found him staring.

Izaya's smile flashed easier. Being territorial was a thing Gunther never denied. Clearly, that was in relation only to the objects he owned. *She* had been another story.

"I didn't book the cruise, didn't pay attention to the information packet on the ship when I boarded and I'm sure the name of the ship's owner didn't matter much to my staff."

He nodded at her explanation and took time to rake her petite frame with striking familiarity.

Izaya swallowed down more water when she noticed his stare lingering on her chest. She stood straighter then. "So is that all you wanted?" she asked, refusing to be a victim of her own unease any longer.

Though still maddeningly cool, Gunther's gaze narrowed just a tad in surprise. He recovered a split second later, strolling slowly as he closed the distance between them. "You really had no idea I was here? Not even a...*funny* feeling?" he inquired, standing close.

"Not even a twinge." She didn't hesitate to voice the lie, refusing to even hint at how much she'd been pining for him. Unfortunately, the longer he stood near, the more she felt like melting onto him.

Gunther's dark gaze roamed every inch of her lovely face. With subtleness only he could manage, his stare journeyed lower to enjoy a closer look at the body he'd dreamed of almost nightly for the past year. "How'd you like the captain's table?" he almost whispered.

Her eyes set on his mouth for the second time that night. "Very much." She cleared her throat abruptly.

His amusement was evident. "Glad you enjoyed it."

"You?" Izaya stepped closer. "*You* arranged that? Why?"

"You're welcome."

"Why, Gun?"

He wanted to kiss her then. "We've been on this boat almost a week," he said, ignoring the urge. "I've seen you every day. At least, I thought I was seeing you." His mouth twisted into a guilty smirk. "Needed to prove it to myself, I guess."

"But why?" she insisted, cursing silently when her lashes fluttered in response to his cologne drifting beneath her nose. The shudder rippling through her joined the fluttering lashes when he raised a hand to lightly cup her chin.

Gunther seemed mesmerized as his thumb brushed the tiny scar along her jaw. She'd worn the mark since childhood and had always been self conscious of it. He thought it was one of the loveliest things about her.

"Congratulations on your award, Izzy." He brushed the scar a few seconds longer, and then turned to leave.

Izaya's legs gave beneath her the instant the door closed at his back. When the bell sounded moments later, she bolted off the chair and whipped the door open to Tammy.

"Hey, I saw..."

Tammy didn't have the chance to finish her question. Not a problem, since she got her answer when Izaya fell into her arms and loosened the tether on her emotions.

"Honestly, Sam, a person doesn't have to have an enviable sex life to be able to write steamy sex scenes."

Refreshed and lovely, Izaya arrived for breakfast the next morning. A full day of conference obligations awaited her, and she was set on giving her best. She'd just approached the magnificent buffet when she noticed one of her dinner companions from the previous evening. She watched Sam Baxter rush over.

Izaya had to admit, she was a little stunned by his interest. Of course, she figured it was just the pilot's way of arranging a more intimate encounter later on. As he spoke, however, she got the distinct impression that he was truly interested in the dynamic of erotica and romance writing as a whole.

"Never fails to surprise me, the sort of people who are interested in the genre." Izaya watched Sam grab a plate and a roll of silverware. She shook her head. "I'd never believe a hard-nosed pilot like you would be so curious about it."

Sam shrugged. "I've read quite a few titles in the genre." His easiness faded a little. "But I'm still one who'll hide the book I'm really interested in behind the one I could care less about."

Izaya burst into laughter while adding a healthy portion of eggs to her plate.

Gunther didn't know if it was luck or a cruel twist of fate that landed him and Izaya in the same room that morning. When her laughter rang out, his expression darkened and his sigh sounded heavily at the table. Apparently, only one other person at the table of execs seemed to notice.

"You alright?" Misty leaned close to ask.

Gunther pushed his chair away from the table and stood. "I'm about to be."

Izaya and Sam had just agreed on a booth when they were approached. Izaya set her plate on the table with more clatter than necessary when she heard Sam speaking to Gunther.

"This is an impressive ship, Datari. I didn't have a chance to tell you that last night," Sam said.

Gunther couldn't help smiling. "I appreciate that."

Sam nodded. "Must be unreal to imagine a beautiful thing and then see it vibrant and real before your eyes."

"You have no idea," Gunther agreed, his gaze riveted on Izaya. "Listen, um, would you mind if I had a few minutes with Ms. Charles?"

Sam spread his hands and grinned. "Not a problem. Catch up with you later." He squeezed Izaya's arm before grabbing his plate from the table.

"You guys seemed to hit it off," Gunther commented once Sam moved on.

Izaya's smile was genuine. "He's really fun to talk to. I wanted to ask more about what being a pilot was like, but he was so interested in talking about the genre—"

Gunther's hearty laughter was an effective interruption. "Do you honestly believe that's what sparked that conversation?"

Izaya blinked and a frown furrowed her brow.Gunther still appeared amused though something harsh began to mingle with his expression. His gaze spanned the white bikini visible beneath her cream crocheted cover-up. "You really believe he was interested in the books you write?"

Izaya's temper warmed to full simmer. She raked his face and body with a look that was anything but appreciative. "Not everyone lies about being interested in my work to get me into bed, Gun."

The blow hit home, and Gunther straightened. When they were together, he had rarely asked about her writing or looked twice at her books. In the year they'd been apart, he'd read every one of her titles and closely followed all business endeavors regarding Charles House.

Izaya made a move to step closer, but changed her mind. "Gunther, I don't know what went wrong between us." He winced and she decided to move forward with, "I do know that we aren't going to be able to avoid each other on this ship, or for the rest of our lives. Especially since we live in the same town. Isn't there a way we can coexist?" She gave a resigned shrug. "Maybe we can find a way to be friends."

"Friends?" He uttered the word with cool firmness and stepped closer until Izaya was wedged between him and the table. "You think I could ever be your friend, Izzy? That I'd even want to be?"

Izaya was grateful to have the table nearby. Her legs turned to water and she wilted upon it.

"And what will you have to drink with your breakfast, ma'am?"

Izaya barely registered the server's question but was glad for the interruption. "I'd like to take my meal with me," she told the smiling young man who nodded immediately and collected her food. Edging away from Gunther, she didn't bother looking his way as she followed the server to the front of the dining room.

The day had gone surprisingly well considering its disastrous start. Izaya conducted a day of workshops and Q&As with the ease of the pro that she was. Of course, the exquisite atmosphere made everything easier. Everything, that was, except the real-life drama building with Gunther. Not even the sun-drenched Gulf and blue skies could diminish the agitations there.

Why had she even bothered to utter that stupid remark about them being friends? After their run-in that morning, Izaya had taken her breakfast in one of the private dining rooms reserved for editors, agents and publishers attending the conference. She'd enjoyed the delicious meal, but still she felt dazed. The feeling lingered even when she dressed and headed out for her first workshop. Once the event had gotten underway, her conversation with Gunther was forgotten. As always, her professional life made the uncertainties of her private one more bearable.

Now back in her suite, Izaya settled into the daring yet surprisingly comfortable bikini she had begun her day in. It was late afternoon and the balcony had become her favorite spot at the end of the day. Sunset was an hour or so off, but she'd taken solace there to try and make sense of Gunther Datari. All the years she'd put into their relationship, she thought she knew him. Then, in the blink of an eye...God, he didn't even want to be her friend.

"Dammit," she hissed softly. Squeezing her eyes shut, she willed anger to arrive and fight off the tears that were pressuring her eyes.

The bell rang and Izaya rejoiced at the sound. Perhaps it was Tammy and the two of them could go out and toss back a few. That thought and several others fled her mind when she saw Gunther in the hall.

"Sam's not here," she said.

Gunther nodded, accepting the sarcastic blow. "May I come in?"

Izaya wearily slapped her hands to her bare thighs. "Why?"

"I need to apologize."

She bristled.

"Please, Izzy."

The phrase was her undoing, and she turned away from the door.

"I'm sorry, Izaya," he said once he'd shut the door. "I never should've said that. I shouldn't have taken whatever was frustrating me out on you." If he'd had a hat it would've been in his hands. "I never meant to hurt you and I can tell that I did."

Izaya wasn't moved. "Why stop now? Especially when you've gotten so good at it?"

"Izzy, please,"

"Please what?" She waved a hand in the air when he said nothing more. "Get out, Gun."

He stood rooted to the spot.

"I said, get out. Go on!" The anger she prayed for arrived, bringing along tears just the same. Furious over her loss of control and that once again Gunther Datari was at the root of it all, she charged in and beat her fists against his chest.

Gunther absorbed the blows, his hands going to her hips to keep her steady as she pummeled him. His supportive hold easily merged into something more and felt like a massage, as though he were reacquaniting himself with her shape. He nudged her temple with his nose and trailed it along the side of her face, and then her jaw until it outlined the curve of her mouth.

His tongue stifled Izaya's sobs when it thrust past her lips. She moaned, instantly pliant in his arms. Then, as quickly as she wilted, she began to sizzle with need for him. Gunther's hands were everywhere, squeezing her hips and bottom, cupping her breasts...The bikini had toyed with his imagination for the better part of the day. He'd snapped at her due, in part, to the thought of pulling it away and helping himself to what lay beneath.

Izaya nudged against him, soothing puckered nipples with the friction of the shirt covering the granite slabs of his chest. His hold on her bottom firmed and she felt him carrying her. She didn't care where, only that it kept her in his arms. She locked her legs around his waist.

Gunther took her to the balcony, securing her between himself and the sliding glass doors. The hint of a growl rose in his chest when he deepened their kiss. Simultaneously, he tortured her nipples with light maddening strokes from his thumbs. Izaya's whimpering fed the crazed desire that had lain dormant for almost a year. It now funneled unrestrained.

"Stop me," he whispered, kissing his way down her chest. Impatiently, he tugged aside one cup of the bikini top and suckled a firm nipple between his teeth.

Shamelessly, Izaya rubbed against him. She shivered, his whimper touching her ears.

Gunther pulled back, surprising them. Bracing his hand on the door, he summoned deep breaths to fill his lungs.

"Why, Gun?" she asked, her voice hushed. Wearily, she leaned against the door and watched him. "What did I do? Did I get too close? Hmm?" she added when he slanted her a look. "Were those years just a game to you? When you realized I was playing for keeps, is that why you pushed me away?"

Gunther took Izaya's hand and pulled her near. "I'm sorry." He lightly touched his forehead to hers.

Izaya shoved at his chest. "Save your apology. I want an explanation."

She shook her head, seeing that he wasn't ready to give her one. "Get out," she ordered after whipping open the door. He obeyed without argument, and she steeled herself against showing any remorse. She knocked her fist against the door after slamming it at his back.

Chapter Three

The Umbrella Terrace had a sweet name, but the goings on inside the grand bar club were anything but sweet. Following the maiden voyage of *The Destiny*, the area was designated to be one of the ship's main hubs for hedonism.

The executive staff at Charles House decided it would be the perfect spot to host their Cover Models Drop In. The event was a definite success. The readers in attendance proved that the moment they entered the plush dance hall. The reinforced glass of the dance floor offered artificial but no less stunning images of the ocean depths. Lighting effects offered true impressions of the water's shimmering effects.

Charles House had guaranteed models from their sizzling erotica covers would be in attendance and they made good on it. More than eighty deliciously attractive men mingled with a number of very pleased conference attendees.

Following yet another dramatic encounter with Gunther, Izaya had considered begging off for the event. Tammy quickly informed her that any attempts to back out would be unacceptable. If need be, they'd move the event to Izaya's cabin

Izaya had seen her editor-in-chief make good on such threats once too often, and she had no intention of calling the woman's bluff.

"Now, aren't you glad you let me bully you?" Tammy stirred the oversized straw in her piña colad

Izaya managed a smile. "I needed to put in an appearance anyway." She smiled at the young waiter who arrived with her third margarita. "It is *my* House putting on the damn party."

"Mmm, yeah, that's *one* reason to be here." Tammy savored her creamy drink and closed her eyes in pure delight.

Izaya could tell the woman wasn't buying her rationale. In no mood to discuss the other reasons, she settled back to enjoy her refill.

"I hope I won't have to sit here and beg you to talk to me, Izaya."

"Tammy please..."

"Please what? Watch you mope and groan over Gunther Dartari?" Tammy locked gazes with Izaya before she could argue. "And don't you dare tell me this isn't about him."

Losing her taste for her drink, Izaya set it on the table and toyed with the stem of the glass.

Taking pity, Tammy leaned close to tug on a tassel dangling from the quarter-length sleeve of Izaya's lavender wrap dress. "Honey, what happened? At least admit to me that this is about Gunther."

Izaya rolled her eyes and reached for her glass.

"Uh uh." Tammy eased it out of her way. "I think you've had enough margaritas to loosen that tongue. Start talkin'."

"Alright!" Izaya hissed, clasping her hands to her head. "It's Gunther? Are you satisfied?"

"Not as satisfied as I thought I'd be. I already knew he was the reason, I just don't know why. So stop stallin' and give up the goods."

Izaya motioned toward her glass and took a sip when Tammy nodded her consent. She gave a short yet complete version of what happened in the cabin with Gunther.

"Do you think that was a smart move?" Tammy took a sip of her drink and noticed Izaya's glare. "Telling him to leave," she clarified. "Maybe he would've—"

"What, Tam?" Izaya sat up a little straighter. "What would he have done? Told me what I wanted to know? He's kept quiet for over a year, in case you forgot."

Poised to argue, Tammy decided on another swig of her drink instead.

Izaya had already noticed her reaction. "What?" she urged. "Tammy?"

"Have you ever considered that maybe he's finally ready to tell you why he handled things that way?"

Izaya lost some of the steam fueling her agitation. Defeated, she slumped back on the cushioned bar chair. "Since the day he ended things, I waited...waited for him to call or stop by, to tell me why he..." She bristled and fixed Tammy with a hard stare. "The fact that we're both here on this ship is total coincidence. He's got no more intention to talk to me now than he had a year ago."

Tammy cleared her throat and took a hasty swallow of her drink. When she glanced at Izaya and then looked away, Izaya cursed.

"Tell me you didn't?"

"Iz..."

"Tammy!"

"Alright! Alright," she whispered. "I ran into Misty—"

"Unbelievable..." Izaya murmured, already knowing where the story was heading.

Tammy had the decency to shrug. "Anyway, I ran into Misty a while back," she admitted, referring to Gunther's right hand woman. Tammy seemed to calm and leaned back to observe the festivities in the room. "Misty asked how you were doing, and I told her the truth–rotten." She pursed her lips when Izaya's gold-brown gaze narrowed. "She told me the same when I asked her about Gunther. She said he was doing as bad as you." Tammy shrugged. "We started putting our heads together. You know she's always been a big fan of the genre. She told me they'd gotten several events booked for one of Gunther's new ships—one of 'em was Slam Jam..."

Izaya groaned and massaged the bridge of her nose.

"I'm sorry." Tammy's whine was purely uncharacteristic. Still, the apology reflected in her almond-shaped eyes was hard to deny.

Izaya waved a hand, appreciating her friend's concern. "You were just trying to help, you both were. I'm just sorry you and Misty went to all that trouble to have it fizzle this way."

Gesturing for a refill from a passing server, Tammy's expression brightened. "I don't think anything's fizzled. In fact, I think it's all gonna work out fine, so you'll understand if I'm not ready to concede failure just yet."

Smirking, Izaya swirled the crushed ice in her drink. "Whatever works for you," she sang, her mood brightening when two Charles House cover models approached the table.

"You don't have to be here, you know," Misty told Gunther, watching him crush a linen napkin in his fist for the better part of five minutes.

"It was your idea that I come here, remember?"

Misty paid no heed to his snapping tone. "*Here* meaning, *here*, at this particular event, which is for women, our...enjoyment." She clarified while gazing helplessly at a model who flashed her a dazzling smile in passing.

Gunther rolled his eyes, muttering an obscenity.

"Honey, why are you torturing yourself like this?" She followed the line of Gunther's onyx stare, which targeted Izaya and Tammy across the room. "So you're determined to give yourself a triple dose of torture tonight, is that it? Izaya, looking gorgeous as hell, *and* being hit on by almost every incredible male specimen in the place? Torture, indeed." She sighed.

Gunther raked a hand through his dark hair as though the gesture would soothe what ailed him. "I screwed up, Misty. Made the biggest mistake of my life so far."

"With Izaya."

"I need to tell her that. I've got no idea, not one damn clue how to do it."

"And that I find hard to believe." Misty didn't blink when he slanted a stare at her. She leaned close and shared an idea of her own. "I know you're this big shipping magnate and all, but is it really so hard to tell the woman you love that you were wrong?" She tugged at the cuff of the cream shirt peeking from his jacket sleeve. "Or is it really even about that?"

Gunther gestured to the waiter for another Scotch instead of answering Misty's question.

"Do you think she won't take you back once you tell her what an idiot you were?" Misty guessed and watched the answer flash in his midnight eyes. "Honey, why don't you just talk to her? You won't know a damn thing until you open up the lines of communication."

"God Misty, spare me the analysis tonight, alright?" Gunther took the fresh Scotch from the waiter before he could place it on the table.

"Call my bluff, then. Go talk to her."

"This isn't the place."

"Baby, it's never *the place* when you're scared."

"You're comin' very close to being fired, Mis." Gunther downed the rest of the Scotch.

Misty pretended to bite her manicured nails. "Wow! Now *I'm* scared. Guess that makes

us two of a kind, huh?"

Gunther growled something harsh, pushed his chair from the table, and bolted off.

"I'm not very good at slow dancing," Izaya told one of her cover models.

Justin Jackson gave Izaya's arm a reassuring squeeze. "Don't stress it. Just follow my lead and put yourself in my hands."

Izaya laughed while glancing toward the incredible stage, where a vocalist belted out a sultry ballad. "That's not calming me any."

Justin felt a tap on his shoulder before he could pull Izaya into the proper embrace.

"Sorry, Justin, do you mind?"

Justin's grin broadened. "Can't very well deny the owner of the ship, can I? Mr. Datari," he greeted with a handshake. After kissing Izaya's cheek, Justin left the dance floor.

Izaya tried not to stiffen, knowing she would only crush her breasts into Gunther's chest when he pulled her close. She failed. "So you also know my cover models, I see."

He smiled, noticing when her striking gaze lowered to the dent in his chin. "Don't you think I should know my passengers?"

"What do you want?"

"To talk." He sobered instantly. "There are things I need to say to you."

"Save 'em," she grown tired of playing the victim. "I don't need your explanation. Thought I did, thought I'd die unless you told me why." She inhaled, squeezing Gunther's hand tight, wishing she could crush it. "Guess I finally realized you weren't going to give me one. I'll deal with it."

"I need to tell you this, Izzy."

She wrenched her hand from his. "And what about what I need? What about that, Gun? Do you even know what that is? Do you even care? Did you ever?" She narrowed her eyes. "I need to be left alone. I need for this damned cruise to be over so I can get the hell out of here." With a shove to his chest, she left him on the dance floor.

Izaya had called herself an idiot from the time she left her stateroom to the second before she knocked on Gunther's door. Following her strong exit from The Umbrella Terrace, she set off, determined to remain hidden in her room until the awards banquet in two days.

When she locked herself in, however, all she could focus on was what she wouldn't let Gunther say. She'd remained in her plush hideaway for over an hour before accepting that she'd been a fool to walk away. The explanation she'd wanted for over a year was now only a few corridor lengths away. She wanted it. More importantly, she wanted...him. And now, she was outside his door, wishing for a chance at both.

When his door opened, it seemed her wishes would be granted.

Gunther dragged a hand across his face, sure the sight of Izaya standing in his doorway was a hallucination. When she left him earlier, he had stifled the desire to go after her and make her hear him out. Instead, he had returned to his room to lick his wounds. Unfortunately, that had only increased the hurt. A few shots of tequila had taken care of that quite nicely. The numbing effects of the drink hadn't lasted for long. He'd been heading to the bar with a firm decision to finish the bottle when the bell sounded.

"Izaya." He'd scarcely whispered her name before his hand hooked behind her neck and he drew her into a throaty kiss.

Izaya whimpered the second their lips melded. Her body was limp against his solid frame but she kissed him with unmistakable fire, her tongue delving into his mouth, desperate to taste every crevice. She suckled his tongue erotically slow, then hungry and fiery.

"Put your hands on me, Gun. Please," she murmured, not the least bit ashamed to beg. She had craved his touch far too long to let anything rob her of it now.

Gunther strengthened his stance. Spreading his legs, he prayed they would continue to support him. Every part of his body felt rigid with need, his fingers kneaded her upper arms beneath the silky fabric of her dress. Raggedly, he scraped his teeth down her neck and across her collarbone, inhaling the coconut fragrance always clinging to her skin. Her lovely frock,nothing more than a hindrance, he relieved her of it with expert speed, leaving her clothed in her wispy lace bra and panties.

Izaya kicked off her strappy heels when he lifted her, carrying her through the darkened stateroom. She felt the plush comfort of his bed beneath her back moments later.

Gunther was still clothed. His jacket had been tossed aside and his shirt freed from his trousers and unbuttoned shortly after he returned to the room. Thoughts of what she'd feel like when they were both naked and wrapped around each other were almost driving him mad. When she moaned and splayed her hands across his bare chest, a wave of possession wrenched through him. He whipped the shirt off his back, the sight of her willing and needy with desire for him as dizzying as it was ego-stroking.

"Gunther, inside me...please...please, I need you there."

He ignored her throaty plea, intent on reacquainting himself with what he'd been denied for far too many nights. Slowly, he dragged his mouth across her chest. Cupping one breast, he tortured a firm nipple with suckling while his thumb manipulated its twin.

Izaya dragged her fingers through his hair and bit her lip at the sensation of the silk bedsheets against her skin. He cupped her bottom and instinctively, she ground herself against the part of him she most craved.

"Gunther, please..."

Again, he ignored her, trailing his kisses farther down her dark, curvy frame and held her thighs apart in a gentle yet unbreakable hold while his head disappeared between them.

Izaya sobbed when she felt his tongue filling and rotating inside her. Instantly, she began riding the thrusting organ even as she regretted that it wasn't the organ she truly wanted. Grasping at his broad shoulders, she tried to urge him upward.

Intoxicated by her taste, he simply wanted to savor the act. Izaya didn't want to reach orgasm, but it rapidly approached. Sensed how close she was to the brink, Gunther pulled back and covered her with his chiseled frame.

Izaya was happy to kiss herself from his tongue but hadn't lost sight of what she was after. Her nails grazed his carved abdomen to the belt surrounding his lean waist. She'd gotten it undone and was working on his trousers when he stopped her.

"Gunther, dammit!" She shuddered when he trapped her hand on a pillow. Deciding to turn the tables, she dragged her teeth along the powerful chords in his neck, smiling as he groaned and arched higher to enjoy more. Once he'd arched high enough, she leaned close and captured his nipple between her teeth. He cursed and went weak with arousal.

His reaction allowed her to push him onto his back and take the power position. She tortured his nipples with more strokes, loving the way it affected him. She unfastened his trousers and tugged down the zipper, taking the long, heavy length of his erection into her hand. She pulled away from his chest, the urgency to see him overpowering. She only had a few moments to marvel over his shape and size before Gunther grabbed her wrist and dragged her beneath him. She moaned her disagreement even as his mouth returned to the heart of her. In seconds, the languid thrusts of his tongue had her crying out in pleasure. Yearning for release, she stopped complaining.

Gunther smiled at her submission. While she was occupied with what his tongue was doing, he doffed his socks, trousers and boxers. Her eyes closed, she writhed on the bed; he pulled away to grab protection from the bedside table.

He plunged deep, kissing the shock from her when she felt him inside her. She convulsed sharply, her eyelashes fluttering as his stiffness threatened to overwhelm her. She cursed softly, a mound of her creamy moisture oozing around his length. Seconds from climax and regretting the approaching conclusion, she didn't want to be without him. How could she survive being without him again?

Gunther kept Izaya's arms at her sides. Sounds of the ocean waves mingled with their whispered words of desire. Gunther's fingers laced intimately through hers. As Izaya's orgasm grew, his thrusts deepened impossibly, deliciously. He groaned his love for her as they savored satisfaction in unison.

Izaya opened her eyes slowly and expelled a relieved sigh when she was sure she was alone in Gunther's suite. It was past 8 am, the morning slightly overcast. She considered that a blessing since this was definitely not the morning she wanted to greet the sun beaming happily into her face.

She had gotten what she'd wanted. Part of it, anyway...Whatever the case, it had been worth it to feel him next to her, a part of her. Regrettably, that fact simply raised the drama level on what would happen between them next. Would he still be willing to share his explanation, now that he'd gotten what she'd so very enthusiastically demanded of him?

Izaya kicked back the thick cotton linens and decided it was far too early to ponder such weighty matters. She left the bed, shimmied into her under things and dress, and was heading back to her cabin within minutes. She stepped inside the room, thankful no one caught her rushing down the corridors in last night's clothes.

She celebrated too soon. Tammy was already there and relaxing in the living area on a loveseat with a cup of hot green tea. Forgetting the tea, Tammy's eyes widened and she pointed. "Oooh!"

Chapter Four

Izaya opened the door to her room just as she realized she'd left her canvas bag on the sofa in the living area. It only took a few seconds to retrieve the tote, and she turned back to the open door to find Gunther leaning against the frame. Izaya silently praised her ability to resist shrieking at his surprise visit. But that ability didn't stop her from clutching a fist to her chest at finding him there.

"Leaving?" he inquired, cocking a sleek brow as he took in the bag she held.

Unclenching her fist, Izaya managed a slight nod and an even slighter smile. "Need some sun," she explained through a suddenly dry throat.

"Not enough?" Gunther tilted his head toward the sun-drenched balcony just beyond the living area.

"I think I've spent too much time in the cabins on this ship," she chided, easing the tote straps to her shoulder.

Gunther's mouth curved into a soft smile. "Is that a bad thing?"

"That would depend."

"On?" Gunther pushed off the door frame.

Izaya refused to let him rile her. "Whether it was a fluke."

"Ah," he moved forward, smirking when he saw that she refused to budge. "A fluke, a *one*-time thing?"

Izaya took a step back.

"Is that a challenge, Ms. Charles?"

"Gunther..." Izaya set down the tote and massaged the growing tension in her neck. "What are you doing?"

"Hoping to continue what we did last night," he smoothed the back of his hand across her scar, "hoping to continue what we did this morning."

"Why?" She groaned, her cheeks burning when his devilish chuckle touched her ears.

"May I show you instead of telling you?"

She refused to smile. "Last night...*and* this morning were incredible. We were lonely and we gave in..." Despite the skimpiness of the bathing suit she now wore, she was roasting. "To give in again will only make things harder."

His chuckle merged into a roar of laughter. "Damn right."

"Gunther, please..."

"I'd like to." The back of his hand ventured down along her neck and across her collarbone.

"This was never our problem." She gasped, biting her lip on the moan that was about to follow.

"I remember."

"It won't settle anything. Aside from the obvious," she hastily added with a glance below his waist.

"Why'd you leave this morning?" The teasing left his voice and expression.

"You weren't there."

"And had I been there, would you have stayed?"

"Yes."

"Even though it wouldn't have solved anything?"

"Gunther..."

"Izaya?"

"Alright, I would've stayed whether it solved anything or not." She withdrew from his loose embrace. "Why does that matter?" Gunther caught her halfway to the sofa. "It matters, Izzy."

"Why?" She strained against his hold. "Because pleasure is of utmost importance?"

"Right now. Yes."

She had to admire his honesty. It was what made his charm so irresistible. "And later?"

"Can we discuss it *later*? After?" His voice was weak with desire.

"I've only got an hour to myself before I have to meet with my group." She tried to step around him.

Gunther blocked her way. "Let Tammy handle it."

She wouldn't look up at him. "It's my responsibility."

He crowded her until she was wedged between him and the wall. "Can't your staff handle it?" His voice faded to a whisper seconds before his mouth touched her skin.

"I have to."

"But do you want to?" Gunther's fingers dipped past the strings securing her bikini bottom. "Hmm?"

Izaya couldn't think beyond his teeth raking her skin, biting softly into her shoulder, tugging at the multicolored spaghetti straps. "This isn't fair..."

"I know," he grunted, his fingers sliding into the crotch of her bikini to discover a well of heavy moisture. "Just please don't stop me, Izaya." He begged, thrusting his fingers deep.

A wavering whimper lilted from her throat. Reflexively, Izaya edged her knee along the powerful length of his thigh.

Gunther's handsome face hid in the crook of her neck while he cherished the feel of his middle finger stroking her to bliss, wishing another part of his anatomy carried out the act.

Izaya curled weak hands into the hunter-green fabric of his shirt. The feel of his chest below her fingertips was as much an aphrodisiac as the lunges and rotations of his fingers inside her.

Satisfaction curved Gunther's mouth when he heard her begging him not to stop. Izaya needed no additional assistance to reach climax, but his wicked murmurs in her ear intensified the pleasure jackknifing through her.

When she was spent, any thoughts of arguing a continuation of that morning's activities were forgotten. She curled into Gunther's embrace when he carried her from the front room.

Izaya prided herself on being an equal partner when lovemaking was in session. When Gunther placed her in the middle of the bed, a wave of selfishness overwhelmed her. She wanted pleasure, the pleasure only he could provide. She moaned, curving her hands around the powerful forearms bared by his rolled-up sleeves. His hands were fisted on either side of her head. He touched her only with his lips, which trailed over skin glistening with a thin sheen of sweat.

Izaya's hands fell away from his forearms to rest upon the bed coverings tangling beneath her writhing. He'd removed her bikini top using only his teeth. She arched like a bow when his lips nibbled all around her breasts, purposefully ignoring the yearning tips. Threading her fingers through his thick hair, she tried to direct his head there and wanted to scream when he chuckled, refusing her silent request.

Gunther outlined the perfect roundness of her bosom with the tip of his nose. The coconut scent clinging to her skin drove him mad and practically disintegrated his restraint. Still, he resisted.

Gunther's hormones had no qualms about rushing. They pulsed and demanded he take her fast and ruthlessly. The fact that he'd had her only hours earlier didn't diminish the renewed need raging through him.

Izaya welcomed the urgency in his touch. Desperate to feel him, she unfastened his shirt buttons, craving the wall of his chest beneath her palms. Gunther muttered a deep curse moments before his tongue pummeled her mouth with wicked lunges. Izaya participated eagerly in the kiss. She took his hand, directing it over her breast and biting her lip when his palm grazed the nipple. Crying out softly, she rubbed against his hand, delighting in the friction and begging for more. His kiss was a mixture of persuasion and possession. Izaya suckled fervently on his tongue when she felt him caressing her sex. His fingers dipped and explored before abandoning their play to massage her inner thighs.

Izaya was lost even as she reached down to undo the button fly of his jeans. She almost laughed over the fact that he didn't try to stop her...Quickening her task, she was reaching inside his boxers seconds later and shuddering her pleasure when he lay hard and heavy in her hands.

Gunther nuzzled the crook of her neck, deeply inhaling her scent before he journeyed lower. At last, his lips were soothing and tugging at her nipples. He smirked knowingly when she spasmed and sobbed at the pleasure he brought her. His lips slackened around the tip when her thumb grazed the crown of his sex with slow strokes.

Feverishly, he tugged at his loose jeans until they were just past his buttocks. Izaya gripped him there, loving the firmness filling her hands.

Gunther, still suckling madly at her bosom, broke briefly to trail his tongue along the deep valley between them. Awkwardly, he patted his jeans where they lay past his butt and began to root around in the pockets. Izaya produced a throaty laugh when he slipped a condom packet between her fingers.

She cupped her hands around his jaw and urged him up for a kiss that he willingly accepted. Izaya shivered when tiny, torturous sounds rose from his throat. Knowing that she was responsible for affecting him so filled her with a truly heady sensation. She put the condom on him and wasted no time guiding him inside her.

Gunther weakened, all of his strength headed right to the source of his pleasure. His hands grazed her body, gripping and squeezing along the way until they locked on her thighs and held them farther apart.

Izaya pushed her head deeper into the coverings and met his devilish thrusts with a fire of her own. Gunther rose to his knees, deepening the penetration and their pleasure. Izaya's cries heightened with each lengthy, stiff stroke. Blindly, she reached for his shirt and clutched the tails to support her while she slammed against him.

Izaya dug the heels of her hands into her eyes once more before again trying to focus on the face looming above hers.

"Gun?"

His soft smile deepened. "She remembers," he whispered.

She studied him in disbelief. "You're still here?"

"You didn't really expect me to go, did you?"

"Well...I..."

"Listen, I talked to Tammy."

"Tammy."

"Asked if she'd mind taking over the rest of the day and night." He shrugged.

Izaya laughed. "I bet that went over well."

Gunther's handsome face would've flushed had he been anything other than molasses dark. "It was surprising how fast she turned you over to my care."

Slowly, Izaya rose to brace her weight on her elbows. "Gunther..."

"Hey," he brushed his thumb across her parted lips, "I won't deny that I've missed you. So much at times, I thought I'd lose my mind." His gaze caressed her face and hair in wonder and then he settled on her eyes. "Do you suppose we could avoid the very heavy conversations we need to have, just for tonight?"

"Tonight?"

"I'd like to take you out."

Izaya bit her lip and glanced around her plush digs. "Can't get more *out* than a cruise ship, Gun."

"Trust me."

Her heart wedged in her throat.

"Pick you up in two hours?"

What the hell, Izaya decided, in no hurry to bring an end to the time they'd shared that day. She kept telling herself that it wasn't safe to fall for him again--but she had never gotten over him in the first place.

"Two hours," she accepted with a nod.

Gunther leaned in for a kiss and lingered far longer than he intended.

"Incognito?!" Izaya's brown-gold stare was as wide as an excited child's. She watched the stage, where one of her favorite jazz groups performed. "I can't believe you remembered how much I love them."

"Did you expect me to forget?" Gunther grazed his fingers along the satiny line leading from her wrist to elbow.

Izaya followed the caress and then looked back toward the dazzling stage across the sea of jazz lovers. "I never expected to see you again, Gunther."

"Is that your way of telling me you've been getting on with your life?"

Izaya swayed in time to the smooth music. "If you like," she chimed.

Gunther resisted the urge to crush the beaded glass he held. "Boston's a small town."

"Yes, but it's surprisingly close to lots of larger ones."

"We've only been apart a year."

"And I'm sure you haven't been a hermit all that time."

He had. Wondering whether or not *she* had was threatening to shred the last of his ability to quell his temper.

"I'll have another," Izaya told the waitress who approached their table. "And this isn't a conversation we should get into," she told Gunther, watching his jaw clench. "You may not like what you hear."

Amazingly, Gunther's mounting temper seemed to diminish. "Then maybe we should change the subject?"

Izaya blinked, not bothering to mask her surprise. "Good idea."

"So is this why you backed off earlier? You didn't want me to decline an invite back to your room?"

Gunther grinned in spite of himself. "You know me too well, Izzy."

"Thought I did," she sighed, dropping her purse to an end table in the spacious living area. Gunther slanted her a look but didn't offer a reply. Izaya quietly celebrated his decision.

Gunther headed for the balcony. The expansive area was set with a table for two, chilling champagne and beer, a CD changer where the sounds of Incognito raised sweet and light. Izaya strolled the area on slow steps. Her eyes were narrowed as she focused on the item that intrigued her the most.

"Is this why we didn't order dinner?"

Gunther smiled but didn't look Izaya's way while taking shrimp kabobs and steaks from a small fridge in the corner of the balcony. "I figured it'd been a while since you'd eaten food from a grill." He shrugged while rising to his full height. "Maybe this is one of those things

you've enjoyed in those larger towns close to Boston."

"May I?" Izaya gestured toward the chilling champagne bottle and helped herself to a glass when Gunther waved. "Afraid I haven't had the pleasure since the last time we did this."

"Right..." Gunther lit the charcoals and waited for the flame to catch. "The last time we did this...hmphf, did we ever get around to eating?"

Feeling more at ease, Izaya stepped from her rose-blush peek-a-boo pumps. "We got around to it...eventually."

"Yeah we did..." Gunther smiled as if suddenly embarrassed by whatever scandalous memory had flashed to mind.

Izaya took a seat on one of the cushioned lounges near the CD changer. Taking a sip of the flavorful champagne, she rested her head against the lounge while savoring the taste bubbling at the back of her tongue. She indulged in her own trip down memory lane, thinking of evenings spent at her place or at Gunther's. He often grilled, telling her he simply preferred the taste of food that had come off an outdoor grill as opposed to that cooked on an indoor stove. Izaya had always loved a good barbeque, but developed a new respect for the art once Gunther introduced her to all the culinary delights that were possible.

"So doesn't the designer of all this luxury have better things to do with his time than grill steaks for a guest?"

"Depends on the guest."

"Lots of special guests on this ship." Izaya turned to her side and watched him while she sipped from the champagne flute. "I can think of any number of them who'd love to be in my seat."

"Can't blame 'em for that." He set the grill rack in place and slid a wicked look across the racy, cream tube dress she wore. "*I'd* love to be in your seat myself."

Izaya burst into laughter a split second before Gunther.

"I couldn't resist that one."

Izaya shrugged. "Well, I put it right out there for you." She felt so incredible, so relaxed, and it had nothing to do with the champagne.

In spite of the lightness they enjoyed, a sobering mood gradually swept in. Gunther decided to take advantage and shared another admission.

"You know my family never approved of me seeing you."

The soft confession had Izaya sitting straighter on the lounge. "Your father and uncle," she guessed, watching Gunther nod. She mimicked the action. "That doesn't really surprise me. Remember, I only met them two, maybe three times. Guess that's why, huh? Because they didn't approve."

"Unless it was about business, I preferred spending as little time around them as I had to."

"And still you..."

Gunther finished seasoning the steaks and placed them on the red hot grill racks. Afterwards, he joined Izaya on the lounge.

"And still I...?" he probed.

"Dumped me." Izaya forced herself not to break eye contact.

Gunther blinked. "You think I did that because they told me to?"

"It's easier to believe than the alternative."

"Which is?"

She couldn't answer and would've looked away had it not been for his hand cupping her chin.

"Which is?" he insisted.

She could feel her lip trembling, but pressed on. "That you threw away what took eight years to build, because you felt like it."

"Izaya..."

The scent from the grill combined with the champagne she'd downed were beginning to make her nauseous. "I should go."

Gunther smothered her hand beneath his. "Don't."

"This walk down memory lane was nice." She edged off the lounge. "I think it was a mistake. We can't go back."

"To hell with going back." He stood and caught hold of her arm when she tried to pass. "It doesn't change the fact that we need to talk."

"I can't," Izaya breathed, feeling the influence of his sex appeal mix with her desire for him. She wouldn't lose herself with him—she couldn't.

"Good night, Gun," she whispered, relieved when he didn't resist her pulling her arm from his grip. Quickly, she collected her things and rushed from the cabin.

Chapter Five

The most highly touted Slam Jam events took center stage a few days later. Brunch to honor the EMMA Award nominees began around 11 am one morning.

From her seat at one of the head tables, Izaya compared the event to her own soiree, which had taken place a few nights prior. There were scores of cover models mixing and mingling from her House and several others. Of course, the readers were just as enthused and incredible as before.

This time around,the readers couldn't outdo the members of Izaya's own House. Their brash and naughty remarks to some of the models had more than a few of the devastating men grinning from embarrassment.

"My God," Rebecca Harvey sighed and tilted her head to get a better look.

"What girl?" Jessica Hume asked the editorial assistant.

Rebecca gave a slight nod and idly twirled a lock of her auburn hair. "*He* must be from one of the other houses' covers. I'd remember him if he were ours."

The table of women turned in the direction Rebecca and Jessica's gazes were focused.

While the rest of her table partners murmured agreement, Izaya whipped her head in the opposite direction.

The bawdy compliments regarding Gunther Datari continued to flow around the table. Eventually, Jessica recalled who he was and winced when she looked over at Izaya.

"Honey, I'm sorry," she leaned over to whisper.

"What's he doing at an event for Slam Jam?" Izaya asked, risking a glance at Gunther across the crowded room.

Jessica shrugged. "Well, he *is* the owner of the ship. Maybe it's about that." She turned to tell the rest of the women whom they drooled over.

"Right." Izaya pursed her lips, clearly not buying that one. She took a healthy swallow of her tea, praying the man wouldn't make a point of stopping by the table.

She hadn't seen him since they'd parted ways a few nights earlier. The *Destiny* had docked in the Grand Caymans, and she'd spent the time sightseeing and shopping with her crew. So much for obtaining that explanation she told him she *didn't* want...

"Good morning, ladies." Gunther finally made his rounds to the Charles House table.

"Good morning, Mr. Datari," the women drawled like school girls swooning over a cute teacher.

Gunther nodded, gracing each woman with a smile. "I wanted to stop by and thank you all for being a part of the *Destiny*'s maiden voyage."

"It's our pleasure, Mr. Datari. This is a phenomenal ship." Rebecca raved as her colleagues nodded their agreement.

Once the light conversation and intros were done, Gunther's dark, deep eyes locked on Izaya. "May I have a moment?"

Izaya gave a soft smile and stood, ignoring the curious stares that followed.

"We haven't finished our conversation," Gunther said once he'd led them to a quiet area across the banquet hall.

Izaya smiled. "Things got out of hand, I guess."

His expression was grim. "That's an understatement. But this still needs to be said."

"Is it really that important, Gun?"

"It is to me," Gunther moved suddenly, towering over Izaya then. "It's very important to me, and you're lying if you tell me it's not important to you."

"Why? Because you think I've been pining for you all this time?"

He shook his head. "Only you know the answer to that one, Izzy." His gaze was soft as it caressed her face. "I need to explain this to you."

"And then what?" Izaya gave herself a mental kick for voicing the question. Thankfully, she didn't have to wait for a response. Applause swelled. The event was beginning, and she gave Gunther a pitiful smile before rushing off.

Following the lovely nominees brunch, the conference workday began. Izaya had workshops in addition to a business meeting regarding the start of the Charles House Network.

Izaya had to commend her contact Mitchell Payne on his tenacity. The man was determined to have the venture go forward and had booked passage on the five-day cruise to do just that. Heading across the lobby to the restaurant, where she was meeting Mitchell, she bumped into an old friend."

"Quite impressive. Everyone I know can't say enough about how incredible this ship is. Including me," Izaya told Misty Terrell once they shared hugs and briefly caught up.

Misty hugged herself, looking up at the lofty expanse of the *Destiny*'s Eastern Corridor. "Yeah, Gunther put a lot of himself into this. First ship he's ever had total authority to design."

"So when did his dad retire?"

Misty frowned, appearing momentarily surprised by Izaya's question. "Well...Mr. Javaris passed away a little over a year ago," she said, referring to Gunther's father.

Izaya stood silent, realizing that was around the time Gunther had ended things between them.

"That was one of the reasons we wanted him onboard for the maiden voyage, to celebrate his success, you know?"

"Mmm...and also because I'd be here, too, right?" Izaya shook her head when Misty winced. "It's alright," she shrugged. "Tammy can't keep much hidden from me for long."

Misty rolled her eyes. "And that fool bet *I'd* be the first one to spill the beans to Gunther."

Izaya squeezed her arm. "Sorry you guys wasted your time planning this."

Misty stepped closer. "I know he wants to talk to you, to *really* talk to you about what happened before."

"You know, Misty, I'm starting to think it's all just best left alone..."

Misty was already shaking her head. "Why don't you hear what he has to say first, hmm?" With that advice, Misty kissed Izaya's cheek and strolled away.

Mitchell Payne expelled a low whistle when Izaya entered the cigar bar and was escorted to a table.

Gunther, sitting next to Mitchell at the bar, frowned when he realized the target of Mitchell's whistle.

Mitch offered a guilty smirk and half-shrug. "Forgive me, but in my line of work, you rarely come in contact with a lovely like that."

Gunther reached for something to squeeze in his fists. "And how much...contact have you had with her?"

"Not as much as I'd like," Mitchell blurted. "It's all business, so far. She's interested in launching a satellite network for her publishing house." He noticed Gunther's frown had become an all-out murderous glare. "What?"

"You really don't know who she is?" Gunther muttered a curse at Mitchell's blank stare. "You had no idea that she's mine?" He cleared his throat after his territorial slip. "You didn't know we used to see each other?"

Mitchell flushed slightly beneath his rich tan. "Sorry, Gun, I had no clue. Hell," he raked a hand through his unruly brown hair, "I accepted that invite of yours for the maiden voyage because I knew she'd be here."

Gunther nodded, accepting the explanation. Silently, he acknowledged that Mitch had no way of knowing about him and Izaya. Mitch had been in California for the past four years and had never met Izaya when Gunther was seeing her.

"So I take it the relationship is dead?"

Gunther's frown returned.

Mitchell raised his hands in defense. "I'm just asking if it was a mutual thing."

"I broke up with her." Gunther admitted.

"Well, then...guess that means..."

"Doesn't mean a damn thing," Gunther clarified, knowing where the man's thoughts were focused.

Mitchell laughed and pushed back from the bar. "Don't go regretting it all now because you made an idiot move." He clapped Gunther's shoulder. "I'm not big on speeches, so let me just say—thanks."

Gunther watched Mitchell stroll off and proceeded to tear his napkin into pieces.

Following a very productive meeting with Mitchell Payne, Izaya was more confident than ever about her next venture. Perhaps a satellite channel wasn't as farfetched an idea as she'd once believed.

Her easy smile froze when she felt a hand tight on her elbow and found Gunther at her side.

"A moment of your time, Izzy?" He didn't wait for a reply, but escorted her none too sweetly towards the ship's executive wing.

The trip was lengthy and silent. Thankfully, the route wasn't heavily travelled. Izaya celebrated the fact that she didn't have to wear a phony smile to mask her tension.

The executive wing was in a dim, elegant area where the soothing hum of the cooling unit provided the only sound. Rich navy and burgundy carpeting muffled their footsteps.

The lengthy corridor branched off into two sections, the captain's office on one end, an unlabeled door on the other. Gunther escorted Izaya to the unlabeled door. Once inside the room, she spent a moment adoring the cool architectural style. Sophisticated and professional, it maintained warmth and comfort, enticing her to kick off her pumps.

"How long have you known Mitch?"

Izaya blinked, momentarily mesmerized by the depth and softness of his voice. "I'm hoping to launch a station through his company. I, um...I didn't realize that you knew him."

Nodding, Gunther scanned the smart suit encasing Izaya's figure. His gaze lingered on the flippy skirt that flared above her knees. "Yeah, guess Boston's a much smaller place than we both thought. Mitch must want your business pretty bad," he said upon realizing he'd been staring at her chest, which was enticingly encased beneath the short waist blazer. "I've known him for a long time. He's more of a workaholic than either of us. Makes sense now why he accepted my ticket for this cruise."

Izaya smiled as it all began to click for her as well. "He made his being here seem like it was all part of his professional service."

Gunther strolled the office before taking a spot on the edge of the desk filling a corner of the room. "Is that all he offered? His...professional service?"

Izaya forgot her musings over Mitchell Payne and studied her ex more closely. Regardless of how relaxed he appeared leaning against the desk, his loafer-shod feet crossed one at the ankles and his arms folded across the midnight blue shirt that did nothing to mask the power of his chest, the truth was glaringly clear. "Are you jealous?" she breathed.

He didn't so much as blink. "Only interested."

"Oh please." Izaya tossed her portfolio to a nearby chair. "And if I said there was more? That he was offering me a prime rate for his *personal* services, then what?"

He was still maddeningly cool, though a tight smile began to play around his mouth. "Then I'd ask if you were trying to get him hurt,"

Izaya crossed the room. "And why would you even say that when you were the one who ended things? This all makes about as much sense as why you ended things in the first place." She graced him with a scathing look before bolting for the door. She made it about halfway before his hand was on her arm again.

"Why don't you take off the territorial cap, Gun?" She wrenched her arm out of his hold. "I'm not yours anymore. You saw to that quite nicely."

He secured her against his chest. "You really believe that?"

"More and more every day," she sneered.

"Is that right?"

Izaya noticed the change in his smile and dark gaze about a second too late. Her only response was a moan when his hands went to work on her body and his tongue plunged deep inside her mouth. His fingers raged upward along her thighs and she simultaneously regretted and cheered her decision not to wear hose.

The kiss deepened, growing lustier as his hands rose higher to knead her bottom until lacy panties covering it had been smoothed down. He broke the kiss and Izaya could only gasp around the sob and moan filling her throat. His teeth scraped the line of her collarbone, venturing lower until his nose was buried in the opening of her blazer. She whimpered, watching as he undid the single button with his teeth. His powerful hands still squeezed her derriere, lifting her steadily until her sex was lodged neatly against his.

Izaya cursed their clothing and cherished the friction when she ground on the stiffness straining the front of his trousers. She'd pressed her palms to his chest intending to push him away. Instead, she used the granite wall to support her mock thrusts on his arousal.

Gunther had tugged aside one lacy bra cup and feasted on a nipple until it firmed and puckered. Whimpers of need were forced from his throat as well. He suckled and bathed her breasts until moans ripped free of her throat and filled the office.

Gunther dragged Izaya with him to the desk and kept her trapped in the spot he'd just vacated. He rested his forehead on her chest, more intent then on searching out what he craved inside her panties. They both shuddered when his middle finger plunged deep inside her to encounter a wealth of need.

She was unashamed yet cursed her weakness for him even as she rode the thrusting finger. When he added his index finger to the seduction, she bit her lip and welcomed the approaching orgasm.

Gunther continued to stroke her even as she trembled from sheer delight. When her shudders began to ebb, he extracted his fingers and set her clothes in place. Cupping her cheek, he kissed her there and whispered in her ear.

"Is that right?"

Repetition of his earlier question forced her to look away. Gunther saw the tear stream down her cheek and experienced an instant stab of remorse and disgust over his actions.

Izaya edged away from him. "It's been over a year." She didn't look his way but headed for the door. "And what you did still hurts as much now as it did then but...more in *this* moment, seeing you, being with you..." She grabbed her portfolio and tucked it under her arm. Her hand closed on the doorknob. "Heaven help me, I still love you and what you're doing now, your hands on me...God, I've thought about it every night." She smirked and bowed her head. "Sweet as a whisper and still it hurts like a fist because I know it's not real for you." Raising her head, she turned the knob and walked past the doorway without a backward glance.

The day of the Emma Awards Gala arrived, and with it came anticipation, excitement and a faint twinge of sorrow that a truly magical time was nearing its end. Izaya basked in the magic surrounding the EMMAs as much as anyone, but all she wanted was to get back to her life in Boston and make a more honest effort at forgetting she'd ever known Gunther Datari.

Seeing him after all that had happened was like finding a pretty box beneath the tree on Christmas morning and opening it only to find sour apples. Her hopes that the impromptu trip might bring about another chance for her and Gunther were dashed, leaving her as hollow as the core of one of those apples.

Still, she had a job to do and a smiling face to wear for her employees and the loyal readers who'd come to support her and those in her profession.

Izaya was first to arrive on deck, where Tammy had arranged a special breakfast for Charles House staff. Relishing the solitude, Izaya took a few moments to indulge in the beautiful view of the Caribbean. She lost herself in the awesomeness of the sea. Miles upon miles of blue water connected with the vivid blue sky produced an effect that took her breath away and made her feel as though she could stare out in wonder forever.

She was still gazing out over the ocean while tugging the wispy cover-up from the coral and black swimsuit she wore. She spent several moments absently pulling at the material when she realized she was being assisted. Turning, she found Gunther behind her.

His dark eyes followed the path of the cover-up as he eased it from her shoulders. He kept the garment in his hands, kneading and caressing it as if it were Izaya between his palms. He tossed it aside suddenly and moved forward to urge her backward until she was sitting in one of the chairs surrounding the table. He settled into the one next to her.

"My father died the night I told you it was over."

Izaya's mouth fell open. She forgot all the tension that had existed between them. She reached out, but he squeezed her hand and set it back on her lap.

"You know he and my uncle raised me." He grimaced when she nodded. "They were great men, great business men. As family men, they sucked." He tried to smile and failed. "But if they strived to teach me one thing, it was that women weren't to be trusted with your money or your heart." He leaned forward, bracing his elbows on his knees. "They'd both loved and lost and it broke their hearts. Second time around, they loved and lost and it hardened their hearts." Gunther studied his hands, rubbing them one on top of the other. "They came out of it bitter, distrustful and they were determined that I not follow in their footsteps.

"The night my father died..." He cleared his throat, determined to press on past the emotion wedging there. "The night my father died, I was there at his side. He was in a world of pain; the cancer had eaten away what stomach he had left. In spite of all that pain, he told me he was happy." He uttered a soft chuckle and slanted a glance toward the sea. "After the second marriages failed, my dad and my uncle, they just lost focus on the business. It was my shot and I ran with it." A more pronounced smile tugged at his mouth.

"My dad said he was proud I was his son. I'd brought Datari back from the brink. Then he was gone. First time he ever spoke a word of approval to me, and the night he does it's the last night I ever talk to him." He groaned, steeling himself against tears by pressing thumb and forefinger to the bridge of his nose.

"I was angry, angrier than I could ever remember being. All I could think about was how I was robbed of more time with him and blaming the gold digger he had the misfortune to hook up with. Then, I came home." He reached for Izaya's hand. "There you were, loving me and telling me how you wanted us to be all that we could be." He nudged her chin with the back of his hand and brushed her scar with his thumb. "You said you were mine and you wanted me to be all yours..." His expression darkened. "I should've been proud and feeling stupid in love. I just felt angry and determined not to go down like those two idiots did. and I snapped."

His hands fell away from hers and he leaned back in the chair, massaging his forehead when he closed his eyes. "When you were gone, it took me a week to admit what a brain dead thing I'd done. The way I hurt you, humiliated you... I felt like shit, but something wouldn't let me come find you and tell you that."

Izaya's smile was sympathetic. "I guess that pride kicked in after all."

Gunther managed a smile. "Yeah...it's as simple and as stupid as that, Izzy. That's what happened that night."

"And what about later?" Izaya's voice was small while she focused on the gold watch peeking from the cuff of his gray cotton shirt. "It's been a year, Gun. Why haven't you come to me? You had to know..."

"But I didn't." He leaned forward again. "Izzy, I didn't know, couldn't be sure if..."

"Gun?"

"I couldn't be sure you'd forgive me. If you'd take me back." He shrugged. "Why should you after the way I acted? I was a jackass and I hurt you. Asking your forgiveness scared the living hell out of me, but not as much as hearing you say I'd never have another chance with you."

Izaya's heart thudded so loudly, it was practically deafening. The most she'd ever hoped for was an explanation. Being back in his life was something she'd wished for and fantasized about. Until the trip, she'd never even entertained the thought that he might feel the same.

He glanced past her shoulder and scooted to the edge of his chair. "I should let you go." His heart thudded too, as the true measure of the statement hit him. He looked over her shoulder again, where he'd spotted her colleagues heading toward the table.

"Thanks for listening, Izzy." He stood but leaned close to press a lingering kiss to her ear. "I love you," he whispered before leaving.

Izaya was frozen to her seat until she felt a hand brush her shoulder. She turned with Gunther's name on her lips.

"Honey?" Tammy knelt beside Izaya's chair and patted her knee. "Everything okay?"

Izaya could only respond with a slow nod.

The rest of the day passed in a whirlwind of talks, signings and other networking events. Izaya had little time to dwell on Gunther's confession.

The Grande Ballroom of the *Destiny* had been reserved for the awards gala and the EMMAs commenced with all the pomp it was known for. Elaborate gowns and chic tuxedos were the order of dress. Men stood handsome and at their most devastating, the women alongside them the epitome of feminine allure.

Izaya felt as much like a fairy princess as any woman there, though her heart was heavy. At least she looked the part in a classic yet chic design. The butter rum satin creation emphasized the flawless rich caramel of her skin. The gown's hoop skirt accentuated her small waist and the fullness of her bosom. Dainty cream slippers peeked from beneath a billowing skirt and matched the cream piping lining the square bodice.

Izaya had stopped searching for Gunther in the massive crowd after craning her neck for the better part of the first hour of the event. She remembered to clap for the authors who won for titles published by Charles House. When the nominations were read for the final category, Publisher of the Year, Izaya's emotions were divided. She was excited about the honor she hoped to take home, but also anticipated the conclusion of the festivities so she could find Gunther.

"...and here to present the award is a man we've all seen and swooned over at least once during the last several days. Not only is he the owner of this incredibly beautiful ship, but he's also its designer. Ladies and gentlemen, please help me in welcoming Mr. Gunther Datari!"

Izaya blinked owlishly and watched Gunther thank the event coordinator, Marsha Reynolds. He went on to thank the audience, and for the first time that evening, Izaya took in the festivities with true interest filling her brown-gold gaze. She thought he was more beautiful than usual in the dark tux with its loose tie and three-quarter length coat. Izaya forced her attention away from his body and face and onto the words he spoke.

"...the EMMA Award for Publisher of the Year goes to...a woman that I love to distraction." Gunther looked in Izaya's direction. "As men—as human beings—we sometimes allow pride to dictate many things in our lives. Many times, the results are disastrous. But if we're lucky we realize our mistakes and...if we're blessed, the one we wronged will forgive us for our vast stupidity. Izaya..."

Izaya heard someone at the table shriek her name and that Charles House had won. The room burst into applause. Tammy rushed around to nudge the dumbfounded Publisher of the Year from her chair.

In slow motion, Izaya stood, and in even slower motion, she closed the distance between her and Gunther. He'd stepped down from the stage and tugged her into his arms before greeting her with a throaty kiss that raised the volume in the ballroom another few decibels.

"What are you doing?" Izaya whispered, her eyes shining with happy years as she searched his face.

Gunther shrugged and brushed his thumb across her scar. "You know me. I'm not above using my clout to get my way."

Izaya's gaze narrowed playfully. "So did I win this thing fair and square?"

"Fair and square," he confirmed, sobering as he drew his sleek brows close. "The honor you came for is onstage, but I pray you'll do *me* the honor of accepting my proposal."

Izaya's lips parted. "Proposal? You really want that?"

"Only if your feelings haven't changed."

"They never did." She gave a tiny sniffle. "I love you."
He nudged her nose with his. "Still?"
"Always."

The End

Author Bio-

AlTonya Washington has been a published romance novelist for 6 years. Her novel *Finding Love Again* won the *Romantic Times* Reviewer's Choice Award for Best Multicultural Romance 2004. In July 2008, she released her twelfth novel *A Lover's Worth*. August 2009 marked the release of her thirteenth and fourteenth novels: *Rival's Desire* and *Passion's Furies*. In addition to teaching a community college course entitled *Writing the Romance Novel* she works as a Senior Library Assistant and resides in North Carolina. AlTonya will release her fifteenth novel Hudson's Crossing in March 2009. In March 2009, AlTonya- writing as T. Onyx- released an electronic version of her debut erotica title *Truth In Sensuality*. In August 2009 she will release her debut audio title *Another Love* and the final installment in her Ramsey series *A Lover's Soul*.

Red Rose Publishing
As a Whisper

BET-
Remember Love,
Guarded Love
Finding Love Again
Love Scheme
A Lover's Dream

Genesis Press-
Wild Ravens
Passions Furies

Dafina-Kensington
In The Midst of Passion

Harlequin
 A Lover's Pretens
A Lover's Mask

Pride & Consequence
Rival's Desire
Hudson's Crossing

Show Me!
By
Barbara Keaton

Chapter One

"I'm too nervous," Camille Kohl, known as Cammie to everyone, breathed out as she wrung her hands one over the other before tossing another article of clothing into the suitcase that would carry her belongings on a five-day cruise to the Southern Caribbean with stops in the Grand Cayman Islands and Jamaica.

"Mom, it's going to be okay." Lottie took her mother's hands in hers, stilling them. "There's nothing to be nervous about."

"So you say. You're not meeting anyone. You're married."

"And?"

"And I'm too old for this, Lottie." Pouting, Cammie plopped down onto the king-sized bed. She thought of Jacques Champion, the man whose whole idea it had been, the one she'd gone along with without hesitation when he'd first mentioned it to her a month ago. Back then, they had been indulging in a little pillow talk, and her head had swum with thoughts she hadn't had in years.

It had been some time since the death of her husband Lawrence, from prostate cancer—four years to be exact. They had been married for twenty-three years when he died, and up until she'd met Jacques, she hadn't been interested in another man.

She thought more about Lawrence and how she had watched the man she had known since she was sixteen, lose a battle he wouldn't have had to if he had listened to her in the first place and seen a doctor. He had silently suffered for over a year with the pain. By the time she had bullied and cajoled him into going to see a doctor, the cancer had spread to his liver and lymph nodes. Within six months, he was gone. Lawrence had been her everything, next to her children, and now her granddaughter, her namesake, Camille.

"It's about time you shed the pall, Mother." Lottie picked up a pair of linen shorts, folded them and placed them in her mother's luggage. Between her and her three siblings, she was most adamant that their mother dated again. "You're way too young, Mom. You're forty-seven and don't look a day over thirty. Shoot, one of my co-workers asked if you were my sister and did you have a man."

Cammie chuckled as she walked over to the floor-to-ceiling mirror on one side of the bedroom. Her mocha complexion belied her true age, for most took her to be no older than thirty-five. She noted the fine smile lines around her lush mouth, her round, doe eyes and short nose. Cammie liked what looked back at her. Though it had taken some time, she had grown to love the skin she was in. Her bust line a generous 36C, her waist had enough to hold onto and her behind was still round and full, filling out a pair of jeans just the way she liked. She looked over at her oldest.

Lottie had come into the world twenty-three years ago with a mother wit and humor unlike any she'd seen. And she was also the one with the most common sense. Cammie had always been amazed by how in-tune Lottie was to those around her, her ability to wade through people's "garbage," as Lawrence had said, to see the truth and her ability to throw caution to the wind and step out on blind faith. Lottie had inherited most of her personality and fearlessness from her maternal grandmother, Momma Lott E.

"It's just been a long time since I've courted, Lottie. Your father was the only man I dated." Cammie raked her hands through her short cut; her whiskey eyes stared at her daughter.

"That's sad." Lottie had thought she whispered low enough to evade her mother's hearing.

"It is not." Cammie turned from the mirror. "And I wanted it that way. I've watched enough of my female friends go from pillar to post over men and too many of them are either on Prozac or damn near close to a nervous breakdown." Cammie smiled when she thought of Lawrence. "Your father was easygoing and non-drama. Whatever I wanted, he provided. I don't think I did too badly."

"No, Mom, you didn't. But you also don't know the difference."

Cammie's eyes widened as she sat on the bed. "What is that supposed to mean, young lady?" This was the part of Lottie no one cared for—her blunt assessments.

Cammie wasn't sure she wanted to have this discussion with her daughter. True, it had been Cammie who'd spoken with her four children about sex, but that was it. They knew the consequences of unprotected sex and knew that she expected each of them to be married before bringing children into the world. Anything else, Cammie hadn't discussed it.

"Mom, I mean no disrespect, but can I ask you a personal question?" Lottie sat down near her mother. "Do you know what passion is?"

Cammie thought about the times she had been intimate with Lawrence. While she thought it good, she really had no frame of reference. He had been her first and only lover. They were both seventeen and virgins when they'd slept together the first time. And though they had been born during the free loving' sixties, they had been raised by strict, moral, churchgoing parents who frowned on experimentation of any kind. The one time she had wanted to explore different intimate acts with Lawrence was after she'd given birth to their second child, Lawrence Jr. Shortly thereafter, Cammie's sister, Candi, had given her *The Joy of Sex* to read. *But because of Lawrence's adverse reaction, Cammie had* quickly dismissed any ideas of experimenting. He had been so embarrassed and flustered, asking her if she was happy and didn't he please her, that she hadn't broached the subject again. So, outside of the missionary position, she and Lawrence hadn't been very creative in the bedroom.

"That is none of your business. " Cammie rose and began moving around the room, aimlessly picking up items and placing them who knows where and why as her mind twirled around one of the last conversations she had with Jacques.

"Have you ever made love in the rain, Camille?" he'd asked her when they talked about the current wet weather in her home state of Illinois and the onslaught of storms in his home state of Washington. The question had come out of the blue, and Cammie wasm't sure how to respond— and she wasn't sure she even wanted to. But she also knew that the question of intimacy would eventually arise. Jacques was thirty-four-years-old to her forty-six, and he had a teenage son.. Something about the handsome, divorced man spoke of unadulterated, unequivocal, hot, insatiable passion. And that was what she was most afraid of. She had no experience with passion.

She first met Jacques at the annual Black MBA conference in Las Vegas. And though she hadn't noticed him when he walked in her workshop—he was one of nearly 100 participants—his offbeat analogy of the expansion of gambling empires and its effect on meaningful minority participation caught her attention. He had stood and strolled, almost glided, to the microphone near the front of the room. The first thing she noticed about him was his warm chocolate face, his eyes focused on her. His ensuing question had been in keeping with her workshop on minority participation in growing business enterprises.

"Where do we stand, Ms. Kohl?" his deep, resonate voice, a cross between James Earl Jones and Barry White, skimmed along her spine, down her legs and back up across her chest. She had inhaled deeply, suddenly quite warm in her red power suit.

But their interaction hadn't ended with her response to his question. He'd sought her out during the entire conference, and they shared countless conversations over drinks, breakfast, late-night snacks and early morning coffees. By the time the weeklong conference had ended, Cammie and Jacques had exchanged every number and means of communication they owned.

And in the three months since, Cammie and Jacques had used those varying forms of communication to talk, laugh, flirt, question and even suggest going past this one barrier and meeting to discuss the what ifs in person.

Up to that point, their conversations had been tame, talking about their families, their lives, their jobs—he the CEO of a food manufacturing company in Philadelphia and she the CEO and President of a well-oiled nonprofit organization—but they hadn't talked about the fierce attraction they fed daily.

Cammie broke from her reverie and looked at Lottie, whose eyes, exact replicas of her own, stared back at her. She was proud of her daughter, a soon-to-be surgeon. She hadn't let the birth of little Cammie prevent her from beginning what had been a lifelong dream. All of her children were bright, but Lottie possessed a quick mind for numbers and a photographic memory that acted like a trap door catching any and all information, and Cammie had one hell of a recall.

"Go in the bathroom and get my nightgown, robe and toiletry kit." Cammie watched as Lottie left the room. She peered around the door, making sure Lottie was gone, and then rushed back into her room. Dropping to her knees at the side of her bed, she reached under the mattress and pulled out a kit of "goodies" her sister Candace had given her.

She had spoken to Candi about Jacques and told her how she was afraid of the "What's next." Candi had been so candid that Cammie had blanched even as she grew heated with the intimate scenarios her oldest sister had outlined.

"Girl, I can't do that," Cammie had stated loudly, standing near Candi at the third hole of their Saturday morning golf outing. The only two girls in a brood of eight, they were extremely close, and Cammie found herself relying more and more on her sister's advice as they got older.

"Yes, you can, Cammie. These positions of intimacy are natural." She stepped up to the ball lying in the grass, then pitched it forward onto the green. Candi looked back at her sister. "And if I were you, I'd be on that man the minute the ship left port." She leaned on her 4H golf club and grinned.

Cammie took her shot and had wondered if Candi and her husband Donald had performed such intimate acts with each other. As if reading her mind, Candi let out a raucous laugh. "Girl, I have no less than three orgasms each time Donald and I make love. And he don't need no Viagra, either."

Cammie had stared at her sister, who was four years her senior. Donald was Candi's second husband. Her first husband, Lawrence's brother JD, short for James David, had fathered her three children, the first one before they married. Their marriage was what folks back then had called shotgun. As the years progressed, Cammie could see that neither of them were happy, with JD cattin' around and Candi flirting shamelessly with every handsome man she came in contact with on the police force. After fifteen years, they finally threw in the towel, much to everyone's relief. And since then, Candi hadn't seen one dateless day. Even though she had insisted that she would never marry again, she had somehow found herself attached to Donald, who was ten years older.

"And once I hit this menopause, girl, the sex was so great and so uninhibited. I don't have any fears of an unwanted pregnancy. And the different types of condoms that are out there will blow wind up your skirt." Candi waved an imaginary fan across her face. "Umph, my sister, you don't know what you're missing." Candi ended as she putted the ball into the hole.

Her mind returning to the task at hand, Cammie had yet to open the package her sister had given her. She hadn't a clue as to what was in the black, felt-like box. Hearing Lottie's footsteps, Cammie hurriedly placed the black box in her suitcase and covered it up with clothing.

"Mom, I didn't see your nightgown, but I found the robe." She held the toiletry case under her left arm while she held out the robe on her finger, dangling it as she frowned. She most certainly didn't want her mother to take either article.

"Um, it must be downstairs. I'll get it. Do me a favor, sweetie. Please finish putting that stuff in my suitcase." Cammie pointed to several stack of clothing before leaving the room.

Lottie put the robe on the side of the bed, and then placed the kit in the suitcase. She tiptoed to the door and watched as her mother disappeared down the stairs. Working quickly, Lottie rushed to the bedroom she slept in the first seventeen years of her life. Kneeling, she pulled a large bag from under the bed and ran back to her mother's room. Lottie pulled two short sheer nightgowns, one cream and one black with matching sheer robes and high-heeled slippers, along with several colorful bra and panty sets and a deep red and cream tankini bathing suit from the pink-striped bag. She laid them quickly in the suitcase, placing her mother's everyday wear on top of them. Lottie snorted, thinking how crazy her mom was for wanting to pack an old nightgown and polyester robe to wear on a cruise that was to be shared with a sexy man who more than likely wanted to get his groovy cool on. And she knew her mother hadn't a clue that she was well aware that Jacques, was twelve years her junior.

"You go, girl, wit cha bad self," Lottie chuckled, adding the last of the articles to the suitcase.

Hearing her mother's footsteps, Lottie sat near the suitcase and watched as her mother added that old robe and nightgown. She stifled a wicked laugh when her mother nodded her head in triumph.

"Oh, I almost forgot my outfit for the captain's dinner," Cammie said, going to the walk-in closet.

Lottie turned up her nose at the robe and nightgown. The sound of the phone pulled her mother from the closet, a long teal, sparkling spaghetti strap dress and black shawl hanging from the hanger in her hand. She tossed them onto the bed as she headed to answer the phone in her home office. Lottie guessed it must have been Jacques.

She leaned to one side, listening to her mother's voice as she snatched the old robe and nightgown out of the suitcase. She balled them up, then kicked them under the bed. She neatly folded the sundress, placed it in the suitcase, following with the shawl on top. Lottie smiled when she heard her mother ring off with a deep, girlish chuckle. That's what she wanted for her mother. She hadn't wanted her mother to shut down and stop living when her father died. And while she loved him dearly and missed him something fierce, Lottie hadn't wanted her mother to curl up and die with him.

"Well," Cammie said as she waltzed into the bedroom, "I guess that's it." She looked at the watch on her wrist. "Time to head out."

"Ready when you are, Mom."

Cammie watched her daughter, so like her father in coloring but with soft features. She was every bit a woman in her own right. She loved all of her children, Lottie, LJ, and the twins, Edward and Eliza, equally, but Lottie was her favorite.

"Thank you, baby. I know what you're trying to do, and I do appreciate it—I really do." Cammie opened her arms to her oldest. "I love you, baby." She wrapped her in her arms and hugged her tightly.

"I love you, too, Mom. And I want you to go and have a great time. You don't have to worry about a thing. With the twins away at college, I'll check on the house and bring in the mail." Lottie kissed her mother lightly on the cheek.

"Thank you." She patted her arm. "Okay, time to go." Cammie shut the suitcase and placed it on the floor. She pulled the handle from its hiding place and rolled it to the door.

"I'm going to pull the car out of the garage." Lottie said as she left the bedroom.

Cammie nodded, then looked behind her at the room she had shared with Lawrence for their last eighteen years of marriage. A part of her felt guilty while another part of her knew that had she been the one to have died, Lawrence would have probably married within two years. She wasn't angry at that thought—it was what it was. Lawrence wasn't the type of man to be alone—even when she went out of town on business, he had traveled with her.

Something inside gave her the idea that when she returned, a part of her would be different, changed. And in an odd way she was looking forward to that change, regardless of the fact that she was frightened and excited and aroused all at the same time.

Chapter Two

Jacques looked around his room. The deep mahogany and honey gold colors of his bedding matched the hunter green of the walls. He had painted the room in very masculine colors following his divorce. The room, when his ex-wife shared it, had been a hideous pea soup green, and the bedding had had more flowers than a botanical garden. After her betrayal, he'd made several changes, including the bedroom, tossing out the bed and all. He could have lived with all the girly, frilly stuff if she hadn't brought another man into their lives and their bed.

He'd questioned himself, from his manhood to how he'd treated her over the fourteen years they'd been together, ten in marriage. Jacques had always been a one-woman man. Running from one bed to another wasn't his idea of fun or masculine. When he'd pledged Omega Psi Phi in college, his lamps and frat brothers had teased him— at nineteen he'd still been a virgin. But he hadn't ended his virginity like Half Pint in *School Days*—no, he'd met Skylar during a frat party and had been smitten with the lanky sister, who had a butt to die for and legs for days. He was a butt and leg man, for sure, but what he had loved about Skylar was her zeal and zest for life. And she had seemed to be into him as much as he had been into her. Even though he'd heard the rumors that there were other men, he'd felt the slight shift whenever they were together. But he had ignored his instincts and plowed forward, marrying her after four years of dating and the birth of their only child, Ronnie.

Once it became clear to him that Skylar was not and had never been faithful to him, he filed for divorce and full custody of their son. He hadn't wanted to drag his son's mother in the dirt, so he'd insisted that she settle amicably. She agreed, and he'd settled into raising Ronnie into manhood.

Jacques thought about Camille. She had been with her husband for almost twenty-four years when he died. And he assumed, as he'd listened to her talk about her late husband, that he had been the only man in her life. That pleased him in an odd way, for her desire for one man had outlasted most marriages that he knew of. It had taken the better part of the past five years to get Skylar and her betrayal out of his system. He'd had several dates, a few that resulted in physical trysts, but he hadn't felt that something that made him want to give his all.

Then he'd gone to the conference and sat in muted silence as she walked from one side of the room to the other as she gave her presentation. He'd watched the sway of her hips in her red silk suit. Her full mouth, the odd, sensuous color of her eyes and her stylish short haircut made up what he thought was a total package—beauty, brains and a body to die for. And she had cohones. He liked a woman who could hold her own, and Cammie, as she liked to be called, could do just that. He'd read that in the three years she'd been CEO and President of the nonprofit agency, she had turned a failing organization into one of the most financially secure and innovative social service agencies in the Midwest. She had acquired several other agencies, turning hers into a multimillion-dollar industry. Word was that she was a fierce negotiator and tended to take no prisoners. It was all or nothing and Jacques liked that. *That,* he mused, *took guts.*

But when he'd stood and opened up the discussion, he had watched her reaction. He'd watched her watch him, her body leaning forward just enough to let him know that she was checking him out. Following the workshop, he'd asked her to join him after the mixer for a nightcap, and he'd held his breath, her hand in his, as he waited for her response. He could sense her hesitation and then was relieved when her eyes softened moments before she agreed. *And the rest,* he chuckled to himself, *was history.*

She had no idea that he had admired her from afar for many years. Since receiving his MBA, he'd joined the local chapter of the Black MBA association and had read several articles she'd penned on minorities in various industries which appeared in the association's quarterly newsletter. He'd enjoyed reading her articles, to which the presidents of local chapters were expected to contribute at least one article a year in addition to facilitating workshops. The same newsletter informed him that she'd been widowed. This year, when he'd decided to attend the conference, he was glad to see that she was a workshop facilitator after a nearly four-year hiatus.

Jacques stole a glance at the clock resting on his nightstand. He had two hours to finish packing, get Bossy, the Greyhound he and Ronnie rescued from the races, to the doggy hotel, and Ronnie to his brother's for the next several days, in which he would wine, dine and love up the woman whom he'd fallen for just through conversation.

He knew she wouldn't believe how deep his feelings had become, but since their meeting and subsequent forays together during the conference, followed by their constant contacts, he'd begun looking forward to hearing her soft, melodic voice several times a day, especially at night before he'd fall asleep. The past month had been hard on him—he couldn't sleep without dreaming of her—dreaming of holding her, of melding his lips to hers, of sinking so deep inside of her that she wouldn't know where he began and she ended. He would awaken in such a hard, vicious state of arousal that he was glad his son had finally taken to sleeping in his own bed over a year ago. True, he and Ronnie had talked about sex and where babies come from, seeing as how his son was beginning to show hair in strategic places, but he wasn't quite ready to explain the how's and whys of his own arousal.

"Dad, Uncle Jackson is on the phone." Ronnie appeared in the doorway, and then stepped over the threshold holding the cordless phone. Jacques hadn't heard the phone ring, which meant Ronnie had been on the other line.

"You finished with your call?" Jacques asked as he took the phone out of his hand. Ronnie nodded in the affirmative. "Don't nod your head son, I don't read head."

"Yes, I'm finished."

"Okay, are you done packing?"

"Yes, I'm finished packing. You need me to pull the car out?" he said as he quickly left the room with Jacques on his heels.

"No, I don't need you to pull the car out. Find Bossy's vet papers so we can get out of here." He placed the phone to his ear. "What's up, man?"

"Just calling to see what time you're heading this way. You still want me to drop you at the airport, right?"

"I'm leaving in about another hour. I'm just about finished packing, and then we're going to drop off the dog and be on our way to you. And yes, I still need a ride to the airport."

"This must be some honey. You done shelled out a lot of loot to be with this sister. How old did you say she was again?"

Jacques turned up his lips. He hadn't told Jackson Cammie's age for a reason. He knew that he would suffer unending, unmerciful teasing from him if he knew that Cammie was twelve years his senior. Even he had been surprised when he asked her age. He figured her a few years older, but had no idea that she was well into her forties and creeping up on her fifties. *Damn, she looks mighty good.*

"I didn't say. I'll see you later." Jacques hung up on his oldest brother. It wasn't that he hadn't shared some things about Cammie with Jackson; he wasn't prepared for the back pats and vicious overtures about younger men and older women. The last thing he wanted anyone to say was that Cammie was a cougar.

"Where'd that dumb expression come from anyway?" he said aloud as he finished packing, placing his iPod and two small speakers

68

into a carry-on bag. The iPod had been loaded with several slow songs as an accompaniment to the flowers, champagne and oils he had planned for Cammie during their cruise. *Oh yeah, this sister is about to find out what Jacques Champion is made of.*

Jacques had planned a romantic getaway once he was sure she would agree to the cruise. And he planned it for when a large group of readers of Black Romance would be celebrating something called the Slam Jam onboard. He had recalled Cammie talking about how much she liked the writers who had created larger than life men with larger than life appetites.

Jacques had never been a fan of romance novels, even though his mother and sister read them incessantly. So when he asked Janie, his sister, about some popular Black romance writers, she had come back with a slew of titles and a few for him to read. Once he'd finished several, he understood why women loved the billion-dollar genre. The writers created a level of fantasy that most of their readers weren't getting in real life. He thought of Cammie. *I'll be her fantasy,* he'd thought to himself after reading one book in particular by A.C. Arthur. Even he had to admit that the steamy love scenes had been page burners. Shoot, he couldn't help getting aroused as he'd read it.

Jacques checked his luggage one last time, making sure he had everything he needed. From shoes to boxer brief underwear, shorts, shirts and swim gear, he went over each item. But something was missing. He looked around the room, his long fingers stroking his goatee then sliding over his bald head. Snapping his fingers, he rushed into his bathroom. Emerging several moments later, Jacques placed the variety samples of condoms and massage oils into his suitcase, then zipped it up and headed toward his son's room.

Yes, he nodded, whistling to himself, this cruise would either bring them closer or let them know they should be apart. But something in Jacques said that this was only the beginning of him and Ms. Camille Kohl.

"Ronnie, Bossy, let's go," he called out as he headed down the stairs toward the attached garage. He waited for his son, seeing the dog first as she ran toward her master.

"Good dog, Bossy." He stroked the dog's tan, short hair before opening the door to the Mercedes SUV. "Up, Bossy, up," he commanded and watched as the dog jumped into the back seat. "Ronnie, let's go!" Jacques yelled out again. He shook his head as he went back into the house and noticed Ronnie dragging a large duffle bag.

"Ronnie, son, what's in the bag?"

"My Wii and my X-box." He looked up slightly.

Jacques wanted to double over in laughter. At fourteen, Ronnie wasn't quite a man, with his peach fuzz covering his top lip and chin. He was still child-like, so much that he still sat close to Jacques when they watched television together, sometimes laying his head on his shoulder. "Boy, Jackson's got all that."

Ronnie shook his head. "No, he don't. He don't have the Wii."

"Okay, maybe not, but do you have any clothes and underwear in that bag?" Jacques asked as he knelt down and opened his son's duffle bag. Ronnie had packed everything but what Jacques had washed, ironed and placed on the bed for him to pack. "Boy," he stood to his full six feet, four inches. "Go and take that stuff out and put the clothes I placed on your bed in that bag." He pointed toward the stairs. "And hurry up. I don't want to be late."

He turned to see Bossy sitting near the door, her head cocked to one side. "Thank God you don't wear clothes." The dog barked and Jacques laughed as he placed his own luggage in the rear compartment of the SUV. He thought of Cammie and wondered if she was all packed and ready to go. He pulled his cell phone from the clip attached to his hip then dialed her number.

"Hey beautiful," he said when he heard her voice on the other end. "Are you ready to go?"

"Just about. I'm almost finished packing and Lottie is here to take me to the airport. How about you?"

"Well, me and the dog are ready to go, but Ronnie's dragging his feet."

"Maybe something's amiss. Have you talked to him about who you're going on this cruise with?"

Jacques hadn't thought of that. And as he thought about it, his son had been acting a little peculiar lately. "No, I just told him I was going on vacation."

"Do you normally take Ronnie with you?"

He closed his eyes and inhaled deeply. Since the divorce they'd been inseparable accept for when he went out of town on business. This wasn't business and he hadn't explained a thing. "You know I think you've touched on something here. He and I haven't been apart with the exception of when I go out of town for business, which I cut down on once he came to live with me permanently. Shoot, I better talk to my boy as we head to my brother's."

"Sounds like a plan. I'll see you later?"

"Bet on it and I can't wait to see you, beautiful. Can hardly wait," he said right before he rang off.

Jacques looked up in time to see his son heading slowly toward him. "Hey champ, what's up?"

Ronnie shook his head as he placed his duffle bag in the rear of the car. "Nothing."

Jacques placed his hands around his son's shoulders and shook him slightly. "You know, son, I owe you an apology." Ronnie looked up. "I'm heading out of town to be with a really special friend, and I haven't told you a thing. Can you forgive me?"

Ronnie nodded his head then asked, "Who is she? And what's her name?"

"She's a woman I met at the MBA conference a few months ago. Her name is Cammie and we've been talking long distance ever since we met."

"Is she going to be my new mother?"

Jacques inhaled deeply and closed his eyes for a brief second. "You know, to be honest, that's a good question and I don't know. I like her—a lot—that much I do know. As for her becoming your mother, that's too much to tell right now. We've only just started seeing each other."

"Well, do you think she'll like us?" he pointed to himself and then Bossy.

He laughed. His son so wanted to be a man, but was still such a boy. "What's there not to like?" He pulled him into a brief embrace. "And she has four kids of her own, including nineteen-year-old twins."

He watched as his sons eyes took on a look of interest. "Is she pretty?"

"Beautiful. And smart, too."

Jacques watched as his son rounded the vehicle and climbed in. For twenty minutes, his son asked questions about Cammie and her family, ending with when was he going to meet her.

"When I come back, maybe we can make a quick trip. She lives in Chicago."

"I've never been. Cool." He smiled and then placed the ear buds to his iPod in his ears and returned to his world.

Jacques had hoped to assuage the fear and trepidation in his son's mind, for he had yet to get over the fact that the last several times he'd gone to see his mother, she hadn't been available to him. The only thing Jacques could do was ride out his son's disappointment and be there for him.

Finally reaching the airport and skirting his brother's incessant questions about Cammie, a small sheen of perspiration broke out across Jacques's forehead and upper lip as he stood in line waiting to board the flight that would take him to Miami and Cammie. Once he settled into his seat in first class, Jacques pulled out the book of poetry he'd brought. He loved to read, and had every intention of reading several of his favorite poems to Cammie when they lay on the beach in Jamaica. Skip Dexter and Winston, Jacques Champion was a man on a mission to win the heart of a woman who made him want to scoop her up and love her until she'd breathed her last breath. *Yeah*, he mused, his head nodding slightly, *this is going to be five days I'll never forget.*

Chapter Three

Cammie stood on the dock, her eyes shielded by the RayBan's Lottie had brought her for her birthday last month, and smoothed a hand across her white peasant blouse and down her matching Capri pants. The sun caught the glitter of the diamonds sparkling from the tennis bracelet Jacques had sent her for the occasion. She smiled.

The past three months had gone by in a blur. She had last seen him on the final day of the conference, when he'd driven her to McCarron Airport. He had taken her bags from her room, carried them to his rental car, then drove to the airport. He had escorted her as far as security would allow, and they had stood close, Cammie looking up into his smooth, chocolate face.

"Well, I guess it's time for me to get going," Cammie had said as she watched the depths of his warm, dark brown eyes as they bored into her own.

"Um, I guess so," he whispered. "But if you'd be so kind and grant a parched man one wish?"

Cammie laughed. "What is it?"

"Kiss me," came his reply, which seemed more of a command than a question.

She closed her eyes as his face slowly met hers; his soft, full lips touched hers lightly before his tongue darted between her parted lips. She waded into the feast he was setting, his tongue wandering and searching hers for answers she didn't know she had.

"Lord, woman," he exhaled, resting his forehead on hers, and then clearing his throat. "You have a safe flight," he said right before he pulled her quickly into his arms and hugged her close. "And call me when you get home." He winked at her as his long finger lightly stroked her cheek before he pushed her gently toward the security clearance, then turned and left.

Cammie had stood there, transfixed, watching his retreat. For her entire flight, all she could remember was the sound of his deep voice, the heady scent of his cologne and the feel of his full lips on hers.

Her mind came back to the present as she stood on the dock, her eyes searching the gathered crowd. Her fingers touched her lips lightly—she could still feel his lips.

"Hey beautiful," came a voice behind her.

Cammie smiled as she turned. Her eyes widened as she came face to face with a man dressed in a garish floral print shirt, white Bermuda shorts, white, patent leather sandals and sheer, knee high socks. His face was covered in a snow white beard. If she believed in Santa, then the man standing in front of her was him.

"Oh, my apologies. I was looking for ..." His voice trailed off. "I'm so sorry."

Cammie touched the stranger's arm when her instinct said she had nothing to worry about. "None needed. That's okay."

He smiled brightly. "Is this your first time?"

Cammie blinked. *First time for what? What does he mean?*

"First time cruising?"

"Ah, yes, it is."

"Are you waiting for anyone special?" He nodded at her, his bright blue eyes wide. If she didn't know any better, she'd swear the old man was trying to hit on her.

"Yes, she is," sounded an unmistakable, deep voice behind her. "Hey there,beautiful," he said, pulling her into his arms and kissing her sweetly, her body pressed to his. She felt as if she would combust as the heat from his tender lips crept up and down her entire body. She exhaled deeply as they parted.

"Hey you, I was about to worry." She took in his face, the smooth dark complexion, his perfectly round, bald head, his intense dark eyes and neat goatee.

Jacques took Cammie's hand and kissed the back of it. "I'm a man of my word." He led her up the gang plank, then paused when he noticed a cruise ship employee with a camera. "Smile for the camera," he said as he stood next to her and smiled.

"Things do happen, you know."

He nodded his head as he paused to hand their cruise documents to the concierge. "Not even."

"Not even what?" Cammie responded, following him to a bank of elevators, her hand still in his. She took in his attire, noticing how his red polo was a wonderful contrast to his skin.

They both smiled and nodded to various people getting on the elevator with them. They rode the elevator in silence. Cammie looked up at him and found that he was watching her, though he couldn't see her eyes through the sunglasses still perched on her nose.

Once they reached the promenade deck, they stepped out of the elevator and headed toward their room, which was at the very end of the hallway.

Jacques knew his hand was sweating as he held onto Cammie more out of keeping himself from pinching his own arm. This was no dream. Finally, they were together. With one hand, he inserted the key card into the slot, and then pushed open the door. He dropped Cammie's hand as she stepped across the threshold into the lavish suite.

"Jacques," Cammie breathed out his name. "This is so beautiful."

She slowly stepped farther into the parlor of the suite. Her feet felt as if she were walking on a cloud as the abundant plush of the sea green carpet absorbed her footsteps. The suite boasted a couch and a matching floral loveseat accompanied by two bamboo end tables and an oval coffee table. On top of one of the end tables was a large arrangement of her favorite flowers. She smiled at Jacques as she headed farther, pausing to take in the aroma of the roses, baby's breath, orchids and white lilies.

Straightening, she looked up and her eyes widened. She and Jacques stopped in front of cream-colored curtains, a slight breeze slowly moving them enough for her to see a sliding glass door behind them. Cammie pulled the curtains back and gasped.

"Jacques, we have a private balcony!"

He placed his arms around her and nuzzled his face against her head. "Wild horses."

Cammie turned in his arms and looked up into his smiling face. "Wild horses?"

He nodded his head. "Not even wild horses could have kept me away." Jacques removed her sunglasses, and then rubbed his nose against hers. "I've missed you."

Mixed emotions swept over her, fear and desire battled for dominance. For once in her life, she wasn't sure how to respond and the arousal this man was awakening had her so turned on, she wasn't sure she was supposed to feel this way. No man had ever been so open with his emotions. With Lawrence, she just assumed. But with Jacques, she didn't have to guess. She knew where she stood—he always told her. Yet something inside of her wasn't quite sure if she was ready to be that open with him.

Cammie stepped out of his arms. "This is truly a beautiful suite," she said as she wandered around, and then noticed the open door leading to what she assumed was the bedroom. She peeked inside. A beautiful pale citrine duvet with mounds of peach and light pale green pillows strategically place near the headboard covered the king-sized bed. Large abstract paintings adorned the warm tan walls, one hanging over the bed, the other on the facing wall. An armoire with a television sat in a corner near a second patio door, whicht Cammie assumed led to their balcony.

She knew he was standing in the doorway, watching her as she wandered around the room. Cammie didn't dare look up—the seriousness in his dark eyes was sure to be evident, just as it had been when he held her moments before.

What am I doing here? Have I lost my mind? Cammie wondered, her pulse racing a million miles a minute. *I'm not ready for all of this—I don't think.*

"Cammie, is everything okay?" Jacques asked as he took a step further into the bedroom. He had noticed the quick change in her when he'd hugged her. He wasn't sure, but something was wrong. "If you don't like it, we can change. We can move to another cabin."

Cammie turned around and saw for the first time the uncertainty in his own eyes. "Oh, my no, Jacques, this is just beautiful. It's just that..." Her voice trailed off.

"It's just what, baby?" He stepped closer and took her hands in his. "What's wrong, Cammie?"

The sudden sound of a siren reminded them that they had to participate in the evacuation drill.

"Nothing, Jacques. Let's head on to the drill."

Jacques dropped her hands and nodded his head. He turned and headed out of the suite, waiting near the door for Cammie to join him. He now knew what it was and he wasn't too sure he liked what he saw. Fear and uncertainty were evident in her beautiful golden eyes as sure as his name was Jacques Ronald Champion. He knew that if he pushed her too hard, came on too strong, she would bolt like a colt—and that was exactly the last thing he wanted her to do.

"Cammie, wait for me, I left something in the room." He rushed back into the suite and picked up the phone near the couch. "Yes, this is Mr. Champion. I'd like for someone to come and separate the beds while we're at the drill. Can that be done?" Jacques absently nodded his head. "Oh, no, nothing is wrong. The suite is just as I expected. I just need the beds separated." He nodded again. "Thank you. I really appreciate your help. Also, cancel the in-suite dinner for tonight. Ms. Kohl and I will be at the seven o'clock seating for dinner."

Jacques hung up the phone. He had waited for her, had wished for her. Now that she was here, nothing—not even her fear—was going to stand in his way. He just had to show her his intentions.

Chapter Four

Cammie and Jacques laughed as they toured the elaborate ship, which was the length of three football fields. During the drill, Jacques had chatted and joked and then afterward, when the boat pushed from the dock, they had stood at the rail, waving at folks they didn't know. He had stood close to Cammie but hadn't touched her.

"I think we should head to the suite and get some rest before dinner," Jacques said, glancing at his watch. They had a few hours before dinner. "How does that sound?"

"That sounds good to me. I would like to take a nap."

"Actually, I could use a few winks myself," he said as they headed to the elevator that would take them two floors below the deck house where the captain controlled the ship.

Cammie watched Jacques's profile as he opened the door. He handed her a key card and then stepped to the side, allowing her to enter first. She noticed their luggage sitting in the living area. She went over to it.

"No, I'll put them in the room." Jacques rolled the two pieces into the bedroom. "If you like, you can go on and grab a nap."

"What about you?"

"I'll be there in a minute. I want to check on the onboard activities and the island excursions available for day after tomorrow." He looked at Cammie as her head tilted slightly to one side.

"I won't book a thing. I just want to see what they have to offer," he assured her.

"Okay," Cammie agreed, and then stretched her arms over her head.

Jacques swallowed hard, watching the fabric of her blouse stretch over her ample bosom. He fought the need to pull her close, bury his face in her breasts and let her feel the hard planes of his body, of the way she had unknowingly caused his erection.

Without a word, Cammie turned and headed into the bedroom. The first thing she noticed was that the once king-sized bed was now two full-sized beds. She glanced over her shoulder, but Jacques wasn't there.

She sat on the bed closest to the patio and looked out through the railings as the shore rolled past. Yawning, she lay down and continued to watch as the shore became farther and farther away, her mind wandering to the man sitting mere feet away, smelling good, looking good and as sexy as anything she'd ever seen. The way his red shirt showed off his well-formed arms and his pectorals was akin to waving a red flag at a bull. She wanted to charge. But ... Cammie changed her mind, rolled over on her side and began to drift.

Jacques stood on the private balcony and watched the shore disappear. He had wanted to nap with Cammie, but the spooked look in her eyes was etched in his mind. He would take all cues from her. If they made love during this cruise, so be it. If not, so be it. Jacques was a patient man, even though being around Cammie made him want to throw caution to the wind and sink as deep inside her mind, body and soul as he could go. He inhaled deeply; the sea air filled his lungs and his resolve. Yes, he would let her set this pace, and he would be there no matter.

Once he could barely see the shore, Jacques headed back into the suite, then to the bedroom. He listened to the slight snore escaping Cammie. She looked so beautiful lying on her side, her hands in prayer position tucked under her cheek, which rested on an oversized pillow. He slipped off his loafers as he stretched out on the bed nearby. Closing his eyes, his breath regulated with the sound of hers.

Two hours later, Cammie awoke and noticed Jacques stretched out on the bed next to hers, his forearm draped lazily over his eyes. She watched his chest rise and fall. Her eyes took a visual tour of his body, stopping at the muscular thighs peeking out from a pair of jean shorts. She wondered how it would feel to rub her hands up and down his body, her fingers rolling across the dips and cervices that made him man. Lawrence had never really let her touch him the way she'd wanted, so she'd had to do so while he slept, which made her feel like a thief.

"Hey, you," Jacques said.

Cammie's eyes quickly met his. "Hey." She looked away, embarrassed at being caught ogling. She searched for something to say. "I guess we better get ready for dinner." She sat up.

"Guess we should. If you want to take a shower, go ahead. I'll go after you're done."

Cammie nodded and then rose. She walked over to the luggage rack, where Jacques had placed her suitcase. She opened it and began to pull out her clothes. She stopped suddenly when she noticed the sheer nightgowns and matching robes.

Lottie had packed these.

She pulled the gowns out and hugged them close to her as she walked over to the dresser. Quickly, she dumped the articles in the drawer and shut it. Again, Cammie went through her luggage, this time pulling out two swimsuits, a one-piece with a serious dip in the back and a tankini. As she continued going through her luggage, she pulled out more sexy items, including the black container Candi had given her. She didn't dare open it, for it suddenly dawned on her that maybe her sister had given her a toy.

Cammie shook her head. She didn't have a thing to wear to bed. The sheer nightgowns were quite revealing, and the way she was feeling, she wasn't too sure about anything.

She glanced at Jacques, who had sat up and was watching her.

"Something wrong, Cammie?" He stood and headed her way. "You look flushed. Are you feeling sick?"

"Oh, no," she stammered, placing her hands outward, palms facing him. "I'm okay." She quickly turned around and finished unpacking. She listened as Jacques moved around the room, unpacking and placing items on the nightstand near his bed.

They both moved around the suite in silence. Cammie was so unsure of what was next—her mind swam. She had been excited about seeing Jacques again, spending time with him. But once she'd gotten a look at all he'd done, the beautiful suite, the bouquet of flowers and the champagne, she wasn't sure how she was supposed to act. And an even bigger part of her was just plain afraid that he'd be turned off by her lack of experience. Truly a man who looked as good as he did and oozed such blatant sexuality was no novice. But she was.

Deciding a shower would do her some good, she headed to the bathroom. She gasped loudly when she saw the opulence of the bathroom. The glassed-in shower stall boasted five showerheads with a cream ceramic tile bench. The stall was definitely made for two. Pewter fixtures accentuated the marble double sink. On a nearby three-shelf stand sat a stack of plush towels. Two terrycloth robes hung on padded hangers from the hook behind the door.

Stepping gingerly into the shower, Cammie turned on the water and moaned aloud as one of the jets propelled water at her mound, the warm water cascading around her bud. She closed her eyes and leaned against the tiled wall as the erotic sensation shimmied slowly up her torso, the tips of her nipples aching. She fought the urge to touch them, to allow her hand to try and put an end to the wicked arousal that had captured her entire body and was holding her hostage. She thought of Jacques and his large hands. She moaned again.

Feeling as if she were being watched, Cammie opened her eyes quickly and turned. She wasn't sure, but she thought she'd seen his back. Hurrying, Cammie quickly showered, then dressed in a flowing skirt and a silk sleeveless blouse.

She returned to the room to find Jacques rummaging through his clothes. He glanced at her.

"How was your shower?"

Cammie's head snapped around. She looked at him and wondered if he had in fact been in the bathroom when she'd been assaulted by that one strategically placed shower head. "Why?" she asked, and then realized that her voice possibly sounded shrill.

He looked at her. "No, reason. I was just asking." He picked out a pair of slacks and a shirt, then headed to the bathroom, shutting the door behind him.

Jacques looked over at the shower and felt a measure of guilt. He had heard her, thinking she had needed rescuing. What he saw had sent blood rushing to his groin. She needed him alright—needed him to rescue her body. He didn't want to admit to her that he had watched her as her head leaned back, her body being pulsated by the jets. He'd had a good view of her body, the roundness of her breast, the large nipples that he could envision licking, nipping and sucking. And then there was the view of her derrière. It looked firm and round and delectable. That sistah had some serious, beautiful junk in her trunk and he wanted his hands to rummage and roam all around it.

He stroked his hardness and then stopped. He wasn't above masturbation, but he knew that only one woman could assuage the hardness, and she was on the other side of the door running from him.

Jacques removed his clothes, stepped in the shower, bathed and then dressed in record time.

Leaving the room, they headed to dinner. Jacques knew they needed to do something that would have them coming back to the room as late as possible. He wanted to be good and tired, sleep coming quick soon after his head hit the pillow. Anything that would take his mind off Cammie and what he'd seen.

Chapter Five

Cammie stretched and rolled over. Her eyes rested on Jacques, who was sound asleep flat on his back, the covers kicked around his large feet, his lower half clad in a pair of boxers, a T-shirt covering his upper body. *Even asleep,* she thought, *he's superfine,* or as her youngest would say: *He all that.*

She smiled to herself as she thought of the last two evenings onboard the ship. The next day would find them at the Grand Cayman Islands, their first stop.

The late hours of their first night had been spent in the Millionaires Club Casino, one of the largest afloat, where she had won five thousand dollars playing Texas Hold'em. Jacques had stood nearby. Several times she looked back to see him with an amazed expression on his face as she sat among a throng of men and played with a skill and precision he'd probably seen only in professional tournaments on cable television.

At one point during the late hour, a crowd of onlookers had gathered and watched as Cammie and another gentleman bluffed their way toward the pot. In the end, she had won with two of a kind by bluffing her opponent into throwing in his hand.

She had noticed, though, that some trampette had been jockeying for Jacques attention. It seemed everywhere they moved about the casino, she had appeared, and when Cammie had settled into the poker game, she had watched as the woman shamelessly flirted with her man.

Umph, Cammie had thought, *I hadn't been exactly acting like he was her man.*

They had finally returned to the suite around three in the morning. And though Cammie had been exhausted, her body was riddled with nervous energy even more so after she asked Jacques if he had an extra T-shirt she could wear to bed. He hadn't asked any questions. He just pulled a shirt from the bureau of drawers and handed it to her. Donning it in the bathroom, she had stepped out to the bedroom and was met by a smiling Jacques, who was already under the covers.

Cammie had looked at him and saw the unmistakable look of passion mixed with a huge helping of desire. There was no way she could please this man, and she didn't even want to tell him of her experience with sex, or better still, her lack thereof.

The next day, a day at sea, she awoke to the sound of her name slipping from Jacques's beautiful, full lips. He had been asleep, but was calling her name. And just as she thought to wake him, he had rolled over and pulled a pillow closer to him, his arms wrapped possessively about it as he called out her name again.

Wow. Cammie wondered how it would feel to be wrapped in his arms, those long, muscular legs entwined with hers, his lips branding hot and luscious kisses over her body. A knowing wave of arousal crept up and over her. She began to rock, trying to still the errant sensations that seemed to have taken residence and refused to leave. All of this was foreign to her. She had never initiated sex in her life. Her husband had always been the initiator.

Cammie had rolled over, putting her back to him, and looked out the patio door as the vast beauty of the open Atlantic Ocean rolled past. *He's dreaming of me.*

That day found them wandering around the ship, exploring the duty free shops and attending a book signing that featured some of her favorite romance authors. She nearly screamed when she finally got a chance to meet A. C. Arthur. And she was even more astounded when Jacques admitted that he had read her latest romance novel and found the story quite entertaining and hot. She wondered if he had read the bestselling author's novel *Guarding His Body.* When she asked him, she noted the dark, arousing depth of his eyes and she could completely understand. The sex scenes in that book were hot to the point of flaming.

He had admitted that he purposely booked them on the cruise because of the Romance Slam Jam conference. Cammie had hugged and kissed him; their lips met in a searing moment of emotions and pent up frustrations. *If I could only tell him*, she thought as he released her lips but not her body, which he held close to his as she watched the heated look of pure want and need flash across Jacques's face.

Following the book signing, they headed to the Rotunda, where they'd sat and sipped wine, the nine levels of glass and brass giving the area its romance. And even though Cammie hadn't made any movements toward intimacy, Jacques seemed content to spend quality time with her.

She had left him to go shopping at one of the duty-free shops. She had wanted to buy Jacques several colognes she had smelled in a catalog and he seemed to favor. As she shopped, had wondered how she would get Jacques to make the first move. Her body was humming and throbbing and she wasn't sure how much more she could take. It was bad enough she had watched him as he slept, captured by the view of his toned body and the knowing sign of a rather large erection. Cammie fanned herself.

After purchasing several, because she couldn't make up her mind which smelled sexiest, she headed back to the Rotunda in time to overhear the trampette come on to Jacques.

"Hey there, handsome—how are you feeling today?" Cammie heard her ask as the trampette sat next to him. She so close, a little too close. *Dang! Talk about an invasion of personal space.*

"All alone?" Her voice was so husky, Cammie thought it sounded more like it belonged to a man than a woman.

Cammie had watched for a moment. She wanted to see his reaction to the hoochie's advances. He shifted away, his eyes darting around as if he was looking for Cammie.

"You know, you never told me your name." She took his hand in hers and traced lazy circles around it with her long fingernail before scratching his palm.

"Oh no, she didn't." Cammie murmured. "Time for this little tramp to kick rocks."

"Hey, baby," Cammie purred as she had sat next to Jacques, and then looked at the woman who seemed to be everywhere Jacques had been when they were in the casino. And while she wasn't afraid of losing a man, she sure wasn't about to allow a tacky, blonde-haired sistah to dis her.

"Why, handsome, you didn't tell me your mother was on the cruise with you."

Cammie smiled demurely. "And I didn't know that it was Senior Citizen's day. Did you sweetheart?" She leaned over Jacques, who sat between them, and said, "If you scurry, there's a dance contest for those 70 and over." Cammie nodded her head as she waved her fingers toward the exit sign.

The two women stared at each other. Cammie wanted to pull all that phony hair out of that sister's head at the roots. Jacques stood, pulling Cammie to her feet.

She wanted to show that trampette, who was dressed in a too-tight pair of leggings with an itty-bitty, wishing-it-had-a-smaller owner shirt, a thing or two.

"Let's go, sweetheart," Jacques whispered in her ear as he pulled her toward the exit. She wasn't sure where they were heading, but she knew that she'd step off in that tramps butt so far, someone would have to rub Ben Gay on her throat.

"That funky female dog," Cammie hissed and then looked at Jacques. He had a smirk on his face. "What?"

"I didn't think you cared." He leaned his head back and placed his right hand over his chest. "I'm touched."

She looked at the amused expression on his face and began laughing. For the rest of the evening, they continued to enjoy the ship's amenities, even stopping for manicures at the Spa Carnival. And while Jacques had mentioned that he'd like a massage, the gleam in the attendant's eyes warned Cammie that if anyone was to massage this man's body it was going to be her, Cammie Kohl.

By the time they made it back to their suite, following a late dinner and a moonlit stroll on deck, they were tired and quickly slipped into their respective beds.

"Cammie?" Jacques had whispered after the light had been doused.

"Yes, Jacques?"

"Are you enjoying yourself?"

"Immensely, thank you, Jacques. I'll never forget this trip."

"Anything for you, sweetheart—just name it."

And for the second night, the two wrestled with their warring emotions.

"Jacques, this was a great idea," Cammie said as they drove behind other Jeeps, caravan style, along the North Sound of Morgan's Harbor, which would take them to Barker's National Park. As they rolled along the two-lane road, the shore an endless picture, Cammie took in the beauty of the trees, alive with bright green leaves and colorful flowers. Several times, Cammie swore she spotted parrots and a cockatoo.

Once they arrived at Barker's National Park, she spotted a blue iguana and jumped into Jacques's arms as it sauntered slowly in the opposite direction.

"Sweetheart, it's not going to bite you."

Cammie held tight to Jacques. "It's too big and ugly." She hid her face in the crook of his neck. "And don't you dare put me down."

He shook his head and carried her back to the lot where their jeep was parked. Placing her in the seat, he looked down at her face. Her lips formed a pout.

"Aw, sweetheart, I didn't know you weren't too fond of reptiles."

"I don't even like watching them on television," she said, and then shivered involuntarily.

"Okay, why don't we go to the beach?"

Cammie nodded and looked up at Jacques, his eyes shielded by sunglasses. When he had come out of the bathroom earlier that morning, she had wanted to whistle at him. He was dressed in a pair of powder blue shorts and a matching blue-striped, short-sleeved, polo shirt. The shirt hugged his muscles just right while the shorts showed off his incredible legs. She found him scrumptious.

Jacques drove along the road and then spotted an open road that led to a secluded spot along the beach. Parking the jeep, he got out, then assisted Cammie from the cab. She grabbed the mini cooler and box lunches, which had been provided as a part of the excursion.

He took her hand in his and led her to the beach. The enticing breeze off the cobalt ocean soothed him, he thought, as he spotted a large rock formation just off the water's edge. He decided to spread out the blanket nearby.

"Jacques, look at that." She pointed to the clear blue ocean, her eyes fixed on the vast body, her mind wandering as she wondered if the water felt as good as it looked. She suddenly wished she had packed her swimsuit.

"It is beautiful. Seems untouched—almost pure."

They sat on the blanket and ate in silence. Cammie found it comforting, conversation unnecessary. She glanced at him and smiled as he lay on his side facing the ocean. Cammie finished her fruit salad, placed the contained in the mini cooler, and joined him.

"Here, lay this way," he said, positioning her in front of him. "Now lean back against me," he whispered in her ear.

Cammie stifled a moan as his arm came around her, pulling her midsection closer to his. He nuzzled her head with his nose and she closed her eyes and allowed the simple but highly charged act to envelope her.

"I love your hair." His fingers gliding lazily in her hair. "Most women are fixed on long hair. I think short hair on a woman shows her fearlessness."

Cammie wanted to snort aloud. She was afraid. Not of things that go bump in the night, or taking a risk with the agency and new, innovative ways to make money or even of cutting her hair, but of her inexperience and how he'd view her once he found out. Most younger men thought older women were worldly and experienced on many matters, especially sex.

She closed her eyes as his fingers began to roll up and down the side of her body. As his hand rolled across her hip, she reached out and grabbed his hand.

"Sweetheart, I'll never do anything you don't want me to." He rested his hand on her hip.

Shoot, she thought. She wanted him to feel her up and more. *Don't stop!*

Cammie rested her head right below his chin as the sounds of the ocean added to her already heightened senses. She inhaled deeply and allowed Jacques to roll her onto her back. She watched as his face neared hers then stopped.

"Can I kiss you?"

She nodded her head, and then closed her eyes as his lips touched hers. He nibbled at her bottom lip, pulling it into his mouth and suckling on it. For a moment, Cammie imagined her lip was her nipple and knew that if he ever tended to her breasts the same way, he would be in trouble. Heck, *she* would be in trouble.

Jacques's mouth covered hers, his tongue pushing past her lips, demanding entry. She willingly succumbed, allowing his tongue to search hers, to tango with it as his large hands captured her face.

Voices interrupted them. Jacques broke the kiss and held his forehead to hers.

"Too sweet," he said and then sat up. Cammie looked up at him; his eyes bore into hers and spoke of things to come.

"We probably should get back with the group," Cammie suggested. She packed up their empty containers, stood and began walking back to the jeep. Moments later, Jacques joined her, taking her hand in his.

His mind spun with whys. He could see that she was attracted to him—her body reacted every time he was near her. But she was holding back, and he wanted to know why.

"Cammie, I..." he began, and then was interrupted when he spotted the tour guide heading their way.

"We thought you guys were lost," came the island lilt of the guide with his smooth, dark complexion and stark white smile. He had spoken to them but was clearly looking at Cammie. Jacques stepped forward.

"We're not," Jacques replied. He placed the blanket in the rear of the jeep. He wanted to break the guy's hands for taking Cammie's hand and assisting her into the jeep.

Jacques and the guide engaged in a Mexican standoff, ominously staring at each other for a long moment. The guide was the first to look away. Jacques had to bite his tongue. There would be no Dexter for his Cammie!

"Please, stay with the group," the guide chided as he walked to the road and resumed leading the caravan.

Once the excursion was over, they headed back to the ship for a shower and a quick nap before dinner.

Following dinner, they sat in on the Slam Jam Conference award ceremony. Jacques watched as the authors rose to receive the coveted Emma Award, which was named after the founder of the prestigious conference created to honor authors of African-American Romance.

Jacques stood back and watched as Cammie floated around the room following the award ceremony. The sleeveless print dress she wore fell right at her knees and showed off her slender legs, which were accentuated by high-heeled, open-toed sandals. As he watched her, he got a funny feeling deep in the pit of his stomach, as if butterflies were in there, skipping and dancing. The look of delight and contentment on her face as she spoke to one author, and he knew at that moment he'd do anything in his power to make her happy.

An hour later, they headed out of the room and up to the deck for a nightcap. Jacques found an empty chaise lounge and sat. He patted the space near the end for Cammie.

"Did you enjoy your day, sweetheart?"

Cammie smiled and twisted so that she could face him. "I sure did. Did you?"

"Yup. Think you know what you want to do tomorrow when we arrive in Jamaica?"

"Not sure, but I do know I want to do a little shopping. Pick up a few trinkets for the kids and some rum for my sister."

A waiter appeared and took their drink order.

Cammie rolled her neck backward, and then smiled when she felt Jacques hands kneading her neck and shoulders.

"Slide back," he said. She complied and slid her body until she was nestled between his legs. She almost jumped out of her skin when her rear came upon his thick hardness. Cammie bit down on her lower lip.His hands rubbed her shoulders then moved down her sides, close to her breasts. She crossed her legs to keep her hips in place. She wanted to ground her rear into his pelvis, to let him feel the effect he had on her. A part of her wanted to turn around and straddle him, pulling him into her. *So, what's stopping you?* asked a little voice in her head.

"Hey, sweetheart." His breath caressed her ear. "It's a full moon." He kissed her neck, then let his tongue trace a wet trail up and around her earlobe. Cammie pushed her behind backward and let her head lob into his as her hand reached up to hold his head in place. The goose bumps rose hard and fast along her arms as her bud tightened. She clamped her legs together as the throbbing ache battered against her fear. She knew that if she let him take her, make love to her, that she would have to admit to being innexperience.

"Let's head to the suite," he said. Cammie stilled. She knew if they returned to that suite right now, she wouldn't know what to do. She wanted him, wanted to see him in all his magnificent glory, wanted to feel him come inside of her. *Throw caution to the wind, Cammie.* The little voice was back and louder than ever. She took the drink that had been delivered and downed it in three gulps. She then finished the drink Jacques had been sipping on before sliding off the chaise.

Chapter Six

Taking his time, Jacques rose from the chaise, took Cammie by the hand and led her to the bank of elevators that would take them to their suite and what he hoped would be a night of pure blissful paradise.

Arriving in the suite, Jacques had Cammie sit on the couch while he attached the small speakers to his iPod. He then went over to the refrigerator and retrieved the bottle of champagne he'd had brought to the suite the day of their arrival.

"What are we celebrating?" Cammie asked when he sat next to her. She looked into his eyes and noted they had turned dangerously dark. Instead of being frightened by the message in them, the liquor she had consumed coupled with the little voice egging her on helped her welcome it. She scooted closer to him as he poured them each a glass of Moët. They clinked glasses and then she took a sip.

"We are celebrating life, Cammie, and the fact that we are here with each other."

Jacques watched Cammie's eyes go from gold to dark tawny. He wondered if maybe he was about to bite off more than he could chew. For the past two nights, she had kept him at bay, and now here she was scooting closer, her breasts inches from his chest, her legs crossed and swinging. Well, he reasoned, if he was, then he would die a most happy death, for he was going to show this woman what real passion was all about. He leaned over and captured her lips with his as he lay backward, pulling her atop him. He felt her pelvis settle over his and then molded to him

Cammie slowly ground her hips into his as his hands plied, and then cupped her behind. The sensation was exquisite as he continued, pulling the tail of her dress up before he placed his hands inside her lace panties. He captured her lips with his, sliding his tongue suggestively in and out of her mouth. Cammie moaned loudly, her innor core ground out a rhythm in response to his own, her bud as hard as his member.

He slowed long enough to remove the dress from her entirely, the tops of her full breasts peeking between them. He traced circles on the tops of her breasts before his thumbs found her nipples. Jacques clenched his teeth. Her nipples were large and hard, straining to be released from her lace bra. He rubbed them lightly with his thumbs, her moans and the movement of her pelvis against his the signal he'd wanted. But before they even went there, he had to know why she had been pulling back.

"Cammie," he called, and then waited as she looked up into his eyes and became still. The fear he had seen the first night was back and he wanted to know why.

"Sweetheart," he said, rubbing her back. "What's wrong? Did I go too far? Do too much, again?" He sat them up.

Tell him, the little voice said. ***Tell him***.

Cammie buried her face in his chest. She didn't want to see the disappointment in his eyes. "I don't know what to do and I don't want to lose you because I don't." Her words came out in a rush, tumbling over one another.

For a long moment they were still, his hand on her back, her face in his chest. Slowly, he raised her face to look into his. He smiled at her.

"Sweetheart, are you talking about what I think you are?"

Cammie nodded her head. Her golden eyes shimmered with unshed tears.

Jacques threw his head back and began laughing.

"It's not funny, Jacques."

"Oh, I'm not laughing at you. I'm laughing at me."

Cammie looked at him and waited. When he saw she wasn't amused, he stopped laughing.

"Let me explain." He took her hands in his. "When we first arrived, I wanted to make love to you so bad that I ached, but then I saw the reluctance in your eyes and thought I had gone too far with all of this." He nodded his head, indicating the suite. "And then when you didn't respond or say anything, I thought that maybe I had been too presumptuous. But I was also more than happy to let you set the pace, so I tried to keep my hands to myself."

Now Cammie was laughing. "So much for communication." She went on to explain her sexual history and her negative status. Once she was finished, the look in his eyes assured her she had nothing to worry about.

"Sweetheart, that makes two of us. I'm negative and haven't been with anyone without the benefit of a condom for nearly eleven years."

"Well, I can't have children. I've been tied off."

Jacques chuckled. "So am I." He kissed the backs of her hands. "So how about we explore together?" He leaned his head forward and nipped at her nipples through the lace fabric. "You tell me what feels good and I'll do it." He nipped the other nipple. "And if you want me to say naughty things to you, I will." He pulled one bra strap down, releasing a breast from its lacy cup, then took her nipple in his mouth, first licking lightly then suckling. She threw her head back. "And if you want to touch me, do." He suckled harder. "And when I enter you, you set the pace." His voice was deep and husky. "Fast and hard—or slow and easy?" He unsnapped her bra and pulled it from her, throwing it over his head. "Damn, you are built like a brick." He cupped her breasts, laving each nipple with his tongue, one at a time. He inhaled her womanly scent, his head swimming,his member hard as granite.

"Jacques." She cooed. "Baby, what should I do?"

He sucked her harder. She writhed, her scent growing stronger, becoming an aphrodisiac. He was so hard that if he entered her now it would be over for both of them before it started, and he wanted her to truly enjoy making love with him.

He knew, based on the way she was moaning, that she was close. He stroked her bud through her panties, finding her soaking wet. If he licked her just right, he knew she would have one hell of an orgasm.

"Just let me take you to paradise." He picked her up and carried her to the bedroom, placing her on the bed she'd slept in the past two nights. He didn't bother turning on the light, for the moon provided enough light.

Jacques pulled her panties from her and placed them to his nose.

Slowly, he disrobed, allowing her to get used to seeing him naked. Her eyes watched his hands as his boxers slid from his hips to the floor.

He began with her feet, rubbing the soles then kissing them. He traveled up farther, his lips never leaving her as he kissed her legs, kneading her toned calves and thighs. The closer he got to her mound, the stronger the aphrodisiac became, the more he needed the elixir to soothe him and put out the heat threatening to consume him.

Jacques wanted to feel her come apart, to be the one who brought her boundless pleasure.

He continued his oral assault before he ventured south and stopped at her mound. With his fingers, he traced lazy designs around the curls hiding the precious jewel. When he heard her sharp intake of breath, he let his fingers travel past the curls to the lips as he stroked them lightly. She arched her back. He took this as his cue to continue.

Finally, he found what he was looking for and dipped his head to begin the feast, letting his tongue, followed by his lips, to suckle her, pulling her bud into his mouth after licking it. Her hips danced for him—round and round they went the more he suckled. He felt her bud throb just as her back arched off the bed and she let out a loud hiss that included fragments of his name. He held her to his face and allowed the orgasm to sweep over her, her bud throbbing and hardening.

"Oh. My. Jacques. I've never felt anything like that." She looked down at his glistening face. Wondering what she tasted like, she motioned him upward, watching as he rose slowly and crept upward, his member was hard. She opened her legs as the head of his exquisite erection bobbed in her direction.

"You ready?"

Cammie nodded as his lips met hers. She tasted wonderful on his lips as he entered her in one fluid thrust. Her body came off the bed as her pelvis crashed into his, causing him to sink deeper.

"Cammie!" he called out. "Baby, do not move." He held her hips still, his eyes shut tightly. He exhaled loudly. "Damn. You are not only wet but you are tight." He began to move in and out of her slowly, fighting the pull, as her muscles clinched around him. "Open your eyes and look at me."

She did as he requested and saw his raw emotions plainly. His eyes stared into hers as he held her hips and slid in and out of her with long, languid strokes. The feel of him, his fullness, the throbbing had her matching his erotic pull. Her hips circled on their own with her pelvis meeting his again and again.

"Let me roll you over." He pulled out of her and gently turned her to rest on her stomach. He rubbed his hands up and down her rear end, gently massaging and filling his hands with her. Jacques bent over and began kissing her derrière. His lips took their time loving the roundness of her behind. "Woman, my god." He rubbed his cheek along hers, then lay across her back and attempted to rest the majority of his weight on his elbows.

He closed his eyes when Cammie began to rotate her hips under him; her roundness met his erection in an all-out assault. There would be no prisoners tonight as Cammie raised her derrière and Jacques slid inside her once again. He snaked his hand under her and began to coax her bud to life. This time, he wanted her to know the experience of a dual orgasm.

"Jacques, what are you doing to me?"

"Making love to you," he whispered into her ear. "Come for me." He began sliding in and out of her, rolling his own hips as her derrière met him. Time and again, the motion threatened to make him lose it, but he held back, wanting to hear her call out his name, to feel her walls grip him. He rolled his finger gently across her bud as he slid in and out of her. "That's it baby. Take me."

Cammie's muscles began to milk him. Her body quaked as an orgasm unlike the first one skipped erratically across her body. She screamed his name as she reached back and pulled him closer, causing him to go deeper.

She went rigid as the aftershock rocked over her body, her walls clenching, her bud throbbing. Never had she experienced such pleasure. And just when she thought he was finished, he pulled out and rolled her over once again, then slid back inside, wrapping her in his arms as he kissed her endlessly.

Cammie wrapped her legs around his waist and he sank farther inside her, his muscular body moving with hers as they made love, holding onto the other as if this day would be their last. In her life, she had loved one man, without reservation. Now, she was falling for another man who had awakened the sleeping beauty and damn near turned her out.

"Cammie," he called out as her walls milked him, pulling every drop from him as he pumped several more times before collapsing onto her.

Jacques lay still as Cammie rubbed her hand up and down his wide back.

For the rest of the night they lay in each other's arms, the passion awakened as they made love several times before sunrise.

Chapter Seven

Jacques awoke and reached out to Cammie. He opened one eye when he realized that she was no longer in bed next to him. Opening both eyes, he looked at the bedside clock. It was nearly noon and they were in Jamaica.

He sat up and swung his legs over the side of the bed, rubbing a hand down his face. The last thing he remembered before passing out was Cammie showing him the sexy nightgowns her daughter had packed and the little black box her sister had given her. He had her model the gowns, which he told her that he found temptingly sexy. And when she handed over the little black box, she'd admitted that she hadn't look inside. When she brought the box back to the beds— which Jacques had pushed back together— he was just as curious about its contents as she. She handed him the box. Jacques began laughing when he saw that her sister had given her "The Bullet."

"What does it do?" she had asked, looking at him in wide-eyed wonder.

"I can show you better than I can tell you," had been his only reply before using the toy to bring her to yet another orgasm.

He smiled broadly, his member stirring to life, and he thought of how his Cammie was a quick study. He loved her reaction to him. By the time they were finally sated enough to sleep, she was riding him into oblivion.

Jacques rose from the bed and walked out to the living area. He was disappointed when he didn't see her. He headed to the bathroom, expecting her there. *Her scent is everywhere*, he thought, inhaling deeply and stepping into the bathroom. No Cammie.

"Maybe she went to get us some breakfast," he mused as he stepped into the shower. Once he finished, he went back out to the living area and saw that she hadn't returned. He dressed quickly and decided that he'd go to the dining area to find her.

He saw the note as he got closer to the door.

"Hey sweetie," Jacques read and then smiled at the term of endearment. "You were sleeping so soundly I didn't want to wake you. I headed ashore. I'll be back at two to see if you're awake. Yours, Cammie."

Jacques titled his head to one side. He wasn't sure how he felt about the note or her going to shore without him.

Cammie wandered around from shop to shop along a strip called the Arena. The various shops had appealed to her taste for items that were a little higher end than the goods sold along the road. In one jewelry store, she found herself fascinated with the exquisite selection. She had already purchased a ruby and diamond tennis bracelet for herself and was looking for a watch for Jacques. And while she liked his Rolex, she thought he should have another watch to wear more casually. She picked out a Movado with a black face and a lizard-skin band.

Leaving that store, she waltzed into another that sold women's clothing. She loved the colorful ankle-length skirts and bought several, for herself, her daughters Lottie and Eliza, and her sister Candi.

Admittedly, Cammie felt a little strange leaving Jacques asleep in the suite, but she had attempted to wake him and all he'd done was smile and roll over, pulling his pillow close. Besides, she needed to roll around in her mind what had happened last night. He had awakened her body and mind, had her climbing the walls and brought her to multiple orgasms. She had wanted to call Candi. When he used The Bullet on her, she just about came out of her skin, the vibration of the toy bringing her to a quick and massive orgasm. And then he'd entered her quickly before the wicked sensation had a chance to ebb. Whew! She began to perspire just thinking about all the things they'd done.

"Hey beautiful."

Cammie turned to see the tour guide from yesterday's excursion standing next to her.

"Why are you shopping alone, beautiful one?" His mellifluous voice was heavy with island patois.

Yesterday she had watched what she thought was a pissing match between Jacques and the guide and dismissed it.

"My sweetie was asleep, and I wanted to surprise him with a few gifts," she said.

"Lucky man," he responded. "May I walk with you?" he asked, nodding his head toward the cobblestone street.

"It's a free country. Sure."

They walked and talked, and Cammie found the guide, Antoine, quite interesting as well as charming. She listened as he told story after story of how the Arena Shops came to be and other tales of growing up in Trinidad. By the time she headed into the men's shop, he had her laughing out loud.

Jacques paced the suite. He felt like a caged animal waiting for Cammie to return. He thought of what he'd read about women going to Jamaica and what went on with them.

"Oh, hell naw," he barked, then headed out of the suite. Foregoing the elevator, Jacques took the stairs to the ship's concierge. He was in the middle of asking if he had seen Cammie and giving him a description of her when the woman assigned to care for their suite paused nearby.

"Mr. Champion," she began. "Miss Kohl went to the Arena." "Arena? Where's that?"

"A cab ride away. It has lots of high end stores and boutiques. And she told me she was going to shop
for you and her family."

Jacques called out thanks as he rushed to the gangplank, hailed a cab and headed to the Arena.

"Antoine, would you mind terribly trying this on?" She held up an off-white linen suit. She knew that the suit would look great with Jacques's beautiful coloring. "You and Jacques are about the same height, even though he has a few pounds on you."

Antoine disappeared behind a curtain and returned moments later wearing the suit. While it was baggy, the length was perfect. Cammie turned to the sales associate. "I'll take it."

After purchasing the suit, she looked at her watch. "Oh my, it's nearly one-thirty. I've got to head back."

"Sure, let me help you."

Cammie and Antoine walked back toward the main road. She blinked several times when she noticed Jacques jump out of a cab, leaving the door open.

"What are you doing with him?" Jacques barked at Cammie.

"What do you mean?" She looked up into his eyes to see a storm brewing. As she watched his face, she realized just what he was asking.

"You know damn well what I mean." He looked Antoine up and down with contempt in his eyes. "Is this why you didn't wake me? So you could hang out with him? I saw how he was ogling you yesterday."

Cammie reared back as if she had just been slapped. If Jacques was accusing her of what she thought he was, then they had a problem.

"What do you think I am, Jacques?"

"You actually may be an innocent in this. These island gigolos are a different story."

Cammie watched as Jacques stepped up to Antoine, who stood by her side holding the packages of items she'd bought for Jacques.

"Antoine, I think you'd better hand him those." She lifted her sunglasses and narrowed her eyes at Jacques. "Cause if I do, they'll be upside his head." She brushed past Jacques and climbed into the waiting cab. The dust from the tires rose around the two men as it disappeared down the road toward the ship.

"Brother, I hate to tell you this, but I think you not only said she didn't know any better but insinuated that she wanted to sleep with me," Antoine said. "Oh, and here." He handed the bags to Jacques. "All she talked about was you and most of these bags are things for you."

Jacques looked at the bags Antoine handed to him, then looked at the road, where the cab had just disappeared. He shook his head. "What is wrong with me?"

"Love, my brother. Love. And she loves you, too."

Antoine pointed to the jewelry shop. "If it's not an engagement ring, it better be a promise ring."

"Promise?"

"Promise that you'll never be this big an idiot again." Antoine shoved the bags into Jacques's hands and walked away.

Cammie opened the door to the suite with so much force, the door hit the wall. She had never in all of her life been so embarrassed and treated as if she were so dumb she didn't know when a man was coming onto her. Antoine had talked nonstop about his wife while she talked about Jacques and how well they got along. That was, until he rushed in and accused her of not owning sense and being naïve, of all things. She might have been inexperienced in bed, but that didn't apply to every aspect of her life. She had been propositioned by several men when Lawrence was alive and soon after his death. Shoot, even her minister had asked her out!

For nearly an hour, Cammie sat in the silence of the suite and fumed. At the sound of the keycard being inserted in the door, she looked up to see Jacques enter, carrying the bags she had left with Antoine.

"Cammie, I'm ..." He started but quieted when she stood and held up her hand.

"Never in my life have I been accused of being naïve and stupid all in the same breath, Jacques Champion." Cammie put her hands on her hips. "I may be a little lax on the sex end, but I most certainly am not dumb. I know when a man is hitting on me. But there is a bigger issue." She wiped at the tear that had rolled down her cheek. "Trust, Jacques.

Trust." She picked up the keycard from the coffee table. "If you don't trust me, then by all means, we have nothing." Cammie walked out of the suite, shutting the door quietly behind her.

She looked around, her eyes clouded with tears. She wished she had someplace to go, then thought of the Spa. She could go there and lay out as she got a massage and cry her heart out. She loved Jacques; she knew. But if he couldn't trust her, there could be no relationship.

Jacques slumped into the overstuffed chair closest to the doors leading to the patio. In less than twenty-four hours they had gone from passion to pain. And until Antoine said that Cammie loved him, he'd had no clue that he was solidly in love with her. So, when he saw Antoine carrying her bags, something he should have been there doing, he thought the worst—that Antoine was attempting to come on to her. He knew men looked at Cammie. He had never met a woman quite like her.

He looked at the bags and decided to see what was in them.

In one bag he found skirts he was sure belonged to her. In another, he found a pair of leather sandals. By the size, he guessed they were for her son. When he looked into yet another bag, he shook his head as he pulled out a plastic garment bag. After removing the plastic, he held up the suit, which was just his size. He noticed a box in the bottom of the bag, opened it, and found the Movado watch.

If he'd felt goofy at the Arena, he felt like a complete cad now. He had overreacted. Big time.

"I'm not going to lose her," he said as he rose from the chair and went to the bar. Picking up the phone, he waited to hear the voice of the concierge on the other end. If anyone could help him put a plan in place, the concierge could.

He had acted impetuously and without thought, but he also knew that the feelings he had for her—the love in his heart—would never subside and he needed her to know it.

Chapter Nine

Cammie lay on the massage bench wrapped in seaweed from neck to ankles, with hot stones strategically placed along her back. Tears rolled down her cheeks, but she felt some relief. After talking to the masseuse, she realized that she loved Jacques with a fierceness and completion that comforted her and frightened her.

After several hours under the expert ministrations of the masseuse, Cammie decided that the best thing for her and Jacques would be to sit down and hash everything out. She needed him to trust her.

She returned to the suite and stopped short when she stepped across the threshold and saw dozens of candles strategically placed around the living area. A small round table covered with a bright white cloth had been set with china and silver. A single red rose sat in the center of the table.

Not seeing Jacques, Cammie headed into the bedroom and saw more candles, and rose petals all over the floor. She smiled, then noticed the note attached to the pillow on her side of the bed. She picked it up and read it.

"I am truly sorry. Jacques."

Cammie folded the note and placed it back on the bed. She went back to the living area and noticed that the patio door was open. Once she reached the door, she looked out to see Jacques standing there in the linen suit she'd purchased, leaning over the railing, facing the ocean.

As if sensing her arrival, he turned, and then stepped away from the railing. He took a tentative step toward her and Cammie could see the plaintive remorse in his dark eyes.

"Jacques ..."

"Cammie ..." He spoke her name at the same time as she called his. He held open his arms and then tilted his head to one side.

Cammie shrugged her shoulders and went to him, allowing him to envelope her in his arms. She placed her head on his chest.

"Sweetheart, I am so sorry for the way I reacted today. I've never acted like that before, and I swear to you that I'll never do it again."

Cammie looked up into his eyes. For years, she'd wondered how it felt to be passionate, to make love to a man who had no hang-ups and to be uninhibited.

"Can you forgive a lovesick dog who didn't use his home training?"

She laughed. "I guess I could try."

Jacques pulled a handkerchief from his pocket and placed it on the floor of the patio. He pulled a small box from his pocket and knelt on one knee before her. "Would you forgive me if I promised to care for you until the end of time?" he said, opening the box.

Cammie gasped, then placed her hand over her mouth.

"Say you love me and that you'll marry me."

A lone tear rolled down her cheek, her headed shaking from side to side. She let him take her left hand and Jacques slid a ruby solitaire surrounded by round diamonds onto her ring finger.

"I've fallen in love with you, Jacques. I really have, but..." She let the last syllable hang in the air.

Jacques looked up at her. "But what, sweetheart?"

"We have a lot to learn. We live miles apart. After what I saw from you today, I have to know, without doubt, that you not only love me but trust me. I'm a one-man woman, Jacques. There's only room for one man in life and in my bed." She inhaled deeply. "And if you don't believe that then we're not going to have much of a relationship. We won't have one at all."

Jacques stood to his full height. He took Cammie's hand in his and headed back inside the suite, then sat down on the couch, bringing Cammie to sit down on his lap. Releasing her hand, he placed his arms around her waist and leaned his head against her. He closed his eyes momentarily and inhaled deeply before looking up into Cammie's warm, whiskey eyes.

"I've been married before, Cammie. You know this. And I loved Skylar. I did. But she wasn't a one-man woman." He shook his head. "Today, when I saw you and the guide, I let my imagination get the best of me, though I knew better. I know you're smart and very intuitive. And my heart tells me that you love me." He took her hand in his again. "All I can say is that I'm truly sorry and I won't ever doubt you again, or react like that without just cause. But I'm not going to lie, if a man comes on to you, it's on."

"Promise?" Cammie asked, looking into his eyes.

With his index finger, he crossed the area where his heart lay under his skin. "Hope to die."

She rested her head against his and stroked his face. "Where will we live?"

Jacques stood, lifting her in his arms.

"Are you saying yes?"

Cammie nodded. "I am."

He kissed her deeply. "Wherever you want to live. But before we go any further, I need to hear it again."

"Hear what, Jacques?" She tilted her head, her eyebrows raised.

He nuzzled his nose to her neck and placed a light kiss right under her ear. "Hear you call out my name," he whispered huskily.

Cammie clamped her thighs together and lowered her eyelids. "How many times?"

He began walking toward the private patio. "As many as you want."

And for the rest of the night, she called out his name over and over, allowing the words of love to float from her lips up to the heavens.

Epilogue

Cammie walked down the beach barefoot, her ankle-length, off-white dress flowed around her ankles as her immediate family waited for her to reach the arch and the man who had promised her passionate nights and loving days. Up to the month before they'd married, he had done just that. Six months after Jacques proposed, they were together every weekend, alternating between their respective cities.

During that time, Cammie and Jacques blended their families, with her children accepting him and Ronnie, who insisted on calling her Momma C.

A month before the wedding, Cammie rented out her house and moved to Philadelphia to move in with Jacques, Ronnie and Bossy, the dog..

At the wedding ceremony, Cammie smiled at Jacques standing under the arch wearing the linen suit she'd bought him during their cruise. Once she reached his side, she placed her hand in his outstretched one and they stared into each other's eyes as the minister began the ceremony.

As Cammie looked at her soon-to-be husband, stared into his warm, dark brown eyes, she thought of the love she shared with him, the way he supported her and how he had loved her with a passion that kept her on cloud nine. *Oh, yeah*, she thought glancing at her family as the minister announced her and Jacques husband and wife, *only heaven knows how special he is to me.*

The End

Author Bio

Barbara Keaton, a native of Chicago, who thinks it's the best city in the world, also enjoys writing. Her first diary is dated December 1975! And since then, Barbara has written articles for *Today's Black Woman Magazine*, Chicago Reader, Chicago Crusader and most recently, True Confessions. In addition, Barbara is an accomplished romance author, having seven titles to her name. Barbara credits her late grandfather, Thomas Hill, and the Oblate Sisters of Providence for instilling in her a love and passion for the written word.

Red Rose Publishing
Show Me!

Genesis Press
All I Ask
An Unfinished Love Affair
Homeland Heroes & Heroines Anthology, V-II
By Design
Blaze
Cupid
Nights Over Egypt

Parker Publishing
Love for All Seasons—Anthology
One in a Million
Good With His Hands—Anthology

Trapped In Paradise

By

Deatri King-Bey

Chapter One

"When Saundra finds out what you've done, you're dead meat," Ashley said from her desk.

"Then I guess she'd best not find out." Miranda pulled various travel brochures off the display rack to expend some of her nervous energy. Of all the cockamamie ideas she had come up with over the years, this one had to be the most cockamamie of them all. Usually her sister, Saundra, kept her from attempting to carry them out, but this time Saundra was the intended target. "She won't find out."

"Oh, she'll find out, and when she does, Marcus will be a widower and those sweet babies of yours..." Ashley sniffed and wiped the crocodile tears from her eyes. "The babies..." She choked up. "Don't leave them without their mother."

"And you call me melodramatic." She plopped the brochures onto her desk. "I know what I'm doing."

"Which makes what you're doing all the more psycho. You are ten kinds of wrong on this. Stop before it's too late."

Though scared to the marrow, Miranda knew she was doing the right thing. "I know you're only trying to help. I appreciate it. I really do, but I have to do what's best for my sister." Feeling less than confident with her plan, she dug in her heels. Nothing anyone could say would change her mind.

"Who are you to say what's best for Saundra? She's happy with her life. I highly suggest you stop interfering."

"I'm her older sister. I know what's best for her by default. Let's just agree to disagree." She straightened her all ready neat desk. "She'll be here any minute, and I need to calm my nerves."

"You're wrong, but I'm done."

"Thank you." Melting into the soft suede of her office chair, she gazed out the window. She had opened *Traveling the Miranda Way* five years ago and prided herself on her professionalism. Eyes closed, she inhaled and exhaled slowly. Even though the economy had turned for the worse, her business still thrived. What she was about to do could ruin her reputation and all she'd worked so hard for. *I have to do this.*

Second, third and forth guessing herself, she whispered, "I have to do this."

"Do what?"

Miranda jumped at the sound of her sister's voice. So caught up in thought, she hadn't heard her enter. "Umm, nothing."

Lips pursed and arms folded over her chest, Saundra didn't even almost look like she believed Miranda. "You're up to something. I just hope I'm out of town when whatever it is blows up in your face."

Ashley began choking. "Oh, excuse me." She fanned her tearing eyes. "Soda...went down...wrong pipe." Still hacking, she pushed away from her desk. "Sorry." She rushed to the back office. "Whatever you're up to must be really big." Saundra settled in one of the armchairs in front of Miranda's desk.

"I'm not up to anything."

"Sure you're not, but I don't even want to know what it is. I'm just here for my travel packet and I'm out. I still have a few calls to make before I pack."

Miranda tsked. "Why do you always think I'm up to something?"

"Because you're *always* up to something."

Miranda unlocked her bottom drawer, took out the packet she had prepared for Saundra and handed it over. "I hope you aren't planning on working. This is a *vacation.*"

"Working vacation." She opened the packet and sorted through the information. "I said I wanted a coach seat. Why does this say first class?"

"You have more than enough money to pay for comfort."

"I'm five-four in heels. Coach is plenty comfortable for me, and I have more than enough money because I spend and invest what I have wisely."

"Fine, I'll downgrade you to coach." Ever since Saundra had given her the initial investment capital needed for *Travel Miranda's Way*, then refused to accept payment for the "loan," Miranda had been making her travel arrangements.

"Thank you."

"You're not seriously going to work, are you?" Proud of her sister, she wished she could tell the world of her accomplishments. Six of the seven last titles she'd written had made it to the *New York Times* Best Sellers list, but since Saundra was a ghost writer, very few people knew of her highly-sought abilities.

"What else is there to do on a boat?"

"I don't know." Miranda hunched her shoulders. "Meet a man, get laid." She covertly checked the time on her computer screen. In the next twenty minutes, the second part of her plan would be walking through the agency's door, so she needed to give her beloved sister the boot.

Laughing, Saundra shook her head. "No thank you."

"You do realize that sex is much better with two than one, right?"

108

"Ha, ha, very funny," Saundra said dryly. "Does your husband know you have such a dirty mind?"

"That's what he loves best." They shared a laugh. "Did I tell you there's a conference going on during the cruise? Readers and writers aplenty for you to hang out with. Please don't stay cooped up in your cabin."

She stood to leave. "Yes, you told me. You also told me it's a romance conference. Yuck! You couldn't pay me to read that garbage."

Truly offended, Miranda grumbled, "You're such a literary snob, you make me sick." She opened her top drawer and pulled out a few books. Ever since Saundra's divorce eight years ago, she had given up on romance, on love. "Read a little Beverly Jenkins and Rochelle Alers before you turn up your nose. Speak from enlightenment instead of ignorance."

"I'm sorry. I know how serious you are about your...romance." She took the books.

"You don't have to say romance like it's a dirty word. There's nothing wrong with falling in love. Look at me and Marcus."

"Don't get me wrong." Hand resting on her chest, Saundra said, "I'm so happy for you two, and my nephews are the cutest little guys ever, but what you have is special."

"You can have it, too."

"I thought what I had with Nathan was special, but it was nothing but a misery filled trap. I know it's hard for you to comprehend, but I'm happy."

"Lonely."

"Alone, not lonely." Saundra hugged her older sister. "I need to get going."

"Call me when you land in Miami."

"I will."

"And promise to read these books."

"I promise. Now let me get out of here."

The door didn't close completely before Ashley returned. "You are going to burn in hell."

"Didn't you say you were done?"

"I changed my mind." She returned to her desk. "After what Nathan put her through, she deserves the right to be alone if she so chooses."

"If she were happy, I'd leave her alone, but she's not. She's more than alone, she's lonely."

"There's no talking sense into you."

"No, there isn't, so why don't you stop trying?"

Miranda searched her book drawer for the perfect novel to recommend to Jeremy, then set it on her desk. Just as Ashley opened her mouth, the man Miranda wanted to see entered and saved her from having to listen to another lecture on what a horrible sister she was for ensuring Saundra wouldn't be lonely.

Jeremy nodded a hello to Ashley as he entered. "How's my favorite travel agent?"

Miranda rounded her desk and gave Jeremy a big hug. "Much better, now that you're here. I thought you would weasel out on me."

"Oh no. I said I'd allow you to make all of the arrangements for my vacation, and I meant it."

She returned to her desk and took out his travel packet. "Well, with you being such a control freak," she teased, "I'm truly honored."

He chuckled. "You should be. So where am I headed?"

"A five-day Jamaican cruise!"

"Cruise? I'm not sure about this."

"Trust me on this. You'll love it." The disdain on his face did not sit well with her. He could be as close-minded as Saundra, reaffirming for her just how perfect they were for each other.

She watched as he sorted through his travel packet. Jeremy loved to read boring books like those Saundra loved to write. Saundra was attracted to older men, and though her sister was a decade younger than Jeremy, she was mature for her thirty-four years. They both owned their own businesses and thought investing was a form of entertainment. A chill went down her back at the thought of the droll conversations both had put her through regarding stock options, and don't get her started on their stupid political blogs. *Oh yeah, these two were made for each other.*

"It looks like you have everything in order."

"That's what I'm here for," she said with a smile. "Now I hope you plan to do more than keep your nose stuck in a book."

"I sure do. I thought I'd keep my nose stuck in several books."

"All you do is work, read, and hang out with married people. You'll never find a wife like that."

"I'm not trying to find a wife. I'm going on a much needed vacation."

"But what if your Mrs. Right is on the cruise, and you miss her because you've stayed hidden in your cabin under a pile of books?"

He tapped the romance setting on her desk. "I'm not the only one who's been reading, I see. Life isn't like in your romance books." He picked up the novel. "I'm not interested in some little girl who just left home. I want a strong, independent woman. Unfortunately, the type of woman I'm interested in has been put through hell and is fed up with giving a man a fair chance. Don't get me wrong. I partially blame myself. I know I helped push many a woman to the brink, but now that I'm ready to settle down..." He hunched his shoulders. "All I'm saying is my 'Mrs. Right' wouldn't see me for who I am. She'd see the pain and disappointment the men before me have put her through."

"And all I'm saying is you know your Mrs. Right has been hurt. Be understanding and patient. If you give her time, she'll see you for who you are." Nathan had pushed Saundra past the brink, but Miranda knew Jeremy could bring her back.

He stared at her.

"What?" she asked.

"It's just...Are you up to something?"

Ashley broke out in a hacking-laughing fit. She quickly excused herself and rushed out the room.

"What are you up to, Miranda?" he asked firmly.

Mouth agape and eyes wide, she drew her hands to her chest. "Me? I am so hurt. Why is everyone always accusing me of being up to something?"

"Because you *always* are."

"Well, I'm not this time," she said hotly. "You're my friend. I just want to make sure you don't close your eyes to what's right in front of you." She saw herself as a conduit of sorts. If she had to tell a little white lie here and there, so be it.

"I'm sorry. I shouldn't have jumped to conclusions." He set the book on her desk.

"No, you keep it. Evelyn Palfrey is one of my favorite romance authors."

"I don't read romance."

"Well start. Her characters are marvelously mature and have been through a lot of what your Mrs. Right has gone through. You might actually learn a little something."

Chapter Two

"I'm kicking myself for not flying first class," Saundra said to her sister as she re-adjusted her cell phone earpiece.

"Why, what happened?"

"As I was boarding the plane, I saw the only man who could make me reconsider one night stands." Giggling, she fanned herself as she walked down the tunnel from the plane into the busy airport. "And wouldn't you know the seat beside him was empty. I'll bet it was mine."

"That's what you get for being cheap. What did he look like? What was he doing? Did he see you...?"

"Slow your roll." She glanced up at the signs for the baggage area. "Whew howdy, his wavy, salt-and-pepper hair called to my fingers."

Miranda giggled. "You and your old men."

"He wasn't old, but mature, and his hair was more pepper than salt."

"Whatever."

"And you know how I like dark chocolate. A man like that could cause some serious diabetes."

"How tall was he?"

"Leg's look to be about fifty feet long."

"Fifty feet?" Miranda laughed. "You should switch from writing nonfiction to fiction."

"Okay, maybe not fifty." Taking her time, she strolled toward the baggage claim area. "But he was well over six feet. He definitely needed the extra room of first class."

"Woman, you ain't but about two foot tall! What is up with you and tall men?"

"I don't know. Let me ask my sister who is shorter than me and whose husband is at least six feet what's the deal with her and tall, dark, and all too fine men." She stopped in front of one of the many gift shops and debated purchasing her nephews a few Miami T-shirts and shipping them off before she left for the cruise. She had promised them she would pick them a little something up on each leg of her trip.

With a giggle in her voice, Miranda said, "I'm just glad you are finally reconsidering the one night stand. It's been eight years. How can you go so long?"

"For one thing, it hasn't been eight. It's been five."

Miranda broke out in another fit of laughter. "Like that's better. You'd better corner the market on condoms, because Jamaica is full of tall, dark and all too fine men waiting on you."

"My name ain't Stella, and I sure don't need to get back my groove."

"Says who? Five years. You need a whole lot more than to get your groove back. And I'm not saying you have to marry the man...men! Shooooot, the one night stand is a beautiful thing."

"You're married. What do you know about one night stands?" She selected Florida Marlin's T-shirts for the boys and a "Too Hot To Trot" T-Shirt for Miranda. She wouldn't tell her sister, but instead of reading on the flight, she had daydreamed about making love with the handsome stranger. Never in her life had she been so attracted to a man. It was frightening. Yesterday after she'd finished packing, she read one of the romance novels Miranda had given her. The Beverly Jenkins novel had turned out to be surprisingly good, but now Saundra was having second thoughts, thinking her reaction to this man had been too "romance novel."

"I know you could use one, two...hell, make it three."

"You are out of your mind." She set her selections on the counter.

"You know I'm only playing with you. I'm just glad to see someone has set a spark in you. It's not about the sex." Miranda paused. "It's not only about the sex. You're a passionate person, but since your divorce, you've shut down."

"I have not." She keyed in her pin number to pay for her purchases. "I'm doing quite well for myself."

"You know that's not what I mean. That spark. Please do me a favor and allow that spark to grow. I'm not saying you have to become promiscuous. That's not you. But neither is this woman who refuses to allow a man close enough to love her as she should be loved. I'm so afraid you'll miss out on your king."

"My *king*?" She giggled. "You're reading way too many romance novels."

"I'm serious."

"Okay...I'll pay along. I thought Nathan was my king, and he turned out to be a cruel dictator."

"You were only twenty when you married. You're older and wiser now. But you're also scared. Don't let fear keep you from your king. I need to get going. The boys are being entirely too quiet. Love you."

"Love you, too. Kiss the babies for me."

Thinking about what Miranda had said, she headed over to baggage claim. Truth be told, she wanted a king. Not to save or protect her. She didn't need saving or protecting. She wanted to share her life with someone special. She wanted what her sister had.

The conveyor belt lurched to a start and jolted her from her musing. A few minutes later, the red and black scarf she had tied onto the handle of her large suitcase caught her attention.

"Excuse me." She squeezed through the people gathered around. Just as she reached for her bag, another passenger bumped her out of the way to grab his suitcase.

"Hey, I'm standing here," she said to the rude man.

"Allow me," came a deep, melodic voice that took her breath away. Tall, Dark and All Too Fine himself reached over and easily grabbed her bag off the conveyor belt, and set it before her.

Rude man completely forgotten, along with her voice, all Saundra could do was stand there and pray she didn't look as flustered as she felt.

"Is that one yours also?" All Too Fine motioned toward the medium-sized southwestern print bag with the black and red scarf tied on the handle.

Wanting to slap the silly schoolgirl jitters into oblivion, she managed a weak, "Yes."

"Here you go, little lady." A bright dimpled smile against dark skin finished her off.

"Thank you. That was really nice of you."

"It was nothing." He glanced toward the belt, then back to her. "Don't move."

Jeans had never looked as good as they did hugging his firm behind when he bent to reach his luggage. Objectifying this man into body parts was wrong on so many levels, but damn. Miranda was right. Five years was too long to go without some good loving.

Before she realized what was happening, he had led her away from the crowd. *Snap out of it*, she chastised herself. He was only a man. Granted, the epitome of drop-dread gorgeous, but still just a man.

"I guess I should properly introduce myself." She held out her hand. "Saundra, Saundra Write."

Amusement flickered in his eyes. "As in Mrs. Right?"

The reaction to her name was odd, yet intriguing at the same time. "Miss Write, actually."

"I'm sorry. I'm not making fun of your name. It's just a friend of mine and I were discussing..." He shook his head. "Let's start over." He held out his hand. "Jeremy, Jeremy King."

"King?" *As in my king? This is straight up out of* The Twilight Zone. *Wait until I tell Miranda. She'll never believe me.* She accepted his hand, and the

114

moment they touched she felt something...*magnetic*...holding them together. Thinking she had only read one romance novel and was already turning into a mush head, she did her best to gather her faculties.

"Yes, King."

She caught him peeking at her left hand. Probably doing the same as she had done to him—checking for a ring.

"I don't want to sound forward, but I didn't eat before the flight. Would you like to have lunch with me?" he asked, releasing her hand.

The loss of contact was much more than their touch ending, which scared and excited the mess out of her. *This is all Miranda's fault. Stupid romance novels.*

Hands up slightly, he said, "No strings attached, just lunch."

"Do you usually pick up women in the airport?"

A full, robust chuckle erupted from him. If she didn't know better, she'd say there was a hint of nervousness mixed in there also.

"This is my first time. How is it going for me?"

"How could I say no to the man who saved my bags?" The flight had left entirely too early for her, and she hadn't eaten. So besides being tired, she was starving.

"Excellent. I need to drop my luggage at the hotel. Would you like to meet somewhere," he checked the time on his cell phone, "around one?"

"I'd love to, except I have no idea what's around here. I've never been to Miami in my life. I eat just about anything, so wherever you'd like to go works for me."

"I don't know about you, but I could eat several horses. Let's take our bags with us." Before she could respond, he picked up the heavier of her two suitcases along with his suitcase, then headed for the taxi stand.

Boy, can this man wear a pair of jeans, she thought as she followed behind, rolling her midsized suitcase. As if he had sensed her checking out his assets, he glanced over his shoulder and flashed a dimpled smile.

In the taxi, Saundra scooted so far over behind the driver's seat that one would have thought she was exiting the car on the opposite side. Nerves skittering, she momentarily contemplated making a run for it. What in the heck was she doing accepting this stranger's offer for lunch? And her heart—it was beating so fast, so hard, she was sure a trip to the emergency room was in her near future. Then there was her attraction to Jeremy. It was too strong, too powerful. *Inhale, exhale, release...*

After ensuring their bags were placed in the trunk to his liking, Jeremy eased into the backseat with her, taking up the center of the seat. His knees touched the backs of the front seats, his left leg resting gently against her right. This simple touch shouldn't be affecting her so. She should be asking him to move further away, not wanting him to remain.

"Where to?" asked the driver as he moved his seat forward.

"What are you hungry for?"

Jeremy's low voice broke into her internal tirade. Mind racing back to reality, she placed things into perspective. They were only two people sharing a taxi and a meal. Nothing more. Nothing less.

"We're in Florida. How about a Cuban restaurant?" she suggested.

"Excellent choice." He turned to the cabbie. "Please take us to the best Cuban restaurant around."

The cabbie nodded his approval, then eased into the busy airport traffic.

A few minutes later, Saundra concentrated on the drizzling rain, the traffic, the people walking about, everything except the man beside her. Why he made her feel as if butterflies had taken domicile in her stomach was beyond her. Her mother's main complaint of her had always been that she knew no strangers and would strike up a conversation with anyone. Yet that skill seemed to have escaped her when she needed it most.

"So what's the last book you've read?" he asked.

A sigh of relief escaped her. Books. How could she have forgotten that she could talk books anytime, anyplace. That he had asked such a question had her thinking he was much more than tall, dark, and all too fine. By the time they arrived at La Rosa Restaurant, the butterflies had been evicted, and she was on her "A" game again.

The hostess was kind enough to keep their luggage in the manager's office.

Seated at the table, Saundra perused through the menu. "Everything looks delicious."

"Have you ever had Cuban cuisine before?"

"No, not really."

"That makes two of us."

"Let's be sure to order two different meals so we can mix and match." Realizing she was eating lunch with a man she'd just met and not a longtime friend, she became mortified. "I'm so sorry. Forget I said that. I have been out before," she joked. "I'm sorry."

"I was going to suggest the same thing."

By the time their cream of split pea soup, shrimp scampi, veal Milanese, and snapper in garlic sauce arrived at the table, conversation had moved from books to politics. Another of her favorite subjects. And Jeremy, to her liking, was into policy—not politics. It never ceased to amaze her how many people didn't fully comprehend the difference.

Another difference came to her mind. Nathan. Confident, intelligent, older men had always been her Achilles heel. Unlike Jeremy, Nathan's confidence was rooted in arrogance instead of security. Thinking back, Nathan was the one who turned her against politics and onto policy. The way he regurgitated "talking points" made him sound like a bad infomercial.

And Jeremy was genuinely interested in her opinion, even when they disagreed. She had taken an opposing view to his on reparations, just to see his reaction. He'd said she was wrong, but respected that she supported her beliefs with facts and figures and looked forward to picking her mind on other issues. Oh yeah, she could get used to having Jeremy around.

Too stuffed from the delicious lunch, they didn't have room for desert, but neither wanted their conversation to end.

"What's wrong?" Jeremy asked.

That voice again. Now she fully understood the saying, "music to my ears." And she loved how he sensed her moods. At first she found it a little unnerving, but now that she knew him, she liked the connection. This was too good to be true. He was too good to be true. How could this man go from being a stranger to...to someone she could see herself falling for, was falling for. And falling quickly.

Boring. Miranda always accused Saundra of being boring, and to some extent she agreed, but this man was just as "boring" as she, yet Saundra found him fascinating. He got it. He got her and she understood him. Which scared the hell out of her.

"Saundra, what's wrong?" he repeated softly.

She couldn't tell him she was falling for him and didn't know how to handle it. No. She needed more time to think this—whatever it was—through. "I used to be a waitress when I was in college and hated it when customers held the tables up. You know how it is. They work for tips."

"I guess we should get going, then."

"I guess so."

After Jeremy called a taxi and retrieved their luggage, they watched the rain as they waited for their rides.

"This isn't it for us, Saundra." He took her hand in his. And though she knew she should pull away, she couldn't.

"I'll call you when I get settled in at the hotel," she said. "Maybe we can go out tonight."

"It's a date. Let's exchange cell numbers now."

No way would Saundra tell Miranda about the afternoon she had spent with Jeremy. Knowing her crazy sister, she would cook up one of her cockamamie plans, and they would all be in trouble. Jeremy was too nice of a man to subject to Miranda.

Going over lunch in her mind, she smiled. Books, books, and more books. The man loved to read and talk books as much as she did. He had even read a few of the books she'd written. But since she was a ghost writer, she didn't tell him who the real author was. He also had his head on straight about politics. It never ceased to amaze her how cavalier Americans were about the power behind their vote. That was one lunch she wished had never ended.

And such a gentleman. At the end of their afternoon, instead of sharing a taxi, he placed her in one of her own and paid her fare, then said he would wait for a second taxi. She had insisted he was going overboard, but he wanted her to feel secure. A stalker. Humph, if anything, she wanted to stalk him! After such a hiatus from men, it just didn't seem fair for God to put a man like Jeremy out of her reach.

Out of her reach because he was too good to be true. Just like Nathan. As Miranda had said, she was older and wiser now, and didn't intend to fall into the same trap. *All that glitters isn't gold.* So instead of calling Jeremy as she had promised, she slipped into a sweat suit, grabbed the second romance novel Miranda had given her, and headed for the hotel lobby to sit in one of their big cushy armchairs to relax. Romance books turned out to be enjoyable fast reads.

Three chapters in, she found herself comparing the novel's hero to Nathan and Jeremy. Early in her relationship with Nathan, she would say he gave the novel hero a run for his money, but after they married, he fell short. Way short. And now there was Jeremy.

The fictional hero was quite nice, but the real thing was so much better. Jeremy's smile, his laugh, his easy way of speaking kept her mind whirling. What if she were wrong about contacting him? Could she be passing up on what she wanted out of fear of repeating history? Should she call and let whatever happens happen? Was she ready to step out there and give love a chance?

Eyes closed, she held the romance novel close to her heart and made a hard admission. Though she didn't want to be like the heroines in the novels, she could see herself falling for Jeremy...had all ready fallen for him. *No. Love at first sight doesn't exist in real life.* She had thought she had fallen "in love" with Nathan, but looking back, that had been infatuation. Always attracted to older men, when he had returned her attentions, she'd fallen head over heels. Next thing she knew, she was married and he was moving her away from her family and everything she knew.

Thoughts of what Nathan had put her through resurfaced with the pain and tried to drown her. She couldn't go back. Wouldn't go back. She would never allow anyone to trap her again. Never.

"Saundra?"

Stuck in the past, she gripped the novel tighter.

"It's all right, baby."

Jeremy's soft voice brought her back to the present. She opened her eyes and saw him stooped before her.

"Jeremy? Jeremy, what are you doing here?"

The concern in his eyes was the only answer she received. He sat on the heavy oak coffee table behind him and continued to watch her.

Uneasy under his gaze, she fidgeted in her seat. "You're making me nervous. Say something."

Elbows resting on his knees, he leaned forward and continued watching her, worry written all over his face.

"I don't usually trip out in hotel lobbies," she teased. "Umm, what are you doing here anyway?"

"I guess we have the same hotel."

"Amazing." She strummed her fingernails on the book.

"I know we just met, but...but something happened between us today. I believe that *something* has scared the hell out of you."

"No, it hasn't."

"Then, why didn't you call?"

Caught, all she could do was smile. "Okay, so you're right."

"I don't know who hurt you, but I'm not him." He stood and pulled her up from the chair. "Let's go."

"Where are we going?"

"I'm walking you to your room."

Without argument, she gave him her room number and allowed him to be her escort. He was right, he wasn't Nathan, but the lessons she had learned from her experience with Nathan overshadowed everything in her life. Alone or lonely. How many times had she told

Miranda she was alone, not lonely, as if wanting companionship, wanting to love and be loved, was something to be ashamed of?

He pointed at the suite next to hers. "You'll never guess who's staying there."

"Who, a movie star?"

He chuckled. "Not quite. Me. You see, fate keeps putting us together."

Eyes and mouth wide open, she couldn't believe her ears. "No way. That is not your room."

He took out his door card and entered the suite next to hers.

"Well, I'll be..." The Twilight Zone *has nothing on this.* A few seconds later, she heard a knock from the interior door of her room, which connected to his. She went inside and opened it. "This is entirely too crazy."

"Isn't it though? If I had known we were in the same hotel, we could have shared the taxi."

"Well." She tossed the novel onto the nightstand. "Want to order a movie?"

"That would be nice." He propped the door open on his side of the connecting suite.

"Thank you, Jeremy King."

"For what?"

"Being you." *And for not being Nathan.*

Chapter Three

Much of Jeremy's time after arriving at the hotel had been spent searching the Internet for every Saundra Right, Wright, Write and Rite he could find. Fortunately, he only found a few instances of any variation of her names. Unfortunately, none of them were his Mrs. Right. Next, he'd begun listing publishing company contact information. She had said she was a ghostwriter, but never stated the genre or if she wrote fiction or nonfiction. During his search, he'd learned of *The Writers Market*, a book listing agents and publishers. He'd hopped over to Amazon and ordered the thousand-plus page book. He hadn't cared if he had to contact every individual listed to find Saundra. Then he realized he was obsessing and stopped. She would either call as she had promised or she would run scared.

He fully understood her fear. For a short time, the fear of the impossible had gripped him until he accepted what was happening between them. When she hadn't called, he had been disappointed, but somehow knew they would meet again. Then he'd seen her in the lobby, and there had been no doubt in his mind that they would be together.

The pain on her face when he first saw her gripping the novel in the chair had him ready to beat someone so badly his driver's license showed the black eye. Whoever had hurt her had really done a job on her, but he would be patient and show her his heart.

As the early morning sun filled the room, he watched her sleep, so calm, so peaceful, so beautiful. Jeremy had woken with his Mrs. Right in his arms. She just didn't know it. Or wasn't ready to admit it. Everything had happened so quickly, too quickly. Before yesterday, he would have said the events of the last twenty-four hours were impossible. Two sensible adults didn't just fall in love over night.

With all of their conversation, they had never mentioned where they came from or where they were going. Not that he hadn't wanted to. When he inquired or tried to give his information, Saundra steered the conversation elsewhere, so he let it go.

The reason behind her actions worried him. She wanted to remain as close yet as distant as possible. Someone had broken more than her heart; he had broken her trust and spirit. As Miranda had said, he would have to be patient. For now, all he could do was enjoy their few remaining hours.

He fingered the soft curls that framed her face. This cruise would now be a working cruise for him. A project manager by trade, winning over his Mrs. Right would be his next assignment.

From the moment Jeremy saw her to the taxi, Saundra felt she was making a mistake, but she couldn't trust her feelings. Sitting on a lounge chair on the deck of the ship, she was glad to be away from his magnetism. With no doubt in her mind he would contact her after their respective vacations, this time and distance apart would give her the space she needed to regroup and decide what her next step would be.

The past twenty-four hours had been overwhelming, to say the least. What was happening to her was all fairy tale, romance novel stuff, not real life. In real life, she'd found who she thought was her king, and he'd turned out to be cruel dictator. What if her instincts were failing her again? What if Jeremy pulled a Nathan?

Being with Jeremy taught her an important lesson: she had never been in love with Nathan. With their breakup, her pride and spirit had been broken, not her heart. Pride was her downfall. Initially, she had been too proud to let her family know she had made a mistake. Then came the shame and guilt of knowing the situation she was in was all her fault. Miranda had warned her against marrying Nathan, and her parents had expressed their misgivings. But she had been too pigheaded, too rebellious to listen. Truly in love with Jeremy, she couldn't fathom the pain of being wrong about him. If Jeremy hurt her, she wouldn't be able to walk away with a just bruised ego.

"What's that you're reading?" asked an attractive, middle-aged woman with a short afro and a billion-watt smile.

Glad for a break from her non-relationship with Jeremy, she answered, "I just finished *Indigo* by Beverly Jenkins. This is my second romance. I actually liked them, which shocked the hell out of me." Saundra's mouth and eyes opened wide in surprise. "Oh, I'm sorry, I didn't mean to curse."

The woman chuckled. "Don't worry yourself. I've said a few colorful words myself from time to time. I'm Bev." She held her hand out to shake.

"Saundra." They shook hands. "Pleased to meet you."

"Are you here for the Romance Slam Jam Conference?"

"Not really, but I'm seriously reconsidering." She glanced down at the second book she was carrying. Miranda had next-day aired it to the hotel and insisted she read it. "Have you ever read anything by Francis Ray?"

"Oh yes, she's quite good."

"Do you actually believe in these romances? I mean the *love conquers all* and *love at first sight* mumbo jumbo?"

With a smile in her voice, she answered, "Yes, I believe in the 'mumbo jumbo.' Why don't you?"

"Don't get me wrong. I used to, but my prince charming turned into a toad after we kissed. A mean, controlling, abusive toad at that."

With a slight nod, Bev said, "I see. You've been burned by the fire once, and don't want to be burned again."

"Exactly! I need to have you talk to my sister. She just doesn't get it. I'm never falling into that trap again. Never."

A compassionate smile tipped Bev's lips. "You know, just because it's hot, doesn't mean there's fire. Passion, love, desire...all hot. I'd even say burning hot, but in a good way." She stood to leave. "I'd best get back inside before they send a search party out for me. Come on down to the conference tomorrow and hang out with us."

"I think I will. It was nice meeting you."

"You, too."

You did good, Miranda. This cruise is just what I need.

"Oh—my—God," a young woman gushed as she rushed across the deck toward Saundra. "Do you know who that was?" She pointed at the door Bev had just stepped through. "That's *the* Beverly Jenkins. I can't believe I'm on the same cruise as Beverly Jenkins. I have got to get her autograph."

Embarrassment warmed Saundra's cheeks. Growing up, it seemed as though just about every other female was named Saundra. With the name Beverly being so common, she hadn't considered the woman she had just met could be the author of the wonderful novel she had just read. "I know I did not just sit here and tell her...Never mind. I think I'll go die now."

Laughing, the young woman said, "Girl, don't worry about it. I've been tripping all afternoon. I was on the elevator and realized Rochelle Alers was standing beside me. I just about fainted." She turned her cell phone screen for Saundra to see. "Look at this picture I took of you two. Would you like me to send it to your phone?"

"Oh thank you, I'll have to forward it to my sister. She's a huge romance fan." She gave her the cell number.

"I'm not trying to get into your business," she said as she keyed in Saundra's cell number, "but why would you let one bad relationship turn you off relationships all together?"

The price of this picture was a little bit too high for Saundra, but it was too late. There was a no return policy on it.

The young woman lifted her hands slightly. "I'm sorry. I shouldn't have asked such a personal question. Don't answer."

"Oh no. It's okay. I wish I knew the answer."

"It's such a calm night. Give it some thought. I'm sure it'll come to you. By the way, my name is Reba."

"I'm Saundra, pleased to meet you."

"I hope to see you at the conference." She stuffed her cell phone into her back pocket. "Let me get back inside and see who else I can just about faint over." She chuckled as she headed for the door.

Saundra relaxed on the lounge chair and looked over the calm sea. The sun had set a while ago, yet she still hadn't gone to her room. She had been told the porters would place her bags outside of her door. She smiled, thinking she might just want to head on down to her room before she had to purchase a new wardrobe.

Why is it so hard? Why can't I move on? She picked up her purse and the two books she'd carried around with her. With four more days of her cruise left, there was plenty of time to do some serious internal scanning for the answers.

As beautiful as it was large, the *Destiny* was a magnificent ship. Whoever wrote the brochure hadn't been kidding when they said the ship was as long as three football fields. Saundra would venture to guess she had walked just about all twelve decks. Once she finally found her room, she was past ready to call it an early night. Just as she had been told, her bags were sitting outside the cabin door.

She slipped in the keycard and entered the room. Surprised, she froze in the narrow entranceway.

Tall, dark, and all too fine, in nothing but a bath towel wrapped around his waist, was exiting the bathroom. A million and one thoughts flashed through her mind in the blink of an eye, from full-blown lust to, *Am I being stalked?*

Jeremy stopped mid stride.

"What are you doing in my room?" they said in unison.

The confusion in his eyes verified he wasn't some sort of high-tech, psycho stalker, but that didn't explain why he was in her room.

He brought her bags into the room and closed the door. "What's going on?"

Dazed, she sat on the bed. No author would write a plot this unbelievable. "This isn't adding up. This is past coincidence. Cruise lines don't make this type of mistake." She closed her eyes as tight as she could and prayed harder than she had in years that what she thought happened hadn't really happened.

"I was supposed to fly first class but switched to coach," she said timidly. "When I boarded, the seat next to yours was empty. Was it ever filled?" She peeked his way.

He shook his head.

Dread filled her. "There's only one explanation."

"Miranda," they said in unison.

"She's dead meat!" Saundra pounded the bed as she rose, then paced the thin walkway from the door to the window. "What in the world was she thinking? Who does she think she is? How could she?" she verbally shot off faster than a speeding bullet. "Trapped. I walked right into her trap." So disgusted she trembled, she bit out, "I knew she was up to something. I knew it!"

"I had a feeling she was up to something also, but this? Wow. Even for Miranda, this is over the top." Jeremy sat on the bed.

Sexy, he was entirely too sexy with the light glisten of moisture on his body waiting for her to lick it off. Oh no. This wouldn't work. She needed distance. Lots of distance. She sat on the bed with her back to him and focused on her anger at Miranda. "I'm so sorry about this. I shouldn't have ignored my instincts."

"I have never used a travel agent before. This isn't quite what I expected," he said with a bit of nervousness.

She turned toward him. "Please don't turn my sister in—"

"Miranda's your sister?"

"I'm afraid so." She blew out a long breath. "I know what she's done is as unethical as you can get, but she's never done anything so..." She couldn't think of an appropriate synonym for insane that wouldn't make Miranda sound like the out of control nut she was.

"It's all right, really." He chuckled. "Miranda is what the young folk call a 'hot mess.' "

"You have noooo idea. She's just bad. Has been her whole life. Instead of Miranda, Mama should have named her Manipulative. Don't get me wrong. She tries to use her *powers* to better mankind," she joked to lighten the mood. "But this is too much. She's gone way past too far."

At a complete loss, she had no idea what to do or say next. Soul mates, every fiber of her being screamed Jeremy was her soul mate, but she'd never considered the possibility of there truly being soul mates. At least not before she had read those dang blasted romance novels. *This is all Miranda's fault.*

"Marcus has his hands full with her."

"You can say that again." Exhausted, she lowered her face into her palms. "So how do you know them?"

While he explained how he and Marcus had pledged the same fraternity, she thought of the many ways she could get even with her meddling sister. Death was too good for her. No, this had to be something long lasting.

"...but I think we should just share the cabin."

"I'm sorry," she said. "I spaced out for a second."

Pearly whites shone bright against his dark skin, and his dimples made an appearance. Sexy and cute equaled dangerous by her calculations. Staying in the cabin with him was a bad idea. A really, really bad idea.

"I said, we should share the cabin."

"I don't think so."

"We are two mature, consenting adults. We shared a bed last night and—"

"That was different. I didn't intend on sleeping with you. I fell asleep."

"I will be on my best behavior. I promise."

"I don't know."

There went that dimpled smile again. Clothes. The man needed to dress so she could think straight. She had life-changing decisions to make, and all she could think about was snatching his towel and ending five years of celibacy.

"First I need to call my beloved sister." She speed dialed Miranda's number.

"Hey, Saundra. How's—"

"Oh my God!" Saundra said as if she'd been running. "The guy from the plane." She drew in a staggered breath. "He's stalking me. He's a stalker." She winked at Jeremy and continued her award-winning performance.

"What? Wait a second."

"No, you don't understand. He's been following me. Everywhere I go, he's there. I'm on my way to security now."

"Wait, wait, wait!"

"No, you're not listening. That guy from the plane has been stalking me since the airport. He followed me to the hotel. He was lurking around my room. How did he find out where my room was? He just entered my cabin on the cruise. I barely got away."

"Slow down. Let me speak."

"I just called to let you know what's going on in case something happens to me. Have the airlines track down every tall, black male who was on my flight."

"But Saundra."

"Oh my God! He's behind me. I have to hurry." She disconnected.

A look of awe on his face, Jeremy slowly said, "That was simply beautiful. You are definitely Miranda's sister."

Brows drawn, lips pursed and arms folded over her chest, she said, "I'm not sure if that's a compliment."

"In this instance, I meant it as a compliment."

"In that case, thank you." Her phone rang, but she didn't answer. "It's Miranda. I can't deal with her right now. I'm going for a walk." She turned the cell phone off, then tossed aside. "I need time to clear my mind." Keycard in hand and purse slung over her shoulder, she walked out.

Chapter Four

When Saundra initially walked into the room, Jeremy thought his mind was playing tricks on him.

"Sisters...wow."

Now he could clearly see the resemblance. Both were attractive, petite women with a propensity toward the melodramatic. Chuckling lightly at Saundra's performance, all he could do was shake his head. If Saundra were even a tenth as "bad" as her sister, Marcus wouldn't be the only one with his hands full. But Jeremy was ready for the challenge.

"Sisters..."

The next move...The next move...What to do...? What to do...? He had thought he would have a week to decide the best way to pursue his reluctant Mrs. Right.

*Sisters...*This new revelation would take a bit to absorb.

He crossed over to the built-in desk, grabbed his cell phone and speed dialed Marcus.

"Hey, Jeremy, what's up?"

"Not much. Is Miranda around?" Though Marcus and Jeremy were best friends, Jeremy never called Miranda directly, even though the calls were to verify if she were cooking a meal or if he should bring carry out from a local restaurant. Somehow, he just felt calling her directly was a bit disrespectful to his and Marcus's friendship.

"She's thumping around up stairs. Wait a minute."

A few seconds later, he heard Marcus saying, "Are you all right, baby? You look sick."

"Oh, no, no, I'm fine," came Miranda's voice.

"Jeremy's on the phone for you."

"Did he sound angry?" she asked shakily.

"What did you do?"

The weary tone of Marcus's voice brought a smile to Jeremy's face. That woman was *always* up to something. There no way Saundra could even be a twentieth as bad as her sister.

"What did he say?" she asked.

Marcus blew out a belabored breath. "Jeremy, what has she done this time?"

"My cabin mate is none other than a certain travel agent's sister, Saundra."

"What...? Miranda!"

"Let me explain," she cried.

Five minutes later, Marcus still hadn't finished chastising Miranda. Jeremy prayed the children were nowhere within a hundred yards of the house to hear their father's tirade.

"Jeremy. Look, man, Miranda will reimburse your vacation and pay to have you moved to a different cabin, won't you Miranda?"

"Yes, yes, of course," he heard in the background.

"That won't be necessary. I just need to speak with Miranda."

"Are you sure? She was so out of line on this one, you can't even call it a line."

"I'm sure. I just need to speak with her about Saundra." He lay back on the bed. Speaking with Miranda was inviting her to meddle in his life, but she knew Saundra better than anyone. Her insight would be invaluable.

"If you change your mind, let me know. How is Saundra?"

"Angry isn't quite strong enough a word."

"Anger is good. She just needs time to cool off, and she'll be her old self again. Miranda, he wants to speak with you."

"I don't want to—"

"Woman, take the damn phone."

A few seconds later, Miranda's voice came on the line. "Jeremy, I'm so sorry. I didn't mean to...I mean, there is no excuse."

"You've got to stop this behavior, Miranda. What are you teaching those boys?"

"I know. I know. It's like I get started and can't stop myself. Please allow me to pay for your vacation."

"That won't be necessary, but I do need your help."

"Yes, anything."

"What happened to Saundra? Who hurt her?"

"Hold up. I thought you two didn't know each other. She just called saying you were stalking her. Are you saying you actually met?"

The thought of Saundra's performance placed laughter in his voice. "Yes, we've gotten to know each other, but—"

"I knew it. I knew it! You two are made for each other!"

"Don't start, Miranda!" came Marcus's angry voice.

"I'm not starting anything, dang. Don't you have some homework to grade?" she asked of her history professor husband. "Now back to you. What was she talking about security? She had me worried to death."

"She was just giving you a dose of your own medicine."

"I've been bamboozled!" Miranda broke out in laughter. "Oh no, she didn't. That was wrong."

"I need to know what happened to her. Who hurt her?"

"Hold up now. Saundra's past is just that, the past. I selected you to be her future, not hold her back in the pain. If I've miscalculated, let me know now."

"Miranda!" Marcus barked.

"Don't Miranda me. I have a right to know if I need to pull the plug on this operation."

"I'm in love with Saundra and want to make her my wife. How can I help her face her demons if I don't know what they are?"

"Excuse me? Did you say...Oh my God! It worked. It worked! I knew it. Marcus, book us a flight to Grand Cayman. I need to call my parents and let them know about the wedding."

"What wedding?" he heard Marcus ask. "Tell Saundra to bring her butt back here and get married properly. Y'all Write women are entirely too dramatic."

"Slow down, Miranda," Jeremy said, sensing Miranda had slipped into controlling, protective big sister mode. If he and Saundra were to have a real chance, he had to draw the line now and let the chips fall where they may. "There is no wedding, yet. I need to know what happened, then for you to step out of my way."

"Excuse you?"

"Don't take this the wrong way, but Saundra and I don't need a matchmaker, plotting and scheming in our lives."

"Need I remind you, you wouldn't be this far without my stepping in the way?"

"It's not that you stepped in the way, it's the how. I love you like a little sister. But Saundra is my heart. She doesn't need or want you trying to control or manipulate her into doing your will."

She sucked air through her teeth. "Fine."

Saundra had met Nathan during her senior year of college. Miranda never liked Nathan and didn't agree with their relationship. It had nothing to do with him being thirteen years older than her baby sister. Something about the man just rubbed Miranda the wrong way. He would monopolize Saundra to ensure she couldn't spend time with her family and friends. Plus Saundra was only twenty at the time, which Miranda thought was much too young to even consider settling down.

A week after Saundra's graduation, she married Nathan. A week after that, he received a job offer in Iowa he just couldn't refuse. Saundra didn't want to leave her family and everything she knew in

Dallas to move up north, but Nathan pointed out she didn't have a job yet and could start her career anywhere.

A month later, Saundra moved across the country with her husband. Things went downhill from there.

"I let her down."

"No, it wasn't your fault."

"But you don't understand. Before she left, we argued. I told her that when he turned on her, not to come running to me. I shut out my own sister. We didn't speak for years, and I was too stubborn to check on her. To busy waiting for the day for her to say I was right. Then the day came..."

All he could hear was her crying. "It's okay, Miranda. You don't need to finish."

"I just wish that day had never come." She choked up.

A few seconds later, Marcus came on the line. "This is too much for Miranda. You go take care of your woman, and let me handle Miranda."

"I fully understand."

"Tell him, Marcus. Tell him the rest," he heard Miranda plead.

"Baby, you need to lie down."

"Tell him!"

Marcus blew out a breath. "Nathan was a first class ass. When Saundra got the courage to call home, she told Miranda everything, and you know how this crazy woman is. She was ready to call out a hit on homeboy. To make a long story short, Miranda *forgot* to tell me what was going on, went to Iowa with a few of her cousins, Nathan ended up in the hospital from a mysterious attack and Saundra returned home to Dallas."

"Oh yeah, that sounds like Miranda. What about the divorce?"

"Saundra lost herself for a while, but came back stronger than before. She filed for divorce and said she wanted nothing from him but for him to leave her alone. He tried to intimidate her into returning to him, but she was with family again. Plus, there was no way in hell I'd allow anyone to harm her, including you. Got me?"

He liked how Marcus looked after Saundra, but that would be his job from now on. "We're good."

"You know I had to make sure the air is clear. Look, I need to take care of my baby girl. Don't let Saundra run."

Saundra wandered about the Promenade deck, through the casino, which was jumping with too much life and excitement for her to deal with, and eventually found herself at the Apollo Bar. Had she just left a half-naked man in her cabin? Not just any naked man, but Jeremy King. The type of man who inspired romance novels.

But what if this wasn't a romance? After ordering a Long Island Iced Tea, she went to find a seat in a corner somewhere to listen to the piano and vegetate.

"Hey, Saundra"

She turned and saw Reba sitting with two other women. "Hey ladies."

Reba stood and introduced Saundra to Toni and Cilla, which was short for Priscilla.

"Pleased to meet you both. Mind if I sit with you."

They all motioned toward the empty seat.

"Are you all here for the romance conference also?" Saundra asked as she took a seat.

"I try to come every year," Toni and Cilla said.

"I have a whole new respect for romance readers and authors," Saundra said, then sipped her drink. She hadn't eaten since breakfast with Jeremy and the *tea* was tasting quite good.

"You sound like you're still going through it," said Reba.

"You have no idea. Have any of you seen *Stranger than Fiction* with Will Farrell?"

All three shook their heads or said no.

"Will's character starts hearing a narrator in his head, like his life were a novel. He begins to think he's crazy, but finds out that his life has become the work in progress of an author, and whatever she writes literally happens to him."

"That sounds really good," said Toni.

"It's a must see. Different than his usual roles." Saundra drank a little more. "Ever since I boarded the plane for Miami, my life has been the making of a romance novel, and I just don't know what to do. I mean, this is real life. What's been happening to me doesn't actually happen to real people."

"If you don't mind my asking, what's happened?" Cilla probed.

Two drinks later, Saundra had spilled her guts about everything that had happened to her since she boarded the plane all the way until she left a towel-clad Jeremy in the cabin.

"Let me make sure I heard correctly." Reba scooted to the edge of her seat. "Did you say you left Mr. Tall Dark and All Too Fine alone in that cabin wearing nothing but a towel?"

"Yes, ma'am."

She tapped Saundra's empty glass. "What are you drinking, because I want to steer clear of it."

All four women burst out in laughter.

"You are so wrong for that." Saundra wiped the laughter tears from her eyes. "Now don't get me wrong. I made walking away sound way easier than it actually was." The thought of making love with Jeremy had her juices flowing—literally. She already had more than enough on her mind. She didn't need anything else clouding her judgment, so she had walked away before she had a chance to give in to the temptation.

"And he held you all night and didn't make a move on you." Reba shook her head. "Girl, you'd better stop tripping. You don't come across good men every day."

"If he's so good, then he will wait until I figure out which way is up. I've been discombobulated since I first saw him on the plane."

Toni and Cilla nodded in agreement.

Reba relaxed in her seat. "I think you are acting 'romance heroine' and blowing this whole thing out of proportion. You have a man who obviously loves you, and you love him. It's cut and dry. Black and white."

"The good news is, since your life has become a romance, you'll have a happy ending," added Toni.

"Let me tell you about the first time I was introduced to 'romance.'" Wishing she had eaten something before she had gone to the bar, Saundra's stomach was beginning to object to the liquor. Just a little while longer, and she would go eat. "One of my friends who knew I was anti-romance novel said they had the perfect romance for me. That I'd love this one. Sooo, I love to read. I figured, why not. I'll give it a try. I *loved* the book. Turned out to be one of my favorite novels of all time."

"So what's the problem?" asked Cilla.

"*Their Eyes Were Watching God* is not a romance, but a romantic tragedy. What if this...this...whatever it is that is happening to me isn't a romance, but a romantic tragedy?"

Toni's eyes lit up. "Oh I love Zora Neale Hurst, but yeah, that's definitely a romantic tragedy." Toni ordered another round of drinks for everyone.

"I really do need to get some food into my stomach." Saundra liked hanging out with this crew. They were so laidback and welcomed her into their fold so easily. She would be sure to attend future Slam Jams with the ladies, but for now, she needed to decide what to do about Jeremy. The hour had grown late, so she might not be able to move to a different cabin until tomorrow.

The thought of another night in his arms took her mind where it shouldn't be—exactly where she wanted to be. But she couldn't.

"Let's finish up this round, then we can all grab something to eat," Reba suggested.

"That'll work," said Saundra.

Cilla toyed with her apple martini. "I think you may be coming at this wrong. The judgment of a twenty-year-old is completely different than that of a thirty-four-year-old. I can't believe this Nathan fellow just turned into a monster overnight. What signs did you miss, and is Jeremy showing any of them?"

Though she felt light-headed, she wanted to continue the conversation. She felt a breakthrough in her near future. "Miranda didn't like Nathan from day one. She's actually a great judge of character."

"Why didn't you listen to her then?" Reba asked.

"Because she's also an attention hog. Nathan was my first serious relationship, and I was spending time with him that I usually spent with her. She accused him of monopolizing my time, and looking back, I see her point. He was really slick with it." She sipped at her drink. "He would plan excursions and dinners out on the town. How could I get mad at him for being attentive?

"But when I'd try to plan something, he'd always make me feel guilty, as if I were saying his plans weren't good enough. And family activities, he would come, but arrange for us to have another date or whatever so we'd have to leave early. He'd also invite Miranda, knowing she wouldn't come. Who wants to be a third wheel? So when Miranda and I would argue, I'd point out that she was invited, and he wanted to spend time getting to know her also, but she was the one who always turned down the invitations." She slowly shook her head and felt as if it were spinning. She leaned back in her seat.

"Needless to say, he was placing a wedge between us, and I fell right into the trap."

"You say you are trapped a lot," Cilla pointed out. "I think it's time we gave your romance of a life a title."

Reba sucked air through her teeth. "All I have to say is she left Mr. Tall, Dark and All Too Fine in nothing but a towel back in the cabin. The man held her *all night long!* The only kind of trap she's been in since she boarded that plane is trapped in paradise. Again, stop acting like a romance heroine. This is real life. Go get your man."

"I'm not feeling very well." Saundra's stomach cramped up something terrible.

"You don't look much better," Reba teased. "I'd be sick too if I left God's gift to women in the cabin wearing *only a towel* while I was out here getting sauced with a bunch of women."

"Don't listen to Reba. She needs to read more romances. Toni and I are the experts. You're in a classic example of the dark moment portion of the novel. Take time to figure out what you ultimately want from Jeremy, then go for it. What do you want?"

It didn't take any soul searching or sobriety for her to know the answer. "Marriage," she reluctantly admitted.

"From all you've said, he's the marrying type and perfect for you," Toni added.

"But we just met. How can I want to marry a man I don't truly know?

"See, that's your problem there." Cilla took another sip of her martini. "You are trying to make an emotional piece fit into a logical hole. It doesn't work like that. Sometimes you just have to step out on faith."

Reba rapped her nails on the table, drawing everyone's attention. "Look at the door. Do you see what I see? That man is *too* fine." The women snuck peeks toward the door.

Saundra's eyes connected with Jeremy's, and her heart did that skip a beat thing she had read about in romance novels. In the past, she had thought for sure that was an indication of some sort of heart attack, but her cynicism was nowhere in sight.

Long, swift strides brought Jeremy to their table, but his movements seemed elongated to her.

"Hello, ladies," he said as he knelt before Saundra.

"Hello, Jeremy." They giggled and tipped their drinks his way.

He took Saundra's hands into his and gazed into her eyes. Oh how she loved the depth of his dark eyes, but right now they reminded her of the richest coffee. She could really use a cup. And a muffin. Make that two. "I don't feel very well."

"How much have you had to drink?"

"Too much. My stomach is on fire and my head is going to pop off any second now."

Chuckling, he wrapped her arms around his neck. "Well, we can't have that, can we?"

"I kind of like my head. I'd like to keep it." She leaned her throbbing head on his shoulder and allowed him to lift her.

"Goodnight, ladies."

"Goodnight, Jeremy..." they cooed with a mixture of giggles.

As Jeremy carried her off, Saundra heard Reba throw out, "You can trap me in paradise with a man like that any day."

Chapter Five

As if it weren't humiliating enough to be carried across a busy ship because she was too sloshed to walk, Saundra knew the liquor in her stomach would be making an appearance soon. Jeremy lowered her onto the bed, and she rushed into the tiny bathroom. Puking into the toilet was not cute no matter what pose you struck, so she didn't even try.

"You need some food in your stomach," he said from the doorway.

Dry heaves followed her Long Island Iced Tea explosion. *Never again*, she swore. Never again would she drink on an empty stomach. He caressed her back, which made her feel even worse. She had become everything she hated about the romance novel heroine stereotype since first setting eyes on Jeremy. Was this what true love reduced you to? If so, she didn't want any parts of it.

He dampened a hand towel, then helped her stand and wiped her face. "You make a cute drunk," he teased.

She licked her tongue out at him and wished the blasted thing would fall out of her mouth. It tasted like something had died on it three weeks ago. "Toothbrush. Have you seen my small duffle?"

He stepped out and returned with her patchwork duffle.

"You are a savior." She dug through it and found her toothbrush and toothpaste. "Thanks for finding me."

"It's no problem. I spoke with Miranda." He leaned his long body against the doorframe.

"I'm afraid to even ask." She began brushing her teeth.

"All I can say is, don't be surprised if there is a wedding party waiting for us in Grand Cayman."

Choking on toothpaste, she fanned at the tears in her eyes. "Grand Cayman?" she barely got out. "She's special."

"You can say that again. The pizza onboard is quite good. I've already had two. What type do you want?"

"How can you ask an inebriated woman such a complicated question?" She brushed her tongue. She was so hungry she didn't care what kind of pizza he brought. "Spinach, goat cheese, artichokes, mushrooms and onions. If they don't have that, pepperoni will do."

He stared at her a few moments, as if to see if she were serious.

"What?" She hunched her shoulders.

"I'm just wondering what you'll eat when you're pregnant with my baby." Before she could comprehend what he'd said, he kissed her on the forehead. "I'll be right back." He left her standing there with a small amount of toothpaste on the front on her shirt.

"Great," she grumbled, dragging herself to her suitcase, which Jeremy had set in the closet. She could have sworn he'd said something about having a baby, but that didn't make sense. It must have been the booze hearing. After pulling out fresh panties and her favorite baggy T-shirt, she undressed and hopped into the shower. This wasn't the first time she'd had a little too much to drink, but this was the first time it sneaked up on her so quickly. The water felt like acid pellets against her skin and sounded like World War III. She quickly lathered up and rinsed off. She wanted to make a call before Jeremy returned.

After dressing, she found her phone and dialed Miranda's number.

"Where have you been? I've left a million messages."

"You are entirely too loud." She pulled back the cushy, down comforter and sheet. "Did I wake you?"

"No."

"Too bad. So explain to me what goes through your mind when you're making arrangements to have your baby sister room with a complete stranger. Nix that. Make it a strange man." She slid into the bed and settled back on the pillows.

"So my methods are a tad bit controversial, the results are what matters."

Saundra's laugh echoed in her head and intensified the throbbing pain. "You really believe that, don't you?"

"You haven't kicked Jeremy out of the cabin, have you?"

"It's late and he hasn't done anything wrong. If anyone is changing cabins, it will be me. Why should he be inconvenienced because I have a nut for a sister? And what is this talk about a Grand Cayman wedding? Stop. Just stop. I'm calling Mama in the morning to make sure you haven't told her any of this craziness."

"It's not craziness. You're in love."

"Why are you so gung ho about this? And please speak softly. I have the makings of a mega-headache coming." Eyes closed, she massaged her temples.

"We've been tiptoeing around our issue for years."

"What issue, you're always meddling in my business? I haven't tiptoed around that. I've asked—flat out told you to stop—but there's no stopping you."

"It's time to lay all of our cards out on the table. We need to go back to what happened between us when you started seeing Nathan."

Regretting this call, especially in her current state, she said, "That's over with."

"No, it's not. You don't trust yourself when it comes to relationships because of what happened."

"I married a man who moved me out to the middle of nowhere so he could beat me whenever the mood hit him. I have legitimate reasons to doubt my judgment in the relationship department."

"But, Saundra."

"Don't 'Saundra' me. Even a drunk could figure that one out."

"Why did you marry Nathan? You didn't love him."

"Yes, I did."

"Liar. Oh, I take it back. You loved him, but you weren't *in* love with him. And I'm ashamed of myself for my part in that disaster, but you married Nathan out of spite."

"I did not." She sat up in bed to defend herself.

"Oh please. Give me a break. Yes, you were interested in him initially, but because I voiced my dislike of him so...shall we say...colorfully, you began seeing him more. The more I objected, the more *in love* with him you claimed to be. I should have backed off, but no. I kept pushing you into his arms."

"It was my choice." Thinking back, she had been rebelling against Miranda, against her family. Who where they to tell her who she could and couldn't date? She had earned her Bachelor's when she was only twenty years old. Unlike Miranda, she had never been in any serious trouble and was very responsible and mature for her age. A late bloomer, she hadn't even dated until her junior year of college.

"You couldn't see his faults because you were concentrating on me. I knew you couldn't see clearly. I shouldn't have stood by to teach you a lesson." Miranda sniffed.

Tears fell from Saundra's eyes. "It wasn't your fault."

"But I played a role. A major role. When I think of what he put you through...How one of my stupid games hurt you. I'm so sorry. Please, baby. Don't pass on Jeremy because of Nathan. Your judgment is right on. Just as it always has been."

"What you're saying sounds so right, but..."

"But nothing. You were only twenty years old. You can't be held responsible for your actions."

They both released anxious laughter.

"You are my favorite nut of all times." Saundra calmed. "I can't really think straight right now. I've had too much to drink."

Miranda giggled. "No wonder you've let me ramble so long. If you were sober, you would have hung up long ago. Where's Jeremy?"

"He went to get me something to eat." She thought about Marcus and Miranda's relationship. "Aren't opposites supposed to attract?

Jeremy and I are so much alike. How will this work? Look at you and Marcus. Because you two are so different, it works."

"How do I explain this...? Oh, I know. Marcus is so straight and narrow that he needs a high-strung, exciting woman to bring him out of his shell. We balance each other out. Whereas you are already balanced. If you marry a man who isn't balanced, you'll be thrown out of whack. That's why you and Jeremy are perfect for each other. I've never met two more boringly balanced individuals. "

"This is scary." She giggled. "That actually made sense. You're unbalanced and need someone on the straight and narrow to keep you from tipping over."

"You're not funny."

"Yes I am. Jeremy's one of the good guys, isn't he?"

"Yes, he's one of the good guys. Now just remember that when you're sober."

The cabin door opened. "I need to get off the phone."

"Is Jeremy back?"

"It's either Jeremy or a really long arm connected to a pizza box. Do you think an arm can be sexy?"

"Five years is too long to go without. Don't eat too much, you'll throw up. Love you."

"Love you, too." Saundra disconnected.

Jeremy entered the room and went to the bedside. Yeah, five years was way too long in Saundra's estimation. Everything the man did had her ready to rip off his clothes.

"You and Miranda kiss and make up?"

"All is right in the Write sister world." She drew in a deep breath. *Food, food, concentrate on the food, not the man carrying it.* "That smells delicious."

He opened the box and displayed the most beautiful goat cheese, spinach, artichoke, mushroom and onion pizza she had ever seen in her life. Oh yeah, he was definitely a keeper.

"I'm still feeling queasy. I hope this doesn't make a return performance."

"You don't drink much, do you?"

"No, not really. I can count the times I've had too much on three fingers." She patted the bed beside her. "Eat with me."

The hunger in Saundra's eyes was for more than the pizza she was devouring, but Jeremy couldn't make love to her yet. When they made love, she would have a clear mind. Until then, he'd have to settle for ice-cold showers. He lathered up the bar of soap and prepared for the long night ahead of holding the woman he loved without being able to make love with her.

His patience had already worn thin. Usually, when he saw what he wanted, he went for it. *I have to be me.* He smoothed the lather over his face. "I have to be me."

They had done the impossible and fallen in love romance-novel style. The how didn't matter. All that mattered was she was his, and after tomorrow, she wouldn't be able to live in denial any longer.

Chapter Six

Saundra lay in bed and watched Jeremy sleep. After his abrupt shower last night, he had crawled into bed with her without a word and held her until she'd fallen asleep. Just what she had needed.

With the rising of the sun came quite a bit of clarity. The points Miranda had made during their conversation had remained with her. She had been only twenty and in a completely different frame of mind when she'd met Nathan than she was now. But as loopy as she'd been acting since they'd met, she wouldn't blame Jeremy for running as fast and as far away as he could. Add Miranda with her own brand of craziness, and any man in his right mind would avoid her family.

I have been seriously tripping.

In her mind, she'd been worried about the prospect of marriage with him, and the poor man hadn't even said he wanted to be more than friends. Shoot, he hadn't even tried to kiss her. Wright women had a tendency toward the melodramatic and easily blew things out of proportion. With her luck, she had done just that.

Her cell phone beeped, indicating a text message.

The caller ID brought a smile to her face. *Reba.*

We won't be angry if we don't see you today! LOL

Entirely too crazy. I need to introduce her to Miranda. Jeremy stirred behind her. She glanced over her shoulder just in time to see a glimpse of his firm butt as he entered the bathroom. Lord knew he could wear the hell out of a pair of briefs.

She dialed Reba's number.

"What are you doing on this phone, woman? Did you leave that man in a towel again?" Reba teased.

"He's in the shower." *He has got to be the cleanest man ever.*

"Ooh, I see potential there. Girl, I need to work on you. Get off the phone and join him. Remember, condoms are your friends." She disconnected.

I know she didn't just hang up on me. Shaking her head, Saundra re-fluffed her pillow and rested. She had brushed her teeth and freshened up when she first awakened over an hour ago, but she still didn't feel like getting up and starting the day. Maybe by noon she'd be ready to head over to the conference and hang out with the attendees, but for now, she felt like being a slug.

She didn't know what to say to or do about Jeremy. Awkward was putting it lightly. She wished she could rewind the past forty-eight hours and start over or at least rewrite those chapters of her life.

Just as she was dozing off, she felt Jeremy's strong arms spoon her close to his body. Both nights that he had held her, she'd felt his hardness against her backside. But always the gentleman, she also felt him backing away when he would wake. This time he didn't back away, and she was glad.

This was the life. Within his arms, she felt loved. She rested her hand atop his. "I could stay here forever," she whispered.

He nuzzled her neck, softly saying, "I owe you an apology."

With the way her body was warming from the gentle grinding of his hardness, she couldn't imagine what he wanted to apologize for.

"I haven't been myself lately." He nibbled her ear lobe. She had forgotten how good that felt.

"How so?" she barely managed as he rolled her to face him.

Gazing deep into her eyes, he said, "If I were myself, I would have told you two days ago that I've fallen in love with you."

He took her bottom lip into his mouth and nibbled until she tingled. He had this nibbling thing down. The sensations going through her body had her so rattled, she couldn't even comment on what he had said. These sensations had nothing to do with the five-year hiatus she'd had from sex. She had never experienced anything like this before and knew she would never again with anyone else. Jeremy was truly her king. This would be the first time she actually made love.

"I love you," she said, pulling back. "I have since you rescued my luggage from Señor Rude."

"That long?"

"Well, maybe not until you wanted us to sample each other's meals at the restaurant." Her eyes traveled along his athletic torso, enjoying every ripple. Not too large or too small, just right. She pulled her still sensitive bottom lip into her mouth. "Where do we go from here?" she asked nervously.

"Shh." He cupped her face in his hands, bent, and brushed his lips over hers.

The light yet potent brushing touched her core and left her wanting, needing more. Heart and mind racing, she slowly took his bottom lip into her mouth and suckled.

He moaned his satisfaction, wrapped his arms around her, and took control of the kiss. She opened freely, tasting every succulent inch of his mouth. Overwhelmed, she backed away to catch her breath.

He returned his oral assault to her ear, softly saying, "Do you want me to stop?" He slipped his large hand under her T-shirt and fondled her breast.

If he stopped, there *would* be a problem. A half-sighed, half-moaned "No," was the best she could manage as he pulled the T-shirt over her head and tossed it to the side. Every kiss laid on her bare shoulder disseminated warm waves of passion throughout her body. He lowered himself and took one of her chocolate-covered caramel peaks into his mouth, licking, flicking, caressing her into full submission.

Saundra grew weak in his arms. He had melted her, and she couldn't believe it would get any better. But better it became as his thick fingers nudged her panties to the side, then entered her. Nathan and the other man she had been with were straight missionary style with little to no foreplay. This new experience excited and worried her. What if she couldn't pleasure him as he pleasured her?

As if sensing her trepidation, he murmured, "It's alright, baby." He suckled along her inner thigh as he removed her panties, her legs trembling with need. "You're hot and wet for me." He took off his briefs and lay proudly with his hardness resting heavily against her thigh. "Feel me."

Holding him, she wanted to do a whole lot more than touch him. Power, a throbbing power was in her hand. A throbbing that matched the throb between her legs. With her hand wrapped around him, she slowly stroked from tip to base, base to tip, repeating the motion.

"That's it," he groaned as his fingers slipped into her and continued their fancy work. Just as she thought she couldn't stand the intensity anymore, he proved her wrong.

His mouth joined his fingers in a beautiful duet of ecstasy. With every flick and lick of his tongue, sensually-charged shards shot through her. Blindly, she reached to grasp something, anything, before she blew away. He held her waist down and continued his siege until her climax knocked her breath away. Once she returned to earth, he seared a trail of kisses from her panty line, along her waist, between her breasts, along her neck, to her ear.

"I love it when you cry out for me."

Dazed and heart beating dangerously fast, she said, "Teach me how to do the same for you." She wrapped her arms around his neck and pulled him close for a deep, passionate kiss. He eased his hand beneath her and spun them so she'd be on top.

A quick study, while stroking him with her hand, she began with her mouth on his chest. Strokes, licks, flicks, caresses, and kisses pushed him into a frenzy. An odd sense of power flowed through her.

She lowered herself and examined him carefully. "I'm sorry, I've never done this before." She touched his tip with her tongue and swirled the wetness. "Salty," she said, moaning her approval. She licked off the rest, then peeked up and connected with the passion in his eyes. Bev had been correct. Not all heat meant fire, and this form of burning was quite good.

"Did I do something wrong?" she asked. "You look strained."

"No, baby," he caressed her back, "continue exploring. It feels good."

She suckled along his shaft, then took him into her mouth. She'd seen this done, but actually doing it sent a rush through her. In, out, deeper...she could do this all day. Before long, she figured out how to stroke him with her hand and work her mouth and tongue at the same time.

His fingers weaved through her curly hair to her scalp and massaged. "I don't want you to stop, but I need for you to stop." He pulled her up by her arms and rolled on top of her.

Having such a large man over her didn't intimidate her in the least, especially since that man was her king. He reached over to the dresser and grabbed a condom he must have placed there after his shower. He opened the packet and protected them both, then positioned himself between her legs.

A little nervous—a lot nervous—she studied every inch of his handsome face. This was the man she wanted to share her life with, the one who had restored her trust. "I am truly in love with you."

Lowering himself, he kissed her gently, then penetrated oh so shallow and waited. A tight fit. She couldn't remember telling him how long it had been since her last sexual contact. She prayed she hadn't told him when she'd been intoxicated. Either way, she was grateful he was taking it slow. As she became more accustomed to his body, he kept his strokes shallow.

"How is that?" he asked, his voice strained.

"Deeper," she breathed, gyrating beneath him. Each stroke probed deeper and deeper, pushing her closer and closer to the edge.

Her climax threatening to overtake her, she drew in one leg, changing her angle. "Jeremy," she panted. Implosion shouldn't feel so good.

He trapped her knee under his arm and continued pumping. Her body sheathed him perfectly. Caressing, pulling, now tightening with each stroke. His gaze locked onto hers. She gripped his arms in hopes of not flying away as she cried out. Their climaxes ran together, merging, binding their souls together.

They needed to shower, but neither wanted to move. Jeremy brushed his lips over Saundra's. "You're my heart. I love you so much, that if you wanted to leave, I'd let you go."

She lay atop him and rested her head on his chest. "I'm not going anywhere. I plan to stay trapped in paradise with you forever."

Epilogue

The next day, Cayman Islands, Grand Cayman

As the shuttle boat that carried them from the Destiny to the pier readied to dock, Saundra found herself a tad bit disappointed.

Jeremy drew her hand to his heart. "Is something wrong?"

She looked over the throngs of people exiting the boat, rushing to the shops that lined the shore. "I just..." She sighed. "In a way, I expected to see Miranda."

Chuckling, he stood and pulled her along. "That makes two of us. She is out of her mind."

They followed the line of people onto shore, then strolled hand in hand along the boulevard. The shops and street vendors weren't quite ready for customers yet, so they found a shady spot to sit while they people watched.

"There they are!"

Saundra and Jeremy looked down the boulevard and saw Miranda flailing her arms and running toward them.

"It's them! I found them!" Not too far behind were Marcus, the Wright family and some people Saundra didn't know.

A deep belly-laugh erupted from Jeremy as he stood. "That's my parents. She actually did it!" He drew Saundra into his arms. "I pray you want to marry me as much as I want to marry you, because I don't think we have much choice in the matter," he joked.

"I'd love nothing more."

He bent and kissed her.

Miranda stopped short of the couple. "Save that for the honeymoon." She grabbed Saundra by the hand and pulled her into her embrace. "I'm so happy for you." She released her. "We have a ceremony to get ready for."

"Can I at least introduce my fiancée to my parents?" Jeremy asked.

"Yeah, Miranda, he hasn't met Mom and Dad," she got out just as the rest of the family arrived.

"Two minutes, then we have to go. We're on a tight schedule here. The wedding starts at eleven."

"But we don't have proper licensing or anything. I don't know how to get married in another country."

Disappointment clouded Miranda's face. "Who do you think you're dealing with here? I've had this planed for months. Everything has been taken care of."

"Of course you have."

After proper introductions to the family members, the couple was whisked away to begin their happily ever after.

The End

http://www.deewrites.com

Author Bio:
An avid writer since childhood, Deatri has authored several articles, essays, workshops, and books. Deatri's idea of a great afternoon is a trip to the bookstore, followed by hours curled up on the sofa with her newly purchased romance, fantasy, or science fiction novel.

Red Rose Publishing
Trapped In Paradise
Broken Promises-Coming Soon November 2009
Honey and Lemon-Coming Soon
 The Other Realm-Coming Soon
Stolen Heart-Coming Soon
White Rose-Coming Soon

Genesis
Caught Up
Ebony Angel

Parker Publishing
Beauty and the Beast
Whisper Something Sweet (Winner of 2008 Emma for Best Steamy Romance of the year)

Seaside Seduction

By

AC Arthur

Chapter One

"I can't believe I'm doing this," CJ murmured as she scooped up yet another black T-shirt, folded it neatly and placed it in her suitcase.

Mac shook his head and removed the shirt the moment her back was turned. "You're doing this because you're my best friend, and this is the kind of stuff that friends do."

"Where in the Friendship Manual does it say I'm supposed to go on a cruise—at the last minute, mind you—and play Sherlock Holmes with you while you chase that trifling chick you're dating?"

Mac chuckled, the action as natural as breathing, just as CJ's reaction to his request was known to him the moment he concocted this idea. He'd known Corina Josephine Monroe since his fifth birthday party, when her parents were new to the neighborhood and his overly friendly mother had invited them to a cookout. She'd been pretty even then, Mac admitted. Two months older than him, she'd had him in height by about six inches and in weight by ten pounds. Her cherubic face had seemed friendly enough until he'd reached over onto her plate to steal a potato chip and felt the sting of her open palm across the back of his head. From that day forth, they'd been thick as thieves—his grandmother's words, not his.

"On the page right behind the one where I stole James Palmer's clothes out of his locker so he'd run screaming through the gym with a towel barely covering his ass. All because he was two-timing you with Janelle Stevens."

She paused and turned her head in that way that had her shoulder-length hair flipping to one side. "Don't even go there," she said, her lips thinning just a bit.

"Nah, you want to question the Friendship Manual, I can also recall calling Paul Lincoln's house for you to see if he was home, then having to come up with an excuse when you were too afraid to get on the phone and talk to him." Mac was now holding his stomach, he was laughing so hard with the memory. "Two times!" he added, then rolled onto his back on the bed.

It didn't take long for the memories to sweep back into CJ's mind so that she laughed right along with him. "Shut up," she chided and tossed a pillow at him.

"The difference is we're grown now, Mac. If you think she's cheating, why not just cut her loose?"

Getting his bearings, Mac sat up, pushing the pillow aside. CJ had a strange pillow fetish. How she slept in a bed surrounded by all this fluff was beyond him. "Can't cut her loose until I know for sure."

"Then why not just ask her?"

"If you were cheating on your man and he asked you, would you admit it?"

She was already shaking her head, holding up two bathing suits and deciding which one she should take. Mac hated both of them. "The question is void since I don't have a man."

"I'm sure they have shops on the boat," he said when she opted for the navy blue one-piece that snapped at her neck. It was plain and covered everything except CJ's thick thighs, the part of her body she hated most. Mac had always disagreed with her on that point as well.

She stopped before dropping the suit into the suitcase. "What?"

"Don't pack that," he said, reaching for the bathing suit. "It's ugly."

"It is not." She frowned. "I like it."

"Well, I don't." He tossed it back into the drawer and slammed it shut.

"This isn't a pleasure trip," CJ complained.

"Of course not, because then you wouldn't be going." She was even prettier when she was mad. That was strange, but true. So even though she was tapping her foot on the beige carpet, giving him the evil eye, Mac's body still reacted to the sexy tilt of her eyes and the alluring curve of her hips.

"And what's that supposed to mean?"

Mac waited a beat. There were two ways he could answer this question, two of which could have him sailing the Caribbean seas by himself. So with the best outcome in mind, he replied, "If you thought I was going on a cruise to watch women walk around in skimpy bathing suits and see how many of them I could get into my cabin, you wouldn't join me."

She smirked. "You've got that right. I don't have time to watch you play."

CJ didn't have time for much of anything besides work and that was only part of the problem. As owner and primary chef of Fancy Fixins, a five-year-old catering company she'd started with money saved from her internship at the Culinary School of Arts, CJ's time was divided between cooking and bookkeeping. Nowhere was there time for a cruise, especially not in the last nine months, after her latest attempt at finding Mr. Right had gone drastically wrong.

"Look, you need to get away, and I need you there with me for support." *That's not a total lie*, Mac consoled himself, because he'd always been honest with CJ.

"I have work to do," she argued.

"You do not. Your next event isn't for three weeks, and Lera can hold down the fort until then."

"What if a request for a quote comes in?"

"Lera's been with you since the beginning. She's your administrative assistant, and she's working on her master's degree. I'm sure she can crunch some numbers. Besides, you'll only be gone for a week."

CJ sighed, knowing she was losing this battle. "How do you even know for sure Sidra will be on this cruise?"

"There's a romance writers' conference taking place on the cruise next week. She's trying to break into cover modeling, she'll be there."

There was that frown, the one he'd seen on CJ's face each time he talked about Sidra. Was it jealousy? He'd been asking himself that for the last few months, or actually hoping that's what it was. It was that look and a few other incidents that had pushed him to finally look at his feelings for CJ in a more realistic manner.

She was his best friend, yes. People had joked they were closer than brother and sister. They got along, they had their disagreements and they always had each other's backs.

They were the perfect couple...without the intimacy.

That's what Mac wanted to change.

This was a bad idea.

With a sidelong glance at the dark chocolate complexion, trimmed goatee and slightly crooked nose, CJ sighed. A very bad idea indeed.

Mac was her closest friend in this world—had been for more than twenty years. He was her confidant, her sounding board, her card partner, her handyman, and her guinea pig when she needed to test out new recipes. He was simply everything to her. Except lover.

Yeah, right. Tell that to her traitorous dreams. How many mornings had it been now? How many times had she rolled over in her bed, pressing her pillow between her legs to stop the incessant throbbing? How many times had Mac made love to her in her dreams?

Too many to count, and too many to be considered normal. Mac had a girlfriend. In fact, he had several girlfriends, just like her older brothers, Porter and Kai. Why men couldn't be satisfied with one woman at a time was beyond her. Her father had even cheated on her mother, which was why Londa Monroe, had been arrested and charged with first-degree assault and battery.when CJ was ten and Porter and Kai were thirteen and fifteen, respectively. When Londa caught Duke Monroe in bed with their next door neighbor, she'd beaten the hell out of both of them while they were still in the bed naked as the day they were born.

Londa had gotten off with probation, but ever since that day CJ had been leery about relationships. She thought she'd developed a sort of system for picking men and taking her time to get to know them. But just last year she'd come to the conclusion that none of that mattered—if a man was going to cheat, he was just going to do it. And it didn't matter how fine he was, how much money was in his bank account or if he worked at Wal-Mart and drove a beat-up Chevy Chevette. A dog was a dog no matter the package he came wrapped in.

And Mackenzi Jackson was definitely a dog. He was her best friend and she loved him as much as she loved Porter and Kai, but he was still a dog. The funny thing was that Mac had been raised in a big family, by his mother and his grandmother—two strong, opinionated women. He had six brothers and sisters, umpteen cousins, uncles, aunts and family friends—like herself—who simply latched on to the Jackson family. There was so much love and commitment in that family, CJ was sure he'd eventually grow up and start his own division of the Jackson clan.

How wrong she'd been. Again.

Mac's problem was his short attention span. He had been medically diagnosed in the third grade, when he found birds eating bread crumbs on the playground more exciting than Mrs. Eubanks's math lesson. The school nurse had suggested Attention Deficit Disorder. Mama Jackson had prescribed a butt whipping and three days punishment from said playground. A few months later he'd told CJ about going to a doctor's appointment where the doctor had explained to his mother that he indeed had ADD. He'd still been plain 'ole Mac to CJ until high school, when she started to notice his restlessness. For that reason and because she knew he would have done the same for her had the tables been turned, CJ had spent most of her evenings helping Mac with the assignments she knew he either hadn't finished in class, or had forgotten.

Looking back, she had to smile, Mac had come such a long way. He was a lead columnist at Serendipity, a top romance and relationship e-zine and print magazine. Yes, Mac with his ADD and infectious laughter was a leading authority on relationships. What was so funny to CJ was that he either didn't want or couldn't handle a committed relationship of his own, so how the hell did he come up with the great advice he did for total strangers?

Still, she had no business dreaming about him. No business wondering how his lips would feel on hers—beyond the chaste goodnight or hello kisses they'd shared over the years. Actually, she was more interested in his tongue. Too many times she'd watch him lick his lips after he'd eaten potato chips or his favorite fried chicken, and her entire body had shivered. It looked so soft, so warm, so enticing.

With a jerk she turned her head so sharply, she probably dislocated a disk in her neck. Taking a deep breath, she tried to focus on the clouds as her plane made its ascent. They were fluffy and white, and and looked just as soft as her sheets had been last night. It had seemed like the moment her head hit the pillow, her had eyes closed and she'd seen his face. A familiar face that meant more to her than it should.

Then he was touching her, whispering explicit messages of what he planned to do to her. Her entire body was on fire by the time his lips first touched hers. And when he'd stripped away all her clothes, she'd been practically begging. Their joining was like a dance; in her mind, in her soul, they moved together in harmony and precision. He was perfect in every way—the kisses, the caresses, the whispers. Hell, she'd even had multiple orgasms, an accomplishment she'd never achieved with another man. When it was over, she was more than sated. She floated. Yep, on one of those great big 'ole fluffy white clouds. That's how sex with Mac made her feel.

Until morning, when her alarm clock blasted her from that cloud, landing her face first in a twist of sheets and pillows, her panties wet—again—and her head hurting from the effort it took to figure out why she was dreaming about her best friend in a carnal way.

By noon she'd decided the whys didn't matter. It was inappropriate and disrespectful to their relationship. So why had she agreed to go on this cruise with him again? Oh yeah, because of that relationship and because he would have done the same for her, in a heartbeat.

They were on their way to Miami to board a cruise ship, *the Destiny*, for a five-day Western Caribbean cruise. CJ definitely needed a vacation, but this, unfortunately, would not be it. Convinced that his companion of three months, Sidra Ellis, was cheating on him, Mac wanted to catch her in the act. Why he wanted to put himself through all this drama, CJ couldn't fathom, but as a friend she knew she needed to be there for him—just as he had been for her when Cliff had shown his true colors.

Sidra hadn't been high on CJ's like-list from the moment they first met. Mac had brought her to the city's annual holiday gala. She'd worn a sultry red gown that left absolutely nothing to the imagination. Her membership to the local gym had been put to good use; her body was tight in all the right places and curved in all the others. Her long hair—definitely a weave of the highest caliber—hung down her back in a waterfall of curls. She was taller than CJ's five foot six and rubbed that fact in as she'd stood beside Mac, wearing four-inch heels looking as if he'd peeled her right off a magazine cover. But that was just the surface summary. Later that night, when Mac had apparently sent Sidra to talk to CJ, the woman had informed her that, "Mackenzi will soon be off the market, for good."

It had taken all CJ's home training to keep from smacking her elegantly made-up face. Truth be told, the woman was wearing so much make-up, CJ didn't want to get it all over her, had a brawl broken out. Instead, she had smiled and simply responded, "Good luck."

To that, Sidra had done the unthinkable—she'd rolled her eyes and stomped away, like a four-year-old playing dress up.Sidra of cheating, which really shouldn't have bothered him since CJ was sure he already had another woman waiting in the trenches. It always seemed that Mac had an endless flow of women in his life. CJ wondered why now, after all these years, that thought made her uncomfortable.

It was nothing, she told herself. The dreams, the weird thoughts of Mac with another woman...all of it was nothing.

Mac was right about one thing: she definitely needed a vacation.

Chapter Two

"Romance Slam Jam," CJ read aloud from the bulletin board at the end of the Guest Relations counter. "Is this what you're supposed to be reporting on?" she asked Mac, who had just finished checking in for them.

"Yeah," he nodded absently looking from the board down to the papers and key cards he'd received from the purser. "That's how I got the magazine to foot the bill for this little trip."

"And you're sure Sidra is booked on this cruise as well?"

Mac hesitated. "Ah, yeah. I told you, she's supposed to be doing some photo shoot for one of the covers in the writing contest the conference sponsors."

"She's going to be on the cover of one of those hot romance novels? I'm impressed."

"Impressed? Why? You knew she was a model." He nodded his head and started moving behind a few other guests that most likely had cabins in the same direction.

CJ picked up the one bag she'd carried on the plane with her and followed him. "Not with Sidra, with the books."

"You still read those things?" he asked over his shoulder.

"In every spare moment I have." CJ chuckled thinking of the two books tucked in her suitcase. One by Gwyneth Bolton and another by Maureen Smith, two of her favorite African-American romance authors.

"They're so contrived. Nobody really falls in love like that," Mac frowned.

"This from the romance and relationship advice columnist."

"Those books are fiction. I write realistic responses to everyday relationship questions. There's a difference."

"No difference. You get paid to tell people how to stay in love and romance authors get paid to show people all the different scenarios in which people can fall in love. It's basically the same."

He never stopped walking but she was right behind him so she heard when he responded, "I'm not writing fake sex scenes and impossible heroes or weak-ass heroines that don't know what they want or how to get it."

"No, you're living that," she quipped.

He stopped so fast and spun around that CJ was very quickly face-to-face with a chest that she'd sworn was just a tad firmer and broader than it had been when she'd last seen him.

"Is that what you really think I'm doing?"

His gaze intense, he looked down at her. CJ opened her mouth to speak then quickly closed it. He was too close, his cologne assaulting her senses and blurring her mind so that she wasn't sure how to answer his question. "I think you're holding up traffic."

He frowned, then turned away from her, continuing down the long hall in silence before stopping at the end. He used his key card to open the door and was moving inside when CJ asked, "Where's my room?"

"The magazine booked the penthouse," he said simply as he held the door for her. "We're sharing."

Unable to move, CJ stared at him, looking ten times the fool, she knew, but still she didn't move. "What? Sharing? Why? Couldn't they afford two rooms? You should have told me, Mac. I could have reserved my own room. We can't stay in here *together*."

Mac's head tilted as he dropped the bag he'd been carrying. "What are you babbling about? We've shared hotel rooms and bedrooms a million times. Come on in here, so I can shut the door and unpack. There's a welcome party in a few hours and I want to tour the ship first."

"But—"

"CJ!" he said in the warning tone he usually reserved for his nieces and nephews when they were showing off.

She frowned and sucked it up. He was right. They had shared rooms more times than she ever had with her brothers or any woman she'd ever known. There had been occasions when they had slept in the same bed to save money on the hotel. So it was crazy to think she was being silly over the room issue. Even though she was, CJ walked in, passing him without a word although her body was all too aware of his closeness.

The room was gorgeous, decorated in tones of orange and gold. The bed was more than big enough for two, but when she looked at it, all CJ saw were scenes from her dreams. Her not so perfectly sculpted bronze body and Mac's muscled ebony form, twisting naked, moaning loudly. Oh God...this was such a bad idea.

Mac certainly had his work cut out for him. CJ's opinion of him was lower than he thought if she really assumed he'd been going through life having sex with women too weak to know what they

160

really wanted. If she believed that, then she didn't really know him at all. Well, okay, she did kind of know him. His high school and college years had borne that exact man—the one who took what he could get and moved on when he'd had enough. But all that had changed; he wasn't that man anymore.

CJ wouldn't know that around the time he was making his change, she was losing the last bit of faith she'd ever had in relationships. Her brother Porter had gotten a woman pregnant and was denying the baby, even after the DNA test proved the child to be his. CJ couldn't believe he was being so callous, so cruel and immature. She'd been pissed off with him just weeks before the blow up with Cliff.

Mac had been more than pissed with Clifton Morris, the man who'd broken CJ's heart. Dragging his hands down his face, Mac tried not to think of all that. CJ's heart and mind were tainted with misconceptions and proof of bad choices when it came to love. So he'd brought her on a Western Caribbean cruise during a romance book convention, no less. He wanted her to see the power of love, the opportunities awaiting her. He wanted her to know how much he loved her, beyond the boundaries of their friendship.

But if she thought he was ten times the dog, she'd never be open to what he needed her to see.

"Damn," he murmured, knowing he had his job cut out for him.

Coming out of the bathroom, he watched as CJ finished unpacking. She moved with the efficiency he'd seen before. She was tense and worried about something but she wouldn't tell him if he asked. So instead, he did what he was sure she wouldn't expect.

"Leave that for later. Let's tour the boat," he said.

"It's a cruise ship," she said over her shoulder. "And I'd rather get this out of the way. You should unpack your stuff, too."

She hadn't looked at him when she spoke, which meant that whatever was bothering her had to do with him.

"Look, CJ, if you want me to try and get you another room, I will." He wouldn't like it, but he'd do it, for her.

She took a deep breath then closed her suitcase and zipped it up, putting it neatly in a corner of the room. "No. This is fine. I don't know why I overreacted. We've stayed in the same room before. It's no big deal."

Yeah, it was, this time. Mac nodded and reached for his own suitcase. "Okay, well, I'll do this real quick and then we can take a tour."

"Looking for Sidra so soon?" she asked.

Mac paused for a moment. Sidra was most likely on this ship but he didn't give a damn one way or the other. He'd already broken up with her because she'd known what he'd been too afraid to admit—he was in love with CJ.

"No. I just want to at least show you a good time. You know, since you're helping me out."

She nodded. "You must really like her."

"Who? Sidra? No. I mean, she's cool and all, but I'm not that into her."

"Really? That's a surprise," CJ remarked, then moved toward the balcony door and pulled it open.

"Hey," he said, following her. "What's that supposed to mean?"

"Nothing."

"Don't be a coward, CJ. If you have something to say to me, just say it."

"Say what? That I don't understand why you're so intent on catching Sidra doing what you've done to women for years?"

"I don't cheat on women, you know that."

"Oh, right you just tell them that you're not into this thing for a relationship, you're just having fun," she said mimicking his deep voice. "Then you sleep with them for as long as they can hold your attention and move on."

He wanted to tell her she was wrong but this was CJ. Pretty lines, flattery, none of that crap would work with her. He'd have to be totally honest, something he was used to doing before he'd fallen in love with her.

"That's called dating in my book. Believe me, I know how to settle down and make a commitment."

"Then why haven't you done so? I mean, we're almost thirty, and you've never had a committed relationship or a relationship that's lasted more than four months. I just wonder how it is that you can guide so many other couples in love, but not yourself." Pushing past him, she went back to unpacking.

Mac took a step closer to her, waiting until she'd slipped her last garments into the dresser door and turned to face him. He didn't touch her because with the mood she was in right now, she was liable to knock him down. But he stood close, close enough that he could see the twin moles at the corner of her left eye and the small scar just above her left temple where she'd jumped off the couch in his grandmother's living room and struck the edge of the coffee table. He could smell the sweet scent of her favorite perfume, Happy by Clinique. And, although it pained him terribly, he could see the etchings of hurt still lingering in her eyes.

"Maybe I just haven't found the right woman to settle down with."

Was it hot in here? *Hell yes*, CJ's mind roared as her chest constricted. God, he was too close. He was too fine, smelled too good, and was generally too tempting. She wanted to kick herself for even going through these motions. It was ridiculous. Maybe she was on the rebound from Cliff, but that had been months ago. This was Mac; he wasn't a romantic prospect. Yet here she was, sharing a penthouse suite with him on a Caribbean cruise during a romance writers conference.

It was just logistics. Right?

"You're never going to find her if you keep sampling all the other merchandise."

"Like you're going to find Mr. Right by hiding behind your family's mistakes."

That stung, then again, he'd known it would. But he'd said it anyway because the nature of their friendship was honesty. CJ could tell Mac the truth and expect he'd do the same with her. Until now. Now, her truth was too shocking and unbelievable to even admit to herself.

"Some people just aren't meant to find Mr. Right."

"You don't really believe that, do you?"

Stepping out of the small space they occupied, CJ was finally able to breathe. She wore slacks and a white wrap blouse that she prayed covered the paunch of her stomach. Very self conscious of her size—although she'd been told that a size fourteen wasn't considered obese or fat or unsightly—she tried to wear clothes that streamlined her more than curvy figure. Suddenly, she felt a little more uncomfortable. Did Mac think she was fat? No, he'd told her time and time again that she had a terrific body. Then again, he wasn't trying to get in her pants, either.

"I believe that some people have a mate they're destined to find. Me? I am destined for heartache. I refuse to be a fool for love again."

"You're no fool, CJ. The men you've chosen have been fools."

She smiled at that. Mac was always one of her biggest champions and she loved him for that. "It's cool. I'm not upset about it and I'm not going to focus on it. But you, I think you might have a lot to offer a woman if you'd stop playing around and get serious."

He raised an eyebrow, slipping his hands into his pockets. "Really? What could I offer you?"

She frowned, wondering what he meant by that question.

Mac cleared his throat then started again. "If you were looking for a man, what would you see when you looked at me?"

CJ relaxed, cursing her wayward thoughts. "I would see a very attractive man with an intelligent mind that he's afraid to use most of the time."

He chuckled.

"I'd see the product of good upbringing and a man with a sense of responsibility and loyalty to those he loved. I'd see lots of potential," she ended, and realized her words were more than true. They were heartfelt.

"Good," Mac said, nodding. "That sounds real good."

She shook her head. "Okay, Mr. Conceited. I'm glad I was able to inflate your ego just a little more. Now let's go take this tour." CJ was already walking towards the door.

Smiling, Mac watched the sway of CJ's bottom in her fitted slacks. Heat rushed through his body. Even after all the women he'd slept with, that heat felt foreign. He knew how CJ felt about her body, but he also knew how he reacted to that body. Beyonce's *Bootylicious* had to have been written with CJ in mind.

With a deep breath and a warning to his growing erection to calm the hell down, Mac made his way to the door. This trip could turn out one of two ways: he could be spending long, hot nights embedded firmly between CJ's soft thighs, or he could lose the best friend he ever had.

Each turnout was emotional and just a tad frightening, but just like the captain of this ship, Mac had charted his course,.and unless there were extreme circumstances, he would not be deterred.

Chapter Three

After the conference's welcome party, as they walked along the Skylight deck, Mac thought of what he would say to her and how he would say it. They only had five days on the cruise. Five days in which he would have CJ's undivided attention. Once they were back on land, she'd be submersed in her work again. He wished she'd slow down, take some time to enjoy the fruits of her labor, but he knew that her upbringing and her unhappiness kept her from doing so.

CJ worked so hard because she wanted to prove to her mother and to herself that she could succeed on her own. Because her mother was a chronic complainer about her circumstances, CJ always swore she'd make her own life what she wanted it to be. Unfortunately, she shared her mother's track record when it came to men. Mac couldn't begin to count how many times he'd wanted to smash in some dude's face for hurting her. But just recently, he'd finally figured out why. He loved her, and he was tired of seeing other men fail where he knew he could succeed.

With that in mind, he took her hand in his. She didn't pull away because this was another one of those natural occurrences between them. They touched frequently, whether holding hands or giving each other hugs or platonic kisses. He always had his hands on her, which was nothing new.

So why did bolts of heat shoot up his arm at the contact? He looked to her with surprise but she was gazing out at the water. Taking a deep breath, Mac tried valiantly to calm his nerves. *There's no need for me to be nervous, this is CJ.* Shaking his head, he realized that was precisely why he needed to be nervous.

"I've been thinking a lot about you lately," he blurted.

She still didn't look at him. "Why? The business is doing well. I'm paying all my bills on time and I even found time to go to the movies last week, remember."

He smiled. He was always after her to relax. It was nice to see she was taking his advice to heart—kind of.. "That's good. But that's not what I've been thinking about."

"Oh. Well, let me see, it's not my turn to pay for drinks at Melba's. For a successful writer, you'd think you could spare twenty or thirty dollars for happy hour."

"Wait a minute," Mac thought suddenly, "I paid for Melba's the last time, so it is your turn."

"It is not. You've got selective memory."

"You want to know what I remember?" he said, stopping, then pulling her over so that they stood at the railing on the Skylight deck.

"What's that?" she asked.

The ocean breeze fluttered through their clothes, lifting the ends of her hair in an alluring flourish. "How pretty you looked the night of our prom," he said.

She blinked, her long dark lashes moving seductively. "Prom? Why do you mention that?"

"I said I've been thinking a lot about you lately. I remember you wore a yellow dress. It wasn't bright like bumblebee yellow, it was pale, like butter. And your hair was pushed up with a bunch of pins that you later pulled out in the backseat of the limo."

Her nose crinkled with the memory. "You know I hate my hair up and those pins stick into your scalp. You'd hate being a girl."

Probably so, because then he couldn't touch her the way he wanted to—and still live to tell about it. But since he was all man, he brushed the tips of his fingers along her jawline. "You wore makeup that night. It was the first time I'd ever seen you in makeup. It made your eyes seem bigger, brighter—"

His words were cut short as she licked her lips and tried to take a step back, suddenly taking in the scenery. A man and a woman, standing on a deck beneath an indigo sky loaded with twinkling little lights that could either be stars or aircraft traveling at a great distance. Way too romantic, way too close for comfort. "That was a long time ago, Mac. No need for this little trip down memory lane."

He nodded. "Okay, then let's talk about the present." He reached out to her again, this time clasping the nape of her neck, holding her still even as his fingers caressed her soft skin. "I like what you do to your eyes. I don't know what it is exactly but I like the length of your lashes and I like how they tilt upward at the corners."

"It's called eyeliner and mascara," she said, her voice a bit on the shaky side. "I'm not in high school anymore. I've learned how to apply makeup well."

He continued, ignoring her sarcasm because he knew it was a defense mechanism. Her eyes seemed to dart all over the place, perhaps finding it harder and harder to stay on him. Could it be? Was he making her nervous? "When you smile, there are these flecks of gold just along the edges, making the ordinary brown color come alive."

"They're just eyes," she said quietly, and because she couldn't move, she simply turned her head.

Mac stepped closer to her, until the tips of her breasts rubbed against his chest. "Your mouth is full, whether you're smiling or pouting or about to curse somebody out. Your lips are..." he hesitated, the hand holding hers moved up her arm, touched her chin and guided her face to his. "Kissable," he whispered, then bent forward, brushing his lips lightly over hers.

It could have been one of their platonic kisses, except that at the last minute, when he would have usually pulled away, he extended his tongue, tracing the seam of her lips, then moving to stroke along the outer rim.

"Mac," she said, surprised, struggling to break free of his grasp.

It was now or never.

"You've tried so hard, CJ. Tried to find the right man or just a man that made you feel good and whole for the moment. And repeatedly you've failed. Don't you think there's a reason for that?"

She was already shaking her head. "What are you talking about? You're no better at the love game than I am. Case in point." She lifted her arms, motioning towards the ship and the fact that they were supposedly there to catch Sidra in the act.

"That's true. But you see, I've figured out that love isn't a game. It's not a race to see who will make it to the finish line first, who will break up with whom first, or who will outlast the other. It's deeper than that, more substantial, more important."

"Is this from one of your articles?"

"I wish it were that easy." Mac dragged a hand down his face, then leaned on the railing. If he wasn't one hundred percent cool, he could at least look the part.

"When I say I've been thinking a lot about you, I mean, I've been thinking about you and me. Together."

She eyed him closely and Mac could tell her wheels were already turning. There were times when CJ could be dangerously perceptive where he was concerned. Tonight, that might actually work in his favor.

"We're always together," she said tentatively.

"I mean together as in a couple, CJ. An intimate couple."

She was quiet. Hell, it seemed everything around them grew quiet. Everything except for the crashing of the waves against the side of the ship.

"We're best friends, Mac."

"The best lovers are friends first."

She was shaking her head.

"Don't tell me you've never thought about it. You said so yourself, we're together all the time. We've been through so much, have been there for each through thick and thin."

"That's the sign of true friendship."

Mac nodded. He should have known CJ wasn't going to be easy. *Of all the women in all the world*, he thought with a chuckle. "Here's the deal. I'm just going to spit it out since you're determined to play ignorant."

"You always get testy when you're nervous," she said offhandedly. Mac didn't get nervous often, that thought alone had her dreading the rest of this conversation.

"I'm not nervous," he said, although his stomach twisted and turned as he attempted to tell her the truth.

"I think I'm in love," he said quickly He held his breath, waiting for her reply.

"With Sidra?"

"With you."

"Stop playing."

"CJ."

He said her name so simply, so convincingly. "Look, you're all twisted up over this situation with your girlfriend," CJ insisted. "Once we get that squared away, you'll be just fine. You'll leave Sidra behind and find someone else."

"I'm not looking for anyone else because I've already found her. She's been right in front of me all along."

"Stop it," she said. "Is the sea air messing with your brain? We've been friends for years. I was the one you told when you had your first wet dream."

"Yeah, did I ever mention that the dream was about you?"

"No." She was shaking her head again, her long earrings swinging to brush against her cheeks. Bringing up wet dreams was definitely a mistake considering the ones she'd been having. "Did I ever mention you were an idiot!"

He laughed

She didn't know what else to say. She wrung her hands, her chest was heaving

He'd told her the truth and she hadn't run, physically, but he could tell by her stance and the defiance in her shoulders that she had every intention of running emotionally. "I agree. I've been an idiot for taking so long to come to my senses. But I can see that I'm not the only one." Taking a step closer to her, he wrapped one arm around her waist and pulled her to his chest. "Look me in the eye and tell me you've never wondered what it would be like. That you've never fantasized about you and me."

She tried, she really did, but his arm was holding her too tightly. The sea air was clouding her mind, clogging her lungs. She couldn't think straight and she couldn't breathe. "Let me go, Mac."

He looked down at her seriously. "I don't think I can."

Her heart pounded in her chest, her thighs humming and her center purring, wanting, needing...him. *No!* her mind screamed. This wasn't right. Mac was her friend. This was lust between them, pure and simple. They were on this romantic cruise with couples all around them, along with a couple hundred writers and readers of fine African-American romance. Sex and seduction was in the air. No wonder he was inhaling it, spouting it at her as if it were gospel.

"I said, let...me...go." She finally wrenched herself from his grip. When she'd backed away from him, she continued, "Take a dip in the pool and cool yourself off. When you do, you'll find it was only your imagination."

With that, she turned and walked away before he could come up with a retort, before he could reach those long strong arms out to grab hold of her again. Before he could see how much his words, his touch, his kiss had truly effected her.

Now she was really confused. Using the key card to enter the room, CJ went straight to the bathroom, closing and locking the door just in case Mac had followed her back. Lord, she prayed he'd give her some time alone. How did he expect her to react to what he'd just said? Why in the world had he even said it?

This was too much. Coupled with her dreams, it was beyond the normal amount of emotions she could handle in one day. So Mac thought he loved her. She chuckled as she stared at her reflection in the mirror. He was crazier than she'd thought all these years. He was not in love with her. It just wasn't feasible. Love was not in the cards for her. And especially not with Mac. What would happen to their friendship?

Grabbing a wash cloth and the make up bag she'd placed in the bathroom earlier, CJ began cleaning her face. Once finished, she pulled her hair into a loose ponytail, and then reached behind her to unzip the dress she'd worn to the party.

The evening had started off just fine, with her and Mac changing into eveningwear for the Romance Slam Jam welcome party. By that time she'd had to admit she was thankful for Mac's career and this assignment—even if it had ulterior motives. Otherwise, she probably would never have gotten the chance to meet her favorite romance authors and many more in attendance.

By the end of the party, she'd smiled and chatted so much, the flyers they had slipped her about tomorrow's book discussions were even more appealing. Mac had frowned, saying he didn't want to spend half the morning listening to women talk about their favorite romance characters. But when CJ reminded him that he still needed to turn in a story to the magazine at the end of the trip, he reluctantly agreed to attend with her.

Then they'd decided to walk, which had seemed innocent enough. However, CJ had noted how quiet Mac had grown since leaving the party. They hadn't seen Sidra once, so she figured he was thinking about her and what they might encounter when they did see her. So she'd remained quiet as well, giving him time to come to grips with his situation.

As they had approached the Skylight deck, she'd been a little leery, remembering the scene in Titanic where Jack had to pull Rose back over the railing. The memory gave her a slight start but then she realized she was not a depressed and sulky Rose, and Mac was not the poor, optimistic artist Jack, who would ultimately save Rose's life in more ways than one. Still, the view had been amazing, the water as dark as the sky, the air just a bit chilly.

She'd figured they would stay there, enjoy the sights for a few minutes, then return to the cabin. Mac had other ideas.

He'd been thinking about her a lot lately, he loved her, had she ever thought of them together? His words came rushing back and CJ shivered as if she were still standing out on the Skylight deck. Leaving the bathroom, she tried to push them out of her mind as she found a nightshirt in the dresser drawer and slipped out of the dress she'd worn, hastily pulling the nightshirt over her head. She wanted to be fast asleep before Mac came back to the room, or at least looking as if she were fast asleep.

CJ was thinking as her head hit the pillow. She pulled the covers up to her neck and scooted until she was almost hanging off the edge of the bed. What if Mac really was in love with her? How would this play out? Would they spend four months screwing each other's brains out then drift apart when he found someone more exciting? That was Mac's normal MO. Actually, it was everyone in her family's MO. So as far as she was concerned, she was tainted with the same curse, only she didn't cheat; she was the one who was always cheated on.

No, she valued her friendship with Mac too much to let something as inconsequential as lust get in the way. Because that's all

170

there was to it...he was in lust with her. Confusing the "l" words came natural for men. He wanted to sleep with her just as she wanted to sleep with him. That was all. They were *not* in love with each other. They couldn't be.

She'd known it all along. In fact, she'd been the one to tell Mackenzi to stop the denial act. To which he'd replied stiffly, "I don't have to lie to you about anything. We're not committed."

Those words stung, and in that instant, Sidra decided she would make him pay for saying them. As soon as he tried to approach the workaholic, mean-spirited woman he called his best friend and she turned him down. While Sidra believed that Mackenzi was in love with Corina, that silly, childish and boyish nickname "CJ" too much for her to actually use, she doubted very seriously that the woman would slow down long enough to want to build something with him. CJ had feelings for Mac, Sidra was even willing to bet she might secretly be in love with him, too. But she'd never act on it. Her misguided morals and focused attention on her company would put a stop to it.

So, whether he loved another woman or not, Sidra was certain Mackenzi would come running back to her.

She practically fumed at the sight before her, Mackenzi and his little friend hugged up on the deck looking like lovers enjoying a tropical vacation. They had actually looked happy until Corina stiffened and spat some words that didn't sit too well with Mackenzi. That had been the only consolation, the look on Mackenzi's face as he stared at Corina walking away. It was a small victory, one she wholeheartedly intended to exploit.

Chapter Four

Mac thought he was dreaming. But on the second moan he'd rolled over and clicked on the lamp on the nightstand. He could have slept in one of the pull-outs in the other room, but since they'd slept together before, they had been a day late and a dollar short on that thought.

Maybe they should have reconsidered that decision.

Not two feet away, CJ lay on her back, one arm resting over her midsection, the other riding closer to her breast—the breast that wasn't covered by the comforter and only barely hidden by her thin nightshirt. He swallowed, sending a silent message to the erection lengthening in his boxers.

But before his message could be digested, or possibly in spite of the pitiful message in the first place, CJ moaned again, this time her lips parting slightly. Like a diving rod, the part of him Mac rarely let overrule common sense took charge, poking through the hole in his boxers, urging him to get the lead out and scoot closer to the object of its desire.

Still, Mac did not move. It was a battle, one he prayed to win for the sake of their friendship.

Her chest rose and fell in rapid movements, making her breasts look large then smaller every few seconds. He wondered what or who she was dreaming about.

On the next moan, the hand closest to her breast moved upward and Mac's eyes almost crossed. *Please. Please. Please.* The word swirled through his mind just as his own hand was lifting, his arm reaching until it hovered just above hers. *Touch it. Touch it. Touch it.*

Her head thrashed, her mouth opening as she panted. Mac hadn't realized he'd scooted closer to her until a knee came dangerously close to unmanning him. She was opening her legs. *Breathe*, he reminded himself. Breathe and count to ten.

But the numbers were lost somewhere between two and three and she did exactly as he wanted, her palm stretched over her breast. As if there were a magnet attached, his hand lowered slowly so that it covered hers, his fingers closing along with hers around the swollen mound.

"Heaven," he whispered, his eyes narrowing to mere slits, focusing on his hand on CJ's breast.

"Yes," she exhaled in a breathy sigh, and Mac's gaze flew to her face. Her eyes were closed. She was still asleep. Like a splash of cold water, the pervert complex washed over him.

Here he was, sharing a bed with the woman he was trying to convince he loved, and he was feeling her up while she slept, like some deranged sex fiend. With a curse he pulled his hand away. He wasn't going to win her over with sex. He'd done that with too many women, too many times, and after the lust there was nothing else. CJ was too important for that.

He moved back to his side of the bed, closing his eyes as his erection continued to pulse. Silent messages weren't getting through to him and CJ was moaning as though her release were just moments away. He jumped up out of the bed, taking a quick second to acclimate himself to the swaying of the ship, then stalked around the bed. His intention was to go into the bathroom, take a cold shower, or a hot one with plenty of soap, that would certainly ease his pain. But mid-stride he stopped, went to the side of the bed where CJ still slept and dreamed of having a good time. Without a second thought he reached out, grabbed her shoulder and shook her until her eyes flew open.

"Wake up," he snipped. "You're having a bad dream." Then he stomped off, closing the bathroom door with a bang. If he wasn't getting any play, she certainly wasn't going to be dreaming about any!

Mac and CJ walked into the room where the first session of book discussions were being held. They had awakened three hours ago, gotten dressed in virtual silence, then went to breakfast.

Over the meal they'd exchanged general conversation, both treading lightly around last night's revelations. Mac figured he should say something but he was dealing with yet another issue this morning: Sidra had called him on his cell phone. He'd heard that connectivity on cruise ships was weak so the vibration across his dresser had been a little jolting. Seeing the number illuminating the screen had been even worse. He had no idea what she wanted. Maybe she'd seen him on the boat, or worse, with CJ. Well, that would just prove her right and she could move on, just as he'd told her to.

He should have known that Sidra was too spoiled to let go of something she wanted just because it wasn't available to her. Maybe this cruise wasn't the best idea. Mac's head had actually begun to hurt as CJ led him to the second row of seats facing two authors and their collage of books.

"Tell me why we're here again?" he asked once they were seated.

"To discuss the authors' books."

"But I didn't read them."

"I told you I had one of them in my suitcase. You could have read parts of it before coming."

"I didn't want to."

"Well, then just sit there and take notes. Do you have your Dictaphone or notepad?"

"Yeah," he sighed. "But I don't know what you think I'm going to get out of these discussions."

CJ didn't know either, nor did she care. She wanted to be here, and if he was supposed to be writing an article about the conference, he should attend some of the events.

So the first author began to speak, talking about the characters in her novel and how they were reunited after years of being separated by a misunderstanding. The hero hadn't given up on love but he was pretty angry with the heroine. The heroine was hurt and still confused over their fallout. The discussion was lively as readers delved into the characters' psyches, wanting to know more.

"He should have just left the lying trick alone," Mac leaned over and said, referring to the discussion.

"She only lied to protect herself from further scrutiny and to protect the hero."

"He was a big boy. He could have held his own. She had no business sneaking off with his friend."

"They didn't sneak."

"You're right, they left town right in front of old boy's face. If you ask me, she never loved him to begin with."

"Maybe she loved him too much. Maybe she didn't want anything to taint the love they'd shared and so she walked away."

"Maybe she should have been woman enough to tell him what was on her mind. If their love was that strong they could have worked it out."

"What if she thought their relationship would change after she told him?"

"Change isn't always a bad thing."

"But it could inadvertently mess up a good thing."

"Or it could make a good thing even better." He'd paused his Dictaphone and wasn't writing a word. Instead, Mac stared at her intently knowing exactly what she hinted at.

She looked down at her clasped hands. "I'm not good with relationships. My track record proves that."

He reached out, lifting her chin until she looked at him. "You know better than that. You're a strong, independent woman, who's

174

managed to build her own business in the face of scrutiny and adversity from your family. You've had men, yes, and they've been punk asses, but you saw them for what they were and you cut them loose with dignity. If you ask me, it's their track record that's screwed up."

She wanted to throw her arms around him, to thank him profusely for saying what she needed to hear. But they were sitting close to the front in a room full of people. So instead she motioned for them to leave. Mac looked all too pleased with that idea.

They were barely out of the room before Mac was taking her hands in his. "I didn't plan this, CJ. It just sort of happened. And for the record, I've been fighting it for a while, for all the same reasons I know are going through your mind. You don't want our friendship to change. And I can't honestly promise you a positive outcome. But what I can promise is that I won't hurt you. I'll treat you with the same respect and trust that we've always shared."

Oh man, his words sounded good. If only they were coming from a stranger and not her best friend. But then she'd be less inclined to believe them.

"I don't think you understand what I've had to deal with, Mac. I mean, I know you went through these breakups with me, but this last one..." she drifted off and was pleased that he gave her a few minutes to get her thoughts together.

"Cliff broke my heart," she said.

He cupped her cheek, praying she wouldn't cry. She'd cried the night Cliff had broken up with her and Mac's own heart had been wrenched at the sight. "I know that, CJ. And that's why the moment he left your house, I followed him and broke his jaw. But love doesn't end with Cliff."

She blinked, then stared at him curiously. "You were at my house that night?"

The moment she asked her question, Mac could have tossed himself right over the railing into the sea. Because once he answered her, she'd be ready to do the same thing.

Instead, he simply cleared his throat. "I was."

"Why? We didn't have any plans."

And he knew that, especially since he'd been with Cliff when he'd called CJ to make plans to talk to her that night.

"I know." He'd come on this trip to finally tell CJ the truth, to put all his cards on the table. And he'd just promised to treat her with the respect and trust they'd always shared. For better or worse, backing out now was not an option. "I knew Cliff was going to be there."

"And how did you know that?"

"I'd talked to him earlier."

She frowned. "About what?"

Mac took a deep breath. This wasn't the truth he wanted to come clean about but if CJ needed to get past the breakup with Cliff to open her eyes to what was between the two of them, then he'd tell her whatever she needed to hear.

"I found out he was married and I confronted him about it."

"You what?" she screeched, pulling herself away from him.

Her fingers flexed at her sides and a vein in her neck jumped. "The night before, I saw him with another woman at a restaurant. The next day I went to his job and asked him who she was. He told me she was his wife. I told him he needed to tell you before I did."

"And he called me saying we needed to talk," she said slowly. "He came to my house to break up with me and you stood outside waiting. Why?"

"Because I knew you would need someone to talk to when he left."

"If you hadn't sent him to break my heart, I wouldn't have needed to talk to anybody."

"He was married, CJ. He was sleeping with you, making plans for a future with you that he'd never be able to uphold. You deserved the truth."

"I deserve to be happy!" she screamed. "One man after another, one heartbreak after another, just like my mother. You know I watch my brothers doing this same thing, sleeping with women, then dumping them. I'm sick and tired of it! I deserve a good relationship, someone to love me, happily ever after and all that Cinderella crap!"

He could have chuckled at her reference to the fairy tale she hated most. She'd always said how Cinderella was stuck on stupid for waiting on her stepmother and stepsisters all those years. Instead, he recognized that she was absolutely right; she deserved the best a man could give her. "I know you do, CJ and I want to give that to you."

"You took that away from me!"

"I didn't tell Cliff to lie to you."

She turned away from him refusing to cry, refusing to let a lost relationship continue to hinder her future. She wasn't pissed at Mac as much as at herself. There was no excuse for missing the signs where Cliff was concerned. And if Mac did the things he said he'd done, which she had no doubt he did, especially breaking Cliff's jaw, then he was a better friend than she'd ever thought.

"I know," she finally managed to say. "I let him lie to me."

Coming up behind her, Mac placed his hands on her shoulders, drawing her back against his chest. "It was never about you, CJ. It was about Cliff and his selfishness. I don't want you carrying any blame for what that joker did."

"And you were right there," she said, turning in his arms. "Just like always."

"I was where I wanted to be, just like always."

And in that moment there was nothing chaste, nothing platonic about the kiss they shared. His lips took hers in a sort of exploration, his mouth slanting over hers, his tongue plunging deeper and deeper. CJ didn't even bother to fight it. What was the point? She'd been dreaming of this and he'd been thinking of this, they might as well get it out of their systems. Thinking about what would happen next would have to wait.

Chapter Five

Like an Olympic swimmer, CJ plunged into Mac's mouth the moment they were in the cabin, the door closed behind them. And just like that it began. She took his mouth in a blaze of heat, holding his lips, his tongue hostage until his body and his mind had no choice but to acquiesce.

With great effort Mac managed to pull away, draw in a breath, then sink right back into the wonder of her mouth. She seared him with her kisses, his entire body heating with her touch. His erection pressed painfully against his zipper. She moaned and pushed him against the door, her hands moving quickly over his chest, down his abs, to fumble with his belt and buckle.

"CJ," he murmured.

"Yes?" she answered between sucking on his bottom lip and nipping her teeth along his jaw.

"Hurry up."

She smiled, then pulled at his pants, hearing the coarse sound of a forced zipper. With quick hands, she pushed his pants down his thighs. For a moment her fingers lingered there, loving the feel of toned, muscled thighs sprinkled with dark hair. She'd dreamt about this, about touching him and feeling him. Now was the time to live the dream.

On a mission of their own, her hands found the front slit of his boxers and released the object of her affection. He was huge. Well, not, grotesque huge like in the porn magazines her brothers kept, but a nice, enticing size that had her thighs shivering.

She couldn't wait. She wanted the seduction, the slow and gentle exploration. But she needed the release, the hot fiery sensation of Mac driving her crazy.

His hands were buried in her hair, tugging until tiny spikes of pain rippled through her scalp. He was saying something, or wait, was he groaning? She wasn't quite sure but none of it sounded like 'Stop, I've changed my mind,' so she continued.

Getting the rest of his clothes off wasn't the easiest task, but once he was naked, beautifully so, she couldn't keep her hands off him.

"We...need...bed...", he mumbled as she nibbled his right pectoral, flattening her tongue then tracing a slow, tortuously hot trail down to his stomach.

"I need now," she said.

Always ready to oblige, Mac yanked at the sash tying her blouse at her side. The fabric tore, but he didn't give a damn. He wanted her naked.

It took some maneuvering, but it was all worth it when he saw her standing in front of him, her caramel cream-colored skin looking soft and probably tasting decadent. Only one way to find out.

He had her flat on the floor in seconds, opening his mouth and sucking in one large dark nipple. It instantly puckered in his mouth, rubbing enticingly against his tongue. She arched her back and he palmed the other breast, kneading it while he sucked the other.

"Mac, please," was her plea.

"Yes, CJ. Yes."

Spreading her legs, he thrust into her with one smooth stroke, gritting his teeth at the tightness of her walls around him. His mind blurred and then everything disappeared. Everything but CJ. Her body lush beneath his, her arms around his neck, holding him tightly, the agile lift of her thick thighs clasping around his waist, holding him deep inside.

He shifted, rotated his hips and felt her walls clench even tighter around him. It was as if he were her first lover. That's what he told himself as he pulled slightly out then sank back into her silken heat once more. Warmth cascaded through his body as he deepened each stroke, pushed farther and farther. He wanted to be so deep in her that she couldn't think of anyone else. Not Cliff, not her family or her failures. Just him.

"Mac," she whispered, and he shivered.

That's all she could say, the only syllable her lips would form. He'd looked at her as if she was precious, like a gem he wanted desperately to hold on to. He kissed her as if she were the love of his life, touched her as though she were the center of his desire. He stroked her, his delectable erection moving in and out of her with sensual ease.

And she loved every minute of it.

She loved the feel of his broad shoulders beneath her hands, the width of him between her legs, the warmth of his breath as he breathed deeply in the crook of her neck. God, she loved him.

It was a glittering revelation, sprinkling over the warm haze of lust that his thrusts evoked. The realization and acceptance of her feelings for him made each stroke, each murmured endearment so much more powerful, meaningful. His skills in the area of sex weren't just good, but the emotion behind each stroke, each thrust, each kiss, lifted her higher, higher than she'd ever been before. Her heart beat steadily, filling with complete and utter adoration.

With that thought she moved her hips, matching his movements, and she loved the depth that created. They moved as one, their minds and bodies in sync.

"Never before," she whispered.

Mac pulled back, gazing into her eyes as he thrust powerfully into her once more. "Never again," he promised, pushing them right over the edge.

<hr/>

"Mornin' sunshine," Mac said cheerfully as he spied CJ's eyes finally peeping open. She'd been sleeping so soundly after their long night of vigorous lovemaking while he'd been too pumped to lay in bed a moment longer. Although he loved the way her body fit perfectly against his, her soft thighs rested along his muscled hairy ones, he'd uncurled himself from that exquisite pleasure to make their plans for the day.

He'd actually just returned to the room—and not a moment too soon since she was now struggling to sit up in the bed and keep the sheet pulled up over her naked body—and was stirring the cream and sugar he'd already put in the coffee he'd picked up for her.

"Just the way you like it," he said, offering her the cup, then sitting on the side of the bed. He leaned forward for a kiss.

Her lips were swollen and for one brief second he felt guilty. He couldn't get enough of kissing her. It was like a drug that he was happily addicted to. She complied, taking the cup out of his hand while puckering up for him. Man, he could get used to this.

"You are way too chipper this morning," she said, then blew over the coffee before taking a sip. "Mmm, perfect."

"I know what you like." In addition to not being able to keep his lips off her, his hands followed suit, cupping the back of her neck, then sliding to the smooth curve of her shoulders.

The sheet slipped and she tried to readjust it. "Don't even try it. Now that I've seen that gorgeous body of yours without clothing, I may just keep you that way from now on."

"Working in the nude is not exactly the reputation I'd like to gain." But she loved that he enjoyed seeing her naked. Her skin warmed with a blush as he pushed the sheet the rest of the way down, his eyes drinking her in as slowly and languorously as she was sipping her coffee.

He bent forward to take one dark nipple into his mouth, and she shivered. She put her coffee down before she made a mess. His hands gripped her breasts, his mouth gorging on one. She held the back of his head, keeping him in place.

In moments she was on her back, Mac climbing on top of her. He was fully dressed so his clothes scraped over her already sensitive skin. She pulled at his shirt as she spread her legs. He pulled away from her breast, grinning.

"You're greedy aren't you?"

"Don't play with me," she said, swatting his back as she struggled to breathe normally. "You're the one serving coffee and kisses first thing in the morning."

"Yeah," he chuckled. "But we don't have time right now."

"What?" she exclaimed as he climbed off her, gave her body one more appreciative glance, then reached for her hands.

"Get up and get a shower. We've got plans for the day."

"What plans? I didn't see that the conference had anything scheduled for the day."

"They don't. We're going ashore."

CJ blinked at him as she climbed out of bed. She grabbed her coffee cup and started moving in the direction of the dresser to get her clothes for the day. "Ashore? Where, oh to Grand Cayman. So we're going sightseeing?"

Mac, ahead of her by two steps,turned, pushing her undergarments into her hand. "Ah, not exactly. I've made some reservations for us but you need to hurry up and get dressed."

"Stop rushing me. I'm trying to drink my coffee."

He took the cup out of her hand. "After you get your shower."

"I have to get my clothes out, Mac."

"Already done." He moved aside so she could see where he'd lain her clothes out on the lounge chair.

CJ moved closer. He'd picked out khaki capris with their matching white and beige striped shirt. Her white tennis shoes were neatly placed on the floor with her ankle socks poking out of them.

"My, my, my, you've been busy this morning."

"Well, tee time's at noon," he said, guiding her to the bathroom and pushing her inside.

"Tee time?" she asked when she dropped her undergarments on the vanity and turned back to him.

Mac was smiling as he closed the door.

"Mackenzi Jackson! I am not playing golf with you! You'd better make some other plans!"

Mac laughed so hard as he held the bathroom door shut, he could barely breathe. CJ hated golf because it was the only sport that she wasn't neck and neck with him. He'd planned this day perfectly, because being with her last night was more than he could have ever hoped for. Things were looking up for them and he wasn't about to lose sight of that.

Of course, he had some other plans for today, but a nice competitive game of golf would get them going. The rest of the island tour would be all about her. And this evening, would be all about them.

He sighed when he finally heard the water turn on. Leaning against the door he whispered, "Life is good."

"This is gorgeous," CJ said while waiting for Mac. Going into the final hole of the back nine, she was way over her normal handicap and on pace to finish the winner. Mac, on the other hand, needed an eagle or better to win, and he was more than a little pissed off about it. Yet that was the only reason CJ was aware of the results. Unlike other aspects of her life, golf wasn't one that she over-studied, over-thought, or over-played. Wow, she really was obsessive.

For years she'd just considered it ambitious, but with long and lazy days of sun-filled skies and glistening sea water, and nights heavy with the aura of romance and relaxation on the cruise, she was beginning to rethink her stance. Again, Mac was right—she had a successful business, a good life—she should enjoy it more. So what if her family was dysfunctional? One-third of American families were. Her mother's failings and her brothers' continuous bad choices were not hers, nor her cross to bear. It was time she let all that go and focused on what made her happy, what made her life worth living.

He cursed and she tore her gaze away from the crystal blue sky to gaze at Mac. He looked the same, basically. His biceps bulged a little more this morning but that could be due to his close-fitting polo shirt. His linen slacks hung seductively on his hips while the dark brown Kenneth Cole Yacht Club loafers gave him a male model sort of look. His dark-brown skin seemed sun-kissed and enticing. All that was certainly due to seeing him in the buff last night.

Mac had never been shy, and last night had been no different. He'd moved around their cabin in naked bliss, and she'd watched ever step he took, waiting with bated breath until he returned to the bed, to her.

"I'm glad this is almost over," he said grimly.

With her most sugary sweet voice, she asked, "What's the matter, you don't like losing?"

Cutting her an annoyed glare, he murmured, "Don't get all excited. It's a one-time thing, a fluke. Probably because we're on this island and the tropical breeze is messing with my concentration."

"Well," she said, smiling and inhaling a deep whiff of said breeze, "it's working wonders for me."

She closed her eyes to the sunshine, letting the warm air soothe her skin.. She was taken off guard by his hug. His arms came around her waist from behind and she melted into the embrace. He kissed her neck and she sighed.

"I'm glad you're enjoying yourself," he whispered.

"Oh yeah, I'm definitely enjoying myself," she responded, rubbing her hands along his arms. "Especially after last night."

Mac smiled. "If you think that was something, just wait until I get you back in that penthouse tonight."

With a wiggle of her bottom against his burgeoning erection, she replied, "Promises, promises."

She looked pretty damned pleased with herself as she waltzed from the casino where she'd left Mac, most likely headed towards their room. They'd been ashore all day, Sidra knew, because she'd been looking for them. The ship was huge, so she'd spent an extremely long time looking for them before it dawned on her that with the ship docked, most of the passengers had gone ashore.

This cruise was about more to Sidra than seeing some stupid island or even posing for some sappy romance novel. Although the male model she'd been paired with was delicious and made her tremble slightly during the embrace that would hopefully be selected to grace the next cover.

But now they were back and Sidra had business to take care of. She caught CJ just as she was turning the corner that led down the hallway to their room. Mac had booked the penthouse suite. Too bad he wasn't sharing it with her. But that would be fixed quickly enough.

"So you've finally come out of your career shell long enough to see what was right in front of you."

Startled, CJ turned quickly, a hand going to her chest. "Oh, Sidra. It's you," she said, taking a deep breath. "What are you doing skulking in the halls?"

"Not skulking, Corina. Waiting."

"My name is CJ, as I've told you before."

"Let's just cut to the chase, shall we?"

CJ lifted a brow then crossed her arms over her chest. She and Mac had enjoyed a glorious day in Grand Cayman; the last thing she needed was to spend time with Sidra. Maybe she could get the woman to simply admit that she was cheating on Mac so CJ could tell him. Then again, did it even matter to him after what he'd admitted to her?

Funny, she hadn't thought about Sidra as she related to Mac up until this point.

"Say what you have to say so I can go," CJ managed although a lot of thoughts were going through her mind at this moment.

"You've always wanted him. I don't know why he never saw it. But I did. That night we first met, I could tell by the way you were so protective of him."

"Assuming you're talking about Mac, I was protective of him because he means a lot to me. He's my best friend."

"Best friends my ass, you're in love with him!"

Because her words were true, CJ couldn't deny them. "Look, whatever I may or may not be feeling has nothing to do with you cheating on Mac. If you don't want him, you should be woman enough to just tell him that."

"You're insane." Sidra gave a shrill laugh. "You and Mac both are in denial. I'm not the one who cheated on him. He's the one who wanted someone else. He wants you. Or at least he thinks he does. But when I tell him you're sleeping with a married man, he'll change his tune."

How did she know about Cliff? And what difference did it make to her whether or not she was sleeping with a married man? Sidra wasn't the one married to him. "We're not talking about me," CJ said. "We're talking about you and Mac. You should have just told him you'd moved on, instead of sneaking behind his back."

"You are so naïve. That's probably how Cliff got over on you for so long. Yes, I know about Cliff. How? Because I slept with him, too. Only I didn't fall for his charms or his lies. I knew the game and I played it right along with him. You, on the other hand, could never be as smart as I am."

"Or as pitiful," CJ laughed, although she was anything but happy. "So here's the deal. Either you tell Mac it's over, or I'll do it for you."

With a tilt of her head, Sidra's long curly black hair swayed past her shoulders. "He didn't tell you, CJ? You're supposed to be best friends and he didn't tell you."

Her temples ached as she opened her mouth to ask. She should probably have walked away, but her feet seemed rooted to that spot, her gaze on the woman Mac had come on this cruise to look for. "Tell me what?"

Sidra threw her head back and laughed. "Now who's the pitiful one?"

CJ took a step towards her, and only the grace of God held her back from punching Sidra. "Don't play games with me. Not right now, Sidra."

"This is too cute and too easy," she quipped. "Mac broke up with me weeks ago because I made him see that he was really in love with you. Now, why would I do that? Because I like my men to know the score. You're not good enough for him and I wanted him to figure that out for himself. Now, I guess I'll just have to tell him about your homewrecking ways and be the shoulder he'll need to cry on."

Her words rang in CJ's head as she struggled to latch on to them. Mac had lied to her. Another man had lied to her. He said he wanted to catch Sidra in the act. But he'd already broken up with her. The why's didn't even matter at this point. The dishonesty stuck out like the black spot that it was. If she couldn't trust Mac, her best friend, then relationships truly were hopeless.

"He doesn't want you," she spoke with all the contempt she felt. "If he did, he would have stayed with you, no matter what you said to him. This whole scene is childish and I'm through with it."

Sidra chuckled. "You're definitely through."

"And you're too pathetic to waste my time any longer." Turning and walking away was easy. Forgetting Sidra's words wasn't.

Chapter Six

He'd spent two hours and probably a good portion of his last paycheck in the Millionaire's Club casino. But that was all good, because he'd also taken quite a bit of the casino's money. Stopping at the duty-free gift stores, he'd purchased a hot little negligee and couldn't wait to return to the room to have CJ model it. So he was in high spirits when he rounded the Rotunda, heading for the elevators.

He saw her the moment she stood. He knew that she knew the second she saw him, and his good mood sank a level.

He knew she'd be here. Hadn't she been his excuse to get CJ here? But he hadn't really anticipated having to speak to her. Their affair was over, a fact made perfectly clear more than a month ago. Still, Sidra, in all her polished beauty, was walking straight towards him. And when she was close enough, she laced her arm through his and turned him in the other direction.

"Heading back to your room?" she asked sweetly.

"I am."

"Good. Then I'm right on time."

"Right on time for what? And where are we going?" He pulled his arm away from hers.

"Come on, Mackenzi, let's not make a scene."

Clusters of people milled about, visiting the shops or heading towards the Palladium balcony for whatever event was scheduled for the night.

"What do you want, Sidra?" he asked when they were off to the side, closer to the elevators.

"That's simple enough. You."

Mac sighed. "That's over. You told me so, remember."

"Oh no," she said, reaching a slim hand with claw-like nails up to cup his cheek. "That's not what I told you at all. I merely wanted you to admit where your feelings truly were."

"And since they're not with you, we decided our involvement was over."

"You decided our involvement was over. See, Mackenzi, I'm a simple woman and I want simple things."

"That's a lie."

She tilted her head, then chuckled. "Yes, I guess it is. At any rate, I don't like complications in my life. So being with you, knowing there were none of those pesky emotions, was just fine with me."

"It wasn't fine with me, Sidra. I need more than sex and arm candy."

"You didn't before."

"I always have. I just waited until I actually found it before admitting that fact."

"And you think you've found it with Corina?"

"CJ and I very well suited."

"You know," she said thoughtfully, "That's not really what she told me earlier."

"What? When did you see her?"

"A couple of hours ago," she answered. "She seemed to be under the impression that I was cheating on you. But I set her straight with that and also informed her that we were still very much an item. She shouldn't mind since she's sleeping with a married man."

"You lied to her?" he asked incredulously, already figuring CJ was packing up his clothes and sitting them outside their cabin. Dammit! Why hadn't he told her the truth about him and Sidra the other day, when they were purging their secrets? CJ's first thought was most likely to be that he was just like every other man she knew.

"I told her what she needed to hear. There's nothing for you two. The friendship thing has probably even run its course."

He grabbed her arm, then thought better of shaking the hell out of her and pushed her away. "You don't know a damned thing, about me, what I want or who my friends are."

"I know that we were happy together."

"You were good in bed. Let's not mistake that for happiness," he said, turning to push the button for the elevator. "Now, let me make myself perfectly clear," he spoke slowly. "You and I are through. And if I ever find out you're spitting lies to CJ again, you'll regret it."

"Is that a threat, Mackenzi?" She asked just as the elevator door opened.

Mac stepped inside, hit the button for the floor he wanted, and looked at her one last time. "No, Sidra. That's a promise."

She was not going to panic. There had to be an explanation. One that prayerfully didn't end with her being used by her closest friend.

The door clicked and CJ took a deep breath. He was back. She wonderd how to broach the subject of seeing Sidra, of hearing that they'd already broken up, of asking Mac why he lied.

When he came to sit on the bed beside her, taking her hand in his, she realized she wouldn't have to.

187

"You saw Sidra," he said, looking down at her hand as if he'd never seen it before.

"Yeah," she answered in a weak voice, then cleared her throat and looked at him. "She told me you two had broken up prior to coming on the ship."

Mac had to chuckle at that. Sidra had always been good at games. Hadn't she just told him she didn't consider their last conversation a break up? Yeah, she was playing a game, but just as he'd told her only moments before, it stopped now. He wasn't a child so games had been off his agenda for a long time. He was not going to tolerate her interference in his relationship with CJ.

"That's true." He held up a hand the moment he saw her open her mouth, the questions in her mind ready to break free. "I told you I needed your help because I knew that was the only way to get you here. You never take vacations and like I said before we left, if you thought you were coming along to watch me have fun and ogle women, you wouldn't have joined me. So I made up the situation with Sidra knowing you wouldn't want me walking into something like that without you."

"You sure do presume to know a lot about me."

"That's because you are a part of me. You have been since you slapped my hand for stealing your chips."

As angry as she wanted to be with him, CJ couldn't help smiling.

"I think I've been in love with you from that day. It just took me twenty plus years to figure it out."

"So when you did figure it out, you lie to me? You should have just told me, Mac. You didn't have to take me on a cruise to say the words."

"No, not to say the words, but to set the scene. I wanted you totally relaxed and open to new possibilities. You've never cruised before so that was new enough. I had the perfect seduction planned."

"Oh, really? And what was that?"

"Things moved a little faster than I'd anticipated, but originally I'd been counting on your romantic mood being set by the writers conference. How could I forget how much you loved to read about black love, even though you believed you'd never find it? I figured that after a few days surrounded by scorching hot sex scenes and tales of finding your one true mate, you'd be primed and open to what I had to say.

"So I figured we could take a shore excursion to one of the private beaches on Grand Cayman or Ochos Rico. That's where I planned to tell you I loved you. And when you denied it, like I knew you would—just like you did on deck—I was going to seduce you. With the white sand beneath your naked body, I was going to make love to you. Yes, make love, not have sex, because you are so much more to me than any other woman I've ever met. Than anyone I'll ever meet."

Her mind reeled, her heart thumping, her body warm all over. She was supposed to be angry with him. She remembered that and tried to focus on it. But when his hand moved to grasp her neck, pulling her face closer to his, she forgot the words.

"We're not on the beach, but it doesn't matter," he whispered against her mouth. "Let me seduce you, CJ. Let me show you how much I love you, how much I've always loved you."

His lips touched hers and she trembled. Maybe she could be angry tomorrow. For now, she pressed her lips to his, moaning as his tongue traced the length of her mouth.

"Seduced at sea," she murmured. "I think I like the sound of that."

The End

Author Bio

Artist C. Arthur was born and raised in Baltimore, Maryland where she currently resides with her husband and three children. An active imagination and a love for reading encouraged her to begin writing in high school and she hasn't stopped since.

Working in the legal field for almost thirteen years now she seen lots of horrific things and longs for the safe haven reading romance novel brings. Her debut novel Object of His Desire was written when a picture of an Italian villa sparked the idea of an African-American/Italian hero. Determined to bring a new edge to romance, she continues to develop intriguing plots, sensual love scenes racy characters and fresh dialogue—thus keeping the readers on their toes!

Red Rose Publishing
Seaside Seduction
Kimani Romance, Harlequin
Full House Seduction
Defying Desire
Second Chance Baby
Guarding His Body
A Cinderella Affair
Love Me Like No Other

Genesis Press
Object of His Desire
Office Policy
Unconditional
Love Me Carefully
Corporate Seduction
Within the Shadows
Heart of the Phoenix
Office Policy
Object of His Desire

Parker Publishing
Love for All Seasons

Wanting You

On My Knees

By

Dyanne Davis

Chapter One

The pale champagne, silk blouse shimmered in the twinkling sunlight. Carmen Harris ran her hand over the fabric before tucking it into her small bag. It was hard to believe that she was actually going on a cruise. A sigh fell from her lips. She couldn't help thinking about the last time she'd planned and paid for a cruise—her then—fiancée had cancelled at the last moment, telling her to go alone or invite a friend. Carmen had not wanted to do that. Why should she? The cruise had been intended as a honeymoon. A honeymoon that had never happened. Now here she was leaving New York for Miami in order to board a ship and sleep in a cabin alone. An unwanted sigh slid from deep within her. She'd much rather not be flying solo let alone going on a cruise by herself. But it was what it was.

Taking a last look around the hotel room for any forgotten belongings, Carmen sighed again, this time shaking her head at her reflection in the mirror, for the foolish waste of money. She couldn't help but think that all of her grand plans were bound to lead to trouble. What she was about to do wasn't who she was. It didn't fit. For the past three weeks, she'd lived in one hotel room after the other, forced to because of all the traveling for her job as a real estate investor. Five days on a cruise was just what she needed to make a decision. She'd accepted a challenge to change, to try harder to have fun, to understand more than facts and figures, to believe in magic and love. She'd believed strongly in those things for many years, but the past year or so, her beliefs had taken a beating.

Another sigh escaped. How could they not? She was barely ever home—when would she have time for magic? This cruise was her panacea. She had something to prove to herself, she could do this, she wanted to do this. Heat to her core hit her at that moment causing her to squeeze her legs together. She needed to be touched n the worst way. Moving her hand slowly downward toward her throbbing mound she stopped barley able to breathe for the fire that was incinerating her. It wasn't her fingers her body craved but the touch of a strong loving man.

Carmen shivered as fear through her. Maybe she was placing far too many hopes on a five day cruise. Maybe, important decisions shouldn't be made on the outcome of wishes, bets or deep blue water and pampering. The ache between her thighs called her a liar. She was going on the cruise with hope that her needs would be met. If nothing else, the view of the ocean from a ship should prove fantastic.

No sooner had she talked herself out of her self-induced funk the doubts returned. What if she didn't have fun? What if she didn't have a shipboard romance like she'd read about in the couple of romance novels she'd skimmed? *So what*, was the answer she whispered in her mind. She wasn't really the kind of woman who would allow a man into her cabin, into her body without knowing him thoroughly anyway. But what if the plan didn't work? What if her questions weren't answered?

Despite all her good intention not to, Carmen was disgusted at herself as yet another heavy sigh came from her. She hated sighing. She hated even more that her sighing was pulling at her as memories of the failed honeymoon cruise returned. Sometimes disappointment happened no matter how well you thought you knew someone.

It was time to go. Her bags had been packed weeks before and left at home. They would be taken to the ship. The only thing she had to worry about was this small carry on, good thing too. Now when she went out of town on business she packed as little as she could possibly get away with. With all the recent changes in the airlines she didn't relish paying for luggage. Force of habit made Carmen pray for things to go well. *With God, all things are possibl*, she thought and exited the room turning the lights off in the process.

Aaron was annoyed. He'd begged and even gotten down on his damn knees to plead with his woman to come with him on the cruise. Like always, she'd refused leaving him to go alone, not willing to share in one of the things that brought him great joy. Being with her, traveling with her brought him joy. He hated traveling alone. It was not what he wanted. She'd have fun if only she'd allow herself to and not keep worrying about what he did for a living. With a sigh Aaron snapped the last bag closed. He grabbed a copy of his latest book, *All for love*, by Lillie White.

The feel of the book in his hand brought a grin to his face, as always. He loved having taken on a female persona to break into the romance world. If only his woman had seen it as that. An unbearable ache filled him as he thought of the last time he'd touched her, the last time he'd held her, made love to her. An instant erection drew his attention and he moved his hand over the bulge giving his flesh a quick squeeze wishing he could bury himself inside the familiar warmth of his woman's body. Even if he had the time she wasn't home. Hell she was never home when he needed or wanted her. Something had to give he thought as his flesh gave a jerk in protest. Well, it was too late to worry about that now...now it was time to leave. He glanced at the wall clock then at the watch on his wrist, a present from his woman. Aaron gritted his teeth against the annoyance. This cruise was for change and he'd planned everything out to ensure that it was a fabulous time. He'd spent a damn fortune, twice the amount he should have paid.

Three bags filled with more clothes than were necessary and a tidy sum for the airlines for the overage charges dominated his thoughts. It was too late now to leave something behind. Besides, he had no real way of knowing what might be needed, he reasoned as he wheeled the bags down the stairs of his home and out into the double driveway to the waiting limo. This damn cruise had better be worth all the hell he'd gone through in the past months. He'd gotten mighty tired of begging and even more tired of not knowing the right thing to do.

Carmen walked up the gangplank, her papers and passport in her hand. She wondered about the smiling crew greeting her as if they knew her personally. Here and there she heard squealing women as they appeared to have found each other. *Must be friends*, she thought. Then her eye caught a huge red banner, and she noticed the flyer in her hand a crewmen had given her announcing a party. Romance Slam Jam Fifteenth Anniversary.

Oh Lord, what in the world was she doing on a ship that would undoubtedly be taken over by hundreds of romance readers and writers? She wasn't a diehard romance reader though she'd read a few. And granted, she was on this cruise partially to find romance. Still, she had her reasons for not wanting to be overrun by a ship filled with romance writers. Her stomach clenched. She'd promised to give new things a chance so she might as well begin by trying to put herself in the right frame of mind. *So be it*, she thought. As soon as her name was given to the crew, Carmen would no longer be using it. She was taking on a different persona. For the next five days she'd decided to be someone else. But who? She looked at the women rushing to get inside the ship and glanced once more at the banner. She wanted a name that sounded romantic, that would roll off a man's lips and sing over her skin. She wanted a name that wasn't her. Eva, Cindy, Niveah, ohh..., she liked Niveah. It had enough syllables that a man would be able to caress it if he said it correctly. That's it; she would be Niveah Cain for the duration of the cruise. What ever happened would happen to her and Carmen could walk away unscathed. She patted the bag on her hip that held two boxes of condoms. She almost grinned at the thought of the glow in the dark ones she'd bought on impulse. With a shrug she braced herself. Okay, this was it, she was here and it was too late to go home.

Greetings past, Carmen made her way to her cabin. Glancing around the room, she noted that her bags had been delivered. The open door of the closet revealed they'd been unpacked as well. Oh damn! She'd not wanted anyone to touch her things. Her face burned at the thought of the new crotchless panties she'd bought on a dare. Annoyance pulled at her features. She should have given better instructions.

Okay, she was here. Now what? She turned to look at her accommodations mentally calculating the cost of this little excursion. This was costing twice the amount it should have, *almost a sinful waste*, she thought. Then the knock on the door interrupted her thoughts.

A welcome gift.

Carmen stared in surprise as the tray was brought in. Dom Pérignon, fresh fruit, cheese and crackers and chocolates. Spotting the chocolate covered strawberries her taste buds went into overdrive instantly making her mouth water. She smiled again, reaching for her wallet to take out a ten. At this rate the tips would almost equal the cost of the trip.

Popping one of the strawberries in her mouth, she savored the flavor. *Good move*, she thought. Chocolate covered strawberries were one of her weaknesses. Glancing around the room Carmen stared at the double bed. It was covered in rose petals. She narrowed her eyes then smiled. Maybe the exorbitant amount spent on the cruise was going to be worth it after all. She hating admitting that she loved the room. It was much larger than expected.

Reaching for another strawberry Carmen bit into the juicy fruit and made her way into the bathroom. Her first thought, to shower and change and ease into her new skin. She would become Niveah Cain and knew just how to do it.

Aaron stood inside the main lounge. He'd been told it was the first one the passengers returned to after boarding. He'd been on the ship for hours, from the moment passenger had been allowed to board. He'd done the things on his to do list and returned to him own cabin to shower and change. Having a lot to do at times he'd wavered between annoyance and delight. *How could anyone not enjoy a cruise?* he wondered. It would be downright impossible, he decided and ordered his mind to think of more pleasant things. The weather was made to order as well as other things. He grinned in anticipation of the memories he would take away from this cruise. He wondered if he'd be able to use any of it in his next romance novel.

"L.W." The squeal of feminine voices made Aaron laugh. He shook his head at the women and opened his arms to them in a welcoming manner. Then he smiled his most provocative smile at the group of women rushing toward him. These were his fans, women who knew Lillie White was only a pseudonym but who enjoyed reading what he wrote. These were women who didn't think it took anything away from his manliness. Hell, how could it when everything about his writing screamed he loved women way too much to ever want to be one. But he did love being around them. As Aaron spoke with the women, he spotted Barbara Keaton and Lisa G. Riley coming toward him. This time the grin was larger and for real. "Hey ladies," he said hugging each of them

"Hey Lillie," Barb flirted a little, as always.

"Stop that right now. You know damn well my name's Aaron. Use it."

"But Lillie seems to suit you."

"Don't play," Aaron teased, "or you might find yourself in trouble."

"Please, brother man," Barb quipped right back.

"So, Lisa G, why are you so quiet? I hear you're up for an Emma this year for Best Hero. Good luck. You too, Barb, for Best Book."

"With all the writers I'm up against in my category, I stand a slim chance of winning it. But thanks for the good wishes. I guess as happy as I am about that I wish my book would have made it in some of the other contests I entered it into. I just don't like that it didn't final anywhere else."

"Well, you should have been listening to me." Barb rolled her eyes and got ready to deliver her famous lecture, ignoring the grin on Aaron's face and the please-don't-say-it-again look on Lisa's. "Ya'll's gots to stop thinking someone else's ice water is colder. It isn't."

"And you've got to stop talking like this; Ms. got two master's degrees, one in English. We both know what Lisa's talking about." Aaron turned his attention to Lisa. "Come on, Lisa G. It's going to be okay," Aaron crooned. "I rather like having Romance Slam Jam be a little known conference. And I like being one of the few males in the henhouse." No sooner had he said that than he was whisked away by a group of women. A thought lurked in his mind. This was what his woman was worried about. But this was about business, nothing more.

Carmen stood for a moment in the new crotchlesss panties. She'd promised, but she couldn't go through with it. She wasn't even sure if being Niveah would help with that. She ripped the underwear from her hips and tucked it into the back of the drawer. *Maybe later*, she thought, just not right now. Settling for the champagne colored silk blouse, she paired it with matching silk pants and reached for a regular pair of silk panties in the same muted color. *That feels better, more like me*, she thought as the feel of her silk underwear glided easily over her body. Gazing at herself in the mirror, she frowned. She was supposed to be going for different. She pulled the black mini skirt from the hanger and exchanged it for the pants. A smile graced her lips at her reflection in the mirror. This was different alright.

She made her way to the main lounge for the welcome aboard party feeling a little self-conscious at being alone, thinking that she must be standing out like a sore thumb. She almost turned to go back to her room but lifted her head as she felt the heat of a man's gaze upon her. She stared across the room at him and he smiled. Carmen's heart skipped a beat and the now constant ache between her thighs returned with a vengeance. As he made a move in her direction, she released the breath she was holding when a group of women surrounded the man and pulled him to a table with them.

A crazy sense of loss permeated her spirit and she gave herself a mental command. She would not turn tail and run. She would remain in this room and she would talk to people if they didn't talk to her. Thankfully, that wasn't the case. She bumped into someone and started to say she was sorry when a young woman in her mid-thirties smiled and put a postcard in her hand.

"Hi, my name's Abigail McKenley and my first book came out not too long ago. It's, Forbidden Masala."

"Congratulations," Carmen replied. "My name's...my name is Niveah...Niveah Cain."

Aaron was as nervous as a schoolboy about to go on his first date. He'd anticipated this cruise and its outcome for months. Every few seconds his gaze went to the entrance of the ballroom and every single time he'd swallowed down his disappointment. A strange electric current was emanating from somewhere in the room making the hairs on his arm stand at attention. Once again he searched the room, stopped and stared as a woman entered, obviously alone. She was uncomfortable, that much he could tell from across the room. His heart pounded with a primal beat. All of his blood pooled in one area and this time his hand was meant to cover his arousal, not relieve it. A groan came unbidden from him that quickly turned into a growl. Like a predatory animal his body laid claim to the woman. Need fought with common sense and lost. He was hard as a rock, not a good thing to be while cornered by so many women. Undoubtedly one of them would get the wrong idea if they looked down. As his penis remained at full mast a thread of caution returned. He stared hard at the woman. Was it her? Would she be able to give him what his heart and body needed? But there was something about her that made him wonder if he was wrong. She moved farther into the room and he perused her body, taking in her saucy hair cut.

Aaron stared opened-mouthed as he allowed his vision to skim quickly past the semi-low neckline of her blouse. Heat rushed through his body, settling in his center. He moaned deep in his throat and forced his gaze downward to her shapely legs, then back up to her miniskirt, a very short miniskirt. Damn. Need so intense it hurt reminded him of how long it had been since he'd last made love. The knowledge caused him to reach out a hand to the bar in order to steady himself. He'd found the woman he wanted to make love to.

A strange sense of possessiveness tore at Aaron as he watched several men walk up to her. He watched in annoyance as he saw her smile up at them. Glancing around the room his fingers tapped the bar when he saw several more men who hadn't yet worked up the courage to make their move, checking her out. He'd better hurry. He knew the beauty looking nervously about the room was the key to his having a good time on the cruise.

There was a beating in Aaron's chest that hadn't been there in a while. He wanted nothing more than to rush across the room, claim the woman for whose attention several men were now vying, pull her into his arms and kiss her senseless. But right now he was having a bit of trouble even moving toward her. With every step he took another woman, a fan, stopped him until suddenly he was totally surrounded by women. The one woman he wanted to be with was lost from view. He glanced frantically around and didn't see her. Perhaps she'd left the room, perhaps with another man. His heart sank. No, that wouldn't be the case, he knew that. She was there for him.

Aaron smiled at the group of women surrounding him. A breeze blew and a familiar sent filled his nostrils. He glanced at the women, knowing it didn't come from one of them. It was a unique blend of vanilla, lavender and cinnamon. He knew it well. He looked up suddenly and found her, the woman who had immediately caught his attention. Heat surged once again into his loins. For a moment he'd thought she was someone else and had almost turned away. It was the haircut that had fooled him. His gut told him she was the one with the signature scent he loved. He noted with pleasure that she was holding his gaze, smiling at him. Then just as suddenly a new group of women encircled the ones already there and he was swallowed up in a sea of femininity. He tried looking over their heads for the woman but she'd looked away and was walking away from him. Damn! Aaron didn't blame her. This was the second time they'd made a connection and the second time he'd been swarmed by women. He didn't think he'd get a third chance with her.

"Excuse me ladies," Aaron murmured and walked away toward the woman who'd caught and held his attention. When he drew near, he paused in disbelief at the reaction his body was having. Pure unadulterated lust wove its magic through his body. He shook his head slightly and sighed, glad that he wasn't wearing jeans. At least in his relaxed fit slacks, he had room for his rapidly burgeoning arousal. Never in his life had his body reacted so quickly to wanting someone. This woman was special, he knew that much. His heart pounding he walked up to her. The urge to fold her in his arms and kiss her was strong. He reached out, and as though she'd anticipated his lust, she reached for a glass from the tray of a passing waiter and shoved a champagne flute into his hand. He blinked, stared, then smiled.

"That was what you were looking for wasn't it?"

"Not really," Aaron said, "but I guess with all of these people standing here I'd embarrass us both if I did what I wanted." He stared at her, long and hard not hiding his desire or admiration. "I'm so glad you're on this cruise," Aaron said honestly. "It would not have been the same without you."

"Hold up."

Aaron waited, wondering what was coming.

"I have a specific reason for coming on this cruise."

"To meet me."

"Maybe," Carmen flirted, "but I came on this cruise to not be me, to loosen up, relax, and have an adventure. My old life hasn't been working as well as I'd like and for a few days I want to pretend. I've been told I need to make a change so I'm changing everything on this cruise, including my name."

He studied her, finally getting the message. He'd almost forgotten. With the amount of money he'd spent on this cruise, how could he possibly have forgotten. She'd just echoed one of his reasons for being on this particular cruise. His old life wasn't working so well either, but he had every intention of changing that. She moved her head slightly showing a generous expanse of tawny skin that went to the very top of her cleavage showed. Aaron moved away to observe the tiny miniskirt and the brown legs that were showing so beautifully beneath it. He lifted a brow. "How far are you planning to stray from your regular life?" he asked.

"Not as far as you might think."

He laughed. "That's good to know. So, you're not here for totally new options, just a few changes." He looked again at her miniskirt, and the sassy cut of her hair and he felt himself stiffen even more. Then he took in a breath, pulling her scent into his lungs. He was a goner. That scent alone would have snagged him, but her throaty, flirty voice and beautiful brown legs made him want to pick her up and take her back to his cabin or hers, whichever she preferred, and it was enough to make him—

Laughter broke through Aaron's lustful thoughts and he grinned. "You're laughing at me. Are you a mind reader?"

"Not generally, but you're pretty easy to read." Carmen stuck out her hand and smiled. "This is the way I want to start this. Hello, nice to meet you," she laughed again at the initials on his name badge. So your name is just initials? L.W.?"

"What's your name?" Aaron pressed.

"Niveah...Niveah Cain." She watched the way his lips curved into a gentle smile before his eyes twinkled and he stared at her.

"Niveah. I like it."

And she liked the way he'd caressed it. *Nice choice*, she thought. "What's your name?" she asked. She searched his face, knowing the name he would give would be fake, just as the one she'd given him. But so what? They were on an adventure, so why not?

"My name's Rick...Rick Jame—"

"Rick James, you've got to be kidding. L.W does not equal Rick James."

"I was going to say Rick Jameson but you interrupted me with your laughter." He tilted his head slightly. "I like the sound of your laughter. It's nice." He studied her. "I also like your hair. You almost reminded me of someone."

Carmen ran her hand over her newly shorn locks. "Your woman?" she asked.

Their gazes met and held but he didn't answer. "What do you do for a living, Niveah?"

"I'm a real-estate investor. I buy up all kinds of property all over the country. And you?"

"I'm a romance writer." He pointed across the room at a group of women eyeing him. "A lot of those women are on this cruise to see me." He gave her a self deprecating smile and added, "along with about a hundred other African-American romance authors, that is."

"You use the name Rick Jameson, in your writing?"

"No, I'm using Rick just for you. In my writing I use the name Lillie White."

"Ahh... L.W. Now I see. Why a woman's name?"

Aaron pursed his lips, observing her eyes, waiting for them to perhaps change with distaste perhaps. "Generally the writing of the genre is mostly done by women and to get in I decided to write using a pseudonym to get women to read my work, to trust me. I know about women and what most of them want," he said casually.

"Do you really?"

"Well, I try but you know how it is. The person you want to know you the best somehow is always excluded from that group. Not only are they not impressed by what you do but they are a bit annoyed with the time that you have to put into a public career. A lot of women can't handle it...having other women fawn over their man," he said, watching her eyes. "I guess it would be hard unless the woman trusted the man completely and knew that he loved her in spite of all the women standing around him."

Carmen swallowed. "Tall order," she said, "but I guess if the woman loved the man the same way, she'd try."

Before Aaron could answer her, he was grinning at the sudden intrusion of Barb as she stood there planted between them. It was obvious from the way she was staring at him that she was attempting to keep him out of trouble. She'd never met his woman but somehow felt it her duty to make sure he didn't stray. Later, he'd tell her a secret. This trip was to end his old life. He didn't need her to have his back on this one. If everything went according to plan he'd soon leave behind the life he'd led for the past few months. His gaze landed on Niveah, the soft smile that played around her lips, the slight suspicion in her eyes as she waited for him to introduce her.

"Niveah Cain, this is Barbara Keaton, my friend and one of my favorite romance authors."

"What about me?" Lisa asked, pretending to pout.

Aaron turned from Niveah and smiled at Lisa. "I said one of my favorites, not 'the' favorite or the only writer I like. You see what I have to contend with?" he playfully asked Niveah. but he could tell her smile was forced. She was uncomfortable. He made quick work of the introductions. Two seconds before he would have asked them to leave, Lisa got the message and turned to go tugging on Barb's hand taking her away.

"Can't you tell he wants us gone?" Lisa had said, rolling her eyes.

"But I want to stay," Barb laughed. "I want to talk to Niveah, too."

"Whatever Barb," Lisa said and walked away with Barb, laughing.

"Your friends seem awfully protective of you."

What was she thinking? Aaron wondered. He sighed and teased his top lip with his tongue before deciding the best way to answer Niveah's question. "We all look out for each other when we're at conferences. Sometimes there are fans that come on a little strong. We're there to remind each other that we have our real lives waiting for us after we leave the conference and not to mess up." He sighed. "But I'm here to let go of my old life, remember? They just don't know that yet. They don't mean any harm, though. They're just trying to be my friend, make sure I don't mess up."

"And they think you'd be messing up with me?"

"It really doesn't matter what they think does it? I'm right where I want to be, sitting here with you."

"You're on this cruise to network."

"Only partly. Mostly I'm here to get my shit together." He shrugged. "Sorry. I'm here to make needed changes in my life, to remember how it feels to be happy." He held her gaze then reached for her hand. "I want to be happy again. Don't you want to be happy?"

Aaron looked at Carmen's left ring finger and found it empty. He frowned slightly, his question forgotten. "No encumbrances, I see."

"Not on this trip," she replied. "How about you?"

"As much as I might not like it, the truth is that I have no one sharing my cabin." He grinned then. "But who knows, maybe before the end of the cruise...maybe even tonight." He slid his left hand into the pocket of his slacks. After a few moments, Aaron brought his hand back out and smiled at her. "I like the way you're planning to spend your time on the cruise. I think I like the part about no encumbrances. I don't know about you but I know I want to make love to you," he leaned over and whispered into her ear." He held up his hand. "Don't get offended at the truth. We only have a few days on this ship. We're adults with no ties." He held up his left hand for her inspection. "Why should we sleep alone?"

"The one thing I've never done is hop in bed with a man straight off the bat. Call me old fashioned, call me a prude, but that's who I am."

"This trip is costing a fortune." The moment the words were out Aaron knew he'd made a big mistake. He could feel her freezing him out as her eyes narrowed into slits. He rushed to explain. "This trip is costing a fortune and worth every penny. I would have paid three times the amount just to have you smile at me the way you did when we first met."

"Nice save," Niveah shook her head and laughed.

"You're beautiful, Niveah."

"Thank you. I find you very handsome. I love the dimples in your cheeks, your beautiful dark brown eyes and long lashes. I even like your short cropped hair." She grinned. And you're just over 6 feet. The perfect height for me."

"I'm glad."

"Me, too."

"You smell wonderful, Niveah. What's the scent?"

"It was a gift. It's a blend of lavender, vanilla and cinnamon." She smiled. "It's my favorite scent. I'm glad you like it." She picked up her Coke and took a long cool drink as she stared at the man in front of her. She could see why women were attracted to him.

Even with the female moniker he exuded sexuality, a strong chin, straight white teeth, and a killer smile with dimples so deep that she got the shivers just thinking what she'd like to do with him. And his voice, smooth as velvet. He had her already. Her panties were wet and would become wetter still if he continued staring at her as though she were a tasty morsel he couldn't wait to put into his mouth.

Now watching him sitting with her, she was aware that it wouldn't take much for him to have her eating out of his hands. If he kept flirting as he talked to her she'd melt. An ache to be filled with a man's hot arousal zinged through her with the speed of a train. She found herself wanting to touch him, to have him touch her, to run his huge hands across her body and make her nerve endings sing. She wanted his fingers to burrow through her wetness and fan the flame. Her legs clamped together of their own accord as she felt her pulse beat from below. He moved his hand to touch hers and a moan slid from between her lips.

"L.W., can you come over to Evelyn Palfrey's table for a moment? There are a group of aspiring authors that want to meet you."

Carmen looked up to see Barbara, the writer he'd introduced her to earlier and she took another drink of Coke knowing that Rick, L.W. or whatever his name was would leave with the writer. Regret was in his eyes, she noticed as his glance speared hers. Still, he was rising from the chair. "Come with me," he offered.

"No, I don't think so," she responded wondering if his disappointment was real or part of his carefully constructed façade. "I don't mind, really. You're a writer. You came on this trip to interact with your fans and peers. Please don't let me stop you or I'll feel guilty."

"Are you sure you don't mind? You're not lying, are you?"

"I don't mind, and no, I'm not lying."

206

"Are you angry?" He searched her face, his eyes locking with her. Resignation was what he saw in her eyes. For a moment he'd rather he have seen anger.

"Babe."

She glared.

"I'm sorry," he said quickly. "Niveah, if you don't want me to leave, I won't."

Damn, if that didn't sound like what it was. He was torn and he shouldn't have been. He wanted to remain with Niveah. But he knew he needed to talk to his fans as well. "Niveah," he said, holding her hand, caressing it. She brought her eyes up and their gazes locked. The resignation remained but this time she smiled.

"Go do your job, Rick. You're not the only one on this ship looking for a change. I told you that. I'm letting go of a lot of things. I didn't come here to pick up more bad habits. If you stayed with me now, neither of us would like it. We'll catch up with each other later."

"What are you going to do?"

"This is a huge ship with a ton of activities. Trust me, I can find something to do. Now go." She shoved him gently in the direction of the table where Barb was beckoning him. "Go talk to the aspiring authors and I'll see you later."

Aaron took a few steps away then turned and called out, "Don't eat, wait for me. Have dinner with me?"

Carmen smiled. It was a nice gesture but an unnecessary one. And judging from the crowd quickly gathering around him one he wouldn't be allowed to do. She hadn't come on this cruise to monopolize the time of a romance writer. A sigh slipped out, unbidden. Wishful thinking aside, she wanted to have a good time on this cruise. Although that was her sentiment she couldn't keep her eyes from following Rick's cool, sleek panther 'like' walk. She loved the way his body moved. Heat flared in her nether regions when he turned as if knowing she was watching, and smiled at her. He had her body wanting to do somersaults. Enough staring. Carmen picked up her glass and made her way to the deck wishing for a moment that she really was Niveah Cain and that she was a part of the romance writers' cruise. She leaned against the rail, listening to the water lapping against the boat. Glancing out at the moon she smiled. *A beautiful sight*, she thought, *a moon made for lovers.*

Making her way her way back toward her cabin a disgusted snort came from Carmen over her foolishness. Why had she bothered thinking a full moon would give her her heart's desire? A lover's moon was made to be shared with a lover. Maybe she'd go back out later, perhaps after.... She smiled at his made-up name. Maybe after Rick had talked to his fans she'd come back out. She wanted to be where he'd find her.

Apparently her mind had been on Rick more than it should have. She walked right into a group of women, bumping hard into one. "I'm sorry," she said. "I wasn't watching where I was going." She pulled back and saw the women all wore huge badges with their names. She groaned inwardly and tried to walk around them. "Again, I'm sorry," she said, moving away.

"You have nothing to be sorry for. You were with L.W weren't you? He's gorgeous."

That stopped Carmen dead in her tracks. "You're here for the romance conference?"

"Yes, aren't you?"

Carmen stared at the woman's name badge for a moment. "No, I'm not, Brenda."

"Then why were you with Lillie?"

How she wanted to tell them, but the urge to tell Brenda none of her business had to be dealt with first. Carmen counted to ten before shrugging.

"I've seen him at a few conferences and I've never seen him looking at any woman the way he was looking at you," Brenda said as she studied Carmen. "In fact, I haven't seen him looking at any woman. Brother man is fine and all, but you know he was beginning to make me wonder."

Relief at hearing that Rick wasn't a playa flooded her system. Now to address the belief he might be gay. "Don't wonder," Carmen replied, "he's not."

"Guess not," the woman laughed, taking no offense at the possessiveness in Carmen's voice.

Carmen stared at the women. "So you all know L.W. well, huh? Maybe you can tell me something about him. I'm Niveah Cain," she said, sticking out her hand.

"I'm Viola Brown but my pen name is Mimi Tremont."

"I'm Brenda Willis. I write under A.M. Wells. I have my first book coming out soon. It's title, Susanna's Heart. Also if you check on line you'll see the book trailer I did for Romance Slam Jam."

"I'm Laverne Thompson. I won the aspiring author's contest in 08 and now I'm up for an Emma in favorite new author. You know, L.W. is up for several awards. I think he's going to win. I know I voted for him."

A shiver of doubt rushed in. He hadn't told her.

"I know you must have voted for him," Brenda said.

"I'm not here for the conference. I'm here for the cruise. I came alone," Carmen shrugged.

"Well, you're not alone anymore." Brenda grabbed one arm and Viola the other and they introduced her to at least fifteen other women who had gathered: Patricia, Stephanie, Savannah, Kiki, Crystal, and Seressia. So many names that Carmen knew there was no way she'd remember them all.

Feeling a bit overwhelmed by the women Carmen had to ask. "Do you ladies belong to a book club?"

"You might say that," Viola spoke up. We have an online MSN group, the Interracial Multicultural Romance Readers group. If you're interested, you can join us."

"We'll see, but out of all of my relationships none have been interracial." Carmen smiled. "If things work out with L.W. the way I think they will, I won't have anything to add to an interracial discussion."

"Do you read?" Viola asked.

"Do you believe in love and romance?" Brenda put in.

"Yes, to both of you."

"Then you'd fit in. Now come on and let's go check this tugboat out," Patricia ordered.

Carmen couldn't help smiling. The last thing she'd expected was to be befriended by a group of romance readers and writers. Maybe it was fate. If she was going to be in a relationship with a romance writer, what better way to get to know him than through his fans and peers?

Chapter Two

Aaron thought now as he had many times in the past that he'd had to make many trade-offs in his career spending time with his woman had suffered. No wonder she'd always refused to accompany him to his conferences. He thought of Niveah, a beautiful woman he'd enjoyed talking to and like always he was whisked away to do something else, to do promo. He checked his watch. Damn, where had the time gone? He'd left Niveah over three hours ago and he wondered what she'd been doing. He thought of the short miniskirt she'd been wearing and an unprecedented growl came from his throat. He had to find her.

He'd promised himself this trip would be different. He needed to relax, to find some time for intimate conversation, for quality loving. That wasn't going to happen if he didn't make it happen. He'd seen Niveah as she'd made her way out to the deck of the main ballroom hours ago, her luscious curves swaying, making him want to grab hold of her and kiss her, beg her on his knees to let him make love to her. He held little hope that she'd still be there but it was at least a place to start. *How would my hero win her over?* Aaron wondered. He glanced at a waiter carrying glasses of champagne and snagged two, carrying them out to the deck. Never in his entire life had he wanted a woman so badly and never had he ever made a move on one so quickly. But this was a short cruise, only five days. As his groin tightened, he knew he wanted to spend the night, every night, with Niveah. He wanted to be in his bed or hers with their arms wrapped around each other. They'd figure out the consequences later, after the cruise was over. He spotted her almost instantly and just stood behind her, observing her silhouette in the darkness. She was beautiful. Something was stirring in his heart and his loins. Lust yes, but something more. This woman, Niveah, was what his life needed. It had been over a month since he'd made love to his woman, a month of traveling from city to city. The last time they'd seen each other, they'd fought over his being gone until it was time for him to leave again. That was not a way to have a successful relationship. Maybe it was time to end what they'd had and try something new. Aaron tamped down the guilt that tried to rise up. *Why not*, he thought. If the old no longer fit it was definitely time to get rid of it.

"Hey again," he said sidling up to Niveah and handing her a flute of champagne. "Here, I thought you'd like something other than

Coke."

"I didn't expect to see you again tonight."

For a long moment he stared, trying hard not to glare at her, but he couldn't help it. "Why would you think that? I asked you to have dinner with me."

"But your fans...they take up so much of your time." She glanced at her watch but didn't mention the time.

"You could be a part of this," he said softly.

"I don't see how..." she shrugged. "It's too late anyway. These women paid for the conference. I didn't."

"You can attend the luncheon and the awards dinner. Those are the only official things I have to do, then the rest of the time is mine."

"Why didn't you tell me you were up for awards?"

"I didn't want it to influence any of your decisions. I want you to be with me because you want to be no place else. I don't want you to feel you must hold my hand in sympathy if I should not win. Still, as for the awards, now that you know, now that you're here, I'd love to spend that time with you. In fact, I'd love to spend every moment that we have left on this cruise with you."

Carmen laughed and shook her head. This was not going to happen. She turned and saw Barbara Keaton walking toward them, and smiled. "You sure she's not your woman?"

"She's a friend, a good friend, nothing more."

She wondered why he sounded so offended. Who wouldn't wonder? Every time they were alone, Barb had managed to find them. "I think I'll just have dinner in my room," Carmen said softly. She turned to leave and his hand captured hers. "Please don't," he pleaded. "Have dinner with me. I promise it will be uninterrupted."

"This is your career. You need to do this. Don't allow me to monopolize your time."

"There you're wrong. I want to monopolize your time. I've seen the way the men on the ship have been eying you." Aaron smiled. "I don't like it." He eyed her miniskirt but didn't say anything.

Carmen wanted to tell him that she didn't like the way women flocked to him, but she refused to allow the words to pass her lips. He was a rarity, a male romance writer who'd come on a conference cruise alone. She was only a woman who'd decided to take a cruise and found herself surrounded by bright blue skies, dark, blue. water and a man with dark brown eyes that made her body ache with want. It had been a while. She shook her head and bit back the retort, waiting to see how he'd handle the situation.

"L.W." Barb said, "what are you doing out here? Everybody's looking for you. We were thinking we'd all eat a late dinner together."

Aaron could feel Niveah trying to tug her hand away from his and he held on tighter. "Thanks, but I'm having dinner with Niveah."

"Okay, go ahead, brother. I ain't mad at you. You do know Niveah is welcome to join us right?"

"I know," Aaron replied, "but I think I'd like to spend the first night of the cruise alone with her, looking at this beautiful moon."

Aaron and Barb pounded fists and Barb grinned at Niveah. "Go 'head, sister," she said and laughed as she walked away.

"You didn't have to do that," Niveah said. "I really don't mind you doing what you're on this ship to do."

"Really?"

"Really." Niveah whispered softly expecting him to leave.

He took the glass from her hand and placed it on the rail. "Then with your permission, I'll do what I've wanted to do since I spotted you." With that he kissed her softly, exploring her lips with his tongue, enjoying the warmth of her mouth. She moaned softly and swallowed hard. Apparently it had been as long for her as it had for him. Her arms stayed at her sides but he was determined to change that. He pulled her close. The moment her hip touched his pelvis, he couldn't have stopped his erection if he'd been paid to. He felt her pulling away but held her close.

"Not now," Aaron moaned, "don't make me beg." He was amazed that those were the words that made her drop her defenses and wrap her arms around him. It was definitely time to let go of the old. *Niveah could very well be my future*, he thought as he deepened the kiss. She felt comfortable, familiar yet unknown and he was content. He sighed happily. He was home.

Aaron pushed away from the small dining table set up in Niveah's room. Having dinner in was a good idea. He glanced at her. She was smiling at him and he wondered if the wine had the same effect on her that it had on him. What with the kisses they'd shared and looking at her the entire time they ate, he was hotter than hell.

"Niveah, how many dates do you think it would take before you'd allow me to spend the night?" Her mouth opened into an 'O' of surprise. "Since the moment I spotted you today I haven't been able to think of anything but how much I wanted to make love to you." He waited for her to speak but she kept silent. "Okay... then I guess the first date doesn't work for you." He kissed her lightly on the lips then left the room.

Still seated, Niveah was speechless. What had just happened? One moment she'd been enjoying the company of a very handsome, erotic man, and the next he'd kissed her and left her. She glanced back at her bed. Alone.

A knock on the door shattered the quiet and brought her out of her reverie. Who the heck could want to see her at this hour? Paranoia danced along her spine and she went to the door reaching for her heavy purse on the bedside table with one hand while sliding the chain over the latch with the other. "Who is it?" she asked, not opening the door.

"Rick," came the baritone reply.

With a grin, Carmen opened the door and stood back. "Did you forget something?" she asked.

He stared at her for a moment then shook his head, his tongue worrying one spot on his upper lip. "Did I not tell you how to play this game?" he asked, pushing the door open wider and coming into the room. "No matter. Niveah, this is date number two." He looked at the tray that was still in the room. "I thought we'd have drinks for our second date and talk."

"You're trying to get me drunk."

"Not drunk," he replied, "just relaxed. I would never want a woman to not know what she was doing with me, or in a position to resist if she wanted to." He smiled. "Don't worry, I won't let you go past your limit. Actually, I'm more in the mood for conversation than for wine."

Carmen's brow lifted. "Yeah, right."

"Okay, I'm in the mood for other things, too. But right now for this second date, I want to talk."

"When do you anticipate there being a third date?"

"Oh, about fifteen or twenty minutes after I leave. Do you think I'll be able to make love to you then?" He held up a finger. "I've decided to let nature lead me while I'm on this cruise, to let go of things in my life that aren't working for me. I'd imagine since you're here alone that you're perhaps in the same predicament. Are you?"

She thought about it for a moment, then answered. "You're right, I am. This cruise was meant for me to let go of the past and try to embrace the present and future. I've been a bit uptight and untrusting in my relationships. I'm trying to change."

"You know the changes you make here on the ship don't have to be permanent. Anything that doesn't work, you can drop the moment the ship docks and you return home. What do you think?" Aaron took her hand and pulled her to the door of the balcony to continue their conversation outside. "My cabin isn't nearly as nice as yours. But then, you're a woman and I guess it's only right that you have a roomier cabin."

"I think I'd like to check yours out later just to know that you're not lying." Carmen said looking at him thoughtfully.

Aaron's tone turned serious. "I'd never lie to you," he said. He laid her hand over his heart. "Don't you know that? Don't you trust me?"

"You're a romance writer. That means you know the right thing to say. I think you probably always do."

"Apparently, I don't know the right thing to say when it counts. Maybe by date number four I won't need to talk as much. Perhaps my loving your body will speak for me."

Mercy. Rick was good. Niveah almost swooned. He was very good. Maybe she'd have to read some more of his work. "Okay, just remember this is the second date not the fourth." The chuckle that started deep in his throat turned her knees to liquid butter. He was right. She was on the cruise to not be what or who she'd been. It was time to live a little although maybe she was moving faster than she wanted, knowing once they'd made love he'd return to his cabin or possibly to the adoring fans, that would be waiting for him. His hand slid along her arm sizzling the bare flesh and she decided not to worry about later. She'd just concentrate on now.

The sea breeze caressed them as they stood on the balcony, cooling their bodies, but doing nothing for the heat that flared steadily in her nether regions.

"Do you mind if we have a very serious conversation? I know we're both trying something new, taking on different personas, but somehow I feel the need to take this deeper," Aaron said. "I want you to know all there is to know about me and I want to know all there is to know about you. Are you happy in your life, Niveah?"

The question wasn't altogether unexpected. She shrugged. If she were happy she wouldn't be alone on a cruise. She stared at him. "Why don't you tell me first? Are you happy in your life, Rick?"

"Mostly," he replied, taking a sip from his glass. "I thought I had everything I wanted but found my professional and private life was having a hard time meshing. You see, I do a lot of traveling. I go to a lot of conferences." He ran his finger slowly down the side of her cheek, lingering, enjoying the feel of satiny smooth skin. "It's made for a lot of problems and pain."

Licking her lips, Carmen replied, "Separation can be hard on any relationship. I think I understand what you mean, though. In my job, I also have to travel a lot. You're right; not being home when you should be is stressful."

"Do you like what you do?"

"I like it but more importantly it puts food on the table and money in the bank at intervals I can count on." Carmen took in a deep breath as she watched a frown come to Rick's face, and saw the look that came into his eyes. "It's stable and I like stability. I have a job where the money is mostly steady."

"Mostly?"

"Well, you know what I'm talking about. The housing market has been taking a beating for the last few years. Still, I've managed to do pretty well."

"Money, is it that important to you?"

"Paying my bills is important to me, not getting kicked out of my home is important to me." Her spine stiffened and his did as well. She put down the flute no longer interested in champagne.

"I make extremely good money," Aaron said through gritted teeth. "I pay my bills on time." He tried his best not to become angry, but she'd touched on a sore subject with him. "There's no danger of me losing my home. I felt your comment was a direct dig at me and my profession. Was it, or was I reading things into it that weren't there?"

Carmen wondered how to answer him. His steely gaze demanded the truth. The unfulfilled need burning between her thighs urged her to temper the truth a bit. "My intent was not to insult you or any writers. Reading is my favorite pastime, so that alone tells you I enjoy what you do for a living. I even like the occasional romance. I have a copy of your latest book by the way. I bought it at the airport." She saw the self-satisfied grin and knew she was on the right track.

"Are you enjoying it so far?"

"I am."

"Is that the reason you made the remark?"

This time Carmen decided the truth would be the best answer. "You said we were both on this cruise to let go of things that weren't working in our lives. I agree. You asked me if I were happy and I was trying to think of the things in the past that have made me..." she hesitated, "not unhappy, but concerned. Writing, to me, is a dream dependent on the whims of so many people, the editors, publisher and then the readers."

"Your profession is dependent on more things than mine, Niveah. The state of the economy, the government bailout," he snorted. "I think I'd rather worry about readers any day than be dependent on the government."

"Ouch."

Aaron paused and took inventory of the woman sitting beside him. Chestnut brown complexion, huge, luminous dark eyes and the sweetest, most kissable lips he'd ever had the good fortune to taste. He glanced at her short hair and smiled, then he stared at her, wondering if she knew what just sitting and talking with her was doing to him. "I'd say both of our jobs have their flaws and are undependable. I have a degree in education, though." He looked at her hard. "Should I have to, I could teach for a living, a safe living. I did it for a number of years. I didn't give my dream a try until I thought the future was safe, with money in the bank, all the creature comforts." He shrugged. "I'd received my third contract and my third whopping advance, more than enough to pay off the mortgage on my house. I wasn't the one who didn't want to pay it off." He paused, wincing at the memory of the fight that had ensued over whether to keep the money in the bank or pay off the mortgage. "I didn't gamble with the future. What other objections do you have with my being a writer?"

"I didn't say I had a problem with your writing. I was speaking in generalities."

"But it's me that's sitting here with you right this moment, watching while the moonlight makes your soft skin appear even softer. It's giving you a glow to you that makes you look angelic. I'm being as honest as I can with you. Can't you do the same for me? Tell me what you have against my being a romance writer. Would it be better if I wrote thrillers or mysteries?"

Carmen's eyes shuttered and she felt sadness washing over him, then her, in waves. He was opening up to her and she'd vowed that she was ready to let go of past hurts, past wrongs. "I've had many pretty words muttered to me during my life. I was to have gone on a cruise years ago, a honeymoon cruise. My fiancée couldn't make the cruise because his career came first. He told me to take one of my friends since it was paid for." She took in a deep breath and let it out, hard. "Watching you today, I saw the charisma that you exuded. I guess it's not an altogether bad thing. It was your charm that made me notice you. It's probably that same charisma that makes you a good writer. You seem to know the inner workings of relationships."

"Again, not very well. Right now, all I want to do is kiss you senseless, make love to you, kiss you from the tip of your toes to the top of your head, and I've spent the whole time defending my career." He smiled. "That is so not the way I want this cruise to go. I have a proposition for you." He hit her playfully as she quirked a pretty brow. "Not that," he said. "I've been under stress for a long time now. I'm

216

making mistake after mistake with no idea of what to do next. I do know that I could use a few days of rest. How about you?"

She couldn't help herself. Carmen smiled back at him. "I could use some of that rest you speak of. My life has also been stressful."

"Okay, how about if for the remainder of the cruise, we relieve our stress in each other?" He saw her fidgeting, likely wanting to say no, to maybe usher him out of her room, but he plowed on. "After the cruise, there is always time to assess our lives, see what we want to do after. I'd be willing to fulfill a fantasy for you during this cruise if you'd fulfill one of mine."

"That depends on what your fantasy is," Carmen answered, allowing her suspicion to show in the tone of her voice.

"I want to share this part of my life with you. I want you to meet all of my writer friends, sit at my side during the speeches, dance with me in the evenings and sing karaoke with me."

"Sing karaoke. I can't carry a tune."

"I'm not worried if you can carry a tune. I just want you to sing with me. Will you do it? Will you share this part of my life with me while we're on this cruise?"

What he was asking seemed such an easy thing. Carmen swallowed, some little part of her remembering past hurts. She had to let go of all of that. "You're willing to give me my fantasy?"

"Yes."

"I want quality time." His hand stilled and he moved away. She stared at him. "I didn't say quantity. I'm not asking you not to do what you came on this cruise to do, mix and mingle, network, see your friends. I'm just telling you that if you want me to fulfill your fantasy for the next four days, that I'm willing, if you're willing to fulfill mine."

"Define quality."

"Men and women really do have a different way of speaking, don't they?" She gave him a brittle chuckle. "Have you ever read the language of love?" She continued without waiting for his answer. "Basically, what it boils down to is that people have different ways of needing their needs met, some by touch, service, words, or quality time. Mine is quality time. I hear the words all the time, the, 'I love you,' but ...." She closed her eyes. "On this cruise, I'd love to have quality time with you like we have it now, talking and actually listening to each other without recriminations, just trying to find what works for both of us.

Just then his hand snaked out and he caressed her face with the pad of his finger. "You look like you're hurting. Are you?"

"Maybe just a little."

"Do you think my suggestion on how to spend this cruise will hurt you more?"

"I don't think so...but I don't know if you can just pull me along to a conference I didn't pay for."

"You let me worry about that. Deatri King-Bey is in charge of Romance Slam Jam. She won't mind."

"Have you done this before?" she asked. The light went out of his eyes and joy followed. For a moment, he didn't speak. He rested his elbow on the arm of the deck chair and placed his chin in the palm of his hand, worrying it with his finger, staring at her.

"I've never done this before," he finally said, "and I've never wanted to." He reached for her hand and gave her fingers a squeeze. "The language of love that you spoke of, mine would be touch. I feel loved with a caress, with a kiss, with making love." His eyes burned into hers. "It's been over a month since I've made love. Right now, I could use your touch to heal what hurts."

"You're good."

"I can be better."

Aaron pulled her up from the chair, lifted her in his arms, and headed back into the cabin.

"I thought you were going to wait until the third date."

A groan followed a chuckle, and he eased her to the floor, his hands lingering on her hips. "Niveah, tell me you don't want me to walk out that door."

"No, I don't want you to walk out that door. But I do want that third date first." She pulled his head down to hers. "You said the third date would take place fifteen to twenty minutes after you left the room, Rick. Good things are worth waiting for. Besides, I'd like to shower. She put her hand on his chest and gently pushed him toward the door. "I'll see you in twenty minutes." He groaned. "If you get waylaid by your friends and return late I suggest you remain with them. I won't come second." She caught the first gleam of annoyance as anger quickly flared in his eyes. "You said you've been missing something, well, so have I. You asked me to be a part of your world for the next few days and I've agreed."

Carmen almost censored what she wanted to say, but didn't. "I don't want every second of your time but I won't come second." She shook her head. "I've done that too many times in my life. I'm not doing it any longer."

"I'll be back," he said firmly, "and on time."

Aaron stood outside the door to Niveah's cabin for a couple of moments, banging his head soundly against the door. Why had he given her a time? Those words had just rolled from his lips. Something to say. He hadn't even known she was paying attention. But of course she had. She was a woman, and women were indeed complicated creatures. She wanted him as badly as he wanted her but she was intent on playing out this game, making him adhere to the rules they'd set. Okay, he'd asked her to be a part of his life for the cruise and he'd told her he wanted her. *What more do I have to do?* he wondered, get down on my knees and beg. *If need be,* a voice answered him. Niveah opened the door and stared at him.

"Anything wrong?" she asked.

"Just wondering how I got myself in this fix. I'll see you in a few."

With a sigh of exasperation, Aaron almost ran to his cabin to shower as well. Ten minutes to the good, he was making his way back to Niveah's cabin. He groaned when he saw Lisa and Barb approaching him.

"Hey, Lillie," Barb called out. "Man, where you been?"

"Spending quality time with a beautiful woman," he answered, not bothering to slow down and shoot the breeze. Barb was a good friend but they were only friends, nothing more, no romance, and tonight he needed romance. He needed to be touched in the act of love. There was no way he was going to be late. He sprinted into a run. *No damn way will I be late,* he thought as he knocked on Niveah's door a couple of minutes later, out of breath.

"You're early."

"Actually I'm much later than I wanted to be," he said, and kicked the door closed with his foot. He stood for a moment, gazing at creamy brown flesh peeking from the silky peach negligee she was wearing. It hadn't been necessary—he was already hot. He turned back to the door bolted it, took out his cell looked at her and powered it off. "Quality time," he said. "No interruptions."

Carmen had not expected him to return on time. She'd had a glimpse into his world and saw the demand on his time. She wondered if he'd been late, would she really have not allowed him in. Giving herself a mental shrug, she let go of what ifs. They didn't matter. He'd returned and she was more than willing to be Niveah Cain and see what life held in store for the fictional character for the remainder of the cruise.

His eyes were appraising her, sending heat to her cells, rewriting her DNA code so that she would forever remember him. He smiled, flashing his deep dimples, then he pulled her into his arms and kissed her, soft gentle kisses, not pushing anything on her that she wasn't ready for. He moved her backwards toward the bed, removing his hand for only a moment to pull the cashmere sweater from his body.

Carmen drew in a breath at the sight of his naked chest. She understood how Rick felt. A month was a long time. It had been a little over a month for her as well. A surprised gasp came from her as he pushed her gently down on the bed and fell next to her, bringing her body in alignment with his own. He found her breast and pressed his mouth to the nipple as he suckled her. The intense pleasure rocked her to her core and her muscles tightened. Her hand found the snap of his pants and she dived eagerly inside. touching him, teasing the hard length of him. He shuddered at her touch and that gave her pleasure. It told her it had been some time for him, that he was telling the truth. He raised his hips making it easy for her to slide the pants from his beautiful masculine body.

Carmen leaned on her elbow to better observe him. She was salivating at the sight of him. He had the firmness of a heavy laborer, not of a writer. His hips were lean, his legs corded with muscle. She could feel power emanating from him and a deep moan took her. She could imagine this man becoming the center of her world, of getting lost in him and losing herself. She couldn't do this. This cruise was about reinventing herself. His hand slid beneath the flimsy gown and she tried hard to remember she didn't want to become lost to his touch. But she was already addicted, there was no denying that. He touched and she burned. The need was there between them, raw. She would have expected them to go at it fast and hard but they didn't. He was taking it extraordinarily slow.

"For the first time, we could just go ahead and do it," Carmen said slowly, "then we can take our time after."

"This isn't about quantity but quality," he whispered softly, feeling her urgency. "You deserve to be treated as the precious gift that you are. You're second to no one and nothing. I want to make love to you slowly and show you that." Aaron chuckled, his voice made harsh by his need. "That was a lie. Right at this moment I want to be inside you, feeling your heat. But that's the urgency of the moment, and damn baby, it might not even be near to quality if I did that. So in a way, I'm taking it slow for both of us so I can breathe again. Okay?"

"Okay," Carmen agreed, as though she hadn't wanted to. She almost thought to tell him that she no longer wanted to pretend to be Niveah Cain, that it didn't matter, that for now they could ease the fever, ease the pain. But if she did that, she'd be telling him that he could go back on their agreement, that she didn't matter. And she did matter. She had to matter. Within seconds they were divested of the rest of their clothes.

"I have something," Carmen nearly purred, reaching into the bedside table and pulling out a handful of assorted condoms.

"Glow in the dark?" Aaron picked one up and gave her a curious look. "It looks like you came on this cruise loaded for bear. I'm glad I'm the one in here with you."

"So am I," Carmen all but purred and lay back. She moved her hand slowly over his body, shivering as his moved over her. He touched her core and she jumped. It had been so long, a month too long. He moved over her, trailing kisses from her eyelids to her nose, a soft one on the corners of her lips, her neck.

Mercy, she was hot. Then he began using his tongue, creating liquid heat along the path he was blazing. The side of her neck tensed and the shiver reached clear to her womb. Still he lingered and continued. He was killing her, but it felt so good. He kissed the base of her neck moving his tongue in the hollow of her throat, nipping her gently, his hand below stoking the fires. She felt the insertion of one, then two and ohhh, three fingers and she moaned grinding her pelvis upwards as he took her right nipple into his mouth and suckled her, pulling and teasing, treating her as though she were his queen and he was worshiping her body.

Carmen pushed back memories of anything but now. She wanted this with everything that was in her. It was right. She was glad she'd agreed to his proposition to go with her feelings on this cruise, to liberate her body and her mind, to be sexually satisfied and think not about the missed opportunities, or the canceled honeymoon.

He was moving again trailing kisses in the crevice of her breasts, the valley that joined the two. And then he took the opposite nipple in his mouth and suckled, all the while his right hand caressed her, feeding the fire and his left trailed over her body touching her. He grunted, his voice hoarse, his arousal pulsing and hard in her hand, throbbing with his need. Carmen felt his wetness and knew he was more than ready to enter her body. She was ready for him to. She wouldn't stop it. So what if she came? But she didn't want to. She rarely had more than one orgasm during lovemaking; she wanted it to be with him inside her, for them to come together. But if he kept touching her like that she knew for sure she wasn't going to make it. She was biting her lips to keep from begging him to enter her. Her part of the deal was for quality. This was indeed quality.

Aaron was dying a slow, slow tortuous death as his tongue was fed a treat that he'd been missing. Soap and lavender scented her body.

She was so soft, so damn soft, and she tasted so good. He jumped when her finger moved over the top of his arousal. She was squeezing him, groping him in just the way he liked and it was all he could do to hold it together. His breath was harsh. Hell, it was amazing he could even breathe, but he wasn't done yet. She was close. Petite orgasms flooded her body. She was so wet. He moved his tongue down the plane of her belly. He didn't know if either of them would be able to take much more but he wanted to taste her. His flesh jerked under the attention he was receiving, causing him to put his hand over hers. "Baby, hold up for a second or two, or I'm going to come."

For an answer she gave another squeeze and he grunted. Damn. She was killing him. "Stop that," he scolded mildly. "I'm serious, believe me I am. I told you before it's been awhile. It won't take much more to make me come, and as good as it feels, I don't want to come now, not while I'm not inside your body."

"Then..."

"No," he repeated. "We're going to do this right." When she reached to grab him again he caught her hand and held it, and gave a short laugh. "Just a few seconds, okay? Give me a chance to get it together."

As he held her hand in his, he returned to his journey of exploration making his way to the indention in the middle of her torso, nipping at her tender flesh, swirling his tongue into her navel. Her belly was flat and smooth. No child had been cradled there yet, he thought and continued on his journey. He parted her thighs and relented as her hand once again found him ready. He tasted her. *Sweet*, he thought. This was what he'd missed, this taste of femininity. He feasted on her sensing her body's surge toward release. She tried to pull away, but he held her tightly, his hands biting into her hips to keep her to him. With a small gasp of surprise, she came and her body shook, sending shockwaves of pleasure though him. He stayed where he was, taking the last of her juices as she rode out the powerful orgasm. Only when her legs began to relax did he move upward.

It was time. He sheathed himself in one of her glow-in-the-dark condoms and entered her gently at first, then he stared into her eyes. "You're beautiful," he stated meaning every word. Then his own need took over and he rode her hard, thrusting over and over again. Her nails dug into him and he felt liquid fire surrounding him. Heat threatened to burn him, turn him and her to ash. Her legs were around his waist and she was holding on tightly as he rode her. His lips captured hers in a demanding kiss and he knew she was going to come again.

222

"Rick," Carmen tried to call his name, but no sound would come out, only a moan. Besides, his real name wasn't Rick. That was the role he was playing, the character. She didn't want to use his character name when she came. Her body was on fire, she never wanted the feeling to end. His thrusts were deep and powerful. Faster and faster he thrust, giving her what happened only a dozen times in her life. He was making her come again. She could feel the crescendo building. Her head was spinning and she was glad he was kissing her, her taste grounding her to him, to the fact that she wanted him. Carmen released every barrier that her mind was trying to throw up. *No*, she thought. *I want this*. And she did. She felt him readying, heard the growl in his throat, felt him shatter, and she followed. *Oh God*, she thought, clutching him to her. She yielded to him, becoming a part of him. It had not been like this in longer than she cared to remember.

A sob tore from her throat. He stroked her, still pumping into her until there was nothing left and they were both too tired to do anything but kiss. He was kissing her senseless, kissing the tears that fell, quietly licking them away, not asking any questions, just accepting her tears as he'd accepted her lovemaking. He was holding on to her so tightly, like he never wanted her to let him go.

Chapter Three

Carmen's hand slid over to the other side of the bed and found it empty. Rick was gone. She smiled remembering their night of lovemaking, wondering if she'd regret her decision in the light of day. Last night, everything had been magical—the way he'd gazed at her, kissed her and made love to her and the way they'd finally fallen asleep in each other arms, sated. She swallowed. If only...she stopped. No regrets, no recriminations. It was what it was. She'd chosen to have an adventure on this cruise. And she'd chosen to make love to a very sexy male romance writer who was surrounded by hundreds of adoring female fans. She punched her pillow, willing the stress to leave her body. Surely the past night wasn't all that there would be on this trip. Still, she should have thought about it a bit more. They'd talked. He was on the cruise to do a job and maybe indulge in a little bit of pretend. She was there trying to recapture magic, to make herself over into a woman she wanted to be. And for a few hours as Niveah Cain it had worked. Now it was morning and she'd have to deal with whatever happened next.

Just as she stepped her foot from the bed, a soft knock sounded on her door and she heard Rick calling her name. *So he came back*, she thought, and padded to the door.

"Good morning," he said, coming in and moving to kiss her. She moved back.

"Something wrong?" he asked.

"You left last night after I fell asleep."

Her words had the sound of an accusation. Anger flared quickly but he tamped it down determined not to allow it to destroy the beautiful night they'd had together. He studied her instead, his gaze intense and unwavering. "I woke about an hour ago and showered. Then I went and found Deatri, to pay the conference fee for you." He held out a bag to her.

Romance Slam Jam Fifteenth Anniversary was emblazoned across one side. Carmen looked inside and saw a tee-shirt with the same logo. "Thanks," she whispered, knowing she should apologize for what she'd almost accused him of but deciding not to. She'd already said 'I'm sorry' too many times in her life. This cruise was to be different. She was different.

"Did you really think I'd make love to you and get up and leave without a word?"

"You have your own cabin," she said, hating the accusatory tone of her voice. She was trying so hard not to be the kind of woman she hated. "You came on this cruise to work, to be a writer, to promote yourself, not to babysit me. That was never our deal. I'm a big girl. I can take care of myself. You have no need to spend every waking or sleeping moment with me. "God, I hate it when I behave this way. Rick, I'm sorry. You did nothing wrong. You didn't deserve that. My tirade came from old baggage I'm trying to get rid of," she finished softly and turned away.

"I should have woke you before I left the room, so you wouldn't have had to remember old baggage."

"Seriously, I have myself together now. You don't have to spend all of your time with me."

"I want to spend every moment with you. Take your shower and come to breakfast with me. On second thought..." He stopped and began pulling his sweater over his head. He dropped it on the bed, then looked at her and gave a smile. He slid out of his shoes before unsnapping his jeans then stepping out of them. She was staring at him one hand on her hip. He gave a shrug then dropped his boxers on the heap. Hunger returned in a big way. "You're overdressed," he said, moving toward her, running his hand over the bottom of her negligee before bringing the silky fabric down her shoulders, kissing her flesh, and in one movement, leaving her undressed.

"Tell me something, Niveah," he said. "Would you like to fulfill another fantasy of mine?"

"What?" she groaned.

"Nothing much. Do you have some crotchless panties?"

"Yes."

"Will you wear them for me today?"

"Why?"

"So that anytime I'm near you I can touch you."

Carmen burst out laughing. "I'll wear them but no way am I going to let you touch me in public."

"The ship has a theater. We could watch a movie and I could touch you in the dark."

"Stop looking at me like that, Rick," she said softly. Carmen found herself getting wet just from the way he was looking at her, the lust in his eyes, the adoration. The adoration was the thing that was getting to her. A woman could become addicted to that.

"Why?"

225

"Because if you don't, we'll never make it out of this room, and I've decided that I am going to try your world today." She smiled. "I already have the shirt." She looked at the other items that had tumbled from the bag. "And I have a name badge." She backed away as Rick moved forward. One quick glance at his erection and she knew it would be hours before they left the room. "No, Rick, I'm taking a shower."

"The shower would be a good place to start and to finish up."

She wouldn't have been able to stop him from following her into the shower even if she'd had a mind to. And she didn't have a mind to. When Rick had her pinned to the wall of the shower, he began kissing her, nuzzling her neck, making her want to scream out as he ran his tongue along her collarbone. He was doing things to her that should be illegal. She was burning and she wanted him. She could feel his hardness against her thigh and raised her hips for him, wrapping her legs around his waist. "Are we going to do it standing?" she asked.

For an answer he just grinned.

"Rick, grab a condom off the top of the sink. I didn't come on this cruise to return home pregnant."

"Just one?'

"Okay, grab a handful."

Hours later they were finally sated, showered and ready for food. Rick had his arm securely around Niveah's waist holding her possessively to him. He liked the way she smiled when he called her Niveah. Maybe one day he'd write her a story and use that name. He heard a tiny growl from Niveah's stomach and laughed. The good thing about being on a cruise ship was that food was available twenty-four hours a day

"Yeah, me too. Let's eat."

Sure enough, twenty seconds after they began eating the table filled with Rick's friends. He glanced at Niveah to see how she was taking all of it and then he discreetly dropped his hand beneath the table and snaked it up her thigh. Her eyes snapped wide open and she stared at him. He grinned at her.

"It's okay, Rick. I'm not going anywhere." She smiled but not at Rick. "Brenda, Viola, how are you this morning? Come have breakfast with us."

This time it was Rick watching her in surprise, wondering when she'd had time to meet and make friends.

"These ladies are aspiring writers and fans of yours, L.W."

Aaron's lips twitched in a smile. It was the first time she'd called him L.W. He stared hard at her trying to decipher the meaning behind her words. She was happy, she was laughing, enjoying his world with him. The tightness in his chest dissipated and he swallowed. His decision to start over had been the right one. When Barb and Lisa sat down at the table and Niveah turned to them smiling, introducing them to her friends he wanted to thank the powers that be. His gaze caught hers and all he wanted at that moment was to return to her cabin, or maybe this time take her to his and make love to her, over and over. He couldn't help himself, he ran a finger along the side of her face and she caught it as he palmed her chin. Everyone at the table stilled as he kissed her hand. She had his heart. Why pretend?

"Damn! Should we leave?" Barb asked, rising from her chair.

"Yes," Aaron said.

"No," Carmen came back. "Remember our deal. You want me to get to know your world I'm willing. In fact I'm going to join Brenda and Viola for the book discussion later today.

"What about our spending time together?" Aaron ignored the other women at the table and the fact that their ears were perked up and listening to every spoken and unspoken word. "I wanted to get some skeet shooting in today. I wanted to teach you," he said wistfully, not liking the way his voice sounded at the end, almost as though he was pleading with her to spend time with him. He could feel Barb's eyes burning a hole in the back of his head, but he didn't care. He'd waited too long to share his life. Now he wanted to have Niveah to himself.

"Just tell me what time and where you want me to meet you, and I'll be there. Until then, you can hang with your fans and I can meet the other writers and readers on this cruise." Carmen tilted her head and gave him a smile filled with promise. "I've been told you know exactly what women want and that your male characters are so real. I think I'll get a real education on the working of your mind if I hang out with the people who seem to know you best."

"Most of that is fiction. I have a muse." Aaron dropped his eyes to Niveah's lips, her kissable soft lips. He swallowed, wanting her, knowing she knew it. Knowing also that she wanted him too.

"Would you two stop it or go somewhere else?" Lisa broke in. "Dag, don't anybody want to look at you two looking at each other like that."

Aaron shook his head and laughed. They'd needed the figurative bucket of cold water that Lisa had dumped on their heads. Cooling off was the only option. "Go with your friends," Aaron told Niveah, "and meet me here at noon. We'll get a little shooting in, then we'll have lunch." He turned slowly toward the other women. "A private lunch," he added.

"Too much information," Brenda quipped standing and preparing to leave and the other women rose with her.

Carmen laughed as she was pulled in for a kiss. If they knew her thoughts at the moment it would prove to be way too much information. She laughed again and walked away with the women.

"What the heck did you do to L.W? He has never as far as I've known even given a woman hope." Barb whispered behind her hand. "Girl what you got? I want to bottle it up and sell it or at least write about it."

High fives and laughter accompanied Barb's remark and had Niveah laughing. She'd decided she liked Barb. In fact she liked all of the women. But now wasn't the time for them to know all that had transpired between her and Rick. They'd both decided this cruise would be one of mystery. They'd each worn their assumed identities well and that had to have made for some of the excitement. She looked at the women, *No*, she thought, *I won't tell. I'll never tell.*

"So L.W. doesn't hit on women at these conferences?" Carmen turned her attention solely on Barb, his friend and fellow writer. She watched as a knowing smiled curved Barb's lips and a question appeared in her eyes, a question that wouldn't be answered.

"You like him, huh?"

"Yeah, I like him."

"You know, people get carried away on cruise ships and sometimes the romances don't hold up. A sister has to be real careful and not get caught up in all of that, take it for what it is and nothing more. I'm all for having fun but I like to be careful. Most times people don't even use their real names." She paused. "For instance, I heard you call L.W. Rick earlier. Do you know his real name?"

"Yes."

"You know it's not Rick, right?"

"I know that," Carmen answered.

"And is your real name Niveah Cain?"

"For the duration of this cruise it is." Carmen held firm. She was not going to give an inch. Niveah Cain was having a fantastic time and she didn't mind in the least having Rick Jameson make sweet love to her.

"You know the man is a romance writer," Barb continued. "He makes women want the men he writes about for a living. He's very good at what he does and all I'm saying is that you need to watch out."

"She's an adult, Barb. Leave her alone and let her enjoy her dream in paradise. You know you're going to be writing about Niveah and Lillie the moment the ship dock," Lisa scolded.

Carmen turned to Barb. "Will you, Barb?"

"That's what writers do. We make most of it up. We fictionalize real life. Whatever happens between you and Lillie could make interesting reading. I mean, if he turns out to have a woman at home and she comes after you that could take a romance to ...urban fiction... mainstream women's fiction. There are lots of possibilities. I prefer romance and for that you need one man, one woman. Just remember that Lillie could very well have a woman at home. He could even be married for all you know. You're a woman and my first responsibility is to make sure women don't get played. Lillie's my boy, but he is a man. You be careful with your heart, sister."

Carmen studied Barb for a few seconds before she spoke. She was glad Barb was Rick's friend. She could only hope when this cruise was over Barb would want to be her friend also. She was someone who could be trusted. "I'll be careful, Barb. Thanks for having my back."

Aaron stopped in his signing of a book for Louise Brown. She was one of his most loyal fans and came to every signing that he had that was within one hundred miles of her. "Excuse me, Louise," he said, then peered at Barb. She'd been standing there nudging him for almost five minutes. "What's up?"

"Finish signing this book, then come with me. I need to talk to you."

"Is it important?" he asked, wondering what the heck was going on. He was not particular about Niveah coming around a corner and finding him cuddled somewhere with Barb for a private conversation. She believed him that he and Barb were just friends, but he didn't intend to push it. More importantly, she was willing to give his world a chance. He didn't want to blow it, not now. Since he'd begun this journey he'd wanted to share it with the woman he loved. No one had to tell him that the woman would be Niveah.

He finished signing the book with a flourish, then kissed Louise on the cheek. "I'll see you later," he said, and walked off with Barb. He skirted around the bar Barb headed for. "No," he said, shaking his head. "We're going to talk out in the open with a bunch of people around."

"Man, why are you tripping?"

"I'm not tripping. I don't want to give the wrong impression to Niveah."

"I don't want your behind."

Aaron laughed. "What's wrong with my behind?" he teased. But for an answer he received only a glare. "Okay, what is it?"

"You're leading Niveah, or whatever her name is, on. She's going to get hurt and you might also. I'm just trying to look out for you, but you have that woman going around this ship with stars in her eyes. She has it bad."

Aaron grinned.

"So do you."

"I know."

"But you have a wife, man. What about that?"

For a long moment Aaron stared at Barb. She was one of his best friends. "You like Niveah?" he asked."

"What does that have to do with anything? You're a damn married man. You're going to hurt that woman and she doesn't deserve it."

"I thought you believed in live and let live and finding love on a cruise ship. You joked about this not a few months ago. You said, 'Wouldn't it be funny if we came on the cruise and found the love of our lives?'"

"I was joking."

"But it happened. I've found the love of my life. I found love and romance. Thanks for wanting to help but I have no plans to back away from Niveah. I'm going to see her every minute that I can." He stared pointedly. "That's why we're sitting out here in the open. I don't want her to see us and get any wrong ideas."

"But you've never—"

"No...I've never and I never will again, not with any woman other than Niveah." He laughed. "Stop worrying, Barb. I know what I'm doing."

"Brother, she has your nose wide open. I've never seen you like this."

"I've been like this for a long time. I just forgot how good feeling like this is. Damn," he muttered softly. "For a romance writer, I forgot the most basic rules." He smiled. "I'm cool, really I am. I'm exactly where I want to be and I'm with whom...well not at the moment, but Niveah is the woman I want to be with." He pursed his lips. "For the rest of my life."

"But..."

"Leave it, Barb. I promise you, I'm not making a mistake." He saw the genuine concern for him in her eyes. "Maybe I'll tell you more later." He glanced at his watch. "Right now I have to find Niveah. We're going to do a little skeet shooting."

The weather couldn't have been more perfect if he'd ordered it. Aaron took a look at the azure sky and the white clouds that dotted it. The water was sparkling as the waves crashed against the side of the ship. As he spotted Niveah he thought again of the money he'd spent for the cruise, and this time he only cringed a little. She had her arms around her body, hugging herself as though she were cold. Putting out his arm to feel the breeze Aaron wondered about that. It was perfect weather. He watched Niveah for a moment as she gazed around corners, no doubt looking for him. Then he knew what was wrong. She was wondering if he'd show. He could tell she was trying hard not to look at her watch by the way she'd look quickly at her wrist then away.

Walking up quietly behind her Aaron slid his arms around Niveah's waist and nuzzled her neck. "Been waiting long?" he whispered. He felt her shiver.

"Not very."

"Were you afraid I wouldn't come?"

"I wasn't sure."

He turned her to face him. "Wow, when did this happen? Where did that come from?" He shook his head. "Barb had a talk with me. She wanted to warn me about hurting you. She thinks you're in love with me..." He paused when she smiled at him. "And she thinks you have my nose wide open. She likes you. She doesn't want me to hurt you."

"Barb also had a talk with me. She warned me that shipboard romances don't always make it past the ship."

"I don't think that's going to be the case with us. I think we have what it takes to make it long term. I have made many mistakes in my life. You will not be another mistake. I can promise you that. But do you want to know what bothers me more than Barb thinking I'm going to hurt you? It's you, that you'd think I'd make a date with you and then break it. You haven't trusted me from the moment you stepped onboard and I'll admit you had good reason not to. This cruise is as much for me to learn the things I've been doing wrong as....I want to change. I know what's important to me," Aaron whispered. "But I've always known what was important to me. You'd think I'd be doing a better job of this."

"You're doing fine."

"You sure?"

"Yeah."

His lips closed over hers and he drew her closer, kissing her, sliding his tongue into the warmth of her mouth, savoring her unique taste. His heart pounded fiercely. He was holding all that he'd ever wanted right here in his arms, kissing her as though there were no tomorrow, kissing her in front of everyone.

As he held her tighter, a small moan slipped from her lips and Aaron paused. Then he realized she was kissing him back, holding him just as tightly. When the kiss ended, he looked at her, allowing his love for her to show in his eyes. "Thank you for coming on this cruise, for fulfilling my fantasy, for being a part of my work." He touched a finger to her chin. Her skin was so soft, her eyes were shining with her emotions. She wanted him as much as he wanted her. Thank God. But he wanted her to do the things they'd planned. He pulled away from her a little and shuddered out a breath.

"Skeet shooting," Aaron shook his head slightly, and accepted the waiting rife. He hefted it to his shoulder testing its weight, then handed it to her. Giving her instructions he moved to the side. "Be ready, you're in control of this. The moment you say pull they will release the clay plates."

Carmen was jumping with glee when her turn was over demanding another one. She'd done quite well and was impressed with her talents. Finally her eyes fell on his. He wanted to give it a go, to impress her with his manly shooting prowess. She placed the weapon into his hands and grinned. It didn't take long for him to shoot the plates to bits even as they soared higher and farther away with each call. He didn't miss a single one. With a self-satisfied grin, he relinquished the weapon as well as a tip for the skeetmaster.

"You're awesome," Niveah smiled at him. He stuck his chest out for a moment then looked at her. "Marines," he said.

"I know."

Aaron reached for her hand, kissed the palm, and stared at her. "Thank you for being there for me when I needed you most."

Carmen wondered how true that was. She knew she wanted to be there for him when he needed her and when he didn't. She gave his hand a squeeze. "You always know just the right thing to say."

"Not always, but it seems to work when I speak from my heart." He ran a hand lightly down the center of her back. A tremor played along her spine. He shuddered on a hard breath as want and need vied with his intentions of showing her a good time. It had been only a few hours since they'd made love, but now it seemed almost distant and a mere appetizer. Still, he supposed he should feed her to keep her strength up. He grinned.

"What are you looking so smug about?" Carmen asked.

"I was debating whether to feed your body or your soul."

"And your decision?"

He groaned. "Feeding your body won out."

"It depends on how you plan to feed my body. If you're talking salad and soup...hmm that sounds good. But if you're talking *you* that sounds even better."

"Are you kidding me?"

"What do you think?"

"Aren't you going to miss all the things that will be happening, all the food?"

"We can have food brought to our room."

"But..."

"I'm serious," Carmen whispered as she looked at him determined to block out the resurgences of a failed honeymoon cruise. Then didn't matter. It was now that counted.

"Rick, your cabin's too small. We should go to mine." Carmen half turned toward the door but he caught her hand.

"No way. You've got me so hot that there is no way I'm moving from this room. Besides, we've made love in your cabin. It's only fair that we christen mine as well, or it really will be a waste—"

"Don't you dare say waste of money."

Aaron groaned and pulled her close. "It's too bad that I can't stay in my persona as well as you. I keep putting my foot in my mouth."

"Perhaps you need to use your mouth for other things besides talking. I always say a man gets in trouble the moment he starts to speak." Carmen laughed and framed his face in her hands. She slid her tongue into his slightly opened mouth. She pressed her body closer to his and felt the need quickly rise. They moved apart and begin tearing at their clothes. "I still like my cabin better. Yours is cramped." She laughed.

"I wonder why?" Aaron feasted his eyes on the beauty before him. He shook his head in awe. "You're exquisitely beautiful. Do you know that? You really and truly are."

"It's been a long time since I've heard those words."

"What a pity. Your man must need to have his head examined not to have told you what a true treasure you are."

"Maybe I'm the one that needed to have my head examined. Maybe I was the one in the wrong, the one not willing to give."

"Do you regret being here with me?"

"Not on your life. This is one of the best decisions I ever made. I almost didn't come." He gripped her hand tightly as he bit down on his lip. She saw the look of fear that came to his eyes. "Almost, I said. But then I had a dream and you were in it. I knew you'd be here and that we'd make love, and I knew I'd find myself and you and that the changes I wanted to make in my life would happen. I knew that I wanted that to happen above all else." Her voice caught on a sob and she couldn't continue. She stared into the eyes of the man who'd given her back her dreams, had fulfilled her hopes and had made love to her as though she were the most precious woman on the planet. His gaze locked on hers and wistfulness replaced hunger.

"I'm the romance writer but you just made my heart fill to overflowing. I'm so glad that you let go of almost, and came here. I don't know what I would have done on this cruise if you had not come."

"Would you have been tempted?" she asked, regretting the words the moment they were spoken. "I'm sorry," she muttered. "I know you've never been guilty of the things in my mind. My own insecurities made me blurt that. You don't have to answer that question."

With the pad of a finger he tilted her head so he could once again look into her eyes. "I would have not been tempted. If you had not been on this cruise, I would have slept alone. I was waiting for you and only you. Know that, please, tell me you believe me."

"I do and again, I'm sorry that that slipped out."

"You still have doubts but when this cruise is over you won't." He kissed her eyelids felt the little rush of air and kissed the other. He kissed a trail down the center of her neck and along her collarbone, then bent her back just a bit. "You're so beautiful." He dipped, lifted her into his arms and carried her the few feet to the bed and laid her on it. Then he returned to the exploration of her beautiful brown body. She shivered slightly from desire.

Aaron smiled and took one perfectly puckered nipple into his mouth. He allowed his hand free rein to tease and titillate, to investigate her hidden treasures. He buried his hand between her thighs finding her wet, and ready for him. But he wasn't ready yet. He still had to erase all of her doubts, one by one, and he'd love her body for hours until the very last doubt was gone.

He felt her cresting. It wasn't time. He removed his head and suckled her other breast, twirling his tongue around the nipple, giving her light nips. He could feel the effect down below and he used his finger to create more heat, inserting a second finger, feeling her tighten around them, feeling her hips moving upward. He smiled inwardly, making his way slowly down her body, kissing every inch of her belly. For the first time the thought of a baby came to him without making him choke. He wanted kids, several of them and without a doubt he wanted them with the woman in his arms. He lifted his head up to gaze upon her.

"What are you doing?"

"I'm wondering what kissing your belly while you're carrying my child would feel like." He saw the hesitation in her eyes.

"You're moving too fast, Rick."

"I didn't mean right this moment. What's wrong?"

"I stopped taking the pills and all the condoms I have are in my cabin." she squirmed. "I'm not ready for a baby."

Aaron gave her a small smile. "I don't have all the colorful ones that you do, but I have some. I promise I won't ever do anything that you don't want or try to force any decisions on you." He caught her look. "I didn't say I wouldn't try and persuade you." He moved his fingers inside her. She was thinking about too many things, the right or wrong of what they were doing and he didn't want that. He wanted them to just enjoy each other. Her eyes closed and he continued his journey, groaning as her hand circled his erection.

"You're making me believe in forever," Carmen whispered. "Did my changing into Niveah do that? Are Niveah and Rick the ones making love now or us, just plan us? I want you to make love to me, to Carmen, not to Niveah."

"And I want to make love to Carmen. In fact, I thought I was. It's not the fake name. It was never the fake name. It was you. Just as I hope that you're making love to me, Aaron was your goal, not Rick Jameson not L.W. But you know if we give up our personas, we'll have to take personal responsibility for the things we do now. We can't blame them on Niveah or Rick. It will be us, Carmen and Aaron. We will be the ones in charge of or lives. It will no longer be pretend. We cannot leave the ship as the same people who came onboard. A shipboard romance is fun and playing make believe has been exciting, but when we leave this ship, I want to continue what we've found and I want to continue it as Carmen and Aaron. Agreed?"

"Agreed."

"Okay, if that's all settled do you mind if I make love to you? You keep stopping me." He moved back up taking her mouth in a passionate kiss. "Carmen, you have the most kissable lips. I could lose my soul in your kisses and my mind in your body. I already have." He kissed her again making love to her until they were both well sated and sleepy.

Carmen glanced at Aaron as he pulled the jeans over his slim hips. Her eyes were riveted to his ever present bulge of his erection. He eyed her and she shook her head and laughed. "I can't believe this," she said. "You're insatiable."

"Me. What about you?"

"I guess I am, but I'm also hungry...for food this time," she chuckled. "Besides I hear there's karaoke somewhere on the ship. I want to hear you sing."

He pulled her hand into his and tucked it possessively inside. "Then your wish is my command."

Several hours later, they were full, but still munching. They'd enjoyed the Emma awards and were now listening to people taking their turns singing. They sat with Barb, Lisa, and the women Carmen had befriended. One after the other the winners' names had been called and it pleased Carmen that she knew them all. Laverne was beaming from her Emma win as was Abigail. Carmen looked around her at all the other winners at their table, Barb, Lisa, A.M. Wells for cover designer. Her eyes rested on Aaron. His was the best win of all. Not only had he won her over but he'd won three Emmas. She was so proud of him. She caught Barb looking at them with a worried mother hen look of affection. Carmen leaned over and whispered into Aaron's ear. "Should we tell Barb that this is a bit more than a shipboard romance and that we're going to carry this off the cruise?"

"No, let her sweat," he grinned. "It's good for her. Come on." He pulled Carmen to her feet as the first strains of a Peaches & Herb song came on. She looked at him in surprise as 'Reunited' began to play.

Carmen felt the sting of tears and held them back. Her heart shuddered and she gazed at Aaron, saw the way he was looking at her and stumbled over the words to the song. She was trying to look anywhere but at him, afraid the tears would fall if she did. But he was making it difficult. He touched her lightly, and when she looked at him, his gaze held her hostage. His lips were moving closer to hers. She knew without him saying it that he was going to kiss her and he did. The moment they finished the song ended he pulled her into his arms and kissed her again, a light pressing of his lips to hers. There was a promise of more to come in his eyes.

"Okay. Do I look stupid?" Barb scolded them as they left the makeshift stage.

"What?" Carmen and Aaron answered innocently.

"You two," Barb shouted and pointed at the women gathered at the table. "We all know something is going on. You're not going to keep trying to tell me that you just met this woman on this damn boat, no way. The way she's been looking at you, the possessive way you look at her, the instant jealousy if another man even peeps at her. No way. What gives? Is this your wife? Come on, I already know her name's not Niveah. Tell the truth."

Carmen started laughing. She looked at her husband, who was trying his best to keep pretending. It wasn't working. The song had been the last piece in their puzzle of pretense.

"Yes, I'm Carmen. I wasn't out to fool anyone. Aaron and I decided our marriage needed a shake up."

"But why did you go to all the trouble of getting two cabins? Damn, that had to have a cost a pretty penny."

"Barb, you're a bigger cheapskate than I am. Believe me, this cruise has made me loosen my wallet a tad. Don't you see the romance in that? Money was never the object," Aaron said then laughed. "Well, if it was, it shouldn't have been," he admitted.

"Don't even play." Barb swatted at Aaron. "You're trying to make this cruise be a write off. You're here fronting with your own damn wife, playing make believe for research. You were just using Romance Slam Jam as a front. I'm telling the IRS. No wonder you couldn't keep your eyes off of her when the men were looking at her in that miniskirt." She turned to Carmen. "Gurl, if you ever want to make your man crazy, just put on that skirt when you're around other men. That'll do it."

"I don't want to make him crazy," Carmen confessed. "I just wanted to make him open his eyes and see me as a woman and not just his wife."

"You did," Aaron said softly, then leaned to whisper so no one else would hear. Now if you'd just wear those crotchless panties I bought for you and let me touch you..." he stopped at the look on his wife's face and grinned.

"Ohhh you two are being nasty," Barb laughed, but before either Aaron or Carmen could answer her she was running for the mike.

"She can't sing a note. I think it'll be safer to take a walk. Come on," he said, holding out his hand to his wife.

"You okay with your fans knowing you're married?" Carmen asked.

"I never tried to hide that fact." He nuzzled the back of her neck. "Okay, I never advertised it either, but baby no, I'm not afraid of my fans knowing I'm happily married and have been for five years. I'll grant you the last year has been harder than it should have been. But we weren't going down without a fight. I was determined to save us, save our marriage."

"Me, too," Carmen admitted.

"And the cruise?"

"You know me so well. Yes, I thought more than once that you'd canceled our honeymoon for your career and I thought not to come, that it would teach you a lesson for putting a deadline before us. But I didn't want to teach you a lesson. I've missed you. Not having you touch me for a month was the hardest month of my life. I don't care to repeat it. I came here for a change and I did change. We're going to be in this together. You were right. Romance writers and readers are a nice bunch of people."

"You're really having a good time aren't you? You're not just saying it because of me."

"Yes, I am having a good time. The writers and readers are a lot of fun. In fact we're planning to go on a little excursion when the ship docks in Jamaica."

Aaron examined his wife's eyes, his head tilted slightly. "In spite of the fun you're having, I still sense sadness in your eyes on occasion."

"Just old memories," Carmen replied and looked away.

He used his finger to bring her back to face him. "I wanted to give you all new memories to chase away all the old and unpleasant ones."

"You've done that and more. Any unpleasantness that lingers, the fault lies with me, not you." She gave a shrug. "But I'm trying. I promise."

"I know you're trying. Thank you."

A smile tugged at Carmen's lips. "You meant it didn't you?"

"What?"

"It's really important to you that I become a part of your life..." she paused, "and your career. It's important to you that I understand and approve of what you do." Sadness tugged at her for taking so long to recognize that. "Aaron, you should have never had to doubt or ask for it. Your career is important to you so it's important to me. I want to be a part of every aspect of your life. One of the changes I plan to make will be to let the man I love know just how important he is to me. All of your official duties for Romance Slam Jam are over. We're going to enjoy the rest of this cruise and then we're going home together and implement more changes."

"We can't go directly home after the cruise." Aaron saw his wife's eyes narrow and rushed to explain. "The first time I asked you to marry me, I didn't do it properly. " Aaron fell on his knees and held Carmen's hand. "I love you, baby, and I want to stay married to you for the rest of our lives. There are so many things I regret but nothing as much as not taking you on the honeymoon cruise."

"I love you too and there's nothing I want more than to be your wife forever. Now get up." Carmen reached out and helped him up

"This cruise has more than balanced the scales for the one we didn't take."

"Not really," Aaron continued. "This was in part for my career. You were right about that but I'm not totally clueless. I made plans for a real honeymoon as soon as this cruise is over."

"What's our destination?"

"Destination romance," Aaron said. "As a husband, that's my primary job. Forgive me for not remembering that, for falling down on the job. It will never happen again." He pulled his wife to him. "Carmen," he whispered into her mouth breathing in her breath. "I love you, always have and always will."

The End

www.dyannedavis.com

Author Bio

Award winning author of twelve published novels, Dyanne Davis lives in a Chicago suburb. She retired from nursing to pursue her dream of becoming a published author.

An avid reader, Dyanne's love of the written word turned into a desire to write. She has been a presenter of numerous workshops. She hosts a local cable show in her hometown to give writing tips to aspiring writers.

Dyanne also writes a vampire series under the name of F. D. Davis.

Dyanne loves to hear feedback from her readers. You can reach her at davisdyanne@aol.com. www.dyannedavis.com Http://dyannedavis.blogspot.com Her alter ego ADAM OMEGA can be reached at adamomegavampire@aol.com www.adamomega.com

Red Rose Publishing
On My Knees- Destination Romance Series

Genesis Press
The Color of Trouble
The Wedding Gown
Misty Blue
Lets Get It On
Two Sides to Every Story
Many Shades of Gray

Parker Publishing
Forever and a Day
In The Beginning
Another Man's Baby
The Critic
In Blood We Trust
The Lotus Blossom Chronicles: Book 2
Carnivale Diabolique - The Good Side of Evil by F.D. Davis

More & More

By

Niobia Bryant

Prologue

"We *have* to do this more often."

Mocha Nivens smiled softly at her lover's heated words, looking down into his handsome and broad face as she slowly rode his hard heat in the middle of the hotel bed. The entire length of Dean Kincaid's tall and muscular frame shivered as she circled her hips clockwise and then counterclockwise. "Yes we do," she agreed huskily, looking down at her lover with her lids half closed over her wide eyes.

The very look of him had the power to excite her. Everything about him was a pleasure to her. The jet black, deep waves of his fade hinting at his grandfather being half Cherokee. The deep bronze of his caramel complexion with his slashing brows, deep-set eyes, high cheekbones and square chin. She moaned and bit her bottom lips as she brought her hand up to trace the outline of his full mouth. And she smiled as she thought of the twin dimples that sank into his cheeks whenever he smiled.

"You are one fine man, Dean Kincaid," she told him huskily as she paused her ride, easing her hips up until her fleshy and moist lips lightly clutched his thick tip.

His lips pursed before he flicked his head just enough to draw her finger deeply into his mouth.

Mocha shivered before swiftly lowering her hips to draw all of him into her.

Dean gasped, the breadth of his wide athletic chest spreading. "Girl, you bad," he whispered up to her, his eyes taking her in by the moonlight peeking through the curtains.

Mocha was any man's dream. Her round face, the deceptively innocent wide-set eyes framed with long, lush lashes, her pug nose, and the fullest heart-shaped mouth, which he loved to kiss. Her hair changed like the seasons, and tonight the jet-black riot of curls framed her face perfectly, offsetting the deep, bronzed tone of her skin. Mocha was an odd mix of adorable cuteness and sultry beauty all at once. And her body, that thick and voluptuous frame was ideal for him. Every inch of her full hourglass shape was softness welcoming the hard contours of his body. He loved it all.

With shaking hands, he reached up to try his best to lift up her voluminous breasts. Her soft, deep brown flesh overflowed them.

Mocha's breasts could put many a woman to shame and mesmerize many a man with their movement.

Mocha eased her finger from his mouth and lowered her head to press her plump, heart-shaped mouth against his lips.

Dean moaned in pleasure at the feel of her tongue outlining his mouth as he brought his hands up to deeply hold her gyrating hips. "This can get to be addictive," he admitted, his heart pounding furiously and a fine sheen of sweat coating his muscled frame.

Mocha said nothing and instead pressed her tongue into his mouth to circle his provocatively. She brought her hands up to hold his face and closed her eyes, getting lost in the heat they created. Their unique vibe. That explosive chemistry.

In that moment, Mocha wanted nothing more but to enjoy their sexy tryst. To please and be pleased. No words. No promises of more.

As she broke the kiss and guided Dean's head until his mouth brushed against her aching nipples, she increased the rhythm of her ride. She loved the feel of his hard shaft filling her completely as it deeply stroked against her swollen bud. "Oh my God," she moaned, letting her head fall back until her curly weave tickled the middle of her back.

Dean bent his legs and pressed his back against the leather-padded headboard as he began to work his own hips in perfect sync to her motions. He was rewarded with Mocha arching her back and roughly crying out as he licked and deeply sucked her chocolate nipples.

And that's the way it always was between them.

Six years, and the crazy chemistry between them had only intensified.

Mocha leaned back. Her breast popped free of his mouth as she placed her hands behind her and pressed down into the softness of the bed. She brought her head up and locked eyes with him. "Ready?" she asked, pausing her ride with her moist and swollen lips lightly clutching and releasing the tip of his thick hardness.

Dean bit his bottom lip and shook his head as he fought for control. He wasn't ready for his peak. Not yet.

But control was completely out of his hands as Mocha began to work her hips so that her intimacy circled his thick tip several times before she dipped down to take all of his hot hardness inside of her. "Mocha," he cried out as he reached out almost blindly to grasp her full breasts, his climax building swiftly.

"Come on, baby," she urged him, her eyes clouded with desire as she, too, welcomed that familiar anticipation building inside of her.

With agility that defied her solid, curvaceous size-sixteen frame, Mocha squatted with his rod still deeply planted within her. She knew he loved this and she cockily looked down at him with her head tilted to the side as his entire body tightened. She felt his shaft spasm with his explosive release. She worked the muscles of her walls as she continued that up and down motion, draining him as she began to tremble with her own release.

Dean cried out hoarsely.

Mocha chorused him.

Even after her explosive climax took the strength from her solid legs, Mocha continued to work her hips. She was relentless. She worked her rigid walls until she was sure she'd drawn out every bit of what he had to offer. "Who's the best?" she asked throatily, her heart racing wildly in unison with the steady pulsing of her bud and his shaft.

Dean licked his lips as his entire body went limp beneath her. "I traveled...three thousand miles...for this. You...*know*...you're...the best," he told her between gasps.

Mocha's soft, husky laughter filled the steamy air.

Chapter One

Five months later: April

Mocha released a dejected sigh as she stood on the balcony of the *Destiny.* Considering this was the start of a weeklong cruise to paradise and the annual Romance Slam Jam, she knew she should be in a better mindset. But it was hard to look forward to something as romantic as a cruise when your own six-year relationship was as tattered as a year-old weave.

"Maybe the conference will take my mind off of Dean," she muttered to the softly blowing wind as she looked out at the port of Miami.

The Romance Slam Jam Conference, an annual event since 1995, brought together readers and authors of African-American romance. Every year, the event was sponsored in a different state, and this year the conference was celebrating its fifteen-year anniversary with a one-week cruise to Jamaica and the Cayman Islands.

Mocha was the president and founder of her book club, and she knew she had to put up a strong front and not ruin the good time for the nine club members attending the conference with her. She was the sassy, lively and outspoken one in their group, but these days she didn't completely feel like herself—and she didn't like it one bit. "Get it together, Mocha. Life without Dean goes on," she said aloud, walking through the opened glass balcony door into her stateroom.

But as she unpacked her clothing from her favorite Louis Vuitton trunk, she couldn't help but think about the last few months...

Rewind: January

"Everyone's here, Mo."

Mocha looked up from the spreadsheet on her laptop to see Lena, her ultra-tall and skinny manicurist standing in the doorway of her spacious office. "Good. Let me finish here and I'll be right down," she told her, as she ran her fingers through her new bone straight lace front wig.

As soon as the door closed behind her, Mocha immediately dropped her head into her hand atop her desk. She was tired, and as much as she loved her monthly book club meetings, she really wanted to go home and climb under her bed.

Owning and operating a successful and extremely busy full-service salon/day spa was serious as a heart attack—and could cause one if she didn't slow down

Haven was her baby and she spent the last fifteen years of her life turning it into a success. She started out with A Cut Above the Rest salon in a small storefront on Springfield Avenue, hustling almost twenty-four-seven in one chair to create a name for herself.

Today she was proud of Haven, the two-story, stylishly decorated facility in Maplewood, and her ten stylists, four full-time manicurists, two masseuses and aesthetician. That didn't include the support staff of front desk clerks, shampooers and the nightly cleaning crew. She could never deny that she enjoyed the fruits of her labor but a three-thousand-square-foot home, a convertible Volvo and designer clothes wouldn't give her the energy she really needed tonight.

Bzzzz.

Mocha stopped packing her deep red alligator attaché case to pick up her vibrating BlackBerry. A smile filled with pleasure lit her round face as she saw the text message from Dean. Her heart beat as she opened and read it. "Well, well, well," she sighed in heated delight. Her face and her femininity warmed as she absorbed each and every X-rated word.

He was in the middle of a dinner meeting sending her naughty texts about sucking this and licking that, massaging here and stroking there.

Biting her bottom lip she quickly texted him back.

DEEPMOCHA07111: IS THAT A PROMISE?

As she waited for his answer she pressed her BlackBerry to her left nipple, giggling when the PDA's vibrations sent a tingle through her. "Humph, a girl in a long-distance relationship had to a little excitement somewhere. Shoot," Mocha mused to herself.

THEDEANOFALL: AS SOON AS I WALK THROUGH THE DOOR.

And that would be in two weeks. She couldn't wait to lay her eyes, hands, and everything else on Dean "The Dean" Kincaid. Their naughty phone calls, emails, and texts were important to their long-distance relationship but their one-weekend-a-month rendezvous were extremely vital.

Knowing he would call her tonight when he got back to his house, Mocha slid her PDA into the inside pocket of her attaché and pulled out her paperback romance. She loved, loved, loved romance novels, and had ever since she was thirteen and sneaking her mother's Harlequins. But at times, the steamier ones really messed with her with during the weeks without Dean. Over the years, there had been many semi-erotic romance books that sent her deep into her lingerie drawer for "Lil' Dean," a very helpful...toy.

"Okay, I have to get my booty downstairs," Mocha said aloud to herself before she hustled out of her office and down the wide spiral staircase to the main hub of the salon/spa.

The Italian décor, in tones of taupe, deep chocolate and ivory, was very soothing. So soothing that the ten core members of the Soul Love Bookclub insisted on holding their meeting in the salon and not the comfortable break room upstairs. Thankfully, the open floor plan made for a sufficient meeting space.

"Hello, everyone," Mocha greeted the women sitting in the two rows of plush, leather beautician chairs facing each other.

With ease she slid her curves into the center chair on the left side of the wall, crossing her full and solid shapely legs. "I'm happy to see we have a full house tonight to discuss this month's selection. Okay, let's get some club business out of the way."

Mocha placed her book beside her on the chair as she looked and listened to Alaina, the secretary, read the minutes from the last meeting; Oshan, the webmistress, updated them on new features on their interactive website and the growing number of online members from around the country; and Candi, their treasurer, filled them in on the total of their book club savings from dues and fees.

"Also, I'm very proud to announce that all reservations for the 2010 Romance Slam Jam cruise are now paid in full for our ten members. We are all set, ladies!"

"Alright now!" Mocha joined the ladies in their whoops and applause.

"Romance authors and a cruise to Jamaica," Candi said with her usual bubbly enthusiasm as she pushed off making the chair swivel her short and pudgy figure. "Can we go now?"

"I hope I meet me a big, strapping Jamaica boy," Lena said in the worst Jamaican accent ever. She hopped to her feet and started doing the Butterfly.

"But not like Terry," Candi added, holding up her hands, which had a ring or two on every finger. "That's one groove I don't want to get back. Okay?"

"You got that right," someone said.

"Okay, ladies, let's settle ourselves down and stop daydreaming about being sexed and flexed on a beach," Mocha said.

"Yes, 'cause I want to get to this book," Lila said, leaning forward to look at each of the other members with one of her bottle-blond eyebrows raised. "There are a lot of women looking for a good man and Brianna spent the whole dang-on book running from Garrett and all that good love."

Mocha nodded in agreement. She loved to sit back and listen to the other members' takes on a book before she jumped in.

"I didn't start to like her until the end of the book," Ese piped in, her auburn twists flying in an infamous sista girl head roll.

Alaina shook her head as she swung her crossed leg and tapped the end of her pen against her chin. "Yes, but I felt like the author was showing the growth of Brianna and a part of her that needed growth was in her ability to fall in love—"

"Or realize she was already in love," Candi added with a friendly wink of agreement at Alaina as she patted her ledger against her thigh and moved back and forth in her chair.

Evie, a soft-spoken woman with the sweetest personality, raised her slender hand before she spoke—mostly so everyone would quiet down so she could be heard. "To me, she didn't really pull away until he proposed. Maybe it was marriage she feared and not love. Right, Mocha?"

Mocha, whose mind had wandered back to Dean's text, looked up, startled, at the mention of her name. "Huh? What?"

"Well, not to get into your business but you and Dean have been together for four or five years—"

"Six," Mocha supplied, shifting in her seat. All eyes were locked on her.

"Not every woman is dying to get married. Right?" Evie asked.

"Ah...um...well, let's see," Mocha said, biting her bottom lip. "I think...I think that Brianna's situation with Garrett and my own with Dean is entirely different, so the motivation behind them is probably different, too."

"Listen, Brianna's behind was probably used to dogs and once she had a good man—specifically good on pages 100 through 110—she ain't know what to do with all that."

The members loved a good sex scene, and Mocha was glad the discussion shifted away from her. I should be in politics, she thought, knowing her answer wasn't really an answer at all. But it sounded great.

Her relationship with Dean was ideal for her...for them. They were two independent, self-sufficient, successful individuals focusing on building up their businesses. They could have their space and still have a relationship. Mocha couldn't be happier.

She cared a lot for Dean. He was sexy, smart, dynamic, strong and romantic. The ideal package.

Their sex. Explosive.

Their weekends together. Amazing.

Their phone conversations. Comforting.

Their distance. A necessary buffer.

Mocha wasn't looking for anything more.

Mocha kicked off her heels as soon as she walked through the front door of her home in Livingston and switched on the lights in the spacious den. "Whoo," she released with a weary sigh, barely taking in the elegant warmth of the décor as she padded across the polished wood floors to the bar in the corner. After pouring herself a glass of red wine from the bottle in the mini-fridge, Mocha made her way up the wood and wrought iron stairs in the center of the den.

It was nearly eleven and she was so ready for a soak in her Jacuzzi before diving into bed. The ladies had been really riled up about the book and the meeting had run over. She had already cut off her cell and had no plans of answering the phone. Her mother, sisters, and Dean would have to catch up with her tomorrow.

Mocha sighed and took a deep sip of wine as she reached the top step. One half of the nearly eighteen-hundred square feet of the upper level was two spacious guest bedrooms with their own baths. The other half was her bedroom suite, complete with a sitting area, spa bath and balcony.

She glanced over her shoulder once she reached the wooden double doors to her suite, and a vision of little girls, their hair in Afro puffs, running out of the guest bedrooms flashed. Mini-versions of herself. Twin girls. She blinked and the vision disappeared.

With a soft smile filled with a just tinge of regret, Mocha entered her bedroom. Okay, she would love to be a mother, but baby daddies could be just as complicated as husbands.

Several years ago Mocha had approached Dean about having a child together. It had all made sense to her. They were financially secure and mature. They were monogamous and adamant HIV/AIDS activists who were faithfully tested every six months.

Dean had disagreed. He wanted to be active on a daily basis in his child's life and felt he couldn't do that from Texas.

Could she blame him for that? No.

Had it put a wrench in her plans? Yes.

Pushing those thoughts away, Mocha undressed quickly, catching sight of her voluptuous frame in the mirror as she crossed the plush carpeting to her adjoining bath. She gave in to vanity and studied herself, loving her five-feet-seven-inch height, her solid build, and the fullness of her FF breasts. True, her belly wasn't rock hard flat but she was more than happy with her body. She paused with a smile thinking of how Dean couldn't get enough of her body whenever he was near her. Soft belly, big thighs, and all.

With a laugh, Mocha playfully jiggled her breasts. "Oh yes, daddy loves ya'll," she said to her reflection, before turning to walk saucily into the bathroom.

Mocha put away her memories along with her last outfit, which she hung in the closet of her stateroom. Dwelling on the better times of her life when she had Dean was unnecessarily pouring salt on open wounds.

She had just finished a quick shower and changed into a gold one-piece bathing suit when there was a knock on her door. Grabbing her Sail & Sign card—used for onboard purchases and identification—Mocha grabbed her sheer cover-up and opened the door.

She smiled at all nine of her club members crowding in the narrow corridor. They knew her man drama and probably wanted to help her through it. "Okay, ladies, let's see what this cruise ship has to offer," she said brightly, sliding on her shades.

Chapter Two

Dean yawned and stretched his long and muscular frame in th[...] middle of his custom-made, extra-long, king-sized bed. He rolled ont[...] his side and opened his eyes to the sight of Mocha's 5x7 photo on hi[...] bedside table. She was giving him that infectious smile of hers as sh[...] lay out on a beach towel in a gold one-piece bathing suit that worke[...] overtime to keep one of her succulent breasts from literally poppin[...] out.

Mocha was thick and confident—a major turn-on for Dean. T[...] him, there was nothing sexier than a woman comfortable in her skin.

Aroused at the sight of her, Dean forced himself out of bed to ho[...] to his size-thirteen feet. He had another long day ahead of him, an[...] getting so hard that he had to work himself home to a happy endin[...] was not a good idea. A nut would leave him feeling like he carried [...] dozen boulders on his shoulders.

Besides, there was no more Mocha and Dean. That had hurt hi[...] at first, but he had dealt with her decision, and now he had to get use[...] to life without her.

Looking over his shoulder, he eyed the photo. Maybe waking u[...] every morning to her picture wasn't the best way to get over his e[...] Flexing his shoulders, he walked back over to his nightstand an[...] picked up the photo. Did he love Mocha? Yes, and he would for a lor[...] time. But he refused to fight for something that wasn't there...an[...] maybe never was.

Still holding the photo, Dean strode to his walk-in closet an[...] grabbed an empty sneaker box from the floor beneath the neat[...] organized shelves holding all of his footwear. He walked through h[...] entire house, tossing any and every thing that reminded him of Moch[...] into the box.

Too bad it wasn't that easy to put away his memories...

Dean had just rushed through a shower and was standing nude in his walk-[...] closet selecting a suit when the doorbell to his condominium rang. He hurried into [...] pair of boxers before he left his bedroom and made his way down the metal stairca[...] and across the foyer. He opened the door. "Morning, Roderick," he called over h[...] shoulder as he hurried back with strong strides up the stairs.

"Morning, cuz," Roderick called up behind him.

Dean knew Roderick was on his way to the kitchen. At thirty, the man was five years Dean's junior and could eat him under a table. They had become more like brothers than cousins since Dean's return to Dallas. They had worked together, chilled together, and Dean had never had a better friend, confidante, or business associate—the last of particular importance to him.

Dean lifted one of his many bottles of cologne from the ebony island in the center of his spacious closet. All of them were gifts from Mocha. On their very first date, she let him know that she loved for a man—her man—to smell good. He had taken great pleasure in never wearing the same cologne twice in a row around her, and today he sprayed his smooth chocolate frame with Estée Lauder's Pleasures for Men. Quickly he dressed in a charcoal pinstriped suit, a paisley tie, and a crisp custom-made white silk shirt.

"Damn, man, how many pictures of Mocha do you have up in here?" Roderick called up the stairs.

Dean just smiled and ignored him as he slipped his size-thirteen feet into his shoes. His cousin was a consummate player who could never grasp Dean's ardent fidelity to a woman who lived over fifteen-hundred miles away.

"I love her," Dean told his reflection as he straightened his big knot tie.

Tucking his wallet into his pocket, he left his bedroom and jogged down the stairs. "If you're done eating all my food, let's roll."

Lounging on a modern leather chair in the living room, Roderick took a swig from his glass of juice as he pushed the last of whatever he was eating into his mouth. "I'll tell you about this super freak I ran into last night at The House of Dereon. Lawd have mercy," he said, his mouth still full.

Dean briefly looked over at his shorter, lighter-complexioned cousin before double-checking his briefcase. "I can do without the details," he drawled with a tinge of sarcasm.

"Man, you haven't lived until you have a freak put ice cubes—"

"Man, shut up." Dean frowned heavily.

"I'm just trying to bring some freaky into your life, Mr. Relationship," Roderick said as he followed Dean out of the house. "Man, your ass is good as whipped."

Dean slid his designer shades on before walking to his black on black Mercedes Benz SL500 in the driveway. "And you like to be whipped," he shot back.

Roderick feigned confusion. "What's wrong with being whipped?" he asked, and then smiled big enough to show every tooth in his mouth.

Dean climbed into his car. "One day, the right woman is going to have your nose wide open."

"Don't see it." Roderick settled into the passenger seat. "Too many women. So little time."

Dean snorted in derision as he started the car. "So many STDs. So little antibiotics."

"Man, I always strap up."

"I hope so." Dean locked his eyes with his cousin. "Sex is supposed to be fun, not deadly."

They rode in silence through the traffic to reach the offices of KAE—Kincaid Automotive Enterprises. Today was an important day for the family business their grandfather, Walt Kincaid, started back in 1988. With nearly one hundred employees and ten luxury vehicle dealerships across the south and southeast, KAE was one of the top African-American owned businesses in the country. Dean was proud of his work over the last six years in continuing to grow and create an even bigger and better future...but now it was time for change.

Roderick was taking over as CEO of KAE and Dean had spent the last year grooming him for the position. He was ready, and Dean planned to return to his life in Jersey...and Mocha. His new position as General Manager of KAE's newest dealership in Union, New Jersey was several step downs from CEO, but Dean was ready to get serious with Mocha and build toward starting a family—he couldn't do that in Texas.

Dean remembered all of his plans and hopes and wished he didn't feel like a fool...but he did. He strode into the pantry of his Jersey home and roughly slid the box in a corner. Out of sight and hopefully out of mind...one day.

Mocha lounged by the pool, basking in the sunshine as several of the club members enjoyed the pool and other passengers. She hated that she had to fight the desire to call Dean. She felt like a stone-cold fool for even wanting to talk to him. But she did.

"Oh...my...God, Mo, oooh look at this guy," Lena sighed from the lounge chair next to Mocha.

Against her better wishes, Mocha slid her shades down to the tip of her pug nose and shifted her eyes in the direction Lena was looking. Completely against her will, her mouth opened a bit in a gasp. Over six feet of pure muscle dipped in the deepest and darkest chocolate was striding towards them in a bright red bikini that was almost a waste of material. Mocha swallowed over a lump in her throat because the man's body reminded her of Dean's.

"Damn him," she swore to herself as she pushed her shades back up onto her face.

Lena hopped to her feet and pulled her polka-dot bikini out of all the wrong crevices. "Time for a little fling," she said, her eyes locked on the Adonis as he strode past them.

Mocha rolled her eyes as she forced herself not to take another look. "I didn't know you were looking for a cruise fling," she teased.

"Girl, right about now I'd take Isaac from *Love Boat*," Lena flung over her shoulder before easing away on her giraffe-like legs to follow her dream.

This was Mocha's first full-fledged vacation in years. She had even closed the salon for a week so she had no business worries. Touching her new jet black micro braids, she contemplated getting in the pool but decided against it. Pools had a way of draining her.

With a sigh, she tilted her head up to kiss the sun as she forced herself to relax, relate and release it. She couldn't let the anger and hurt Dean caused her to change her. She just couldn't.

"Come on, cuz, the clubs are calling!" Roderick shouted through the door.

Dean grabbed his keys and wallet, checking out his jacket and jeans ensemble before walking out his bedroom in their hotel suite at the Waldorf-Astoria. Roderick had flown in this afternoon to begin looking for possible sites for a dealership in upstate New York. Of course, it was Roderick's urging that they stay in New York City for the remainder of the weekend and have a ball. "Okay, let's roll," Dean said. "Our car should be downstairs by now."

"Trust me, dawg, this is just what you need," Roderick told him with a sound slap to his shoulder as they strode across the stylish suite and out the door. "And I know this ain't the time to say I told you so, but just think of all the women you've turned down over the years, and now you and Mocha aren't even together."

"I have never seen someone so dedicated to making another dude into a whore," Dean drawled.

"I just want you to know what you're missing."

His relationship with Mocha had failed, but Dean firmly believed that Roderick was the one missing out. True, he had been faithful to Mocha, and even now after she had hurt him, he didn't regret his fidelity...

Even in his twenties, Dean had never been much of a club person. The music was too loud, the people too sweaty, and the whole scene just too tiring. Although the restaurant in midtown Dallas was more bar than club, it was a night for celebration and goodbyes for him and Roderick so he couldn't turn down the invite. Still, he would give it only a few hours before he headed home. He wanted to call Mocha before she turned in for the night.

"I'm really going to miss you around the offices, Mr. Kincaid."

Dean was standing at the neon-lit circular bar and looked down to find Ashlee Givens, KAE's receptionist, staring up at him with clear intent and invitation in her almond-shaped eyes. "Thank you, Ashlee. I really appreciate that," he said with a smile before turning back to the bar.

"Um, you know I would love to have a private and very special goodbye celebration," she said with soft eyes and her soft breasts pressed against his forearm.

Dean accepted his Grey Goose and cranberry juice from an amused-looking bartender. He overreached for the drink, effectively freeing his arm of her breasts. "That wouldn't be appropriate. I'm leaving Texas, Ashlee, but I'm still a board member and senior management of KAE," Dean told her with patience, doing a great job avoiding her noticeably erect nipples pressing against the thin silk of her shirt.

She licked her full lips and gave him a full-on flirtatious tilt of the head and lash bow. "I'm very discreet."

"And very persistent," Dean countered sardonically, before turning to walk away. She sidestepped into his path. Annoyance filled him. She was one second from getting her feelings hurt. For real. He didn't want to go there, but he didn't want to be semi-stalked either.

She gave him a slow once over. "Um, um, um, Mocha's a very lucky woman."

Dean watched her turn and seductively walk back to the section of tables where their party was seated. He was glad he didn't have to tell her that she wasn't his type. Her size-six frame was too slender. Her five-foot-five-inch frame too short. Her approach too sexually aggressive.

She was the exact opposite of Mocha.

Turning to set the drink he no longer wanted onto the bar, Dean reached into the inner pocket of his suit jacket for his BlackBerry. As he made his way out of the club, he frowned at the sight of Ashlee now deep up in another man's face.

He could care less, of course.

Outside, his suit jacket offered little protection from the biting January night air. He dialed Mocha's cell as he turned his back to the street to avoid the wind beating against his face.

"Hey, baby," she cooed.

He smiled, causing his dimples to flash as his heart beat harder just from knowing she was on the line with him. "Whatcha doing?"

"I'm closing up the salon and heading out for some drinks and dinner at Mahogany's with my sisters."

Dean nodded and looked up the street as a group of twenty-something women walked in his direction. Each of them eyed him and he gave them a cordial smile. They all smiled back and a few winked. Dean just turned back to the wall, ignoring the woman who called out her number as they passed and entered the bar.

"You, Coko, and Koffee be careful," Dean advised, allowing himself to imagine being in her arms in a few days.

"You and Roderick be good," she said with a smile in her voice.

"And don't have too many men buying those drinks," Dean teased, not at all worried about Mocha's fidelity.

She just gave him one of her soulful laughs that made a man feel like he was home.

Looking up, his eyes locked on his reflection in the tinted glass. "I have a big surprise for you when I get to Jersey this weekend," Dean admitted, his eyes sparkling with mischief.

"Ooh, I love surprises."

Yes, she did love surprises and always had the best way of saying and showing her thanks.

"Uh-oh, that's Coko beeping in. I'm running late."

Dean didn't know which he hated more: hanging up with Mocha or going back in the club. "Bye, baby," he said, just as Roderick poked his head out the door.

"Man, the party inside!" his cousin shouted down to him.

Dean pushed his cell phone back in his pocket as he made his way back into the bar. One hour and I'm out.

For the last six years, Mocha had been enough for him. She would have been enough for the rest of his life. But if this was the way she wanted it, then that's the way it would be.

Chapter Three

The next morning, Mocha rose in better spirits. She pulled on the robe that matched her white satin nightgown before she pulled back the curtain and gazed out at what seemed to be endless miles of ocean. She wanted to enjoy the serenity before a full day of conference activities. She couldn't lie she had a few books in her suitcases that she was dying to get autographed by those authors in attendance. The ladies could be real inspirational. In fact, Mocha remembered reading one of the love scenes to Dean. She had to fan herself remembering how hard it made him and how he had given her nearly an hour of pure passion.

"Those days are behind us and I'm okay with that," she assured herself, opening the door and walking out onto the balcony.

Still, she couldn't deny that their weekends had come to mean a lot to her mentally and sexually. They had shared a chemistry that neither could deny, as if they had no choice...

Mocha fingered her newest weave, a chin-length ultra-wavy look that framed her round and pretty face. She liked to have a new and fresh look for each of her weekends with Dean. It was one of her ways to keep the spice in their relationship.

"Well, that and Kegels," she thought with a mischievous smile as she leaned against a window and watched planes arriving and departing.

In just a few minutes, Dean would be walking his fine self off a plane and into her arms. She could hardly wait. Her pulse was racing. Her stomach was filled with butterflies. She was so ready to be with her man...and to get her surprise.

As soon as Dean's flight was announced, Mocha took off her shades and smoothed her hands over the stylish black belted capelet and fitted jeans she wore. She looked good and felt even better. Everything was always all good on her weekend with Dean.

"Damn, you fine."

Mocha cocked a finely arched brow and looked over her shoulder to find a short, overly muscular, bald brotha eyeing her like a barbeque rib. "Thank you," she said politely, turning away from him with nothing but looking for Dean on her mind.

"Please tell me you ain't waiting on your man."

She spared her admirer a side glance as she walked past him towards the terminal. "I guess today's not your lucky day," she told him over her shoulder, striding away with the confidence only a big-bones sista could have.

"Damn, sure ain't," he called behind her.

Mocha just smiled and kept it moving as if she owned Newark International Airport. One thing her mother had taught her was that there were two things a woman had to give herself before a man would even think about giving it to her: respect and love. Mocha had plenty of both, as did her sisters.

Her BlackBerry began to vibrate in her hand. Mocha looked down at it. Speak of the devil. "Hi, Ma," she said into the phone, on her toes to look over the heads of the crowd walking out of the terminal.

"Did you pick up Dean yet?"

"I'm at the airport right now."

"Well, I want you two to come to church and then dinner at my house Sunday."

Mocha's heart swelled as she caught sight of Dean striding through the crowd in dark denims, a white turtleneck and a camel leather peacoat. She smiled as he caught sight of her and pleasure instantly filled his handsome face.

"There's more to you two than a bed you know," her mom was saying.

Mocha barely heard her as Dean stepped in front of her and wrapped one strong arm around her waist to easily lift her. "Dean," she said softly, looking into his deep-set eyes.

He smiled. "Hey you," he said before dipping his head to capture her full mouth in a kiss.

"Mocha? Mocha, are you listening to me?"

Remembering her mother on the line, Mocha broke the kiss and let her head tilt back as she pressed her BlackBerry back to her ear. "Mom...let me...let me...let me call you back," Mocha fought to get out around Dean's warm kisses and soft bites to her exposed neck.

Mocha was pleased to lock her BlackBerry and drop it into her tote bag. "Welcome home, baby," she said huskily with emotion as she pressed a hand to the back of Dean's head.

Sitting her back down on her feet, Dean said, "Let's get outta here." He reached down and took her hand in his while grabbing the handle of his rolling duffel with the other.

"Where's my surprise?" Mocha asked as they made their way through the crowded airport to the street level exit.

Dean glanced down at her. "Good things come to those who wait."

Mocha smiled as she slid on her shades to fight the winter sun. "Mind I don't make those words haunt you," she teased, just loving being reunited with him for the next three days.

Dean just laughed and brought her hand up to press a kiss to the back of it.

Mocha moaned as she was gently stirred from her deep sleep. She stretched as she opened her eyes, immediately aware that hours had slipped past since she picked Dean up from the airport that morning. She looked down as her silk top sheet was gently eased down from over her breasts.

She looked at the foot of her king-sized bed to find Dean standing there naked, his rippled abs and lengthy erection framed by the moonlight. He continued to pull the sheet and expose her nude frame. With a smile, she raised her arms above her head to grab the edges of the ivory leather headboard as she twirled her hips against the bed.

Dean's hard thickness throbbed up and down, like push-ups.

Mocha could only shake her head as Dean flung the sheet behind him like a cape.

They hadn't left her bedroom suite since that morning, and there was an added level of fierceness to Dean's lovemaking that was completely mind-blowing.

He grabbed her ankles tightly and spread her full legs wide. The sweet scent of her femininity rose in the air. "Ready for round two?" he asked thickly as his penis led him onto the bed and between her open thighs.

Mocha grasped her full breasts, hiking them up enough to tease her hardened chocolate nipples with flicking motions of her tongue. "Actually...it's round three," she told him thickly as she looked up at him with intense eyes.

Dean literally growled as he grabbed her soft thighs, pressed her legs open a bit more and plunged his thick and steely hardness into her with one swift movement of his hips.

Mocha arched her back and cried out in pure unadulterated pleasure as Dean delivered the way only he could...again...and again...and again.

Mercy.

After dragging themselves out of bed around noon the next day, Mocha and Dean were both in clean pajamas and prepared to spend the rest of the day watching movies on the retractable hundred-inch Hi-Def projection screen.

"It's snowing outside." Mocha watched the snowflakes falling out the rear wall of the den that was made up entirely of glass panes. She tucked her feet beneath her on the comfy sofa.

"Now this really does feel like we're away in an isolated cabin in the woods," Dean mused as he handed her an oversized cup of hot chocolate before reclaiming his spot beside her on the sofa.

"Sometimes I can't believe this is my house," Mocha admitted, taking a careful sip of her drink. "This is a long way from the projects in Newark."

"I'm proud of you, too. You worked hard and now you can reap the rewards."

Mocha smiled as she snuggled under the mink throw Dean settled over their laps. "All I ever really wanted to do was have a little shop for me to do hair."

"You can fit five of your first shop in Haven now."

Mocha set her cup down on the leather ottoman serving as a coffee table. "Your advice over the years has helped me so much, Dean, and I really thank you for that. Going to that business course you were teaching at Essex County College was the best decision I ever made...because I met you."

Dean set his own cup down beside hers. "Six years," he said, reaching to pull Mocha over to straddle his lap. "Six good years."

"Six damn good years," she agreed, leaning down to kiss him gently as Dean hitched her flannel nightgown up over her plush hips.

"I love you, Mocha," he whispered into her open and panting mouth before kissing her deeply and passionately until both of their hearts pounded in crazy unison.

They undressed in a rush until their brown, heated skins pressed intimately against one another. As the snow continued to fall, Dean and Mocha made love with a dizzying mix of tenderness and fierceness that left them oblivious to anything but each other.

Mocha shook herself out of the heated memory, knowing she couldn't waste the morning strolling down memory lane. Even one that was so blisteringly erotic.

She allowed herself a few more moments to bask in the sun and let it sink in that she was in the middle of an ocean on a beautiful cruise ship. To top it off, she would get to meet some of her favorite romance authors and get introduced to a few she wasn't familiar with. A bonus to paradise.

After a leisurely shower, Mocha dressed for comfort in a pair of capris, patent leather flats, and a white linen shirt. She wished now that she had brought her mom. Belinda Nivens wasn't a romance reader but she would have gotten a kick out of the ship's amenities and the upcoming shore excursions.

As she left her stateroom to meet the ladies for breakfast on the Lido deck, Mocha decided she would treat her mom and her sister to a cruise. It would be a great family getaway.

"Mocha!"

She turned and saw Candi rushing up the hall to meet her.

"I thought I was the only one enjoying a late start," Mocha told her, looking down at the shorter woman as they continued down the hall towards the elevator.

Candi winked up at her. "Oshun and her husband are still in bed, but I don't blame her."

Oshun and two other book club members had brought their spouses or significant others. Mocha was glad they were able to share such a beautiful experience with someone they loved. She had even surprised Dean with a ticket, but he obviously decided against using it. Sadness touched her deeply.

"Hey, you and Dean will work everything out," Candi told her, grabbing her hand to give her a reassuring squeeze.

Mocha shrugged. "We want different things in life so there's no need wasting each other's time."

Candy wrapped her pudgy arm around Mocha's as they stepped on the elevator. "You young ones have ways of making simple things seem so complicated. Love means compromise, Mocha."

"Yes, but—"

"There is nothing not worth working on when love is involved. Take an old woman's advice."

She doesn't understand, Mocha thought even as she gave half an ear to Candi's rambling on about the power of love and there never being too much to do for love and that being a success at business was great but you had to stop to love.

Mocha was sure Candi had Luther Vandross's greatest hits CD in her collection.

"Good morning, ladies," Mocha greeted as she and Candy reached their tables in the casual but fun dining environment.

"Mocha, you look pretty as always," Alaina said, before taking a sip of her juice.

Mocha smiled her thanks as she took her seat and looked out the window. In Candi's perfect world—or even the romance novels she cherished so much—love had a way of conquering all. But in the real world, things weren't that simple. Sometimes people just didn't click. Didn't work. And sometimes it took a major event for that fact to truly hit home...

"Thank you for coming out of seclusion," Belinda said to Mocha and Dean as they pulled on their coats at the front door of her two-bedroom apartment in Irvington.

"And tell Roderick I said what's up," Coko called from the living room.

Mocha looked up at Dean and playfully rolled her eyes. Coko was convinced she was the woman to put it on Roderick "Hot Rod" Kincaid so good that he would burn his little black book. Her sister was fine, her body a little tighter than Mocha's and her skills in the bedroom were one of her greatest bragging rights, but when it came to a man like Roderick...a dog was a dog was a dog. Bow-wow-wow.

Belinda pressed a plastic supermarket bag with two to-go plates of her Sunday dinner of ham, brown rice, greens with neckbones, macaroni and cheese, and sweet potato pie—all Dean's favorites.

He bent down to kiss her mother's cheek. "Thanks for everything, Ms. Nivens."

Her smile spread like butter. Belinda loved her some Dean.

"Alright, Ma, I'll call you tomorrow," Mocha said, pressing her own kiss to her mother's cheek as she allowed herself to enjoy the ever-present scent of her mother's Tresor perfume.

They left after that, hurrying inside Mocha's car to get out of the cold. She settled her hand on Dean's thigh as he drove through the narrow, slush-covered streets of Irvington with ease. It had been a long day with church and then dinner at her mother's, so Mocha allowed herself to doze off.

"Mocha, baby, come on. It's time for your surprise," Dean whispered close to her ear, awakening her.

"I love surprises." Mocha yawned as she smiled and opened her eyes as Dean hopped out of the car.

They were parked in the driveway of an impressive two-story stone house that she instantly recognized. It was a mile down the road from her own home in Livingston. "What are we doing here?" Mocha asked, as Dean opened the car door for her.

She looked up at him as she exited the car and his dimples were deeper than ever as he smiled in what could only be excitement.

"Do you like it?" Dean asked, throwing an arm around her shoulder as he led her up the stairs built into the hill.

"It's nice," Mocha said warily, her mind running in a dozen different directions. "Why?"

"You'll be spending a lot of time here...with me." Dean paused as they neared the front door. He pulled out a ring of three keys and unlocked the door.

Mocha's bottom lip and her stomach dropped in shock.

"Welcome to my house."

Her heart began to thud and she was getting a headache from the continuing confusion. He tried to steer her inside the empty house but she dug her feet in to stay rooted on the porch. "But...but...you live in Dallas."

"I used to live in Dallas, but I moved back to Jersey."

'Huh? What? Say what? Say who?' Mocha's expression was decidedly shocked as Dean pulled her into the house behind him.

And that was the beginning of the end, Mocha thought, yearning to get the day's activities started so she could fill her brain with anything but that dang on Dean Kincaid!

Chapter Four

Dean reached for a bottle of water from the glass-front fridge in his gym. He was invigorated from the one-hour workout he just put his body through. Using a towel to wipe some of the sweat from his face and neck, Dean left the basement gym and jogged up the stairs directly into his kitchen. He still had a lot of decorating to do in his new home. Foolishly, he imagined Mocha using her innate style to help him. "I imagined a lot of things," he drawled a bit sarcastically as a tiny twinge of pain made his heart literally ache...

"*The construction of the car lot should be complete within the next four weeks, Roderick,*" *Dean said, using the speakerphone on his BlackBerry as he stirred fried ground beef into his pot of spaghetti sauce. His veal parmesan was in the oven.*

"*We're right on schedule then,*" *Roderick replied in satisfaction.* "*The Dean of All strikes again.*"

"*And you know it.*" *Dean turned down the heat under the pot.*

"*Man, what are you doing?*"

"*Cooking dinner for Mocha.*"

"*Lawd have mercy.*" *Roderick groaned.* "*Your ass is whipped.*"

Dean just laughed as he placed spaghetti in the pot of boiling water.

"*Are you even moving into your house when the renovations are done or ya'll shacking right now?*"

"*My house will be ready next week.*" *Dean picked up his can of beer and took a swig.* "*But I've enjoyed living with Mocha these last two weeks.*"

Roderick groaned again.

"*Listen, you should come up here one weekend. Mocha's sister Coko, wants to see you...bad.*"

"*Is that the one with the real short hair?*"

"*Yup.*"

"*Not that it matters, they all fine as hell.*"

"*Hey, hold up, man!*" *Dean said.*

"*What? Mocha is fine. Not fine-for-a-big-girl-fine, just plain fine—*"

"*Man, you better keep your mind on Coko, playa.*"

Roderick's laughter echoed into the kitchen.

Dean shook his head as he washed his hands. "*I gotta go. I want to take a shower before Mo gets home.*"

"A'ight, Mr. Monogamy. And tell Coko if she want some, she can get some."

Dean made a face. "Romance is not your strong suit, cuz," he drawled before ending the call.

He couldn't wait for the right woman to knock some of Roderick's bravado from him. The thought of that made him chuckle as he grabbed the plates to set the table in the den.

He couldn't wait to surprise Mocha with the romantic dinner. Over the last two weeks, he had barely seen his lady any more than when he lived in Texas. She was up by seven and didn't get home until after seven or eight sometimes. He'd really had no clues, until now, just how much time she put in at the salon. Still, he wouldn't trade his move back for anything. He was ready for the next level with Mocha and that couldn't go down with over fifteen-hundred miles between them.

The thing was, he honestly wasn't sure if Mocha was as happy as he was. But that couldn't be. Right?

Dean shook his head because he hadn't missed the signs. He had just ignored them. Roderick wanted him to plow through women to get over Mocha, but that was ridiculous because he truly loved her. He just wondered if she had ever truly loved him or just how good he was in bed.

And for her to be angry at him?

"Mocha you got a lot of nerve," he muttered into his bottle of water before guzzling it down.

"Maybe she'll meet someone new on the cruise," Dean thought, hating the very thought of another man touching her yet knowing he had no right to be jealous.

She had just as much right to date as he did.

Brrrnnnggg.

Sitting the bottle down on the counter, he walked over to pick up the cordless phone on the island. "Hello."

"Dean, hi, this is Belinda."

His heart pounded so hard, he thought he heard drums. "Hi, Ms. Nivens," he said, alarmed. "Is something wrong with Mocha?"

"No, Mocha's on the cruise, remember, and I told her don't bother calling me 'cause it's too expensive."

Relief filled him.

"I actually hate to bother you, but I didn't know anyone else to call."

"What's up?" he asked, grabbing his water bottle and walking into his nearly empty den to settle down on the lone couch before the wall-mounted, flat-screen television.

"I need a ride to church for an afternoon program, and Koffee's car won't start. Would you mind?"

He frowned, thinking it would've been easier and quicker for her to call a cab. But there was no way he could turn down a sweet woman like Ms. Nivens. "Okay, I'm on my way."

"Thank you, Dean."

Unsure if he had time to wash, he grabbed his keys and headed out the house.

Mocha and Lena decided to use their lunch break for some pampering at the spa. The two women worked in a spa daily and never got the chance to indulge so they were determined to be spoiled for once. Plus, Mocha thought she might even pick up some innovative ideas for Haven.

"Can you believe how good this feels?" Mocha sighed in pleasure as she lay on her stomach beneath an orange satiny sheet, receiving a stone massage.

"God no," Lena said, her voice muffled from the table next to Mocha's. "I wish Mr. Adonis wasn't married because I would've loved to see him stretched out on this table."

Mocha laughed, even though the thought of Lena's onboard crush made her think of Dean, or rather, the last time they spent together as a couple...

"How was your book club meeting?" Coko asked, putting on a fresh coat of lip gloss.

Mocha sighed dejectedly as she stirred her fruity drink and looked around Mahogany's, the restaurant/jazz club she and her sisters had agreed to meet at in downtown Newark. "It was good. A nice break from Dean moving, his big, sweaty, leaving his drawers on the floor, drinking out of the jug, hogging the remote, and invading my space self," she said with obvious annoyance. "I am used to doing my own thing, not explaining and not justifying. It's not that he's overbearing. It's just not that I feel like all my space and my freedom is gone. I feel like he wants too much from me."

"Ooh!" Koffee said, making a pity face.

"You ready to freak out, huh?" Coko asked before sipping her drink—leaving almost all of the lip gloss she just applied on the rim of her glass.

Mocha nodded. Her shoulders sank as she released a rather dramatic and comical sigh. "Everything was perfect the way that it was. In six years, Dean and I saw each other just enough to get me some—"

"Once a month?" they both gasped in horror.

Mocha eyed them like poo on her new Choos. "It was enough, okay!" she snapped. "Everything is different with him living here, and he gave me no time to get ready. I just feel like the next step is marriage and I don't want to get married. So yes, I ...am about to...freak...out."

Her BlackBerry vibrated on the table top. Mocha glanced down at Dean's handsome face looking up at her. Like the other call he'd made, she didn't answer, even though she knew he was checking on her since she hadn't gone home after the book club meeting—something he hadn't done when he was in Texas. Dean wanted more of their relationship and Mocha was happy the way that it was.

Koffee signaled for their waitress before turning to face Mocha, looking more like their mother every day. "Let me try to get this straight. You have an intelligent, fine, sexy, built brotha with loot, no kids, no wife, faithful, who loves you and just moved back to be with your crazy ass. That's a problem? Girl, please."

Mocha shifted her eyes to Coko, who only nodded in agreement before they ordered another round of drinks. She should have known her sisters wouldn't understand. To them, she had the perfect life: her business, the house, the car, the clothes, and the great guy. They loved her and they were happy for her, but she knew they honestly thought she shouldn't have a care in the world.

They were so wrong.

She hung out with them a little longer but decided to call it an early night. During the drive home, her mind volleyed the good and the bad of having Dean in town for good.

The house was entirely dark and quiet when Mocha arrived. The first thing she noticed when she turned on the lights of the den was the table in front of the glass wall. It was completely set with roses and melted candles that obviously burned for hours.

Hours waiting for her to get home.

She moved across the room to the table, bringing her hand up to lightly touch her mouth in surprise. Dean had made her a romantic dinner?

"That's why he kept calling," she said softly to herself, her heart pounding because she was completely touched by the gesture.

Yes, she loved Dean and she could easily list a dozen or more reasons to love him, but she couldn't help that every day she literally felt panic, like she was in a hole slowly filling with water that would eventually drown her.

Half of her wanted to simply be happy with Dean, but the other half was genuinely afraid.

Mocha bit her bottom lip as she touched the huge bouquet of roses in the center of the table. She felt bad for ruining his surprise, but it was proof positive that the independent side of herself that she didn't want to let go of wasn't used to thinking ahead and notifying someone that she was going to be late returning to her own home.

Mocha turned and made her way to the kitchen, curious to see what he cooked for them.

"Wow. Veal parmesan and spaghetti," she said, her stomach growling at the sight of her all-time favorite dish.

Mocha kicked off her pumps right there in the kitchen and got to work making herself a plate of food. While the microwave did its thing, she poured a full goblet of wine and sipped it as she leaned against the edge of the counter.

Her stomach clenched and she felt the imaginary water rising as that internal conflict rose. A part of her wanted to go upstairs and wake Dean up to join her for the late night meal, but that other part of her enjoyed the peace, the calm, and the quiet of being alone.

"Maybe things will get better when he moves into his own house," she pondered aloud as she took her plate from the microwave. She moved across the kitchen to ease onto the plush cushioned window seat overlooking her backyard that was surrounded by trees dense enough to be a forest.

Sitting in the semi-darkness of the kitchen, she enjoyed her meal, her wine, and the spring beauty sprouting beneath the moon's light.

"Welcome home."

Mocha didn't let on that Dean scared her as she took a sip of wine before looking over her shoulder to see him walk into the kitchen, naked, wiping sleep from his eyes. "Hey, Dean," she said, forcing her eyes to stay focused on his face because the sight of his body was distracting.

"How's your dinner?" he asked, his eyes leveled on her as he stood beside her seat.

That made it very hard to ignore the muscled contours of his lower half. His dark and thick member was impressive even at rest. "It was delicious, Dean, thanks so much," she said huskily. She sat her plate on the seat beside her and then set her goblet in the center of the plate. "Now it's time for dessert."

She turned to face him, taking his shaft into her hand to massage it to hardness.

"Mocha, we need to talk—"

She wetly licked her lips and the corners of her mouth before dipping her head to stroke his length with her tongue.

"Mocha—"

She purred in the back of her throat, her heart and the bud between her legs pulsing as she deeply sucked his thick and shiny tip into her mouth.

269

Dean hissed as his hips bucked forward and he tightly grabbed a handful of her weaved hair.

Mocha massaged the length of him, his moans echoing her pleasures. Moans that chorused the smacking noises of her mouth.

"No, Mocha." Dean pressed his hand to her forehead and worked his hardness from her mouth by stepping back. "We need to talk."

Mocha released an agitated breath. She snatched up her goblet and downed the rest of her wine. "I don't feel like this shit, Dean!" she snapped, fighting the urge to fling her goblet across the room.

"I'm not happy, Mocha—"

"You're not happy," Mocha drawled sarcastically as she jumped to her feet. "You're the one who hijacked my life."

Dean's face hardened.

Mocha's face immediately filled with regret.

The silence in the kitchen was deafening.

"I was going to tell you that I'm not happy because you're not happy, but now I see I'm only good enough to screw once a month when I'm in town," he finished in a low and angry voice as hard as diamond.

"Dean, I didn't say that."

"What are you saying?" Dean asked, his jaw tense.

"Listen, let's just go to bed and talk about this in the morning." Mocha turned to leave the kitchen.

"No," Dean said shortly.

Mocha turned on her heel to face him with her hands on her ample hips.

"I moved to Jersey to have an adult relationship—a meaningful relationship—with the woman I love, and she makes it clear through her actions and now words that I'm intruding in her life."

Stress made Mocha want to pull her weave out. The truth was she didn't want to lose Dean from her life for good, but she wasn't ready, or ever planning to be ready, for the future he wanted. Her panic resurfaced.

Dean watched her for a long time. "You have no intention of ever marrying me. Do you?" he asked, still watching her like a hawk.

Mocha's eyes shifted away from him.

"So the last six years has been a long ass booty call, Mocha?" Dean asked coldly.

But she heard the pain through the coldness. She heard it and she felt it. But she couldn't lie to him. She couldn't.

"I like my life they way that is, but I do love you, Dean," she told him, tears tightening her throat. She walked over to him, but his hand slashed the air, stopping her from getting close.

He looked at her as if she were a stranger...or maybe even an enemy.

"Well, I've had enough of the booty call, Mocha."

That water level was now at her chin and sending her pulse into overdrive.

"I'm ready for commitment and it's obvious we don't want the same thing."

The water rose another inch and Mocha felt nauseous. "Dean, why does it have to be all or nothing—"

"Too bad my dick is the only thing good enough for you."

His words were as cold as the draft caused by the door swinging as he walked out of the kitchen and out of her life.

Mocha felt emotionally drowned.

Chapter Five

Mocha twirled in front of the mirror and inspected her strapless gold metallic silk shantung dress. The early dinner was in a few minutes and although she wasn't really hungry, she was anxious to be around her friends just having a good time. Tomorrow, the ship would arrive in Ocho Rios and the true sightseeing would begin. The cruise ship was nice, but Jamaica would be nicer.

Her eyes fell on the telephone sitting on the desk. She bit the IMAN glitzy lip gloss from her mouth. Would it be wrong to unplug the phone and throw it out to sea? The thing was tempting her. But it would be ridiculous to pay almost seven dollars a minute to call Dean when she already swore she had nothing to say to him. Ever...

"This book is definitely going in my keeper pile. I absolutely loved it!"

Mocha smiled at Candi's enthusiasm as she held the book to her chest as if it were a newborn baby.

"I agree it had lots of emotions, a great story, and well, the love scenes can inspire any woman with a man to make him very, very happy, and any woman without a man to get one. He-ey!" Lena hopped out of her chair and dropped it like it was hot.

The club members laughed and cheered her on.

"Well, I liked that it was also so romantic," Alaina added. "Too bad a lot of men don't read romances because they could learn a lot."

The ladies all agreed with that one.

Mocha had to admit that her relationship with Dean had been over for two weeks but she could never deny that the man was strong when he needed to be strong, and romantic when he needed to be romantic.

Bzzzz.

Mocha reached down beside her for her vibrating BlackBerry. Her sister Koffee's picture appeared on the screen. "Excuse me, ladies," she said, rotating the beautician's chair to put her back to them.

"Hey, what's up. I'm in my book club meeting."

"Are you coming to Mahogany's after your meeting?" Koffee asked with the sound of talking and music echoing behind her.

Mocha had always been a house person—even more so than her sisters—but recently she had spent more time going out with them to help keep her mind off how much she missed Dean's presence in her life. She never said she wanted to lose all of him. She only wanted to make sure she didn't lose any of herself.

"I'll be there in thirty or so."

"Girl, hurry because the men are wall to wall in here tonight."

Mocha rolled her eyes as she straightened the hem on her pinstripe pants. "A man is the last thing I'm looking for."

If she ever did want to get married, then that man—the only man—would have been Dean.

And now their relationship was dunzo. She had her precious freedom, but it had come at the cost of Dean.

"It's for the best," she tried to console herself as she ended the call.

"Ladies, don't forget to read next month's selection in time because we're having our meeting on one of the last days of the cruise," Alaina called out as the women began to gather their belongings. "Don't forget you need identification for the flight to Miami and to get on the cruise. No passport. No cruise."

Mocha closed up shop after everyone left and was glad to finally hop into her car and leave one more workday behind. Pulling out of the rear parking lot, she made the left to go towards Newark and not the right that would have taken her towards Livingston. As she drove through the busy city streets, she thought of Dean. She missed him. She ached for him. She loved him.

But Dean was looking for the happily ever after and she wasn't. Period. So the best thing was to leave him be to find the white picket fix. With Dean it was all or nothing. Black or white. No shades of gray.

Mocha pulled her car into the fenced parking lot of Mahogany's. She was reaching into the back seat for her large tote when she looked up just in time to see Dean hurrying into Mahogany's.

Her body reacted as though they'd never been apart and she felt breathless. They hadn't spoken or seen one another since that last night at her house. Her first instinct had been to run, but a piece of her wanted to see him and wanted him to see her. Just because their love affair had ended didn't mean they had to be enemies. The last six years was worth more than that.

After double-checking her makeup, Mocha climbed out of the car. She strutted into Mahogany's with the utmost confidence. She would never let Dean know their breakup had killed her appetite and caused a slight acne build up on her chin.

Koffee jumped up from her seat at the bar to rush over and grab Mocha's arm. "Girl, Dean is here," she whispered to her like a runaway slave scared of being caught.

"Okay, that's fine," Mocha said. "We are two mature adults who can handle a situation like this."

"Yeah, uh-huh." Koffee led the way through the crowd back to the bar.

"Hey, Coko." Mocha tried her best not to let on that she was looking around the crowded spot for Dean.

"He's upstairs on the balcony to the right," Coko supplied in a teasing voice.

Mocha's eyes immediately shot up. Sure enough, there he was at a table with five other people, laughing and having a ball...without her.

Throughout the night Mocha's eyes were drawn to him. She felt like a dang ol' stalker or something, just sitting in one spot sipping the same drink and sneaking looks at her ex. Sipping and peeping. Peeping and sipping.

"Check out hot mama in the red dress all up in Dean's face," Koffee whispered to her like Dean was in trouble.

Mocha almost spilled her drink as she whirled around. Her face and her chest tightened at the sight of some video vixen reject pressing her body close to Dean's as he stood by the wrought iron rail. "Why is she all up in my man's face?" Mocha snapped, pure green-eyed jealousy consuming her.

Koffee cleared her throat. "Oh no, little sis, Dean ain't your man. Remember?"

Mocha ignored her as she watched Dean laughing at something the woman whispered in his ear. She couldn't sit back and watch this. She was two seconds from flying up those stairs and acting a straight fool. Mocha grabbed her bag and sat her drink on the bar. "I'll see ya'll later," she mumbled, ignoring their calls as she flew out the building and into a new reality she couldn't handle.

Mocha hated the tears that gathered in her eyes, and she blinked them away before they could fall. That night wasn't the first bit of pain Dean caused her. In the next couple of weeks, Dean became quite a Lothario—she got so sick and tired of being sick and tired over "Dean on a date" sightings.

Dean and some woman coming out of the NJPAC.

Dean and some woman on Rte. 22 shopping.

Dean and some woman. Period.

If Dean was enjoying his single status so much, just what had he been up to in Texas? This was a side of him she didn't know.

She had been glad to get on the plane, but unfortunately all of her drama was still fresh in her mind. "A man will have a woman crying and licking the inside of an empty bucket of Rocky Road ice cream," she muttered.

Mocha eyed the phone again. She had gone to Dean's house one night to blast him out for becoming Roderick's gigolo twin, but she had stood out in the rain for a few moments trying to find the nerve to actually confront a man she had thrown away. She just couldn't find the nerve that night and she didn't yet have it tonight.

"I bet Mocha's not having fun on that cruise," Ms. Nivens said, setting a plate of fried chicken, potato salad, corn on the cob and a buttermilk biscuit in front of Dean.

Dean only shrugged, not sure just how much Ms. Nivens knew about his breakup with her daughter.

She sat at the table with him, still dressed in her white usher's uniform. Her own plate held a much smaller portion of the meal. "Mocha is more sensitive and insightful than my other two girls. She's more like me. She listens first and talks after. I always taught them all that a closed mouth and open ears will get you a long way in life, and Mocha learned it better than the other two. Must be because she's my baby."

Dean dug into his food, still wondering how coming to Irvington to give her a ride to church turned into him fixing Koffee's car. As a teenager, he worked with his grandfather in the car lot's shop. His skills had never left him. Mocha's sisters were making up lost time with the vehicle, which left him, Ms. Nivens and her grands, who were in her den watching music videos.

"I used to always be so proud because Mocha was the one of my three who listened to me without hesitation." Ms. Nivens smiled, illuminating the fifty-nine years of her life in her pretty face. "Oh, she would speak her mind but she always did what I said. Now I wonder if maybe she took my life lessons to heart too much."

Dean looked up at Ms. Nivens and he wished being here didn't remind him so much of Mocha. *Damn, I miss her. I shouldn't. I don't want to. But damn I do.*

"My husband and I were married really young, and I wish I could say there was more good than bad, but there wasn't. I guess it was silly of me to love a man so hard and not love myself enough, especially when he loved drugs and the streets more than me."

He was saddened by the emotion brimming in her eyes.

"I finally got the nerve to leave, and from that day on, I taught my girl to be independent and not to rely on a man. That was my way of shielding them from my own decisions. I meant to teach them to be strong and stand up on their own feet, but I didn't mean to teach them that you don't need love. I was so busy preaching about having your own house, and your own car, and your own bank account."

Dean looked away from the hope he saw in Ms. Nivens' eyes.

"Do you know you're the only boyfriend Mocha has been with longer than a year or two?" she asked as she rose from her seat to retrieve a glass pitcher of lemonade from the fridge.

Dean's face must have revealed his surprise because Ms. Nivens added, "That's right."

Dean thought back to the look on Mocha's face when he asked her if she ever planned to marry him. He could see it clearly.

"You're good for my baby Mocha."

He shook his head. "Mocha and I are on two different paths, Ms. Nivens."

"The amazing thing about life is how roads and paths have a way of intersecting and merging into one."

Dean remained unconvinced.

Chapter Six

Mocha could barely hold all of her purchases as she led the way back aboard the cruise ship. She and her travel companions laughed and recounted funny stories from their day-long excursion to Ocho Rios as they made their way back to the staterooms.

"Come and get me before ya'll go to dinner," Mocha told the ladies before she walked into her stateroom and closed the door with her hip.

She frowned at the sight of a man in her bed. "Who are you?" she roared, dropping her packages onto the sofa. She stalked over to the bed.

The shirtless—and probably bottomless—man rolled over and looked up at her.

"Dean? What the hell are you doing here?" she gasped angrily, even as all her senses flooded with seeing him until she felt weak in the knees.

"Don't yell, Mocha, I've got one helluva headache."

"Dean, this is insane. You moved down the road from me and you had nothing to say to me but you traveled to Jamaica to say what?" she asked as she crossed her arms over her chest and glared down at him. "If you think you have balls enough to bogart my room so you can party it up in my face, Mr. Lover Lover, your ass is mistaken."

Dean flipped the covers back and sat up on the edge of the bed. "Are you done?" he asked patiently.

Mocha turned away from him and walked down the length of the stateroom to drop down on the sofa. This wasn't fair. She was just beginning to enjoy herself and not hurt like a dagger was being twisted in her gut every time she thought of him...and now here he was.

Dean rested his elbows on his knees as he looked over at her.

Still handsome.

Still sexy as all get out.

Still Dean.

"I was so angry at you for not wanting to marry me, Mocha."

She leaned back in her chair and crossed her legs as she locked her eyes with his. "I never said I didn't love you. I never said that," she defended herself fiercely.

"No, you didn't but you didn't love me enough, Mocha, and that hurt." He hit his palm with his fist. "I'm man enough to admit that it hurt to know all of my plans were one-sided."

"So I'm the bad guy. Fine. I'll wear that. So what now?" she asked bitterly, rising to her feet.

"We do what we should have done that night at your house. Talk."

Mocha laughed even as her heart and her soul shivered with nervousness.

"I saw you run out of Mahogany's that night," he admitted in a low voice.

She looked up at him in surprise.

Dean rose to his feet, dressed in pajama bottoms, and walked over to her. "I saw you watching me all night, Mocha, and I thought if I paraded enough women in your face, you would realize that I belong with you and no one else."

"Um, just what an ex wants to see and hear about...especially when she wasn't the one who ended it."

"No, you're just the one who put limits on the relationship."

Mocha held up her hands and forced herself to breathe as she counted to ten in her head. "I need a breather," she finally said, turning to snatch the door open.

"Mocha—" he called.

The door closed behind her as she made her way to Lena's stateroom. Like Mocha, she had booked a private room. But her fist paused before she knocked on the door. Changing her mind, she turned and walked back to her stateroom, dismayed that she forgot her key and had to knock.

Dean opened the door and then leaned against it to look down at her in amusement. "Welcome back," he teased.

She brushed past him to enter the room. "When I brought you that ticket we were still together."

"You didn't cancel it."

"Dean, what do you want? Why are you here?" she asked, turning to face him.

"You," he answered simply. "I'm willing to fight for you, Mocha. You're worth it. We're worth it."

Mocha began to tap her foot in a mix of nervous energy and anxiety.

"Can you look me in the face and say you don't miss me? That you don't have any regrets?" he asked. He walked up close to her and pressed his warm hands to her arms.

Mocha shivered from his touch. "Don't, Dean," she pleaded as she stepped back from his grasp.

But he stepped towards her again and the level of energy bouncing off them and between them intensified.

Mocha looked up into his eyes and she was swamped with love for him.

"I can love you enough and still let you be your own woman, Mocha," he told her seriously. "I never asked you to change who you are because I love you for who you are."

The tears for her fears rose as she continued to look into his eyes. Eyes filled with love, passion, and hope.

"Independence is not a bad thing, Mocha, but living life alone when you have someone to love and cherish you is just crazy." Dean pulled her body close to his as if he was unsure she wouldn't run from his touch. "Tell me you don't love me?"

Mocha adored him.

"Tell me you didn't miss me, Mocha?"

She craved him.

"Tell me that you want to go the rest of your life without me."

She couldn't.

She wouldn't.

Mocha knew that it was all or nothing. She tried to live without him and failed. "All my life I've worked to build my own and to have my own."

"Okay, so you've done that. Now what?" Dean countered.

The feeling of panic was beginning to rise but Mocha forced herself to push it away because she wanted to think with a clear head.

"I'm not asking you to move in with me...right now. I'm not asking you to marry me...right now. But I will one day, that I promise you, Mocha Nivens," he swore fiercely as he kissed her forehead. "But for now, baby, I'd rather be with you than without you."

Suddenly Mocha thought of the little twin girls with the afro puffs running up to her, calling her Mama. Instinctively, she knew Dean was a big part of that vision coming to fruition.

"You know what? For now let's enjoy this vacation." Dean smiled and he pulled her softening body into his grasp. "I just had a five-hour flight and a two-hour cab ride from Montego Bay to get here."

"At least you didn't have to ride a mule or something," she teased, allowing herself to simply enjoy having Dean with her. For now it was enough. She was touched that he came all the way to Jamaica to enjoy this cruise with her and, most importantly, to woo her back.

"Listen, I'm not sorry for moving back to Jersey, but it was a big change in our relationship and maybe I should have talked it over with you. Let you know what was going on."

Mocha nodded as she looked down at the floor. "And maybe I overreacted...a little," she admitted begrudgingly.

Dean laughed as he used the tip of his finger to her chin to lift her head up. "Let's take things slow but let's not stop a good thing, Mocha."

There is nothing not worth working on when love is involved.

When Dean lowered his head to capture her mouth with a kiss, Mocha's body responded before her head could process everything. She trembled. Her breasts hardened in a flash and the bud between her fleshy lips throbbed with an erratic beat all its own. She didn't know if she was taking on more than she was ready for, but in that moment, with Dean pressing her body onto the unmade bed and blessing her neck with kisses and tiny bites, she felt complete. There was no other place she would rather be. She wouldn't be the one to deny them this pleasure.

With a moan she clutched the back of his head as they locked their lips heatedly. No words were spoken as the sun faded and night reigned. Clothes were peeled away until they were able to press their naked flesh together. Even as the book club members gently knocked at the door of the stateroom, Mocha and Dean were lost in their own world and ignored them. The first plunge of his protected hardness within her warm and moist walls caused them both to clutch each other desperately as they shivered uncontrollably. They began a slow grind, completely in sync with one another as they lost themselves in heat and passion.

It was a passionate reunion of not just love, but love.

Dean and Mocha enjoyed the rest of the cruise together, but Mocha liked that he gave her the space to enjoy a lot of her time with her book club members. She completely appreciated and respected him for that.

But the nights were all theirs.

"I think making love on a cruise ship is the best," Mocha sighed as she snuggled against Dean's broad muscular chest.

He chuckled as he played in the damp beads of sweat coating her back. "I agree."

Mocha twirled her finger around his nipple until it hardened. "We really should get some sleep, Dean. Tomorrow all of this comes to an end and it's back to reality."

Dean stiffened. "Is reality so bad?" he asked, his words measured.

Mocha squeezed him close. "Not at all."

His body relaxed before he climbed out of bed to grab the bottle of champagne they ordered earlier. He poured what little was left into two flutes.

Mocha allowed her eyes to follow the hard lines of his body as he walked back to the bed and handed her one. "I thought I poured it all on your chest," she teased, before taking a sip.

Dean laughed. "We have just enough left for a toast," he told her, reaching down to her with his free hand.

Mocha placed her hand in his and eased up from the bed carefully so as not to spill her drink. "Where are you taking me?" she asked, happy to have him back in her life.

Dean nodded towards the balcony just as the picture window seemed to perfectly frame the moonlight.

Mocha freed her hand from Dean long enough to grab the sheet from the bed with a giggle. Out on the balcony, she handed him her drink before she wrapped the sheet around her back, opening and closing it in a playful and erotic fan dance. "Care to join me?" she asked.

Dean stepped forward and Mocha closed the sheet around them both, holding it close with one hand behind his strong back. "This is beautiful," Mocha sighed in pleasure as she accepted her flute from Dean and looked at the glistening, moon-kissed ocean.

"Here's to our future."

Mocha touched her glass to his. "Our future."

Epilogue

What a difference a year makes.

Mocha poured the last of the flower petals onto the center of Dean's bed and then stood back to check out her handiwork. Everything was just the way she wanted it. Perfect.

Champagne chilling.

The air filled with the scent of roses and lilies.

Fresh fruit ready and waiting to be eaten, served, or become a part of their lovemaking.

The stone fireplace of his bedroom lit and crackling.

And she was as naked as the day she was born.

It was a year since their cruise, and now Mocha felt foolish for the horrible misgivings she'd had about Dean. He was a man of his word. Supporting her without smothering her. Allowing her to make her own decisions and have her own friends. Now, instead of seeing him as an intrusion on her independence, he was the icing on the cake.

She heard the front door downstairs close and she hurried to climb onto the bed, in the middle of the petals strewn on the white satin sheets. She loved all the surprises Dean orchestrated for her, but now it was her turn.

"Surprise, daddy," she said in her softest and sexiest voice.

"Wow," was all that he said as he stood in the doorway, taking it all in.

Mocha enjoyed the smoky look that filled his eyes as he unceremoniously dropped his briefcase and slowly undressed, making his way over to the bed.

"What's the occasion?" he asked as he worked his boxers down over his hips and growing erection.

Mocha curled and uncurled her finger as she licked her lips. She smiled as Dean crawled on the bed like a tiger about to pounce on its prey. "Just wondered if you would marry me," she said, tilting her head up to capture his mouth with a kiss as surprise filled his face.

"You're asking me?" he asked, sounding cocky.

Mocha gave him a mock-stern face.

Dean's eyes smoldered as he looked at her with an intensity that made Mocha breathless. "And you're ready?" he asked with the utmost seriousness.

"*More* than ready," she assured him as her hand massaged the length of his muscled arm.

"Just remember when we tell this story to our grandkids that *you* asked *me*," he teased.

"Shut up and kiss me."

Their laughs soon turned to sighs of exquisite pleasure as they cherished the thought of a future with lots more and more to come.

The End

Author Bio:

Niobia Bryant is a highly praised, nationally bestselling and award winning author of romance, mainstream fiction, teen fiction, and urban fiction. She currently writes under a few pseudonyms for multiple publishers. She has over   fifteen books in print and currently divides her time between South Carolina and New Jersey.

Red Rose Publishing
More & More

Writing as Niobia Bryant (Romance-Mass Market Paperbacks)

BET Books/ Arabesque
Admission of Love (2000)
Three Times a Lady (2001)
Heavenly Match (2004)
Can't Get Next to You (2005)

Harlequin/Arabesque
Let's Do it Again (2005)
You Never Know (2006) Anthology
Count on This (2006)

Kensington/Dafina Romance

Heated (2006)
Hot Like Fire (2007)
Make You Mine (2009)
Give Me Fever (5/2010)

Writing as Niobia Bryant (Mainstream-Trade Sized Paperback)

Live and Learn (2007) Kensington/ Dafina
Show and Tell (2008) Kensington/ Dafina
Message From a Mistress (3/2010) Kensington/ Dafina
Writing as Niobia Simone (Erotica)

Caramel Flava edited by Zane (2006) Simone & Schuster/Atria (Anthology Collaboration)

Writing as Meesha Mink (Urban Fiction)

Desperate Hoodwives (1/2008) Simon & Schuster/Touchstone
Shameless Hoodwives (8/2008) Simon & Schuster/Touchstone
The Hood Life (1/2009) Simon & Schuster/Touchstone

Writing as Simone Bryant (Young Adult/YA fiction/Teen Fiction)

Fabulous (2/2010) Harlequin/Kimani Tru
Notorious (Tba) Harlequin/Kimani Tru
Glamorous (Tba) Harlequin/Kimani Tru